English Poetry from the Elizabethans to the Restoration

An Anthology

Edited by
Pramod K. Nayar

Orient BlackSwan

ORIENT BLACKSWAN PRIVATE LIMITED

Registered Office
3-6-752 Himayatnagar, Hyderabad 500 029 (A.P.), India
Email: centraloffice@orientblackswan.com

Other Offices
Bangalore, Bhopal, Bhubaneshwar, Chandigarh, Chennai
Ernakulam, Guwahati, Hyderabad, Jaipur
Kolkata, Lucknow, Mumbai, New Delhi, Noida, Patna

First published 2012

ISBN 978 81 250 4610 3

Typeset in Minion Pro 9.5/11.5
Macrotex Solutions, Chennai 600 088

Printed in India at
Charita Impressions, Hyderabad - 500 020.

Published by
Orient Blackswan Private Limited
3-6-752, Himayatnagar
Hyderabad 500 029
Email: hyderabad@orientblackswan.com

Contents

Editor's Acknowledgements

As always, immeasurable gratitude to Anna Kurian for suggestions regarding the Introduction, help with selection of texts, the bits on 'The Bard', but mainly for her consistent affection and loyal endorsement of all my projects.

It is a pleasure to acknowledge the various roles played by people in the making of this work:

my parents,

Pranav (no, this book does not mention Transformers or Percy Jackson) and Nandini, and my parents-in-law,

Malte Urban of Queen's University, Belfast, for his generous gift of J.J. Cohen's *The Postcolonial Middle Ages*,

Saradindu Bhattacharya for acquiring essential journal essays, and Madhavi Menon and Tapan Das at Orient Blackswan for their support.

Pramod K Nayar
Hyderabad

Introduction

This volume covers the period between the ascension of Elizabeth I to the throne of England (1558) and the restoration of the monarchy after the Civil War (1660). Divided variously into the Elizabethan (1558–1603), Jacobean (1603–1625), Caroline (1625–1649) and the Interregnum (1649–1660), the entire period, from roughly 1500 till around the end of the seventeenth century, is labelled 'early modern' as well. England's early modern was marked by massive controversies over the power of the monarch, tensions between Catholicism and Protestantism, the exodus of the Protestants to the 'new world', the influence of European, especially Italian, Renaissance ideas, the flowering of a vernacular (that is, English) literature (as opposed to the dominance of Latin), the arrival of print, regicide and civil war, the rise of a popular culture in the form of the stage – a domain that would, since his arrival in London as an 'upstart crow', be entirely dominated then, as now, by one man, William Shakespeare – amazing advances in biology, chemistry, medicine, astronomy and scientific thought, explorations of the oceans and distant lands and radically new philosophical ideas. It was a period of great social flux as well. The expressions of these contexts and concerns by men (and, as we shall see, thanks to the archival and historiographic work by scholars since the 1980s, women) present some of the most diverse forms of writing in the English language – from sermons to scientific tracts, pamphlets to poetry, drama to doggerel, amorous verse to a poetry of science, epics to etiquette books. The richness of the early modern ensures that it has never really gone out of fashion among literary scholars, its political themes and contexts – slaving voyages, discovery narratives, new world/settlement texts, cartography and chorography, speculations on utopias, heresies – have energised studies of the very idea of 'modernity'.

The Social and Political Background

London began to emerge as the financial and cultural capital of England during the time of Queen Elizabeth (its population grew by nearly 400 per cent between 1500 and 1600). The English language itself began to take the shape we now know, and the rise of print literacy and the theatre (the first one opened in London in 1576) had a major role to play in this. London also suffered the great plagues (1563 and 1600), losing thousands of its population to the disease.

The Elizabethan and Jacobean periods saw great social transformations. Merchants, for example, acquired property and began to compete with the aristocrats and landed gentry for social status. The resultant social tensions congealed into rituals of social distinction and the rise of categories such as the 'gentleman' (mapped as 'self-fashioning' by Stephen Greenblatt, 1980). Classical learning, Latin and a particular kind of literacy (the ability to write poetry, for instance) began to be seen as markers of distinction. Sumptuary laws, which decreed dress codes for people based on their social standing, were still in existence during the sixteenth century, thus indicating a continuing concern with manners, appearance and social affiliations.[1]

Marriage was based on economic means, and was usually forbidden to apprentices who earned lower wages. Among the aristocratic circles and the upper classes marriage was an instrument of political alliance. Divorce was not permitted.

New notions of privacy emerged in this, the age of social mobility.[2] Gardening and cultivation, for instance, were seen as markers of 'culture' and taste. Country houses, eulogised by Ben Jonson ('To Penshurst'), Andrew Marvell ('Upon Appleton House') among others, became the loci of domestic tourism, where the poorer classes could go and see for themselves how the wealthy lived. These also became symbols of English upper class hospitality and culture (McBride 2001).

The family was treated as a key public concern. One document dated 1600 stated simply that 'on their [families'] good government the commonwealth depends'. The family was the site, Martin Ingram notes, of production and consumption (that is, economic activity), but also 'patriarchal authority and the reproduction of age and gender hierarchies' (2003: 114).

London, the seat of culture and spectacle, as well as court life, was also the site of low life, crime and poverty (even the soldiers who had fought the Armada and helped defend England had not been paid their salaries and lived in abject poverty in and around London). Merchant guilds were powerful and Elizabeth, recognising this, formulated policies to help them. London was also the city of choice for individuals from the countryside, both men and women, to acquire skills and employment. It was also the city where one could see foreigners, arriving on both strange and familiar ships from various parts of the world. Very often these foreigners were the cause of social tensions. For example, there were Africans in England since the 1560s, mainly as a result of the slaving voyages. An edict was issued in 1601 that

1 For a very readable account of everyday life in the Renaissance, see Chamberlain (1967).

2 On social mobility in early modern England, see Lawrence Stone's pioneering work (1966).

called for the expulsion of Africans from England, on the grounds that they were depriving Englishmen of jobs.

Social anxieties congealed around Jews, Africans, Catholics, vagrants and witches in Elizabethan England. The Poor Laws (codified in 1587–98) sought to regulate idleness by penalising and even incarcerating vagrants (called 'masterless men'; see Beier 1985). Alongside the poor, Jews, Africans and women branded as witches were marginalised. Laws against witchcraft were instituted in 1542 (repealed only to be reinstated in a harsher form by Elizabeth). James I wrote a tract on demonology and instituted an Act against witchcraft in 1604 that was not repealed until 1736.[3] After the 1572 Vagabonds Act, state subsidy and support was granted to 'impotent persons' after an examination of their credentials. The other marginalised group, the Jews, practised their religion in secret in an age when Jew-baiting was common (one of the most popular plays of the age was, due to the anti-Jew hysteria, Marlowe's *The Jew of Malta*).

With numerous epidemics prevailing, such as smallpox, plague, measles, among others, there was a huge amount of investment in writings – literary and non-literary – about health. Indeed the very idea of the 'body politic' (to describe in an organic metaphor the kingdom itself) enabled the circulation of ideas of infection, pathology and invasions. James I therefore proposed thus:

> So if we will take the whole people as one body and mass, then as the head is ordained for the body, and not the body for the head; so must a righteous king know himself to be ordained for his people, and not his people for him . . . (accession speech).

And: 'kings are compared to the head of this microcosm of the body of man' (speech of 21 March 1609).[4]

The idea of order was central to such discussions and edicts in early modern Europe and England: it was the Elizabethan 'world view' (Tillyard 1946). The 'great chain of being' was a pervasive idea that suggested that creation consists of many degrees of existence, each linked to the other in a certain order. There was a 'natural' sequence and unity to all forms of life. One's social position was pre-ordained. The state was headed by a monarch, and the people were her/his subjects (see the speeches of James I already quoted). Families were patriarchal. The appropriate place in the cosmos and the social

3 However, as Diane Purkiss (1996) has demonstrated, women's stories about witchcraft were essentially fantasies, created as a means of escaping the anxieties of motherhood and housework.

4 For analyses of the idea of the body politic and the images of invasion and sickness see the exemplary work of Jonathan Gil Harris (2004).

order that Renaissance Europe believed in proceeded from the assumption, and commonly held belief that God created the universe and structured it in terms of clear hierarchies – which could not, therefore, be tampered with. As Shakespeare put it in *Troilus and Cressida*:

> The heavens themselves, the planets, and this centre
> Observe degree, priority, and place
> Infixture, course, proportion, season, form,
> Office and custom, in all line of order.

Bishop Hooker's *Laws of Ecclesiastical Polity* (1593–1597) stated: 'the obedience of creatures unto the law of nature is the stay of the whole world'. Such a sense of ordered cosmos and ordered societies came frequently under threat when vagrants, foreigners, unwed mothers, illegitimate children or the new gentry moved socially or geographically. The collection of information about such social and geographical mobility – through procedures such as census operations, land ownership records, population movements – in early modern England (Edward Higgs refers to it as an 'information state', 2004) was inspired mainly by this anxiety over mobility and the need to preserve order. Institutional mechanisms were developed, therefore, to ensure that people were watched and order was maintained.[5]

Religion

Martin Luther's attack on the Catholic Church which climaxed in his *95 Theses against the Sale of Papal Indulgences* (1517) marked the launch of what we now call the Reformation. The Reformation on the continent was the context within which radical, and often bitterly contested, changes were taking place in England as well. It was to be a century of change, as even a short inventory of the events would show.

In 1534 Henry VIII, who had been invested with a new title, 'The Defender of the Faith', broke with the Roman church and declared himself, through an Act of Supremacy, the head of the Church of England. Soon after, Henry VIII closed the monasteries and convents and confiscated all their properties. Henry's attacks on the authority of the church were only the beginning of a long-drawn, acrimonious and bitter quarrel between monarch and religion that was to provide the most sustained context for the literary production of early modern England.

Under Edward VI's monarchy (1547–1553) – he had been brought up Protestant – more Protestant changes were initiated into England's official religion. The Protestants believed that humankind was utterly without hope

5 These included the Justice of Peace (whose responsibilities were framed by statutes, and overseen by the Privy Council), the hierarchy of courts, ecclesiastical courts, etc.

of redemption because it had sinned. It was God alone who could save humanity, and for this, humanity had to admit its sins and rely entirely on God. Faith was therefore the only thing that could save humanity, and the liturgy and ritual aspects of religion were all, ultimately, shallow.

The first English translation of the Bible was published in 1551. Then, when Mary I became queen, she returned England to Catholicism. The cumulative effect of these many reversals and reactions caused Protestant believers to flee to Europe (mainly Geneva). However, when Elizabeth I came to the throne in 1558 she once again returned England to Protestantism. The bishops appointed by Mary Tudor refused to serve under her, and she therefore simply appointed a new bench. She was eventually excommunicated by the Pope in 1570. Elizabeth, not one to be deterred by the Papal action, initiated and promulgated via her Parliament a series of Acts that prohibited the practice of Catholicism in 1580. To be a Catholic at this time was extremely dangerous – to even harbour one was deemed a felony and chargeable as treason.

Elizabeth also combined elements from both Protestantism and Catholicism to produce a new religion called Anglicanism. These efforts had some effect, and there was considerable religious stability during her reign. Animosity and discontentment did not entirely disappear, however. Critics of Elizabeth's 'settlement' of the religious identity of England as 'Anglican' discerned touches of Catholicism in it. These radical Protestants came to be known as the Puritans. Under James I, England became definitively Protestant. The first authorised version of the Bible appeared in 1611, under orders from James I who then persecuted both the Catholics and the extreme Protestants (the Puritans).[6]

Such extended religious strife and oppression had a different consequence. A group of English Calvinists (described as 'separatists' or 'dissenters'), who had fled England for Holland, now embarked on a ship called the *Mayflower*, arriving at Plymouth, Massachusetts, in 1620. Commonly called the 'Pilgrims', these would become the founders of the new American nation. Though Jamestown in the 'new world' (America) had been settled much before this event, in 1607, it had failed. With the 1620 exodus the new world would become a full-fledged settlement.

After the ascension of Charles I to the throne of England and his subsequent marriage with the French Catholic princess Henrietta Maria, the war of monarchy and church flared up again, especially with the arrival of William Laud as the Archbishop of Canterbury (1633). After the Civil War,

6 The standard work on the English Puritans remains Collinson's *The Elizabethan Puritan Movement* (1967).

Protestantism would become a major political ideology, especially embodied in the Puritan Commonwealth under Oliver Cromwell.

Monarchy, Wars and Rebellions

The power of monarchy and the endless tyrannies and misery the untrammelled power of a monarch could inflict on her/his subjects concerned the greatest playwright of the age: William Shakespeare. And this was for good reasons too. From Elizabeth I through James I and Charles I, the authority of the monarch was the subject of much discussion and dispute. Some, like James I, appropriated God and divinity to demonstrate that they were authorised by divine right to rule, or as the physician of the kingdom come to heal its many ills. Others like Elizabeth portrayed and presented themselves as the 'peoples' queen', loved and therefore obeyed.

Elizabeth I, who declared herself 'mere English', thus foregrounding her pure English roots, remained the 'virgin queen' till her death. In what is surely a remarkable exhibition of tenacity and astute social engineering, Elizabeth thwarted many suitors – her tactic of allowing herself to be courted by foreign suitors ensured that they would not attack England, because they would hope to marry her – and presented herself as dedicated to the nation. As she famously put it: 'I am already bound unto a husband which is the Kingdom of England'. With her victory over the Spanish Armada of 1588 she acquired a reputation as a heroic queen (it proved expensive, and Elizabeth was forced to sell off crown lands to pay for it), one fit to lead the people of England to the glories of 'Great Britain'. Elizabeth sought the love of the people of England and sought to acquire their loyalty as their beloved queen. In her farewell speech to Parliament in 1601 she reiterated this ideology and politics of love:

> I do assure you there is no prince that loves his subjects better, or whose love can countervail our love. There is no jewel, be it of never so rich a price, which I set before this jewel: I mean your love. For I do esteem it more than any treasure or riches; for that we know how to prize, but love and thanks I count invaluable. And, though God hath raised me high, yet this I count the glory of my Crown, that I have reigned with your loves...

During the war against the Armada Elizabeth said in her speech:

> I do not desire to live to distrust my faithful and loving people . . . I have placed my chiefest strength and safeguard in the loyal hearts and good will of my subjects.

This would change with her successor. In order to ingratiate herself better with her subjects Elizabeth travelled throughout England, staying with Earls and Dukes (bringing ruin upon them – they often went bankrupt due to the expenses involved in hosting the Queen), and made herself a very visible monarch (for a study of Elizabeth's travels and the 'politics of place' see McRae 2009, chapter four).

James VI of Scotland (son of Mary Stuart, the executed rival of Elizabeth) ascended the throne of England as James I (hence, quite often his name is written as 'James VI/I'). James I united England and Scotland under his banner. This was a major achievement and James I capitalised upon it, using it to 'prove' that he had the support of God, and going on to claim that the 'Golden Age' had finally come to England. The monarch was guided by Divine Wisdom and so all monarchic decisions had Providence's blessings as well as authority. Continuing the efforts of Elizabeth, James I also spoke of a 'Great Britain', thus reinforcing the idea of a nation. The King would be the 'father' taking care of his subjects, that is, his children. The King was endowed with the divine right to rule, and divinity was inherent to kingship. Together these ideas suggested that the authority of the King was beyond dispute and the subjects, like good children, must therefore *subject* themselves to the care of their father-king. In his accession speech to the Parliament on 19 March 1603:

> I am Head and Governor of all the people in my Dominion who are my natural vassals and subjects, considering them in numbers and distinct rank . . .

Thus, departing from Elizabeth's practice, James sought not love but *obedience* from the people of England. He would write in *Basilikon Doron*:

> God gives not Kings the style of Gods in vain
> for on his throne his sceptre do they sway:
> And as their subjects ought them to obey
> So Kings should fear and serve their God again.

Or, as Ben Jonson put it, 'The King and [the] priest of Peace' are one. Yet there was no complete peace, as was demonstrated by the Gunpowder Plot by Catholics to blow up the Parliament (1605). Later, in his speech to the Parliament on 21 March 1609 James would elaborate his views on absolutist monarchy:

> Kings are justly called gods, for that they exercise a manner or resemblance of divine power upon earth; for if you will consider the attributes to God, you shall see how they agree in the person of a king. God hath power to create or destroy, make war or unmake at his pleasure, to give life or send death, to judge all and to be judged nor accountable to none, to raise low things and to make high things low at his pleasure, and to God are both soul and body due. And the like power have kings: they make and unmake their subjects, they have power of raising

> and casting down, of life and of death, judges over all their subjects and in all causes and yet accountable to none but God only. They have power to exalt low things and abase high things, and make of their subjects, like men at the chess, – a pawn to take a bishop or a knight – and to cry up or down any of their subjects, as they do their money.

Charles I, who succeeded to the English throne in 1625, slowly turned absolutist, and began to reject Parliamentary advice. 'Personal rule', which rejected the authority of Parliament and invested even national happiness in the happiness of the King and his consort, became Charles' hallmark, and all his iconography and the Stuart masques (by William Davenant, Thomas Carew and others), Graham Parry notes (1989), were directed at emphasising this. Indeed, unlike either Elizabeth or James, Charles I was an avid supporter of the arts, and of course manipulated them to reinforce his presence and authority.

The Court in much of these Stuart arts becomes an ideal space, and the monarch is presented as something akin to the divine (for example, we can see Charles I continued James I's principle of demonstrating the divine right of kings), as Carew put it:

> Tourneys, masques, theatres, better become
> Our halcyon days.

In 1628 the Petition of Right was presented to Charles I by Parliament. Angered by the Parliament's refusal to submit to absolute monarchic power, Charles I dissolved it, embarking on a eleven-year 'Personal Rule' (1629–1640). A short Parliament was convened in 1639, but was soon dissolved even as war erupted between England and Scotland. In 1641 the Parliament drew up a list of complaints against the monarch, and the Civil War was sparked off. It raged till 1646 when Charles I surrendered to the Scots and, after a brief lull, a second civil war, with the Scots now intervening on behalf of Charles I, erupted. In 1646 Charles I was executed. Oliver Cromwell defeated the Scots in 1650. Following the same pattern as Charles I, Cromwell dissolved the Parliament in 1653 to become Lord Protector. After his death in 1658, the Protectorate broke down and Charles II was restored to the throne – an event known as the Restoration.

Printing and Literacy

The first recognisably 'English' works were in Middle English, in the form of texts such as *Sir Gawain and the Green Knight*, *Piers Plowman*, *Patience*, *Pearl*, the works of John Gower (1330–1408) and Geoffrey Chaucer (1343–1400). Translations of Latin, Italian and other classical texts into English became more accessible after the arrival of print. Genres such as autobiographies (of which *The Book of Margery Kempe* was perhaps the first by a woman: it was completed around 1436, and first copied out in 1450, before the era of printing), epic poetry, dream poems and romances emerged in Middle English and mark the making of an 'English' literary tradition.

When William Caxton (1422–1491) brought printing to England, he initiated a process of unprecedented social change. The nature and extent of literacy changed radically as pamphlets, broadsides and political tracts began to appear in cheaper form for a more diffused and enlarged audience. Cheaper books meant that the middle classes could also read political debates and scientific advances at a much lower price. In fact it could be argued that the rise and spread of humanistic thought in this age might be traced to the printing press. The issue of language was, understandably, at the centre of concerns in printing and the manufacture of books. The Reformation itself, as Elizabeth Eisenstein has demonstrated in her magisterial *The Printing Press as an Agent of Change* (1980), was made possible by printing which helped disseminate and preserve ideas.

The language of the stage (the masques) began to use the language of the people from the mid-fifteenth century, though with printing, publishing for the masses had begun to use English (rather than language), and helped standardise it (the first English dictionary is still a while away though, appearing only in 1604). In order to emphasise the power of the ruling class, literature and the arts needed to convey ideas and images about England and its rulers in the language of the common man; Latin was not adequate for the purpose. People had to be convinced of the rule of the king. Therefore the plays (the most common form of entertainment) had to use the language of the town-square and the market place. Ideas about monarchy, religion and absolute kingship could be conveyed through common speech and images. The vernacular, which was linked to nationalism and emergent ideas of national identity, was, therefore, central to the social and political ethos of the day, and finds its climactic moment in the 1611 King James Bible and is preceded, in importance, by Edmund Coote's *The English Schoolmaster* (1596), the first textbook intended to teach the illiterate English the vernacular. (In the 1620s Ben Jonson would begin a textbook on grammar, and dozens of grammar treatises appeared right from the Elizabethan times.) Poets and commentators like George Puttenham and George Gascoigne would attempt to craft a tradition of English poetry as part of the drive towards vernacularisation. (Ironically, the emphasis on the development of a vernacular in European nations like England and Spain would lead the early conquistadors to *impose* their languages on the natives of South America, and destroy the natives' own – which they had 'discovered' – from the fifteenth century, see Mignolo 2003 on the link between language and early Renaissance colonisation.)

Everyday speech was now the language of dialogue on stage, thus making entertainment more inclusive in its appeal to a larger section of society. Most importantly, this was itself a major contribution to forging an English identity because plays and entertainments that used political themes – and who did this better than Shakespeare? – could convey ideas about the nation, religion, and the monarchy to the people in their own language. (The power of this social entertainment to raise social consciousness and political unrest might be gauged from the fact that in 1642 plays were deemed subversive and dangerous; the Act of 1642 therefore shut down the public playhouses.)

Travel and Exploration

There was considerable domestic travel within England in the early modern age. Indeed, mobility, argues Andrew McRae, may be read as a signifier of social change, and random and rampant mobility was a matter of concern for the authorities, who saw it as a threat to the social order (McRae 2009). If these domestic travels mapped the changing dynamics of the social order in early modern England, of far greater consequence were the English, and European, travels outward, into distant parts of the world.

European travels for the discovery of new routes to other parts of the earth had been underway since the fifteenth century, climaxing in the historical Columbian arrival, in 1492, on the shores of the New World. The seventeenth century was marked by travels into various parts of the world, driven primarily by commercial reasons (trade). Invented travelogues like that of John Mandeville (the first English edition appeared in 1499), translations of European travel-texts such as those of Dutch traveller Jan Huyghen van Linschoten's (his *Itinerario* was made available in English in 1598) were hugely popular, and gave the English a sense of a world, or worlds, beyond the confines of their island nation.

The voyages of Francis Drake, Walter Raleigh, John Hawkins and others made England a major sea power, though with hindsight their activities might easily qualify as piratical now. (They seized the ships of other nations.) In 1600, on the last day of the year, Elizabeth I granted the charter of trade to a company of merchants from London, permitting them to trade with the eastern nations – an event that would change history forever: this was the creation of the English East India Company (EIC), which would go on to build the greatest empire the world had ever known.

The English, some commentators argue, as a nation, were seeking an empire. Looking eastward they saw the grand Ottoman Empire, and beyond that, the wealthy Mughal one in India. 'Empire' was therefore, also a part of the cultural imaginary from which the EIC and the early English traveller emerged, and much of the early writings on India may be seen as expressing a sense of 'imperial envy' (Maclean 2001). These travels brought the distant

East, the New World (including present-day South America) closer to the Europeans in the form of travellers' accounts. Walter Raleigh's description in *The Discovery of the Large, Rich, and Beautiful Empire of Guiana* (1596) of a race of grotesque creatures captured the cultural imagination of the British, and inspired further quests for the 'ends' of the earth. Richard Knowles' *The Generall Historie of the Turkes* (1603) opened with a description of 'the glorious Empire of the Turkes, the present terror of the world'. The first English edition of Marco Polo's *Il Milione* appeared in 1503. The first English travel publications were translations of foreign travelogues – Richard Eden's *The Decades of the New World* (1555) which carried a history of the Columbian voyage and that of his successors. In 1582 Richard Hakluyt published his *Divers Voyages Concerning the Discovery of America*, following it up with *The Principall Navigations, Voiages, and Discoveries of the English Nation* (1589) and thereby inaugurated a field of textual discovery. In 1577 Monardes' natural history of the Indies appeared in English translation. Other French and Italian texts (such as Ottaviano Bon's *The Sultan's Seraglio*, translated into English in 1625) offered images of the Arab harem that in turn inspired English works like John Fletcher's *The Knight of Malta* (1616) and *The Island Princess* (this one ostensibly set in India), William Daborne's *A Christian Turned Turk* (1612) and Phillip Massinger's *The Renegado* (1624) that offered highly sexualised images of 'Turkish' women. Collections such as Hakluyt's and later, Samuel Purchas' *Hakluytus Posthumus*, or *Purchas His Pilgrimes* (1625) organised narratives of English and European adventure for public consumption, whetting their appetite for not just more description but evidence of the existence of these other places. They constructed a cultural imaginary, and called for a shift from *imagination* about these distant regions to *inquiries* – mercantile, ethnographic, scientific, theological, political – into these other places, as I argue elsewhere (Nayar, forthcoming).[7]

There was also a 'material' introduction of the Orient and the East to the English public. In the 1460s Andrea Barbarigo, a Venetian trader, was selling spices from the Indies. By the time Vasco da Gama arrived in India in 1498, the port of Calicut (where he landed) already had a thriving international trade with European, Muslim and Jewish merchants from North Africa, Turkey, Persia and Egypt. Exotic goods from the Levant Company and the East India Company began to be more or less commonplace by the 1620s. Shipments of Indian calico by the EIC climbed from 250,000 pieces in the 1660s to one million pieces by the 1680s. Cocoa and tobacco came into England. And, as we know, these were the early moments of the British Empire (see Jardine 1996).

7 Europe in general, and not just England, had a strong interest in the Middle East in the 1550–1700 period, and especially in the Ottoman Empire. (For a recent study, see Brentjes 2010.)

There was another kind of travel as well. The slaving voyages, which began from the sixteenth century, transported nearly 10 million Africans in over 35,000 voyages (sub-Saharan Africa alone lost about 12.5 million people between 1525 and 1867, to the slave trade) for work in the sugar plantations in the New World.

In short, the early modern European world was one that was opening up to other cultures, races and people – an exposure that fed directly into English literature in terms of its interest in geography, racial difference and the existence of other cultures. It discovered 'difference'.

Women and Writing

It is only since the 1980s that the contribution of women writers to the English Renaissance and early modern culture has been recognised. Debates as to whether the women writers of the age were only responding to male writers have continued since then. What has emerged with new feminist historiographies is the fact that women writers worked with all existing genres – fiction, the memoir, lyric poetry, drama and non-fictional prose – and translated from other languages, clearly suggesting that the lack of a formal education seems not to have deterred them from acquiring literacy skills. Many scribbled in the margins of printed matter and this kind of 'work', as some marvellous new studies have shown, indicates how women readers acquired creativity and 'personalized' texts for themselves (Snook 2009). Privileged women such as Lady Mary Wroth were of course familiar with European texts and the humanist tradition, and their writings (in prose, particularly) indicates this class-linked literacy.

While women were producing a significant body of work, mainstream publishing focused on creating 'suitable' women. Gender roles were clearly prescribed and described in Elizabethan–Jacobean England with works such as *The Book of Common Prayer* (1559), John Dod's *Exposition of the Ten Commandments* (1604), Dorothy Leigh's *The Mother's Blessing* (1616), *The English Hus-Wife* (1615) and *The Law's Resolution of Women's Rights* (1632) offering advice and instructions on the woman's role as wife and mother, and called for a greater attention to femininity and feminine virtues such as care and gentleness. Cookbooks such as John Partridge's *Treasurie of Commodious Conceites* (1573) targeted women of a particular class who could not afford expensive (those served at the court) dishes, but sought to imitate them.

Even as such social definitions of what it meant to be a woman circulated widely, women of the period had begun to acquire a literacy unheard of in earlier eras. More women began to write and translate (at least a hundred works were translated or composed by women between 1500 and 1640). Motherhood, religion, love and marriage were common topics. Social criticism was also an emerging genre, and one prominent authoress, Anne

Askew, was even arrested for heresy for criticising the gender-discriminatory laws and religion of England. Dramatists like Aemelia Lanyer, Anne Finch and Elizabeth Cary flourished. Margaret Cavendish, the scientist, wrote poetry with scientific themes. Other authors, while supposedly offering advice on household management, also managed to indicate that women might want to take to writing, thus quietly subverting the stereotypical feminine roles. Hannah Woolley in her *The Gentlewoman's Companion* (1673) treated writing as a household art, and scholars have noted the recipe for preparing ink in several recipe collections (Wall 2009).

The Playhouse, the Performers and the Audience

The late medieval period had seen wandering players performing across England. These lacked, given the fact that they lacked patronage of any kind, suitable venues, props and costumes. Further, their choice of subject matter was also limited, especially because Elizabeth I's decree that religion could not be the subject of theatre, meant that a significant theme was always beyond their ken. Groups of players such as Queen's Men (under Elizabeth I's patronage), Leicester's Men (under Robert Dudley, Earl of Leicester) and then the Chamberlain's Men and the Admiral's Men were formed, often performing in open-air playhouses built in the suburbs of towns such as Shoreditch, Bankside and Holywell. Among the Chamberlain's Men was an actor, William Shakespeare, and the performances of this group at the Globe would soon begin to acquire a large fan following. These amphitheatres, with three-tier galleries, could seat up to 3000 people. However, wandering troupes of actors performed even in the grounds of inns and the animal-baiting arenas common to the age. Indoor theatres were exclusive, since the admission rates were beyond the reach of the commoner.

The stage in Shakespeare's time was usually of the open-air variety where the stages extended into the audience (which meant that the audience surrounded the actors on at least three sides). The proscenium arch style became commonplace only after the Restoration. Plays were written primarily for daylight performances, and playwrights could not create scenes exclusively for indoor staging (and therefore controlled lighting).[8]

Innovators such as James Burbage (who actually dismantled a theatre and relocated it to another site in 1598–1599) were at the forefront of the

8 The following websites offer excellent contextual, critical and source materials, in addition to texts, for Shakespeare studies. Embedded links on these sites lead further afield. http://internetshakespeare.uvic.ca/; http://pages.unibas.ch/shine/metasite.html; www.folger.edu; http://shakespeare.palomar.edu/. The web's first edition of the complete Shakespeare is the one hosted by MIT at http://shakespeare.mit.edu/. Vast teaching and primary resources are available at one of the world's great Shakespeare libraries, the Folger (http://www.folger.edu/template.cfm?cid=618).

theatre scene. Aristocrats patronised companies of actors, even though city authorities were often worried about the crowds that gathered to watch the plays, for they recognised the potential in staging plays about the monarchy and the power of the medium to generate and disseminate political opinions. The 1574 Act of Common Council set limits on public performances for this reason. A famous instance of official surveillance of the theatre is of course that of Thomas Nashe and Ben Jonson, whose *Isle of Dogs* attracted the attention of the government for its politics and resulted in both Nashe and Jonson being imprisoned.

Criticism of monarchy, the exploration of human foibles and its capacity for evil, greed and cruelty were common subjects in the Elizabethan and Jacobean plays. Shakespeare's contemporary, Christopher Marlowe, for instance, offered the first real examination of power. *Tamburlaine* and *Edward II* looked at the power of monarchs, the *Jew of Malta* at commercial business power and knowledge-as-power that aligns with the demonic in *Dr Faustus*. The powerfully poetic *Tamburlaine the Great* (1587) was based on the story of Timur the Lame). Tamburlaine is one of the first great characters in English tragedy, and Marlowe captured all his arrogance in some truly poetic passages such as these:

> The god of war resigns his room to me,
> Meaning to make me general of the world:
> Jove, viewing me in arms, looks pale and wan
> Fearing my power should pull him from his throne. . .

Dr Faustus focused on a man's greed for knowledge, and concludes with one of the most touching pleas for mercy:

> O God!
> If thou wilt not have mercy on my soul,
> Yet for Christ's sake whose blood hath ransomed me
> Impose some end to my incessant pain:
> Let Faustus live in hell a thousand years,
> A hundred thousand, and at last be saved!
> O, no end is limited to damned souls!

In his Jacobean phase, or rather, Shakespeare's darker period, similar gloomy themes and characters were to multiply. *Othello* (1603) dealing with human jealousy, distrust and vulnerability, combines the heroic figure with a braggart. *King Lear* (1605) presented the failure of a man unable to recognise evil or virtue. *Macbeth* (1606) is about succession, kingship and the social order. Shakespeare also often linked the fate of the social order, subjects and kingdoms to the greed and short-sightedness of aristocrats and kings in *Antony and Cleopatra* (1607), *Coriolanus* (1609) and *Timon of Athens* (1608).

Thus, it is more than evident that there was a substance to the anti-theatre group's opinion that many of the plays staged conflict, depicted human nature at its worst and carried political overtones.

To return to the production component of these plays, theatre companies shared the properties (actors' costumes were very expensive) and finances of the firm, including sharing rents and licensing fees. The Admiral's Men and the Chamberlain's Men – which became The King's Men after James I took over as patron – were two of the largest companies after 1594. (Shakespeare produced two plays a year for the latter.)

There has been considerable debate about the nature of audiences for these plays. Commentators have proposed that theatres seem to have attracted audiences from across the social spectrum, though many of the working classes may not have been able to afford the penny admittance fees (which would have meant they get to stand in pits around the stage) – the cheapest seats cost three and six pence at the Blackfriars (Gurr 1996).[9] Debates about the influence of the stage on audiences raged furiously during the Elizabethan and Jacobean times, where some saw theatre as corrupting, displacing Sunday religion for entertainment, theatres as the dens of the devil, etc. Philip Stubbes' *Anatomy of Abuses* (1583) called for a complete abolition of the theatre for the threats it posed to both spectators and players. (Thomas Kyd's melodramatic *The Spanish Tragedy* had eight murders and suicides, besides spectacles such as a public hanging, the biting out of a man's tongue, the picture of a lunatic, a play-within-a-play. It went into ten editions before 1634, and was one of the most popular plays of the age.) Others were concerned that women in the audience were particularly inclined to being corrupted, and hence theatre ought to be banned (Kidnie 2003, also Barish 1981).

The Intellectual Background

Elizabethan and Jacobean England were both influenced by the waves of new scientism, philosophy and learning that arose with the European Renaissance (dated from roughly the mid-14th century). Rational thinking, empiricism and Reason (always spelt with 'R' in upper case) reigned and specialised societies founded in the seventeenth century (the Royal Society) disseminated new views in science and philosophy (Abraham Cowley's poem, 'To the Royal Society' is a paean to the work and significance of this society and individuals such as Francis Bacon).

The influence of the Dutch Erasmus and the French Descartes, the scientific discoveries of William Hervey, Robert Hooke and Robert Boyle and the

9 Thomas Deloney was one of the first to situate his fiction in lower class society in *Jack of Newbury* (1597), *Thomas of Reading* (1597) and *The Gentle Craft* (1597). These were essentially satires on London life, its corruption and moral depravity.

writings of Francis Bacon were the engines of great intellectual change and debate in early modern England.

'Renaissance' meant simply a resurgence of the arts and culture, new ways of thinking within philosophy and a greater interest in all forms of knowledge and knowledge-making (by which we mean the processes through which knowledge or 'truth' is acquired, and spread). It also meant a greater interest in human behaviour, which led directly to the rise of an interest in manners and civility, with instruction manuals on etiquette (called courtesy books), fashion and other domains of social interaction, being published during this age. This Renaissance, as contemporary scholars insist, was constituted equally by an interest in the other parts of the world, such as Asia, and had begun to exhibit a proto-colonial tendency to exploration and conquest but also intellectual and cultural exchanges (see Johanyak and Lim 2010; Mignolo 2002).

Against Scholasticism and the New Science

Knowledge was a common concern of philosophers, statesmen and poets alike in the early modern age. Monarchs like James I sought to establish his reputation as an *erudite* monarch with *Demonology* (1597), *Basilikon Doron* (*King's Gift*, 1599) and *A Counterblast to Tobacco* (1604). Embodying the new spirit of knowledge in early modern England is Francis Bacon (1561–1626), one of the most prolific writers of his time. Bacon inaugurated an era of discovery, scientific spirit and rational temper. *The Advancement of Learning* (1605) presented learning as the basis for a national culture. *Novum Organum* (*The New Instrument*, 1620) identified four 'idols' that lure man away from the truth: the tribe, the cave, the market-place and the theatre. Thomas Browne (1605–1682) was a physician by training, who published his private journal, *Religio Medici* ('A Doctor's Religion') in 1642. Like Bacon, faced with religious and scientific truths, Browne suggested that we inquire into God's works. We should seek to read *the* book (the Bible) alongside the *book* of Nature. In *Religio Medici*, he therefore attempts to provide scientific explanations for Biblical miracles. His *Pseudodoxia Epidemica* (1646) discussed the various errors in our ideas about minerals, vegetables, diseases and animals, pointing out superstitions and myths. His antiquarian tract, *Hydrotaphia, or Urn Burial* (1658), was a report on the various Roman funeral urns discovered near Norwich and concludes with a meditative essay on death.

Skepticism was a common position taken up by philosophers in the early modern period (Spolsky 2001). But one of the key moments in early modern philosophical thinking on the very idea of knowledge was the rejection of scholasticism. Scholasticism sought to find the complete 'truth' very often within the bounds of Christian truth. It also demanded an attention to, and reverence for, tradition and classical thought. Scholasticism also proposed that heavenly bodies were incorruptible. Such metaphysical accounts, as Basil Willey suggests in his magnificent study of continued significance, were confronted with newer discoveries of comets, planets and sun-spots, seen through new human technological devices such as the telescope (Willey 1967: 20). In religion, a whole new iconography – and iconoclasm – was instituted with the Reformation. (The effects of this in the visual arts have been studied by Joseph Leo Koerner 2004.)

From the sixteenth century a different ethos emerged, influenced mainly by the Renaissance in Europe. The age of new science might be said to be inaugurated with Copernicus who, in 1543, argued for the heliocentric view of the universe. Discoveries of new planets by Johannes Kepler and Galileo's theories in astronomy radically altered the existing views of the world. Developments in mechanics and optics (this is the age, also, of Isaac Newton, whose own work – including many writings – spanned religious questions, subjects such as alchemy, optics, math, physics and church history[10]) opened up whole new worlds, both distant (in the form of planets and celestial bodies) and internal (the cells in bodies). These suggested that there could be multiple worlds, and hence multiple cultures and multiple gods. William Harvey's discovery of the circulation of blood, Robert Hooke's discovery of the cell, Robert Boyle's discovery of the chemical laws ensured that science became the authoritative interpreter of natural phenomena, and dominated religion in terms of the pursuit of knowledge. The empirical observation of natural phenomena, whether in the heavens or in bodies, became the acceptable and respectable mode of knowledge-making (as opposed to the scholastic mode of explicating texts – *expositio* – and systematic discussion – *quaestio, disputatio* – in order to arrive at the total truth, or *summa*[11]).

Francis Bacon proposed two kinds of truth – one of religion and the other of science, and suggested that these be kept separate. The first was a matter of faith, and therefore internal. The latter was truth mathematically and/ or empirically verifiable, and was external. The central problem, therefore, was how one could be certain of the truth: a question, in other words, about the *nature* of knowledge, or epistemology. With Rene Descartes, the key philosopher of the age, the thinking mind became the one thing any

10 A reliable resource for Isaac Newton is the Newton Project at Sussex (http://www.newtonproject.sussex.ac.uk/prism.php?id=1).

11 Rhetoric was central to argumentation. The Renaissance was a period when rhetoric flourished, and its influences are still visible in contemporary philological studies, narrative theory and literary theory. For a study of Renaissance rhetoric, see Barilli (1989), and for primary texts in the rhetorical tradition, see Bizzell and Herzberg (2001).

individual could be certain of. It is the indisputable truth. Descartes also argued that whatever could be clearly apprehended is necessarily true.

The rise of natural science as a discipline meant that Nature stopped being treated as vile and satanic (which was the case in the medieval ages) but as divine. God, it was argued, revealed Himself to man through the created universe. Only knowledge from particular sources, ratified by certain authorities ('learned' bodies such as the Royal Society) was acceptable *as* knowledge. Knowledge was also seen as the hallmark of particular classes of people, who were curious about things. They were the 'curiosi', essentially gentlemen with the leisure and funds to spend their time seeking knowledge.

After acquiring this empirical knowledge, it had to be systematised, and organised in the form of 'inquiries'. The organisation and presentation of knowledge – with straight narration, and no frills or rhetorical flourishes – was as important as the gathering of knowledge. 'Natural history' and chorographies (descriptions of particular places) combined with 'curiosity cabinets' (the early museums) to become modes of knowledge dissemination among the discerning (that is, the elite) classes. Those like Galileo, Kepler and Huygens treated such knowledge, verified empirically by experts, alone as valid. Galileo is famous for dismissing philosophers in a letter to Johannes Kepler wherein he mocked people who think 'philosophy is a sort of book like the *Aeneid* and the *Odyssey*, and that truth is to be found not in the world or in nature but in the collation of texts'. Translations of classical texts often involved, as Grafton and Siraisi warn in their introduction to a collection of essays on the history of Renaissance natural philosophy, 'appropriation, manipulation and reworking of older forms of knowledge', even occasionally *recasting* classical texts to fit their humanist agenda. Indeed, the knowledge and practice of sciences of nature and mankind itself were humanistically inclined, in addition to being subject to the intersections of the changing nature of disciplines like alchemy, natural history and medicine (1999: 4–5).

Exotic knowledge about other parts of the world was organised alongside detailed information about England. Numerous chorographies and antiquarian research appeared in the seventeenth century. Works like William Dugdale's *Antiquities of Warwickshire* (1656) and Thomas Browne's 'Urn-Burial' (1658) helped develop a sense of place and history. Antiquarianism also enabled an interest in Britain's Roman past (for example in John Speed's influential *History of Great Britain*, 1611). Antiquarianism was influential in developing a sense of English nationhood, with local histories and genealogies occupying pride of place. Works like William Camden's *Brittania* (1586), Michael Drayton's *Poly-Olbion* (1612, 1622) and others mapped England in terms of its traditions, fauna and flora and history. Edmund Spenser's *Faerie Queene* attempted to trace or invent the lineage of the British monarchy. Richard Verstegan's *A Restitution of Delayed*

Intelligence in Antiquities (1605) established an English-Saxon lineage for James I.

Humanism

Studia humanitatis – what we now identify as liberal education – deriving the term from the Latin *humanitas* of the European classical tradition, included language, literature, history and moral philosophy. Florence and Naples were at the vanguard of humanist thought in the Renaissance, and were the centres where humanities as a discipline evolved in the period.

Studia humanitatis includes an interest in the past and the arts of antiquity, philological attention to written texts, but also demonstrates a keen enthusiasm for mathematics, medicine and the law. Humanism was also grounded in serious and intense textual scholarship, mainly of manuscripts, and most humanists built up vast libraries especially after the advent of the printed book. Translations of the classics were a key mode of transmission of learning, and were central to the spread of humanist thought throughout Europe (Davies 1996). Educational developments of the Jacobean period and after were influenced by humanist ideals (Loewenstein 1996).

In English literature humanist thought really makes its presence felt in the sixteenth century. The classical learning that humanism demanded was available only to the upper classes, and the stylistic and rhetorical requirements for writing were not commonplace outside these classes. As translations of Greek and Latin classical texts arrived from the 1470s, many members of these classes acquired them and were influenced by them. Thomas More, the author of *Utopia* (1516, translated into English in 1551) was perhaps England's first humanist writer. Wyatt, Surrey (Henry Howard), Spenser and Sidney were influenced by Petrarch and Ariosto (Carroll 1996), as questions of moral and political reform engaged the English humanists.

A knowledge of history was seen as central to a complete humanist education. Histories were a popular genre after the printing press arrived in England, and one of the first books to be printed by William Caxton was *The Chronicles of England* (1480). Right through the sixteenth century we see chronicles and histories, such as those by John Stow (*Summary of English Chronicles*, 1565) and William Warner (*Albion's England*, 1586), being published and proving extremely popular. Locating the ancestry of the nobility (the work of Edward Hall, in particular, *The Union of the Two Noble and Illustrious Families of Lancaster and York*, 1548), details of the great wars and peerage were subjects of considerable interest to the rich patrons. History itself was deemed central to a complete education, and hence there was a certain pedagogic angle to the publication of these extensive histories. It is not a coincidence that Shakespeare began his career with history plays – plays dealing with the age of Henry VI (which are referred to by Robert

Greene in the course of which he famously dismissed Shakespeare as the 'upstart crow').[12]

Rationality and language were treated as the markers of the human. Animals were central to the construction of the human as a category, as Erica Fudge (2006) shows, even before Descartes' influential beast-machine hypothesis. Reason, the humanists would argue, 'reveals humans' immortality, and animals' irrationality reveals their mortality, their materiality' (Fudge 3). Notions of virtue, excellence, greatness and moral goodness were qualities associated with the human than with the animal species. But it also meant that these qualities were seen as associated with particular classes and races of humans: with Africans, Asians and even women excluded from the ambit of the 'human' (see Tony Davies, 1997 for a summary).

English Poetry, from the Elizabethans to the Restoration

The continental influence on English poetry continued through the fifteenth and sixteenth century, most markedly in sonneteers such as Wyatt and Surrey (the 'Silver Poets'). Elizabethan poetry was mainly courtly, written by earls and dukes. Love poetry was a common form, and descriptions of the psychological states of lovers were an enduring theme. Courtship and wooing, the disinterest of the mistress and the pains of separation were also common themes. It is in Elizabethan poetry that we see the emergence of an indigenous English poetry. The period between the Elizabethan and the Restoration also produced some extraordinary topographical and chorographic poetry. In this section I shall survey some of the more prominent genres in the poetry of this hundred-year period.

Love and religion seem to be the twin poles of the Elizabethan age's thematic in poetry. Allegories of and myth-making about the nation and national identity were embodied in Spenser, Drayton and others. Spenser's *The Faerie Queene* (the first three books appeared in 1590, and the second group of three appeared in 1596, with the famous 'Mutabilitie Cantos' appearing ten years after Spenser's death), often treated as the first truly epic poem in English, was meant as a moral, political and religious allegory, to restore

12 Shakespeare's early history plays *Henry VI*, parts I, II and III, critics agree, encode a nostalgia for a glorious English past. *Henry VI, part I,* opens with a scene of mourning for the dead king (Henry V), even nature takes part in the mourning because 'England ne'er lost a king of so much worth', once again suggesting Shakespeare's nostalgia for an earlier age (Rackin 2003). The later history play, *Richard II*, which opens the second cycle of Shakespeare's history plays, is set in the medieval times, where Shakespeare presents Richard as a king who, like Henry VI, destroyed the heritage of the earlier generations. Chivalry, honour and such 'old world' virtues are mourned in later history plays as well (*Henry IV*, in the figure of Hotspur). *Henry V* presents the king as an embodiment of moral perfection.

the moral function of poetry. The Faerie Queen sends out her knights to overcome monsters and temptations (the twelve moral vices). The triumph of the knights stands for the triumph of a virtuous English monarchy itself. Friendship, loyalty, chastity, grace and courtesy are *defined* for England and its people, critics have noted, in the poem (Pichaske 1977, Archer 1987). The Faerie Queen, Spenser himself said, was the symbol of glory. Themes of nationalism, loyalty, the glory of the monarch and morality were woven into the story of the knights, who themselves symbolise various qualities. John Milton focused on a grander theme: humanity and God.[13]

The Poetry of Love and Courtship

Walter Raleigh (1552–1618), the conqueror of Virginia in the New World, was instrumental in persuading Spenser to publish *The Faerie Queene*. Raleigh's love poetry captured the various moods of the lover:

> Passions are liken'd best to floods and streams:
> The shallow murmur, but the deep are dumb;
> So, when affection yields discourse, it seems
> The bottom is but shallow whence they come.
> They that are rich in words, in words discover
> That they are poor in that which makes a lover.

Philip Sidney (1554–1586) in *Astrophel and Stella* (two editions published in 1591) compiled a collection of 108 sonnets and 11 songs, all dealing with the unfulfilled love of Astrophel for Stella. Courtship here proceeds along certain lines. Sidney from around the 25th sonnet begins to use personification to describe his love, and Stella becomes the personification of all virtue:

> Vertue of late, with vertuous care to ster
> Loue of herself, tooke *Stellas* shape, that she
> To mortall eyes might sweetly shine in her.
> It is most true; for since I her did see,
> Vertues great beauty in that face I proue,
> And find th' effect, for I do burn in loue.

Sidney also posits a connection between the poetry and love: 'love doth hold my hand and makes me write' (sonnet 90). Or:

> My best wits still their own disgrace invent:
> My very inke turns straight to *Stellas* name

13 A useful source book for Spenser is Albert Charles Hamilton's *The Spenser Encyclopedia* (1990).

And because the love is unfulfilled, the sequence ends, appropriately, in mid-sentence: 'That therewith my song is broken'.

Nature and the beloved are linked, in what would set a tradition for love poetry, in Sidney:

> When Nature made her chief worke, *Stella's* eyes,
> In colour blacke why wrapt she beames so bright?
> Would she in beamy blacke, like Painter wise,
> Frame daintiest lustre, mixt of shades and light?

But there is also, perhaps the anxiety, that his love and passion for Stella was blinding him, and diverting him from his true vocation – the service of the prince and state.

The connection between a lush, and therefore pleasurable, nature and the ripe woman (available for pleasuring) that we see in most of these poems, Christine Coch notes in a perspicacious reading (2009), is possibly embedded in the theme of 'pleasure gardening' of the late sixteenth century.[14] Both gardens and women appealed to the senses. And gardens, like women, were prone to running wild, given to the passions rather than to rationality, and hence needed to be tended and controlled. Coch suggests that the entire imagery of gardens and women reveals an ambivalence towards aesthetic pleasures.[15]

Edmund Spenser (1552–1599) published one of the most important poems in the pastoral, *The Shepherd's Calendar* in 1579. It was illustrated with woodcuts, and consisted of 12 eclogues, one for each month of the year. Spenser's wooing of Elizabeth Boyle resulted in the love songs, *Amoretti* and *Epithalamion* (both published in 1595). *Amoretti* is a three-part sequence of sonnets dealing with his love and courtship of Elizabeth Boyle and in *Epithalamion* Spenser celebrated his marriage to Boyle. The twenty-four stanzas of *Epithalamion* represent the twenty-four hours of Midsummer Day (Hieatt 1960). *Prothalamion* (1596) celebrated the double marriage of Lady Elizabeth and Lady Katherine Somerset. In all these poems, marriage is celebrated as the natural fulfilment of the human life cycle. Spenser's religious imagery partakes of both pagan and Christian symbolisms, so that the bride represents the Christian church, the bridegroom, Christ, and the marriage itself the eschatology.[16]

---

14 On the 'ideal' landscape in seventeenth century poetry, see Spencer (1973).

15 The standard study of Elizabethan imagery remains Rosamund Tuve's 1961 work, *Elizabethan and Metaphysical Imagery: Renaissance Poetic and Twentieth Century Critics* and Caroline Spurgeon's *Shakespeare's Imagery and What it Tells Us* (1961).

16 Elsewhere, in the 'Mutabilitie Cantos' (Cantos VI and VII of Book VII of *The Faerie Queene*), Spenser would meditate on change, time and eternity, where man, nature, nations, the cosmos itself becomes subject to mutability. For a quick introduction to the books of Spenser's epic, see Heale (1987).

These poems were also addressed to the woman not only as the poet's lover/beloved, but as the reader of their texts (Spenser explicitly refers to the *Epithalamion* as a 'song made in lieu of many ornaments' for Elizabeth). Spenser also moves from the woman/beloved as an ethereal and transcendent entity to somebody *of this world*. Critics have proposed that poems like *Amoretti* begin by showing the lover/woman as insubstantial (an 'objectified ideal', as one William Johnson put it, 1993, 506) and even an inimical *other* to the male/poet but ends being beneficial to the poetry, and even to the fashioning of the poet's very self.

Abraham Cowley (1618–1667) in *The Mistress* (1647) detailed a lover's suffering in the face of his beloved's indifference. Andrew Marvell (1621–1678), with his intellectual sentimentality and lovely use of metaphysical conceits and immediately resonant themes (such as 'seize the day', or *carpe diem*) in 'To His Coy Mistress', 'The Garden' and other poems, has remained one of the most popular poets of this age.

The Cavaliers had a greater amount of sensuality in their love poems, even though some, like Herrick, entwined love and the country in a form of pastoral poetry:

> I sing of Brooks, of blossoms, birds, and bowers:
> I write of youth, of love…

Most Cavalier poets were concerned with mutability and the passage of time, and their poetry exhorted their beloveds to make use of their youth and the time at their disposal to the best effects, such as love:

> Gather ye rosebuds while ye may,
> Old time is still a-flying:
> And this same flower that smiles to-day
> To-morrow will be dying.

This famous verse from Herrick's 'To the Virgins, to Make Much of Time' captures the entirety of the Cavalier's disposition. Herrick, Suckling and Lovelace have been treated as poets who celebrated life, even if short, and there is a certain careless exuberance of manner in their work. Wit was a characteristic trait, and accompanied by a certain effusive charm, was believed to be the marks of a gentleman (all Cavaliers saw themselves primarily as gentlemen).

An exaggerated courtesy that however often reduced the wooed woman to a sexual object is visible in much of their work. The idealisation of the woman dicussed above with regard to Elizabethan poetry is conspicuously absent here, and references to the carnal component of love are part of the address to the wooed woman in Cavalier poetry which is toned with sexual frankness. John Suckling (1609–1642) wrote poetry full of wit in a tone that is always casual, but biting:

Out upon it, I have loved
Three whole days together,
And am like to love three more,
If it prove fair weather;

His poetry is an example of this kind of loaded imagery:

If where a gentle bee hath fall'n,
And laboured to his power,
A new succeeds not to that flower,
But passes by,
'Tis to be thought, the gallant elsewhere loads his thigh.

For still the flowers ready stand:
One buzzes round about,
One lights, one tastes, gets in, gets out;
All all ways use them,
Till all their sweets are gone, and all again refuse them.

Edmund Waller compares women to food, as edible objects that satisfy the man's craving:

Amoret! as sweet and good
as the most delicious food,
which, but tasted, does impart
life and gladness to the heart.
('To Amoret')

An admonitory tone is visible in others. Suckling's 'Why so pale and wan, fond lover?' deals with the inability to convince the woman to love:

Quit, quit for shame, this will not move,
This cannot take her;
If of herself she will not love,
Nothing can make her;
The devil take her.

In a different line, honour, chivalry and courage mix with amorousness and sensual affection in poems such as Lovelace's famous 'To Lucasta, Going to the Wars', which begins with:

from the nunnery
Of thy chaste breast and quiet mind
To war and arms I fly

He has a 'new mistress' to 'chase' he says. But he justifies his action thus:

I could not love thee (Dear) so much,
Lov'd I not Honour more.

Lovelace, unlike Suckling, casts love alongside religious and civic values. He subsumes the eroticism and the amorousness within these other qualities. His protagonist is at once lover and soldier or, in other words, a gentleman.

Among the metaphysicals like John Donne, the great elegies ('To His Mistress Going to Bed') show remarkable sexual frankness. Donne also appropriated images from geography and astronomy to describe amorousness and love (for example in 'Air and Angels', 'The Good Morrow', 'Love's Alchemy'). In the great songs ('The Canonisation', 'The Expiration', 'A Valediction: Forbidding Morning'), there is an entire range of emotions: from frustration and exasperation to ecstasy.

The Poetry of Faith and Religion

'today
In prayers, and flattering speeches I court God:
Tomorrow I quake with true fear of his rod.'

John Donne's Holy Sonnets, from which the above lines (Sonnet XIX) are taken, inaugurated the highly personalised religious lyric of the seventeenth century. The poetry inscribes devotion with fear, faith with anxiety. The devout individual has an intense relationship with God, but fears God more than loving Him. Hence the tone of the poetry in Donne is one of pleading, wanting and anxiety rather than of any affectionate or trusting relation with the divine. The devout is chided and chastised into worship and faith, as Donne puts it:

Your force, to break, blow, burn, and make me new . . .

This sense of self-doubt and uncertainty over the relationship with God is best exemplified in the work of George Herbert (1593–1633). Like in Donne, adoration mixes with anxiety, happiness with uncertainty in the accounts of the poet's relationship with God. The poetry is intensely personal, as we can see in 'The Collar' or 'The Pulley'. In the former, the speaker opens with a note of anger ('I struck the board, and cried, "No more" '), as though he is annoyed with God. Yet when it concludes it is passive:

But as I raved and grew more fierce and wild
At every word,
Methought I heard one calling, *Child!*
And I replied *My Lord.*

In 'The Pulley', Herbert, like his contemporaries, presents a less-than-kind God, one who wishes to induce fear and restlessness in the faithful, so that they would then turn to Him:

> But keep them with repining restlesnesse:
> Let him be rich and wearie, that at least,
> If goodnesse leade him not, yet wearinesse
> May tosse him to my breast.

Henry Vaughan (1622–1695) was influenced by Herbert in his most famous work, *Silex Scintillans*. The speaker, recognising that he has left his innocence, and perhaps his faith behind and been corrupted, longs for a return in 'The Retreat', another poem about the anxiety over the loss of faith:

> O how I long to travel back,
> And tread again that ancient track!
> That I might once more reach that plain,
> Where first I left my glorious train.

Thomas Traherne (1636–1674) wrote some very self-conscious poetry, imbued with a sense of wonder in his vision of the world. All of these poets exhibit a certain mysticism. Faith, repentance, spiritual progress, perseverance and grace are the central themes in almost all religious poetry here. The speakers seem to be torn between desires and the divine, and this tension is suggested by the violence of imagery in most of the religious poetry (and thus anticipates Gerard Manley Hopkins' works).[17]

The most important poet of the age was of course John Milton (1608–1674), whose career spans the interregnum and the long eighteenth century, and a man whose work has fascinated critics and readers for centuries. *Paradise Lost* (1667, revised and updated in 1674 – this latter, with commendatory poems by Andrew Marvell and others, is treated as the standard edition by Milton scholars) dealt with the creation of the world, the fall of man and the power of God. Milton's great work uses, in addition to Christian theology, pagan mythology, recent scientific theories, and classical literature.[18] It also adapts from a number of genres. Commentators

17 Image makeovers of the cross and other Christian icons were central to the Reformation which, even as the Protestants indulged in iconoclasm, 'renewed' Church art (see Koerner 2004).

18 For Milton's use of classical rhetorical tropes in *PL* see a quick guide hosted by Dartmouth College, http://www.dartmouth.edu/~milton/reading_room/rhetoric/index.shtml. A more elaborate and student-friendly resource for reading the text is http://www.christs.cam.ac.uk/darknessvisible/index.html. A very useful compendium is Edward S. Le Comte's 1969 work *The Milton Dictionary*. Also useful is Hanford

for the past few centuries have worked to unravel influences, genres, adaptations and references in the epic (for a detailed summary of Milton's generic borrowings, see Lewalski 1999). Milton's aims were stated at the beginning of Book I:

> Of Man's First Disobedience, and the Fruit
> Of that Forbidden Tree, whose mortal tast
> Brought Death into the World, and all our woe,
> With loss of Eden, till one greater Man
> Restore us . . .
>
> I thence
> Invoke thy aid to my adventurous Song,
> That with no middle flight intends to soar
> Above th' Ionian Mount, while it pursues
> Things unattempted yet in Prose or Rime.
> And chiefly Thou O Spirit, that dost prefer
> Before all Temples th' upright heart and pure,
> Instruct me, for Thou know'st; Thou from the first
> Wast present, and with mighty wings outspread
> Dove-like satst brooding on the vast Abyss
> And mad'st it pregnant: What in me is dark
> Illumin, what is low raise and support;
> That to the highth of this great Argument
> I may assert Eternal Providence,
> And justifie the wayes of God to men.

The poem therefore does *not* seek to explore God's existence but rather to explain God's *nature* and attitude: 'justifie the wayes of God to men' is how Milton puts it (what is called theodicy). With light and dark, vision and blindness as recurrent tropes (Quint 2010), Milton proceeds to explicate these divine 'ways'.

Besides the (usual) Biblical themes of creation, the fall of Lucifer, the fall of man (on which thousands have commented), *PL* can also be read for its mythopoeic and 'grandiloquent' language. There are also other points of interest. John Leonard points to, for instance, the ease with which Adam acquires language – he is born with it. Adam proceeds to name all that he sees:

---

and Taaffe's *A Milton Handbook* (1970), which offers quick summaries of the books, allusions, Milton's cosmology and literary sources. For more detailed expositions see Marjorie Hope Nicolson's *John Milton: A Reader's Guide to his Poetry* (1970). William Blake's magnificent illustrations to *PL* are archived at http://www.pitt.edu/~ulin/Paradise/Blake1808.htm. A study of Milton's visual imagery may be found in Ronald Mushat Frye (1978).

> I nam'd them, as they pass'd, and understood
> Their Nature, . . .

This ability to name was a sign of his wisdom, which was his birthright in Paradise (Eve has partial rights too – she names flowers). When Adam uses the word 'ask', Leonard notes, it does not imply curiosity about God's work, but serves, rather, to magnify the grandeur of God's creation (1999: 138). Debates about Milton's Satan have also raged, with many scholars claiming that Satan is the real hero of the tale. However, it seems more convincing, given Milton's description, to see his attitude toward Satan as *ambivalent*. John Carey suggests that unlike Adam, Eve and God in the poem who are 'transparent' and exist in the words they speak, Satan has levels that are not revealed to us, but is 'dissimulated' (162). Newer readings detect a concern with the nature of the family, especially in the monarchic family, in Milton's epic (Murphy 2011). It appears that Milton's Eden and its account might have also been influenced by the country-house genre (Song 2010). An interest in the politics of Milton's work, especially the idea of citizenship (Adam and Eve as citizens of Eden, for example), has resulted in interpretations that see a trace of republicanism at the heart of *Paradise Lost*. James Kuzner summarises this position:

> His portrayals of Paradise and Pandemonium, for instance, find value in joining rational disputes and sensual caresses; in the therapeutic pleasures of public argument; in the enjoyable, transformed world made by vulnerable subjects within the space of conversation; and, finally, in forms of 'republican' selfhood that do not depend on the republic's support. (2009: 106)

Temptation, at the heart of *PL*, is the key theme in Milton's *Comus* as well, where the lady has to preserve her chastity in the face of Comus' vile magic. *Samson Agonistes* was published along with *Paradise Regained* in 1671. *Samson Agonistes* emphasises the element of divine revenge in the Old Testament, and *Paradise Regained* is about the devil's attempted temptation of Christ in the wilderness.

The Poetry of Landscape

The Elizabethan Age was a time of nationalism and the construction of the English national identity. Understandably, place and locality, folklore and local histories had a major role to play in the construction of such a sense of 'Englishness'.

William Camden's *Brittania* (1586) had already offered a strong sense of place when he mapped England's fauna and flora, history, antiquities and geography. He did this by travelling county by county; therefore what we have in Camden is nothing short of a political and natural geography. He also mapped families, thus offering the reader a social history and a record of land ownership. Take for instance, at random, his account of East Riding:

> Not far from hence, stands a place seated upon the bank of the river, called *Kirkham*, Kirkham. i.e. *the place of the Church*; for here was a College of Canons, founded by *Walter Espec*, a very great man, whose daughter brought a vast estate by marriage to the family of the *Rosses*. Next, but somewhat lower upon the *Derwent*, there stood a city of the same name, which Antoninus calls Derventio. and makes it seven miles distant from York ... The Company of the *Derventienses* under the General of Britain, that quarter'd here: and in the time of the Saxons it seems to have been the Royal Village situated near the river *Doreventio* (says Bede,) where Eumer, that Assassin (as the same Author has it) made a push with his Sword at Edwin King of Northumberland, and had run him through, if one of his retinue had not interpos'd, and sav'd his master's life with the loss of his own . . . The *Derwent* (which, as oft as it is encreas'd with rains, is apt to overflow the banks, and lay all the neighbouring Meadows a-float) passes from hence to *Wreshil*, Wreshil. A Castle neatly built and fortified by *Thomas Percy* Earl of Worcester. . .

We see here combined, geography, political history and social history of the region as Camden moves from landscape to marriages to ownership and architectural history.

Spenserian pastoralism from *Shepherdes' Calendar* influenced entire generations of English poets. 'Spenserianism' is therefore the term used to describe the work of Joshua Sylvester (1563–1618) and other poets like William Browne. Browne's *Britannia's Pastorals* (1613, 1616) and *Shepherd's Pipe* (1613), George Wither's *Shepherd's Hunting* (1615) were all poems in the Spenserian pastoral tradition, as were William Basse's *Three Pastoral Elegies* (1602) and *Pastorals* (1616). In his *Purple Island* (1633) Phineas Fletcher used the allegoric mode aligning human bodies with geography. Milton's *Lycidas*, a pastoral elegy, was also in this tradition (though, as Samuel Johnson would say dismissively of Milton's effort, it is not genuine passion or sorrow Milton expresses for the simple reason that 'passion runs not after remote allusions and obscure opinions').

In the early seventeenth century Michael Drayton embarked on a project similar to Camden's – of celebrating England in verse. The result was *Poly-Olbion* (1612, 1622). He sets out his task clearly in the title (itself a narrative):

> A Chorographicall Description of all the Tracts, Rivers,
> Mountains, Forests, and Other Parts of this Renowned
> Isle of Great Britain. . . .

He also promised an account of the

> Stories, Antiquities, Wonders, Rarities, Pleasures, and Commodities of the same. . .

Drayton invokes myth to connect England's present to the classical age. He offers a catalogue of its fauna and flora in order to capture what he termed 'the genius of the place'. Here is an example of how he combines geographic description with myth and history:

> By nature strongly fenc'd, which never need to fear
> On Neptune's wat'ry realms when Eolus raiseth wars,
> And ev'ry billow bounds, as though to quench the stars:
> Fair Jersey first of these here scatt'red in the deep,
> Peculiarly that boast'st thy double-horned sheep:
>
> Inferior nor to thee, thou Jernsey, bravely crown'd
> With rough-imbattl'd rocks, whose venom-hating ground
> The hard'ned emeril hath, which thou abroad dost send:
> Thou Ligon, her belov'd, and Serb, that dost attend
> Her pleasure ev'ry hour; as Jethow, them at need,
> With pheasants, fallow deer, and conies, that dost feed:
> Ye Seven small sister Isles, and Sorlings, which to see
> The half-sunk seaman joys, or whatsoe'er you be,
> From fruitful Aurney, near the ancient Celtic shore.
> To Ushant, and the Seams, whereas those Nuns of yore
> Gave answers from their caves, and took what shapes they
> Ye happy Islands set within the British Seas,

Most importantly, Drayton chose to do this in the *vernacular* – thus suggesting that the history of England needed to be recorded for the common readers and not for the Latin-speaking elite. The 'genius of the place' was to be conveyed in the language of the common reader. Similar efforts at recording the genius of the place are to be seen in William Browne's *Brittania's Pastorals* (1613–1616). John Denham (1615–1669) in *Cooper's Hill* (first version, 1642, there were at least four subsequent versions) offered a variation of the chorographic poem when he created the panoptical topographic poem, in which the speaker looks down from a height and describes the scene below:

> So rais'd above the tumult and the crowd
> I see the city, in a thicker cloud
> Of business, than of smoke . . .

Denham introduces English cultural practices as well, most notably, the hunt:

> Here have I seen our Charles, when great affairs
> Give leave to slacken, and unbend his cares,
> Chasing the royal stag, the gallant beast,
> Rous'd with the noise, 'twist hope and fear distress'd,
> Resolves 'tis better to avoid, than meet

His danger, trusting to his winged feet:
But when he sees the dogs, now by the view,
Now by the scent, his speed with speed pursue,
He tries his friends, amongst the lesser herd,
Where he but lately was obey'd, and fear'd,
Safety he seeks: the herd, unkindly wise,
Or chases him from thence, or from him flies.
Like a declining statesman, left forlorn
To his friends' pity, and pursuers' scorn.

Denham, like Drayton, also invokes mythic figures to present a continuity and tradition: Cooper's Hill is Parnassus, Charles and his queen, Henrietta Maria, are Mars and Venus, Philippa is Bellona. Native kings are surveyed, thus tying in history with myth. The history of Windsor Castle in the poem centres the history, geography and culture of England itself. Denham uses topography to present not just a pan-optical view of the country but to suggest a unified view at a time of civil and political strife. The harmony of nature and people, the king and subjects that the poem offers in its imagery actually flies in the wake of this instability, and the poem might therefore be seen as a political statement, or fantasy, about the need for harmony.

Such poetry as Drayton's or Denham's that utilises topography and geography to address larger issues of national identity is also paralleled by another kind of poetry of landscape in the seventeenth century, the country-house poem, most notably by Thomas Carew, Ben Jonson and Andrew Marvell. These were written in praise of manors and the houses of aristocratic patrons, where the house was portrayed as the epicentre of values like hospitality and social order. Carew's 'To Saxham', Robert Herrick's 'A Country Life', Jonson's 'To Penshurst' and Marvell's 'Upon Appleton House' are examples. Thus Jonson's poem opens with an emphasis on the *true* nobility of a great house:

Thou art not, PENSHURST, built to envious show
Of touch, or marble; nor canst boast a row
Of polish'd pillars, or a roof of gold:
Thou hast no lantern whereof tales are told;
Or stair, or courts; but stand'st an ancient pile,
And these grudg'd at, art reverenced the while.
Thou joy'st in better marks, of soil, of air,
Of wood, of water; therein thou art fair.

All the inhabitants of such houses are virtuous, and even the servants and waiters serve the guest generously:

Here no man tells my cups; nor standing by,
A waiter, doth my gluttony envý:

But gives me what I call, and lets me eat,
He knows, below, he shall find plenty of meat.

The sense of order is visible even in the architecture according to Marvell who says in 'Upon Appleton House':

But all things are composed here
Like Nature, orderly and near. . . .

Or in Carew's 'To Saxham':

Yet, Saxham, thou within thy gate
Art of thyself so delicate,
So full of native sweets, that bless
Thy roof with inward happiness.

Even the animals know the necessity of keeping the social order and hierarchies, suggests Carew:

The pheasant, partridge, and the lark
Flew to thy house, as to the Ark.
The willing ox of himself came
Home to the slaughter with the lamb,
And every beast did thither bring
Himself, to be an offering.

These landscape poems are about a way of life, rather than strictly about the place alone. It was meant to convey the owner's taste, virtues of hospitality and chastity, a sense of just social order that could be, or ought to be, emulated. They might be read as the expression of a certain anxiety that traditional lifestyles and social hierarchies were in flux, and in danger of disappearing. The glorification of the country house, or the English landscape with its practices such as the hunt, was an attempt to reinstate older values. Thus the poetry of place sought to capture English identities in the form of landscape, architecture, lifestyle and behaviour, using the building or the place as a symbol of more abstract qualities.

Science and Poetry

Poets and prose writers of the sixteenth and seventeenth centuries had to negotiate the erasure of poetic wonders at the hands of scientists. Astronomers, for example, were busy examining the nature of previously poetic objects such as the moon and stars and revealing their inner workings. The world's mysterious functioning was being unravelled with the discovery of cells, atoms and the gas laws. Margaret Cavendish's poetry therefore engages with these new developments in sciences. New worlds, she wrote, were to be discovered within the motion of atoms (the reference to the 'discovery' of the New World is inescapable here):

> Thus by their severall Motions, and their Formes,
> As severall work-men serve each others turnes.
> And thus, by chance, may a New World create:
> Or else predestined to worke my Fate.

Geography and geographical instruments abound in John Donne:

> As stiff twin compasses are two;
> Thy soul, the fix'd foot, makes no show
> To move, but doth, if th' other do.

'Anatomy' as a science that evolves through the sixteenth and seventeenth centuries, serves as the title of dozens of poems and tracts – non-medical ones – in this period (Philip Stubbes: *Anatomy of Abuses*, Donne: 'The Anatomy of the World'; Burton: *Anatomy of Melancholy*).[19] Even political and philosophical writings used tropes and images from anatomy and mechanistic ideas. Thus Thomas Hobbes (1588–1679), influenced by Descartes and machinist views of nature and humankind, would write in *Leviathan* (1651):

> For seeing life is but a motion of limbs, the beginning whereof is in some sort of principal part within; why may we not say that all automata (engines that move themselves by springs and wheels as does a watch) have an artificial life? For what is the heart, but a spring; and the nerves, but so many strings; and the joints, but so many wheels, giving motion to the whole body.

These examples indicate the extent of the literary and philosophical engagement with the new science. Abraham Cowley's poem in praise of the Royal Society ('To the Royal Society'), prefixed to Thomas Sprat's history of the Society, treats scientists like Francis Bacon as the true heroes of the age, presenting Bacon as explorer and pioneer, thus combining the two key 'moments' of exploratory voyages and the new sciences.

Theories of medicine emergent during this time seriously undermined superstitions and myths about the body and bodily functions. John Rogers (1998) shows how in Andrew Marvell, sexual abstinence is the cornerstone of a peaceful existence (in poems like 'The Garden': 'the happy garden-state/ where man walked without a mate'). Sexual aggressiveness and political

19 For a stimulating study of the influence of dissection and the new cultures of medicine, see Jonathan Sawday (1995).

elements are aligned in Marvell's vision, in Rogers' reading. The tension in Marvell, notes Rogers, is between the *vita contemplativa* and *vita activa* with the latter indicative of an active sexual life as well). Vitalist theories constitute the subtext to works like 'The Garden' and 'Upon Appleton House', the latter containing images of the vitrification of nature. Such a 'philosophical vitalism' is also at the centre of Milton's *Paradise Lost*. Rogers notes that Milton himself, in his theological treatise (*De Doctrina Christina*), produced around the same time as *Paradise Lost*, wrote about the 'co-union' of body and spirit.

*

English literature of the period between Queen Elizabeth and the Restoration has, as can be seen even from this short inventory of themes and contexts, multiple sources of inspiration and influence, anxiety and social pressures. Metaphors, themes and images in poets, dramatists and polemicists – whether of the diseased body or of honourable houses – seem to have been drawn from a bewilderingly diverse set of sources, as noted in the course of this introduction. From science to exploration and religion to the law, from plagues to literacy and from mechanistic views of the body to notions of the body politic, the literature of the 1550–1660 period is an extremely demanding one if we were to historicise texts and readings. This diversity of sources and adaptations in literary texts, it is hoped, is what the poems to follow capture.

References

Archer, Mark. 'The Meaning of "Grace" and "Courtesy": Book VI of *The Faerie Queene*.' *Studies in English Literature* 27.1 (1987): 17–34.

Barilli, Renato. *Rhetoric*. Minneapolis: Univ. of Minnesota Press, 1989.

Barish, Jonas. *The Antitheatrical Prejudice*. Berkeley: Univ. of California Press, 1981.

Beier, A.L. *Masterless Men: The Vagrancy Problem in England 1560–1640*. London: Routledge, 1985.

Bizzell, Patricia and Bruce Herzberg. Eds. *The Rhetorical Tradition: Readings from Classical Times to the Present*. New York: St. Martin's, 2001.

Brentjes, Sonja. *Travellers from Europe in the Ottoman and Safavid Empires, 16th–17th Centuries: Seeking, Transforming, Discarding Knowledge*. Aldershot: Ashgate, 2010.

Carey, John. 'Milton's Satan'. *The Cambridge Companion to Milton*. Cambridge: Cambridge Univ. Press, 1999. 160–74.

Carroll, Clare. 'Humanism and English literature in the Fifteenth and Sixteenth Centuries'. *The Cambridge Companion to Renaissance Humanism*. Ed. Jill Kraye. Cambridge: Cambridge Univ. Press, 1996. 246–68.

Chamberlain, E.R. *Everyday Life in Renaissance Times*. London and New York: B.T. Batsford, G.B. Putnam, 1967.

Coch, Christine. 'The Woman in the Garden: (En)gendering Pleasure in Late Elizabethan Poetry'. *English Literary Renaissance* 39.1 (2009): 97–127.

Collinson, P. *The Elizabethan Puritan Movement*. London: Jonathan Cape, 1967.

Davies, Martin. 'Humanism in Script and Print in the Fifteenth Century'. *The Cambridge Companion to Renaissance Humanism*. Ed. Jill Kraye. Cambridge: Cambridge Univ. Press, 1996. 47–62.

Davies, Tony. *Humanism*. London and New York: Routledge, 1997.

Eisenstein, Elizabeth. *The Printing Press as an Agent of Change: Communications and Cultural Transformations in Early-modern Europe*. Cambridge: Cambridge Univ. Press, 1980.

Fudge, Erica. *Brutal Reasoning: Animals, Rationality, and Humanity in Early Modern England*. Ithaca and London: Cornell Univ. Press, 2006.

Frye, Roland Mushat. *Milton's Imagery and the Visual Arts: Iconographic Tradition in the Epic Poems*. Princeton: Princeton Univ. Press, 1978.

Grafton, Anthony and Nancy Siraisi. 'Introduction.' *Natural Particulars: Nature and the Disciplines in Renaissance Europe*. Ed. Anthony Grafton and Nancy Siraisi. Cambridge: MIT, 1999. 1–21.

Greenblatt, Stephen. *Renaissance Self-fashioning: From More to Shakespeare*. Chicago: Univ. of Chicago Press, 1980.

Gurr, Andrew. *Playgoing in Shakespeare's London*. Cambridge: Cambridge Univ. Press, 1996. 2nd ed.

Hamilton, Albert Charles. *The Spenser Encyclopedia*. Toronto: Univ. of Toronto P, 1990.

Hanford, James Holly and James G. Taaffe. *A Milton Handbook*. New Jersey: Prentice-Hall, 1970. 5th ed.

Harris, Jonathan Gil. *Sick Economies: Drama, Mercantilism, and Disease in Shakespeare's England*. Philadelphia: Univ. of Pennsylvania P, 2004.

Heale, Elizabeth. *The Faerie Queene: A Reader's Guide*. Cambridge: Cambridge Univ. Press, 1987.

Helgerson, Richard. *Forms of Nationhood: The Elizabethan Writing of England*. Chicago: Univ. of Chicago Press, 1992.

Hieatt, A. Kent. *Short Time's Endless Monument: The Symbolism of the Numbers in Edmund Spenser's 'Epithalamion' and 'Prothalamion'*. New York: Columbia Univ. Press, 1960.

Higgs, Edward. *The Information State in England*. London: Palgrave, 2004.

Ingram, Martin. 'Love, Sex, and Marriage'. *Shakespeare: An Oxford Guide*. Ed. Stanley Wells and Lena Cowen Orlin. Oxford: Oxford Univ. Press, 2003. 114–26.

Jardine, Lisa. *Worldly Goods: A New History of the Renaissance*. London: Macmillan, 1996.

Johanyak, Debra and Walter S. H. Lim. Eds. *The English Renaissance, Orientalism, and the Idea of Asia*. London: Palgrave-Macmillan, 2010.

Johnson, William. 'Gender Fashioning and the Dynamics of Mutuality in Spenser's *Amoretti*.' *English Studies* 6 (1993): 503–19.

Kidnie, Margaret Jane. 'Shakespeare's Audiences'. *Shakespeare: An Oxford Guide*. Ed. Stanley Wells and Lena Cowen Orlin. Oxford: Oxford Univ. Press, 2003. 32–43.

Knapp, Jeffrey. *Shakespeare's Tribe: Church, Nation, and Theater in Renaissance England*. Chicago Univ. of Chicago Press, 2002.

Koerner, Joseph Leo. *The Reformation of the Image*. Chicago and London: Univ. of Chicago Press, 2004.

Kuzner, James. 'Habermas Goes to Hell: Pleasure, Public Reason, and the Republicanism of *Paradise Lost*.' *Criticism* 51.1 (2009): 105–45.

Le Comte, Edward S. *The Milton Dictionary*. New York: AMS, 1969.

Leonard, John. 'Language and Knowledge in *Paradise Lost*'. *The Cambridge Companion to Milton*. Cambridge: Cambridge Univ. Press, 1999. 130–43.

Lewalski, Barbara Kiefer. 'The Genres of Paradise Lost'. *The Cambridge Companion to Milton*. Cambridge: Cambridge Univ. Press, 1999. 113–29.

Loewenstein, Joseph. 'Humanism and Seventeenth-century English Literature'. *The Cambridge Companion to Renaissance Humanism*. Ed. Jill Kraye. Cambridge: Cambridge Univ. Press, 1996. 269–93.

MacLean, Gerald. 'Ottomanism before Orientalism? Bishop King Praises Henry Blount, Passenger in the Levant.' *Travel Knowledge: European 'Discoveries' in the Early Modern Period*. Eds. Ivo Kamps and Jyotsna G Singh. London: Palgrave, 2001. 85–96.

McBride, Kari Boyd. *Country House Discourse in Early Modern England*. Aldershot: Ashgate, 2001.

McRae, Andrew. *Literature and Domestic Travel in Early Modern England*. Cambridge: Cambridge Univ. Press, 2009.

Mignolo, Walter D. *The Darker Side of the Renaissance: Literacy, Territoriality, and Colonization*. Ann Arbor: Univ. of Michigan Press, 2003. 2nd ed.

Murphy, Erin. '*Paradise Lost* and the Politics of "Begetting".'*Milton Quarterly* 45.1 (2011): 25–49.

Nayar, Pramod K. *Colonial Voices: The Discourses of Empire*. Malden and Oxford: Wiley-Blackwell, forthcoming.

Nicolson, Marjorie Hope. *John Milton: A Reader's Guide to his Poetry*. London: Thames and Hudson, 1970.

Parry, Graham. *The Seventeenth Century: The Intellectual and Cultural Context of English Literature, 1603–1700*. London and New York: Longman, 1986.

Pichaske, David R. '*The Faerie Queen* IV. ii and iii: Spenser on the Genesis of Friendship.' *Studies in English Literature* 17. 1 (1977): 81–93.

Purkiss, Diane. *The Witch in History: Early Modern and Twentieth-Century Representations*. London: Routledge, 1996.

Quint, David. ' "Things Invisible to Mortal Sight": Light, Vision, and the Unity of Book 3 of *Paradise Lost*.' *Modern Language Quarterly* 71.3 (2010): 229–69.

Rackin, Phyllis. 'English History Plays'. *Shakespeare: An Oxford Guide*. Ed. Stanley Wells and Lena Cowen Orlin. Oxford: Oxford Univ. Press, 2003. 192–202.

Rogers, John. *The Matter of Revolution: Science, Poetry, and Politics in the Age of Milton*. Ithaca: Cornell, 1998.

Sawday, Jonathan. *The Body Emblazoned: Dissection and the Human Body in Renaissance Culture*. London and New York: Routledge, 1995.

Snook, Edith. 'Reading Women'. *The Cambridge Companion to Early Modern Women's Writing*. Ed. Laura Lunger Knoppers. Cambridge: Cambridge Univ. Press, 2009. 40–54.

Song, Eric. 'The Country Estate and the Indies (East and West): The Shifting Scene of Eden in *Paradise Lost*.' *Modern Philology* 108.2 (2009): 199–223.

Spencer, Jeffrey B. *Heroic Nature: Ideal Landscape in English Poetry from Marvell to Thomson*. Evanston: Northwestern Univ. Press, 1973.

Spolsky, Ellen. *Satisfying Skepticism: Embodied Knowledge in the Early Modern World*. Aldershot: Ashgate, 2001.

Spurgeon, Caroline E. *Shakespeare's Imagery and What it Tells Us*. Cambridge: Cambridge Univ. Press, 1961.

Stone, Lawrence. 'Social Mobility in England, 1500–1700', *Past and Present* 33.1 (1966): 16–55.

Tillyard, E.M.W. *The Elizabethan World Picture: A Study of the Idea of Order in Shakespeare, Donne and Milton.* 1959. London: Chatto and Windus, 1973.

Tuve, Rosamund. *Elizabethan and Metaphysical Imagery: Renaissance Poetic and Twentieth Century Critics.* Chicago: Univ. of Chicago P, 1961.

Wall, Wendy. 'Women in the Household'. *The Cambridge Companion to Early Modern Women's Writing.* Ed. Laura Lunger Knoppers. Cambridge: Cambridge Univ. Press, 2009. 97–109.

Wells, Stanley and Lena Cowen Orlin. *Shakespeare: An Oxford Guide.* Oxford: Oxford Univ. Press, 2003.

Willey, Basil. *The Seventeenth Century Background: Studies in the Thought of the Age in Relation to Poetry and Religion.* London: Chatto and Windus, 1967.

Isabella Whitney

Born around 1540 into a poor family of reformists, Whitney seems to have had some kind of an education. Her brother Geoffrey was a writer. Whitney worked as a servant in London for some years and began writing during this time. She might have been the first woman to publish a book of poetry, according to contemporary critics and literary historians. She published *The Copy of a Letter, Lately Written in Meeter, by a Yonge Gentilwoman: to her Unconstant Louer*, perhaps her best known work, in 1567. The year of her death is not known, but is believed to have been between 1570 and 1573.

On her Unconstant Lover

As **close** as you your wedding kept,
  yet now the truth I hear,
Which you (ere now) might me have told —
  what need you nay to swear?

You know I always wished you well,
  so will I during life:
But **sith** you shall a husband be,
  God send you a good wife.

And this (where so you shall become)
  full boldly may you boast:
That once you had as true a love,
  as dwelt in any coast.

Whose constantness had never **quailed**
  if you had not begun:
And yet it is not so far past
  but might again be won.

If you so would, yea, and not change
  so long as life would last,
But if that needs you marry must?
  then farewell — hope is past.

And if you cannot be content
  to lead a single life?

(Although the same right quiet be)
then take me to your wife.

So shall the promises be kept
that you so firmly made:
Now choose whether ye will be true,
or be of **Sinon's** trade.

Whose trade if that you long shall use,
it shall your kindred stain:
Example take by many a one
whose falsehood now is plain.

As by **Aeneas** first of all,
who did poor **Dido** leave,
Causing the Queen by his untruth
with sword her heart to cleave.

Also I find that **Theseus** did
his faithful love forsake,
Stealing away within the night,
before she did awake.

Jason that came of noble race,
two ladies did beguile.
I muse how he durst show his face,
to them that knew his wile.

For when he by Medea's art
had got the Fleece of Gold
And also had of her that time,
all kind of things he would.

He took his ship and fled away
regarding not the vows
That he did make so faithfully
unto his loving spouse.

How durst he trust the surging seas
knowing himself forsworn?
Why did he scape safe to the land
before the ship was torn?

I think king **Aeolus** stayed the winds
and **Neptune** ruled the sea:
Then might he boldly pass the waves
no perils could him **slee**.

But if his **falsehed** had to them
been manifest before,

They would have rent the ship as soon
    as he had gone from shore.

Now may you hear how falseness is
    made manifest in time:
Although they that commit the same
    think it a venial crime.

For they, for their unfaithfulness,
    did get perpetual fame:
Fame? wherefore did I term it so?
    I should have called it shame.

Let Theseus be, let Jason pass,
    let **Paris** also scape
That brought destruction unto Troy
    all through the Grecian rape,

And unto me a **Troylus** be,
    if not you may compare
With any of these persons that
    above expressed are.

But if I can not please your mind
    for **wants** that rest in me,
Wed whom you list, I am content,
    your **refuse** for to be.

It shall suffice me, simple soul,
    of thee to be forsaken:
And it may chance, although not yet,
    you wish you had me taken.

But rather than you should have cause
    to wish this through your wife,
I wish to her, ere you her have,
    no more but love of life.

For she that shall so happy be,
    of thee to be elect,
I wish her virtues to be such,
    she need not be suspect.

I rather wish her Helen's face
    than one of **Helen's trade**:
With chasteness of **Penelope**
    the which did never fade.

A **Lucres** for her constancy,
    and **Thisbie** for her truth:

If such thou have, then **Peto** be,
not Paris, that were **ruth**.

Perchance ye will think this thing rare
in one woman to find:
Save Helen's beauty, **all the rest**
the Gods have me assigned.

These words I do not speak, thinking
from thy new love to turn thee:
Thou know'st by proof what I deserve —
I need not to inform thee.

But let that pass: would God I had
Cassandra's gift me lent:
Then either thy ill chance or mine
my foresight might prevent.

But all in vain for this I seek;
wishes may not attain it.
Therefore may hap to me what shall,
and I cannot **refrain** it.

Wherefore I pray God be my guide
and also thee defend,
No worser than I wish my self,
until thy life shall end.

Which life, I pray God, may again
King **Nestor's** life renew:
And after that your soul may rest
amongst the heavenly crew.

Thereto I wish King **Xerxes'** wealth
or else King **Cressus'** gold,
With as much rest and quietness
as man may have on **mould**.

And when you shall this letter have,
let it be kept in store,
For she that sent the same hath sworn
as yet to send no more.

And now farewell, for why at large
my mind is here exprest,
The which you may perceive if that
you do peruse **the rest**.

Notes

close: secret **sith:** since **quailed:** failed **Sinon:** the Greek spy who betrayed Troy **Aeneas:** Priam's son, survivor of Troy and the subject of Virgil's *Aeneid* **Dido:** the queen of Carthage, was abandoned by Aeneas **Theseus:** He took away King Minos' daughter Ariadne. **Jason:** who obtained the Golden Fleece with Medea's help, but married Creusa, and was later murdered by Medea **Aeolus:** god of the winds **Neptune:** Greek god of the oceans **slee:** slay **falsehed:** falsehood **Paris:** Priam's son, who seduced and took away Helen, and thus provoked the Trojan war **Troylus:** Priam's son, died faithful to Criseid, even though she aligns with the Greek Diomede during the Trojan war. **wants:** lacks **refuse:** rubbish **Helen's trade:** refers to Helen as a symbol of seduction **Penelope:** Odysseus' wife who waited for his return, though besieged by numerous suitors, often treated as a symbol of the faithful wife **Lucres:** or Lucretia, symbol of chastity – she killed herself to protect it. **Thisbie:** Pyramus's lover who killed herself, under the impression that he was dead **Peto:** William Peto, the priest who opposed Henry VIII's divorce of Catherine of Aragon **ruth:** a pity **all the rest/the Gods have me assigned:** The poet suggests that other than Helen's beauty, she has all the other virtues. **Cassandra:** Priam's daughter; she prophesied the fall of Troy. **refrain:** prevent **Nestor:** the wise king of the Greeks **Xerxes:** Persian King; he defeated the Greeks at Thermopylae. **Cressus:** King of Lydia **mould:** here, earth **the rest:** might gesture at the rest of the book

Edmund Spenser

Edmund Spenser (1552–1599) matriculated from Pembroke College, Cambridge, and was translating French poetry from the age of sixteen. At Cambridge he acquired Latin, Greek, French and Italian. He served as secretary to Bishop John Young of Rochester for a period in 1578, soon after which he published *The Shepherdes Calender*. He also served Robert Dudley and was a member of the literary circle of Philip Sidney. He may have married Machabyas Chylde around this time. He began composing *The Faerie Queene* around 1580. Later Spenser moved to Ireland and served its Lord Deputy, Arthur Grey, who was a friend of Sidney's family. For his services in suppressing the rebellions there he was awarded lands in Cork. Spenser acquired vast lands in the area, where his neighbour was Walter Raleigh. Spenser's *The Faerie Queene* was part of his attempt to get a position in the Court, but achieved nothing much for him. His pamphlet, *A View of the Present State of Ireland,* was not published in his lifetime. In this, the embittered Spenser claimed that Irish customs and language must first be destroyed if England wanted to conquer the land. He lost his castle – and perhaps his wife and child, who may have been burnt down with the castle – to Irish rebels in 1598 and had to flee to another property he held. In his later years, Spenser moved to London and died in dire conditions. Wordsworth, Keats, Tennyson and others admitted to Spenser's influence on them. Among the more famous love poems in the English language is Spenser's *Epithalmion*, written in honour of his wedding to the much younger Elizabeth Boyle. The 'Two Cantos of Mutabilitie' (Canto VI and VII of the projected Book VII), and fragments of a third, were first published in 1609 (ten years after Spenser's death).

Epithalamion

Ye learned sisters which have oftentimes
been to me aiding, others to adorn:
Whom ye thought worthy of your graceful rhymes,
That even the greatest did not greatly scorn
To hear their names sung in your simple lays,
But joyèd in their praise.
And when **ye list your own mishaps to mourn**,
Which death, or love, or fortunes wreck did rayse,
Your string could soon to sadder tenor turn,
And teach the woods and waters to lament
Your doleful dreariment.
Now lay those sorrowful complaints aside,
And having all your heads with garlands crowned,
Help me mine own loves praises to resound,
Ne let the fame of any be envied,
So **Orpheus** did for his own bride,
So I unto my self alone will sing,
The woods shall to me answer and my echo ring.

Early before the world's light giving lamp,
His golden beam upon the hills doth spread,
Having dispersed the night's uncheerfull damp,
Do ye awake and with fresh lusty head,
Go to the bower of my beloved love,
My truest turtle dove
Bid her awake; for Hymen is awake,
And long since ready forth his **mask to move**,
With his bright **Taed** that flames with many a flake,

And many a bachelor to wait on him,
In their fresh garments trim.
Bid her awake therefore and soon her dight,
For lo the wished day is come at last,
That shall for all the pains and sorrows past,
Pay to her usury of long delight,
And whilst she doth her dight,
Do ye to her of joy and solace sing,
That all the woods may answer, and your echo ring.

Bring with you all the Nymphs that you can hear
both of the rivers and the forests green:
And of the sea that neighbours to her near,
all with gay garlands goodly well be seen.
And let them also with them bring in hand,
Another gay garland
my fair love of lilies and of roses,
Bound truelove wise with a blue silk riband.
And let them make great store of bridal posies,
And let them eke bring store of other flowers
To deck the bridal bowers.
And let the ground whereas her foot shall tread,
For fear the stones her tender foot should wrong,
Be strewed with fragrant flowers all along,
And **diapered like the discoloured mead**.
Which done, do at her chamber door await,
For she will waken straight,
The while do ye this song unto her sing,
The woods shall to you answer and your echo ring.

Ye Nymphs of **Mulla** which with careful heed,
The silver scaly trouts do tend full well,
and greedy pikes which use therein to feed,
(Those trouts and pikes all others do excel)
And ye likewise which keep the rushy lake,
Where none do fishes take.
Bind up the locks the which hang scattered light,
And in his waters which your mirror make,
Behold your faces as the crystal bright,
That when you come whereas my love doth lie,
No blemish she may spy.
And eke ye lightfoot maids which keep the deer,
That on the hoary mountain use to **tower**,
And the wild wolves which seek them to devour,
With your **steel darts** do chase from coming near
Be also present here,

To help to deck her and to help to sing,
That all the woods may answer, and your echo ring.

Wake now my love, awake; for it is time,
The Rosy Morn long since left **Tithon's** bed,
All ready to her silver couch to climb,
And **Phoebus** gins to shew his glorious head.
Hark how the cheerful birds do chant their lays
And carol of love's praise.
The merry **Lark** her matins sings aloft,
The thrush replies, the **Mavis descant** plays,
The **Ouzel** shrills, the **Ruddock** warbles soft,
So goodly all agree with sweet **consent**,
To this day's merriment.
Ah my dear love why do ye sleep thus long,
When meeter were that ye should now awake,
T'await the coming of your joyous make,
And hearken to the birds' love learnèd song,
The dewy leaves among.
For they of joy and pleasance to you sing.
That all the woods them answer and their echo ring.

My love is now awake out of her dreams,
and her fair eyes like stars that dimmèd were
With darksome cloud, now show their goodly beams
More bright than **Hesperus** his head doth rear.
Come now ye damsels, **daughters of delight**,
Help quickly her to dight,
But first come ye fair hours which were begot
In Joves sweet paradise, of Day and Night,
Which do the seasons of the year allot,
And all that ever in this world is fair
Do make and still repair.
And ye **three handmaids of the Cyprian Queen**,
The which do still adorn her beauty's pride,
Help to adorn my beautifullest bride
And as ye her array, still throw between
Some graces to be seen,
And as ye use to Venus, to her sing,
The whiles the woods shall answer and your echo ring.

Now is my love all ready forth to come,
Let all the virgins therefore well await,
And ye fresh boys that tend upon her groom
Prepare your selves; for he is coming straight.
Set all your things in seemly good array
Fit for so joyfull day,

The joyfull'st day that ever sun did see.
Fair Sun, shew forth thy favourable ray,
let thy lifeful heat not fervent be
For fear of burning her sunshiny face,
Her beauty to **disgrace**.
O fairest **Phoebus, father of the Muse**,
If ever I did honour thee aright,
Or sing the thing that mote thy mind delight,
Do not thy servant's **simple** boon refuse,
But let this day, let this one day be mine,
Let all the rest be thine.
Then I thy sovereign praises loud will sing,
That all the woods shall answer and their echo ring.

Hark how the Minstrels gin to shrill aloud,
Their merry Music that resounds from far,
The pipe, the **tabor**, and the **trembling Croud**,
That well agree withouten breach or jar.
But most of all the damsels do delight,
When they their tymbrels smite,
And thereunto do dance and carol sweet,
That all the senses they do ravish quite,
The whiles the boys run up and down the street,
Crying aloud with strong confusèd noise,
As if it were one voice.
Hymen, lo Hymen, Hymen they do shout,
That even to the heavens their shouting shrill
Doth reach, and all the firmament doth fill,
To which the people standing all about,
As in approvance do thereto applaud
And loud advance her laud,
And evermore they Hymen, Hymen sing,
that all the woods them answer and their echo ring.

Lo where she comes along with **portly** pace,
like **Phoebe** from her chamber of the East,
Arising forth to run her mighty race,
Clad all in white, that seems a virgin best.
So well it her beseems that ye would ween
Some angel she had been.
Her long loose yellow locks like golden wire,
Sprinkled with pearl, and **perling** flowers a **tween**,
Do like a golden mantle her attire,

And being crowned with a garland green,
flowers like some maiden Queen,
Her modest eyes abashed to behold

So many gazers, as on her do stare,
upon the lowly ground affixed are.
Ne dare lift up her countenance too bold,
But blush to hear her praises sung so loud,
So far from being proud.
Nathless do ye still loud her praises sing,
That all the woods may answer and your echo ring.

Tell me ye **merchants' daughters** did ye see
So fair a creature in your town before,
So sweet, so lovely, and so mild as she,
Adorned with beauty's grace and virtue's store,
Her goodly eyes like Saphires shining bright,
Her forehead ivory white,
Her cheeks like apples which the sun hath rudded,
Her lips like cherries charming men to bite,
Her breast like to a bowl of cream **uncrudded**,
Her paps like lilies budded,
Her snowy neck like to a marble tower,
And all her body like a palace fair,
Ascending up with many a stately stair,
To honour's seat and chastity's sweet bower.
Why stand ye still ye virgins in amaze,
upon her so to gaze,
Whiles ye forget your former lay to sing,
To which the woods did answer and your echo ring?

But if ye saw that which no eyes can see,
The inward beauty of her lively spright,
Garnish'd with heavenly gifts of high degree,
Much more then would ye wonder at that sight,
And stand astonisht like to those which read
Medusa's mazeful head.
There dwells sweet love and constant chastity,
unspotted faith and comely womanhood,
Regard of honour and mild modesty,
There virtue reigns as Queen in royal throne,
And giveth laws alone.
The which the base affections do obey,
And yield their services unto her will
Ne thought of thing uncomely ever may
Thereto approach to tempt her mind to ill.
Had ye once seen these her celestial treasures,
And unrevealèd pleasures,
Then would ye wonder and her praises sing,
That all the woods should answer and your echo ring.

Open the temple gates unto my love,
Open them wide that she may enter in,
And all the posts adorn as doth behove,
And all the pillars deck with garlands trim,
For to receive this Saint with honour due,
That cometh in to you.
With trembling steps and humble reverence,
She cometh in, before th' almighty's view,
Of her ye virgins learn obedience,
When so ye come into those holy places,
To humble your proud faces,
Bring her up to th' high altar that she may,
The sacred ceremonies there partake,
The which do endless matrimony make,
And let the roaring Organs loudly play
The praises of the Lord in lively notes,
The whiles with hollow throats,
The Choristers the joyous Anthem sing,
That all the woods may answer, and their echo ring.

Behold whiles she before the altar stands
Hearing the holy priest that to her speaks
And blesseth her with his two happy hands,
How the red roses flush up in her cheeks,
And the pure snow with goodly vermeil stain,
Like crimson dyed in grey,
That even th' Angels which continually,
About the sacred Altar do remain,
Forget their service and about her fly,
Oft peeping in her face that seems more fair,
The more they on it stare.
But her sad eyes still fastened on the ground,
Are governèd with goodly modesty,
That suffers not one look to glance awry,
Which may let in a little thought unsound,
Why blush ye love to give to me your hand,
The pledge of all our band?
Sing ye, sweet Angels, Alleluya sing,
That all the woods may answer and your echo ring.

Now all is done; bring home the bride again,
bring home the triumph of our victory,
Bring home with you the glory of her gain,
With joyance bring her and with jollity.
Never had man more joyfull day then this,
Whom heaven would heap with bliss.

Make feast therefore now all this live long day,
This day for ever to me holy is,
Pour out the wine without restraint or stay,
Pour not by cups, but by the belly full,
Pour out to all that wull,
And sprinkle all the posts and walls with wine,
That they may sweat, and drunken be withall.
Crown ye God Bacchus with a coronal,
And Hymen also crown with wreaths of vine,
And let the Graces dance unto the rest;
For they can do it best:
The whiles the maidens do their carrol sing,
To which the woods shall answer and their echo ring.

Ring ye the bells, ye young men of the town,
And leave your wonted labours for this day:
This day is holy; Do ye write it down,
that ye for ever it remember may.
This day the sun is in his chiefest height,
With **Barnaby the bright**,
From whence declining daily by degrees,
He somewhat loseth of his heat and light,
When once the **Crab** behind his back he sees.
But for this time it ill ordainèd was,
To chose the longest day in all the year,
And shortest night, when longest fitter were:
Yet never day so long, but late would pass.
Ring ye the bells, to make it wear away,
And bonfires make all day,
And dance about them, and about them sing:
that all the woods may answer, and your echo ring.

Ah when will this long weary day have end,
and lend me leave to come unto my love?
How slowly do the hours their numbers spend?
How slowly does sad Time his feathers move?
Haste thee O **fairest Planet** to thy home
Within the Western foam:
Thy tired steeds long since have need of rest.
Long though it be, at last I see it gloom,
And the bright evening star with golden crest
Appear out of the East.
fair child of beauty, glorious **lamp of love**
That all the host of heaven in ranks dost lead,
And guidest lovers through the night's dread,
How cheerfully thou lookest from aboue,

And seemst to laugh atween thy twinkling light
As joying in the sight
Of these glad many which for joy do sing,
That all the woods them answer and their echo ring.

Now cease ye damsels your delights forepast;
Enough is it, that all the day was yours:
Now day is done, and night is nighing fast:
Now bring the Bride into the bridal bowers.
Now night is come, now soon her disarray,
And in her bed her lay;
Lay her in lillies and in violets,
And silken curtains over her display,
The odoured sheets, and **Arras** coverlets,
Behold how goodly my Fair love does lie
In proud humility;
Like unto **Maia**, when as Jove her took,
In **Tempe**, lying on the flowery grass,
Twixt sleep and wake, after she weary was,
With bathing in the **Acidalian** brook.
Now it is night, ye damsels may be gone,
And leave my love alone,
And leave likewise your former lay to sing:
The woods no more shall answer, nor your echo ring.

Now welcome night, thou night so long expected,
that long day's labour dost at last defray,
And all my cares, which cruel love collected,
Hast summed in one, and cancellèd for aye:
Spread thy broad wing over my love and me,
that no man may us see,
And in thy sable mantle us enwrap,
From fear of peril and foul horror free.
Let no false treason seek us to entrap,
Nor any dread disquiet once annoy
the safety of our joy:
But let the night be calm and quietsome,
Without tempestuous storms or sad affray:
like as when Jove with fair **Alcmena** lay,
When he begot the great **Tirynthian groom**:
Or like as when he with thy self did lie,
And begot Majesty.
And let the maids and young men cease to sing:
Ne let the woods them answer, nor their echo ring.

Let no lamenting cries, nor dolefull tears,
Be heard all night within nor yet without:

Ne let false whispers breeding hidden fears,
Break gentle sleep with misconceivèd doubt.
Let no deluding dreams, nor dreadful sights,
Make sudden sad affrights;
Ne let housefires, nor lightning's helpless harms,
Ne let the Puck, nor other evil sprights,
Ne let mischievous witches with their charms,
Ne let hob Goblins, names whose sense we see not,
Fray us with things that be not.
Let not the screech Owl, nor the Stork be heard:
Nor the night Raven that still deadly yells,
Nor damnèd ghosts called up with mighty spells,
Nor griefly vultures make us once affeard:
Ne let th' unpleasant Quire of Frogs still croaking
Make us to wish their choking.
Let none of these their dreary accents sing;
Ne let the woods them answer, nor their echo ring.

But let still Silence true night watches keepe,
That sacred peace may in assurance reign,
And timely sleep, when it is time to sleep,
May Pour his limbs forth on your pleasant plain,
The whiles an hundred little wingèd loves,
Like divers feathered doves,
Shall fly and flutter round about your bed,
And in the secret dark, that none reproves
Their pretty stealths shall work, and snares shall spread
To filch away sweet snatches of delight,
Concealed through covert night.
Ye sons of Venus, play your sports at will,
For greedy pleasure, careless of your toys,
Thinks more upon her paradise of joys,
Than what ye do, albeit good or ill.
All night therefore attend your merry play,
For it will soon be day:
Now none doth hinder you, that say or sing,
Ne will the woods now answer, nor your echo ring.

Who is the same, which at my window peeps?
Or whose is that Fair face, that shines so bright,
Is it not **Cinthia**, she that never sleeps,
But walks about high heaven all the night?
O fairest goddesse, do thou not envy
My love with me to spy:
For thou likewise didst love, though now unthought,
And for a fleece of wool, which **privily**,

The **Latmian shepherd** once unto thee brought,
His pleasures with thee wrought,
Therefore to us be favourable now;
And since of **women's labours** thou hast charge,
And generation goodly dost enlarge,
Encline they will t'effect our wishfull vow,
And the chaste wombe informe with timely seed,
That may our comfort breed:
Till which we cease our hopefull hap to sing,
Ne let the woods us answer, nor our echo ring.

And thou great Juno, which with awful might
the laws of wedlock still dost patronize,
And the religion of the faith first plight
With sacred rites hast taught to solemnize:
And eke for comfort often called art
Of women in their smart,
Eternally bind thou this lovely band,
And all thy blessings unto us impart.
Thou glad Genius, in whose gentle hand,
The bridal bower and genial bed remain,
Without blemish or stain,
And the sweet pleasures of their loves delight
With secret aid dost succour and supply,
Till they bring forth the fruitfull progeny,
Send us the timely fruit of this same night.
And thou fair Hebe, and thou Hymen free,
Grant that it may so be.
Till which we cease your further praise to sing,
Ne any woods shall answer, nor your echo ring.

And ye high heavens, the temple of the gods,
In which a thousand torches flaming bright
Do burn, that to us wretched earthly clods:
In dreadful darkness lend desired light;
And all ye powers which in the same remain,
More then we men can fain,
Pour out your blessing on us plenteously,
And happy influence upon us rain,
That we may raise a large posterity,
Which from the earth, which they may long possess
With lasting happiness,
up to your haughty palaces may mount,
And for the guerdon of their glorious merit
May heavenly tabernacles there inherit,
Of blessed Saints for to increase the count.

So let us rest, sweet love, in hope of this,
And cease till then our timely joys to sing,
The woods no more us answer, nor our echo ring.

Song made in lieu of many ornaments,
With which my love should duly have been decked,
Which cutting off through hasty accidents,
Ye would not stay your due time to expect,
But promist both to recompense,
Be unto her a goodly ornament,
And for short time an endless monument.

Notes

Ye learned sisters: invocation to the Muses **ye list your own mishaps to mourn:** Muses are asked to lament upon the decay in the arts. **Orpheus:** His music brought back his wife, Eurydice, from the dead. **Ye Nymphs:** here, refers to a call to the maidens to wake up his beloved and get her ready **Taed:** wedding torch **diapered like the discoloured mead:** 'diapered' here means woven with a different colour, and 'discoloured' implies 'of various colours'. **mask to move:** a retinue of masked people, accompanied by musicians, dancers – a marriage 'masque' **Mulla:** Spenser's name for the river Awbeg which flowed through his estate **tower:** here, stand aloft **steel darts:** a reference to Diana's silver arrows **Tithon's:** In Greek myth, the lover of Eos, or Titan of the Dawn, he was granted immortality but not eternal youth. **Phoebus:** another name for Apollo **Lark:** symbolic of the dawn **Mavis:** song-thrush **descant:** literally a 'part-song', which has a counter-point song over and above the main one **Ouzel:** blackbird **Ruddock:** robin **consent:** here, meaning both 'approval' and 'singing together' **Hesperus:** both evening and morning star **daughters of delight:** a reference to the 'Graces', the handmaids of Venus **three handmaids of the Cyprian Queen:** Aglia, Euphrosyne, Thalia, the three graces who attend Venus, are taken to be associated with the Muses. **disgrace:** here, disfigure **Phoebus, father of the Muse:** Spenser suggests that Apollo is the father of the Muses. **simple:** single **tabor:** drum **trembling Croud:** a stringed instrument **portly:** here, stately **Phoebe:** Artemis, the twin sister of Phoebus Apollo **perling:** to twist with golden or silver threads **tween:** to entwine **merchants' daughters:** here used to contrast with the aristocratic men and women at traditional marriage processions and ceremonies in poems of this sort **uncrudded:** uncurdled **Medusa:** a Gorgon, she had her head turned into a maze of snakes. It was cursed that anybody who saw her head would be turned to stone. **mazeful:** a play on the maze of Medusa's head, but also meaning 'amazing' **Barnaby the bright:** The feast of St Barnabas that is celebrated on 11th June. According to the old style Julian calendar, 11th June was also the summer solstice. Spenser is also referring to the proverb, 'Bamaby bright, Bamaby bright, / the longest day and the shortest night.' **Crab:** the astrological sign of Cancer **fairest Planet:** Spenser is referring to the sun here. In the older, pre-Galilean and Ptolemaic world-view, the sun was deemed a planet. **lamp of love: a reference to Venus** **Arras:** city in the north of France famous for its tapestries in the medieval and early modern period **Maia:** the mother of Hermes after being seduced by Jove **Tempe:** Traditionally, this is the place associated with the pursuit of Daphne by Jupiter. (Spenser here is mixing up places and myths.) **Acidalian:** the brook where Maia bathed **Alcmena:** She was seduced by Jove when he appeared in the guise of her husband. Jove also delayed the sun rising for three days so he could be with her. Their son was Hercules. **Tirynthian groom:** Hercules, brought up in Tiryns **Cinthia:** goddess Diana, guardian of virgins but also of married women especially those in childbirth **privily:** secretly **Latmian Shepherd:** Diana fell in love with the shepherd **women's labours:** childbirth

The Faerie Queene (extracts)

From: *The Mutabilitie Cantos* (Book VII, Canto VI)

Proud **Change** (*not pleas'd, in mortal Things*
Beneath the **Moon**, *to reign*)
Pretends, *as well of Gods, as Men,*
To be the Sovereign.

What Man that sees the ever-whirling **Wheel**
Of Change, the which all mortal things doth sway,
But that thereby doth find, and plainly feel,
How MUTABILITY in them doth play
Her cruel Sports, to many Mens decay?
Which that to all may better yet appear,
I will **rehearse** that whylom I heard say,
How she at first her self began to real;
Gainst all the Gods, and th' Empire sought from them to bear.

But first, here falleth fittest to unfold
Her antique Race and Linage antient,
As I have found it register'd of old,
In Fairy Land mongst Records permanent:
She was, to weet, a Daughter by descent
Of those old Titans, that did whylome strive
With Saturn's Son for Heaven's **Regiment**.
Whom, though high **Jove of Kingdom did deprive**,
Yet many of their **Stem** long after did survive.

And many of them afterwards obtain'd
Great Power of Jove, and high Authority;
As **Hecate**, in whose Almighty Hand
He plac'd all Rule and Principality,
To be by her disposed diversly,
To Gods, and Men, as she them list divide:
And drad **Bellona**, that doth sound on high
Wars and Alarums unto Nations wide,
That makes both Heaven and Earth to tremble at her Pride.

So likewise did this **Titaness** aspire,
Rule and Dominion to her self to gain;
That as a Goddess, Men might her admire,
And heavenly Honours yield, as to them **twaine**.
And first, on Earth she sought it to obtain;
Where she such Proof and **sad** Examples shew'd
Of her great Power, to many one's great pain,
That not Men only (whom she soon subdu'd)
But eke all other Creatures, her bad doings **ru'd**.

For, she the Face of earthly Things so chang'd,
That all with Nature had establisht first
In good **Estate**, and in meet Order rang'd,
She did **pervert**, and all their Statutes **burst**:
And all the World's fair **Frame** (which none yet durst
Of Gods or Men to alter or misguide)
She alter'd quite, and made them all accurst
That God had blest; and did at first provide
In that **still** happy State for ever to abide.

Ne she the Laws of Nature only broke,
But eke of Justice, and of **Policy**;
And Wrong of Right, and Bad of Good did make,
And Death for Life exchangeth foolishly
Since which, all living Wights have learn'd to die,
And all this World is woxen daily worse.
O piteous Work of MUTABILITY!
By which, we all are subject to that Curse,
And Death instead of Life have sucked from our **Nurse**.

And now, when all the Earth she thus had brought
To her Behest, and thralled to her Might,
She 'gan to **cast** in her ambitious Thought,
T' **attempt** th' Empire of the Heaven's hight,
And Jove himself to shoulder from his Right.
And first, she past the Region of the **Air**,
And of the Fire, whose Substance thin and slight
Made no resistance, ne could her **contrair**,
But ready passage to her pleasure did prepair.

Thence, to the Circle of the Moon she clamb,
Where **Cynthia** reigns in everlasting Glory,
To whose bright shining Palace straight she came,
All fairly deckt with Heaven's goodly story;
Whose silver Gates (by which there sate an hoary
Old aged Sire, with Hour-glass in hand,
Hight **Tyme**) she entred, were he **liefe or sory**:

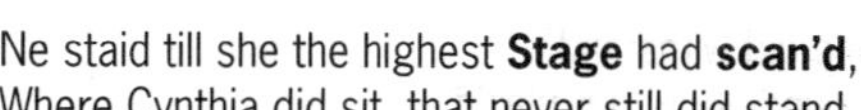

Ne staid till she the highest **Stage** had **scan'd**,
Where Cynthia did sit, that never still did stand.

Her sitting on an Ivory Throne she found,
Drawn of **two Steeds, th' one black, the other white**;
Environ'd with ten thousand Stars around,
That duely her attended Day and Night;
And by her side, there ran her Page, that hight
Vesper, whom we the Evening-Star **intend**:
That with his Torch, still twinkling like Twylight,
Her lighten'd all the way where she should wend,
And Joy to weary wandring Travellers did lend.

Tho when the hardy Titaness beheld
The goodly Building of her Palace bright,
Made of the Heaven's Substance, and up-held
With thousand Crystal Pillors of huge hight,
She 'gan to burn in her ambitious Spright,
And e' envy her that in such Glory reign'd.
Eftsoons she cast by Force and **tortious** Might,
Her to displace; and to her self t' have gain'd
The Kingdom of the Night, and Waters by her **wain'd**.

Boldly she bid the Goddess down descend,
And let her self into that Ivory Throne;
For, she her self more worthy thereof **wend**,
And better able it to guide alone:
Whether to Men, whose Fall she did bemoan,
Or unto Gods, whose State she did **malign**,
Or to **th' infernal Powers, her need give Loan**
Of her fair Light, and Bounty most benign,
Her self of all that Rule she deemed most **condign**.

But she that had to her that Sovereign Seat
By highest Jove assign'd, therein to bear
Night's burning Lamp, regarded not her Threat,
Ne yielded ought for Favour or for Fear;
But with stern Countenance and disdainful **Chear**,
Bending her horned Brows, did put her back:
And boldly blaming her for coming there,
Bade her attonce from Heaven's **Coast** to **pack**,
Or at her peril bide the wrathful **Thunder's wrack**.

Yet nathemore the Giantess forbare:
But boldly pressing-on, **raught** forth her hand
To pluck her down **perforce** from off her Chair;
And there-with lifting up her golden Wand,

Threatned to strike her if she did withstand.
Where-at the Stars, which round about her blaz'd,
And eke the Moon's bright Wagon, still did stand,
All being with so bold Attempt amaz'd,
And on her uncouth Habit and stern Look still gaz'd.

Mean-while, the lower World, which nothing knew
Of all that chanced here, was darkened quite;
And eke the Heavens, and all the heavenly Crew
Of happy Wight, now **unpurvaid** of Light,
Were much afraid, and wondred at that sight;
Fearing lest Chaos broken had his Chain,
And brought again on them eternal Night:
But chiefly **Mercury**, that next doth reign,
Ran forth in haste, unto the King of Gods to '**plain**.

All ran together with a great Out-cry,
To Jove's fair Palace, fixt in Heavens hight;
And beating at his Gates full earnestly,
'Gan call to him aloud with all their Might,
To know what meant that suddain lack of Light.
The Father of the Gods when this he heard,
Was troubled much at their so strange affright,
Doubting left **Typhon** were again uprear'd,
Or other his old Foes, that once him sorely fear'd.

Eftsoons the **Son of Maia** forth he sent
Down to the Circle of the Moon, to know
The cause of this so strange Astonishment,
And why she did her wonted Course **forslowe**;
And if that any were on Earth below
That did with Charms or Magick her molest,
Him to **attache**, and down to Hell to throw:
But, if from Heaven it were, then to arrest
The Author, and him bring before his presence **prest**.

The wing'd-foot God, so fast his Plumes did beat,
That soon he came where-as the Titaness
Was striving with fair Cynthia for her Seat:
At whose strange sight, and haughty **Hardiness**,
He wondered much, and feared her no less.
Yet laying Fear aside to do his charge,
At last, he bade her (with bold steadfastness)
Cease to molest the Moon to walk at large,
Or come before high Jove, her doings to **discharge**.

And there-with-all, he on her shoulder laid
His **snaky-wreathed Mace**, whose awful Power

Doth make both Gods and hellish Fiends afraid:
Where-at the Titaness did sternly **lour**,
And stoutly answer'd, that in evil Hour
He from his Jove such Message to her brought,
To bid her leave fair Cynthia's silver Bower;
Since she his Jove and him esteemed nought,
No more than Cynthia's self; but all their Kingdoms sought.

The Heaven's Herald staid not to reply
But past away, his doings to relate
Unto his Lord; who now in th' highest Sky,
Was placed in his principal Estate,
With all the Gods about him congregate:
To whom when Hermes had his Message told,
It did them an exceedingly **amate**,
Save Jove; who, changing nought his Count'nance bold,
Did unto them at length these Speeches wise unfold.

Harken to me awhile, ye heavenly Powers;
Ye may remember since th' **Earth's cursed Seed**
Sought to assail the Heaven's eternal Towers,
And to us all exceeding Fear did breed:
But how we then defeated all their Deed,
Ye all do know, and them destroyed quite;
Yet not so quite, but that there did succeed
An Off-spring of their Blood, which did alite
Upon the fruitful Earth, which doth us yet despite.

Of that bad Seed is this bold Woman bred,
That now with bold Presumption doth aspire
To thrust fair **Phoebe** from her silver Bed,
And eke our selves from Heaven's high Empire,
If that her Might were match to her Desire:
Wherefore, it now behoves us to **advise**
What way is best to drive her to retire;
Whether by open, Force, or Counsel wise,
Areed ye Sons of God, as best ye can devise.

So having said, he ceast; and with his Brow
(His black Eye brow, whose doomful dreaded **Beck**
Is wont to **wield** the World unto his **Vow**,
And even the highest Powers of Heaven to check)
Made sign to them in their degrees to speak:
Who straight 'gan **cast** their Counsel grave and wise.
Mean-while, th' Earth's Daughter, tho she nought did reck
Of Hermes' Message; yet 'gan now advise,
What Course were best to take in this her bold **Emprize**.

Eftsoons she thus resolv'd; that whilst the Gods
(After return of Hermes' Embassy)
Were troubled, and amongst themselves at odds,
Before they could new Counsels re-ally,
To set upon them in that **extasy**;
And take what Fortune, Time and Place would lend:
So, forth she rose, and through the purest Sky
To Jove's high Palace straight cast to ascend,
To prosecute her Plot: Good On-set boads good End.

She there arriving, boldly in did pass;
Where all the Gods she found in counsel close,
All quite unarm'd, as then their manner was.
At sight of her they suddain all arose
In great amaze, ne wist what way to chose.
But Jove, all fearless, forc'd them to **aby**;
And in his sovereign Throne 'gan straight dispose
Himself more full of Grace and Majesty,
That mote enchear his Friends, and Foes mote terrify.

That, when the haughty Titaness beheld,
All were she fraught with Pride and Impudence,
Yet with the sight thereof was almost quell'd;
And fully quaking, seem'd as **reft** of Sense,
And void of Speech in that drad Audience;
Until that Jove himself, her self bespake:
Speak thou frail Woman, speak with confidence,
Whence art thou, and what dost thou here now **make**?
What idle Errand hast, Earth's Mansion to forsake?

She, half confused with his great Command,
Yet gathering Spirit of her Nature's Pride,
Him boldly answer'd thus to his Demand:
I am a Daughter by the Mother's side,
Of her that is Grand-mother **magnify'd**
Of all the Gods, great Earth, great Chaos' Child:
But by the Father's (be it not **envy'd**)
I greater am in Blood (whereon I build)
Than all the Gods, though wrongfully from Heaven exil'd.

For, Titan (as ye all acknowledg must)
Was Saturn's elder Brother by Birth-right;
Both, Sons of Uranus: but by unjust
And guileful Means, through **Corybantes Slight**,
The younger thrust the elder from his Right:
Since which, thou Jove, **injuriously** hast held
The Heaven's Rule from Titan's Sons by Might;

And them to hellish Dungeons down hast feld:
Witness ye Heavens the truth of all that I have teld.

Whilst she thus spake, the Gods that gave good ear
To her bold Words, and marked well her Grace,
Being of Stature tall as any there
Of all the Gods, and beautiful of Face,
As any of the Goddesses in place,
Stood all astonied, like a sort of Steers,
Mongst whom, some Beast of strange and foreign Race,
Unwares is chaunc'd, far straying from his Peers:
So did their ghastly Gaze **bewray** their hidden Fears.

Till having paus'd awhile, Jove thus bespake;
Will never **mortal Thoughts** cease to aspire,
In this bold sort, to Heaven claim to make,
And touch celestial Seats with earthly Mire?
I would have thought, that bold **Procrustes' Hire**,
Or Typhon's Fall, or proud **Ixion's** Pain,
Or great **Prometheus**, tasting of our Ire,
Would have suffic'd, the rest for to restrain;
And warn'd all Men by their Example to refrain:

But now, this Off-scum of that cursed **Fry**,
Dare to renew the like bold Enterprize,
And **challenge** th' Heritage of this our Sky;
Whom what should hinder, but that we likewise
Should handle as the rest of her Allies,
And thunder-drive to Hell? With that he shook
His Nectar-dewed Locks, with which the Skies
And all the World beneath for terror **quook**,
And **eft** his burning **Levin-brond** in hand he took.

But, when he looked on her lovely Face,
In which fair Beams of Beauty did appear,
That could the greatest Wrath soon turn to Grace
(Such sway doth Beauty even in Heaven bear)
He staid his Hand: and having chang'd his Chear,
He thus again in milder wise began;
But ah! if Gods should strive with **Flesh yfere**,
Then shortly would the Progeny of Man
Be rooted out, if Jove should do still what he can.

But thee fair Titan's Child, I rather ween,
Through some vain Error or **Enducement light**,
To see that mortal Eyes have never seen;
Or through Ensample of thy Sister's Might,

Bellona, whose great Glory thou dost **spight**,
Since thou hast seen her dreadful Power below,
Mongst wretched Men (dismay'd **with her affright**)
To bandy Crowns, and kingdoms to bestow:
And sure thy Worth, no less than hers doth seem to show.

But **wote** thou this, thou hardy Titaness,
That not the Worth of any living Wight
May challenge ought in Heaven's **Interesse**;
Much less the Tide of old Titan's Right:
For, we by Conquest of our sovereign Might,
And by eternal **Doom** of Fate's Decree,
Have won the Empire of the Heavens bright;
Which to our selves we hold, and to whom we
Shall worthy deem Partakers of our Bliss to be.

Then cease thy idle Claim thou foolish Girl,
And seek by Grace and Goodness to obtain
That place from which by Folly Titan fell;
There-to thou may'st perhaps, if so thou **fain**
Have Jove thy Gracious Lord and Sovereign.
So, having said, she thus to him reply'd;
Cease **Saturn's Son**, to seek by Proffers vain
Of idle Hopes t' allure me to thy side,
For to betray my Right, before I have it try'd.

But thee, O Jove, no **equal** Judge I deem
Of my Desert, or of my dueful Right;
That in thine own behalf may'st partial seem:
But to the highest Him, that is **behight**
Father of Gods and Men by equal Might;
To weet, the God of Nature, I appeal.
There-at Jove wexed wroth, and in his Spright
Did inly grudge, yet did it well conceal;
And bade **Dan Phoebus** Scribe her Appellation seal.

Eftsoons the time and place appointed were,
Where all, both heavenly Powers, and earthly Wights,
Before great Nature's Presence should appear.
For trial of their Titles and best Rights:
That was, to weet, upon the highest hights
Of **Arlo-hill** (who knows not **Arlo-hill**?)
That is the highest Head (in all Mens sight)
Of my old Father **Mole**, whom Shepheards Quill
Renowned hath with Hymns fit for a rural Skill.

And, were it not ill fitting for this **File**,
To sing of Hills and Woods, mongst Wars and Knights,

I would **abate** the Sternness of my Stile,
Mongst these stern **Stounds** to mingle soft Delights;
And tell how Arlo through Diana's Spights
(Being of old the best and fairest Hill
That was in all this **Holy-Island's** hights)
Was made the most unpleasant, and most ill.
Mean while, O **Clio**, lend **Calliope**, thy Quill.

Whylome, when IRELAND flourished in Fame
Of Wealth and Goodness, far above the rest
Of all that bear the British Islands Name,
The Gods then us'd (for Pleasure and for Rest)
Oft to resort there-to, when seem'd them best;
But none of all there-in more pleasure found,
Than Cynthia; that is sovereign Queen profest
Of Woods and Forests, which therein abound,
Sprinkled with wholesome Waters, more than most on ground.

But mongst them all, as fittest for her Game,
Either for Chase of Beasts with Hound or Bow,
Or for to shroud in Shade from **Phoebus' flame**,
Or bathe in Fountains that do freshly flow,
Or from high Hills, or from the Dales below,
She chose this Arlo, where she did resort
With all her Nymphs enranged on a row,
With whom the woody Gods did oft consort:
For, with the Nymphs, the Satyrs love to play and sport.

Amongst the which, there was a Nymph that **height**
Molanna; Daughter of old Father Mole,
And Sister unto **Mulla**, fair and bright:
Unto whose Bed **false Bregog** whylome stole,
That Shepheard **Colin** dearly did condole,
And made her luckless Loves well known to be.
But this Molanna, were she not so **shole**,
Were no less fair and beautiful than she:
Yet as she is, a fairer Flood may no Man see.

For, first, she springs out of two marble Rocks,
On which, a Grove of Oaks high mounted grows,
That as a Girlond seems to deck the Locks
Of some fair Bride, brought forth with **pompous** Shows
Out of her Bower, that many Flowers **strows**:
So, through the flowery Dales she tumbling down,
Through many Woods, and shady Coverts flows
(That on each side her silver Channel crown)
Till to the Plain she come, whose Valleys she doth drown.

In her sweet Streams, Diana used oft
(After her sweaty Chace and toilsome Play)
To bathe her self, and after, on the soft
And downy Grass, her dainty Limbs to lay
In covert shade, where none behold her may:
For, much she hated sight of living Eye.
Foolish God **Faunus**, though full many a day
He saw her clad, yet longed foolishly
To see her naked mongst her Nymphs in privily.

No way he found to compass his Desire,
But to corrupt Molanna, this her Maid,
Her to discover for some secret Hire:
So, her with flattering Words he first assay'd;
And after, pleasing Gifts for her purvay'd,
Queen-Apples, and red Cherries from the Tree,
With which he her allured and betray'd,
To tell what time he might her Lady see
When she her self did bathe, that he might secret be.

There-to he promis'd, if she would him pleasure
With this small Boon, to quit her with a better;
To weet, that whereas she had out of measure
Long lov'd the **Fanchin**, who by nought did set her,
That he would undertake, for this to get her
To be his Love, and of him liked well:
Besides all which, he vow'd to be her Debter
For many moe good turns than he would tell;
The least of which, this little Pleasure should excel.

The simple Maid did yield to him **anon**;
And **eft him placed where he close** might view
That never any saw, save only one;
Who, for his Hire to so Fool-hardy due,
Was of his Hounds devour'd in Hunter's **Hue**.
Tho, as her manner was on sunny Day,
Diana, with her Nymphs about her, drew
To this sweet Spring; where, **doffing her Array**,
She bath'd her lovely Limbs, for Jove a likely Prey.

There Faunus saw that pleased much his eye,
And made his Heart to **tickle** in his Breast,
That for great Joy of somewhat he did spy,
He could him not contain in silent rest;
But **breaking forth in Laughter** loud, profest
His foolish Thought. A foolish Faune indeed,

That couldst not hold thy self so hidden blest,
But wouldest needs thine own Conceit **areed**:
Babblers unworthy been of so divine a **Meed**.

The Goddess, all abashed with that noise,
In haste forth started from the **guilty Brook**;
And running straight where-as she heard his Voice,
Enclos'd the Bush about, and there him took,
Like **darred** Lark; not daring up to look
On her whose sight before so much he sought.
Thence, forth they drew him by the Horns, and shook
Nigh all to pieces, that they left him nought;
And then into the open light they forth him brought.

Like as an Huswife, that with busy care
Thinks of her Dairy to make wondrous gain,
Finding whereas some wicked Beast unware
That breaks into her Dair'house, there doth drain
Her creaming Pans, and frustrate all her Pain;
Hath in some Snare or **Gin** set close behind,
Entrapped him, and caught into her **train**,
Then thinks what Punishment were best assign'd,
And thousand Deaths deviseth in her vengeful Mind:

So did Diana and her Maidens all
Use silly Faunus, now within their **Bail**:
They mock and scorn him, and him foul **miscall**;
Some by the Nose him pluck'd, some by the Tail,
And by his goatish Beard some did him hail:
Yet he (poor Soul) with patience all did bear;
For, nought against their wills might countervail;
Ne ought he said whatever he did hear;
But hanging down his Head, did like a **Mome** appear.

At length when they had flouted him their fill,
They 'gan to **cast** what Penance him to give.
Some would have **gelt** him, but that same would spill
The Wood-Gods Breed, which must for ever live:
Others would through the River him have drive,
And ducked deep; but that seem'd Penance light:
But most agreed, and did this Sentence give,
Him in Deer's Skin to clad; and in that **Plight**,
To hunt him with their Hounds, himself save how he might.

But Cynthia's self more angry than the rest,
Thought not enough, to punish him in sport,
And of her Shame to make a gamesom Jest;

But 'gan examine him in **straighter** sort,
Which of her Nymphs, or other close **Consort**,
Him thither brought, and her to him betray'd.
He much afeard, to her confessed **short**,
That 'twas Molanna which her so bewray'd:
Then all at once their Hands upon Molanna laid.

But him (according as they had decreed)
With a Deer's Skin they cover'd, and then chac'd
With all their Hounds, that after him did speed;
But he more speedy, from them fled more fast
Than any Deer: so sore him Dread aghast.
They after follow'd all with shrill Outcry,
Shouting as they the Heavens would have **brast**:
That all the Woods and Dales, where he did fly,
Did ring again, and loud re-eccho to the sky.

So they him follow'd till they weary were;
When back returning to Molann' again,
They by Commandment of Diana, there
Her **whelm'd** with Stones. Yet Faunus (for her Pain)
Of her beloved Fanchin did obtain,
That her he would receive unto his Bed.
So now her Waves pass through a pleasing Plain,
Till with the Fanchin she her self do wed,
And (both combin'd) themselves in one fair River spread.

Nath'less Diana, full of Indignation,
Thenceforth abandon'd her delicious Brook;
In whose sweet Stream, before that bad Occasion,
So much Delight to bathe her Limbs she took:
Ne only her, but also quite forsook
All those fair Forests about Arlo hid,
And all that Mountain, which doth over-look
The richest **Champian** that may **else be rid**,
And the fair **Shure**, in which are thousand Salmons bred.

Them all, and all that she so dear did **way**,
Thenceforth she left; and parting from the Place,
Thereon an heavy **hapless** Curse did lay,
To **weet**, that Wolves, where she was wont to **space**,
Should harbour'd be, and all those Woods deface,
And Thieves should rob and spoil that Coast around.
Since which, those Woods, and all that goodly **Chace**,
Doth to this day with **Wolves and Thieves** abound:
Which too-too true that Land's In-dwellers since have found.

Notes

Change: mutability **Moon:** Spenser here refers to Renaissance cosmography. The worlds above the moon were deemed to be beyond change, those below it, subject to change. Mutability reigns beneath the moon. **Pretends:** here, 'claims' **Wheel:** the wheel of fortune **rehearse:** here, 'to tell' **Regiment:** rule **Jove of Kingdom did deprive:** refers to the wars with the Titans **Stem:** family-line, genealogy **Hecate:** goddess of witchcraft; her powers extend over both heaven and hell. **Bellona:** Roman goddess of war **Titaness:** mutability **twaine:** Hecate and Bellona **sad:** here, serious **ru'd:** to be contrite **Estate:** state **pervert:** overturn **burst:** break **Frame:** structure **still:** here, continually **Policy:** here, government **Nurse:** traditional image of Nature as mother/nurse **cast:** plan **attempt:** attack **Air:** In cosmogony, air occupies the middle region. **contrair:** oppose **Cynthia:** goddess of chastity and hunting **Tyme:** time as the boundary between heaven and earth **liefe or sory:** willing or unwilling **Stage:** celestial station **scan'd:** climbed **two Steeds, th' one black, the other white:** the two phases of the moon **Vesper:** Hesperus, the evening star **intend:** here, call or address **tortious:** wrong, or even wicked **wain'd:** carried along **wend:** thought **malign:** here, envy **th' infernal Powers . . .fair Light:** When the moon is invisible to the earth, she lends her light to the infernal regions. **condign:** valuable or worthy **Chear:** expression **Coast:** The moon is the boundary of the heavens. **pack:** to retreat **Thunder's wrack:** Jove's vengeance **raught:** reached **perforce:** by force **unpurvaid:** deprived **Mercury:** messenger of the Gods, also known as Hermes **'plain:** complain **Typhon:** a Titan, one who waged war against the gods, and was eventually imprisoned by Jove under Mount Aetna **Son of Maia:** Mercury **forslowe:** delay **attache:** here, seize **prest:** immediately **Hardiness:** courage **discharge:** here, justify **snaky-wreathed mace:** Mercury's mace, with powers to summon both the living and the dead **lour:** here, to scowl **amate:** amaze **Earth's cursed seed:** the Titans **despite:** here, anger **Phoebe:** another name for Cynthia **advise:** here, to consider **Areed:** counsel **cast:** delivered **Emprize:** enterprise **beck:** nod **wield:** to control **Vow:** will **extasy:** here, both ecstasy and confusion **aby:** stay **reft:** deprived **make:** here, want **magnify'd:** here, praised **envy'd:** grudged **Corybantes:** priests of the goddess Cybele. They guarded Jove when he was an infant. They were later known for their wild rituals. **Slight:** cunning **injuriously:** wrongfully **mortal Thoughts:** Mutability is part god and part human. Here Jove insults her because she is a lesser god. **bewray:** betray **Procrustes:** Poseidon's son, killed by Theseus. Procrustes would fit his victims to a bed either by stretching them, or by cutting off their limbs (hence the common phrase 'Procrustean. bed') **Hire:** here, rewards **Ixion:** He was tied to a burning wheel by Jove. **Prometheus:** Titan, who stole fire from the gods and was punished by being chained to a rock and having his liver plucked out by an eagle everyday. It would grow back in the night and would be eaten again the next day. **Fry:** brood **quook:** quaked **challenge:** here, lay claim to **eft:** afterward **Levin-brond:** lightning **Flesh yfere:** against flesh **Interesse:** legal right **Enducement light:** promise of rewards **spight:** envied **with her affright:** frightened of her **wote:** know. **Doom:** judgment **fain:** to imagine **Saturn's son:** She asserts her right of succession as Titan's daughter, thwarting Jove's right to rule. **equal:** here, impartial **behight:** summoned **Dan**

Phoebus: Mercury **Arlo-hill:** Spenser's name for Galtymore, the hill outside his home in Ireland **Mole:** the hill ranges in the area of Spenser's home **File:** thread **abate:** stop **Stounds:** conflicts **Holy-Islands:** This refers to the myth that the Irish islands were populated by saints and scholars during the middle ages. **Clio:** the muse of history **Calliope:** now replaces Clio as the narrator of the remaining story **Phoebus flame:** the sun's rays **height:** was called **Molanna:** a river, actually named Behanna, near Spenser's home in Ireland. Spenser combines Mole and Behanna. **Mulla:** another name for the Awbeg river into which four rivulets meet and merge **false Bregog**: in Irish 'Breg' means deceiving. The description here is of rivers that flood suddenly and are therefore untrustworthy. **Colin:** a reference to Spenser's work *Colin Clouts Come Home Again* **shole:** shallow **pompous:** here, magnificent **strows:** scatters **Faunus:** The name might be derived from words for 'foolish' (fatuus). The story originates from Ovid, where Faunus tried to rape Omphale, but was discovered and ended up being ridiculed. **Fanchin:** Spenser's name for the river Funsheon, which joins the Molanna **anon:** at once **close:** secretly **eft him placed where he close:** Acteon saw Diana bathing, and he was turned into a stag and killed by his own hounds as a result. **Hue:** here, form **doffing her Array**: taking off her clothes **tickle:** thrill **breaking forth in Laughter:** suggests incontinence **areed:** reveal **Meed:** reward **guilty Brook:** the Molanna. Spenser treats it as guilty of betraying Diana. **darred:** dazzled (birds used to be dazzled by mirrors and thus caught) **Gin:** trap **train:** snare **Bail:** power **miscall:** insult **Mome:** idiot **Cast:** consider **gelt:** castrated **Plight:** state **straighter:** harsh **Consort:** here, confidante **short:** soon **brast:** burst **whelm'd:** overwhelmed **Champian:** open country **else be rid:** everywhere, common **Shure:** the river Suir **way:** weigh **hapless:** causing misery **weet:** know **space:** walk **Chae:** hunting ground **Wolves and Thieves:** refers to the wolves and thieves that abound in Ireland

Philip Sidney

Philip Sidney (1554–1586) was born into a wealthy family in Kent. Educated at Oxford, he spent several years in France and other parts of Europe in the 1570s. After returning to England he met Penelope Devereaux, the daughter of the Earl of Essex and the Stella of *Astrophel and Stella*. He fell out with Elizabeth and stopped being a part of the Court circle. However, he did win back Elizabeth's favour and was made Member of Parliament in 1581. In the intervening years he had composed several works which would contribute to his stature as a poet and critic: *Astrophel and Stella*, *Arcadia* and *The Defence of Poetry*. Sidney married Frances Walsingham in 1583. His literary circle was now large, and included Edmund Spenser, whose *The Faerie Queene* he recommended to the Queen, and Giordano Bruno – the proponent of the plural worlds theory who would eventually be burnt at the stake as a heretic. He was appointed Governor of Flushing, Netherlands in 1585. In the Battle of Zutphen Sidney was injured and is famously believed to have offered his water-bottle to another injured soldier stating, 'Thy necessity is yet greater than mine'. Sidney died of his injuries a few days later at the age of thirty-one.

Astrophel and Stella (extracts)

Loving in truth, and fain in verse my love to show,
That she (dear She) might take some pleasure of my pain:
Pleasure might cause her read, reading might make her know,
Knowledge might pity win, and pity grace obtain;
I sought fit words to paint the blackest face of woe,
Studying inventions fine, her wits to entertain:
Oft turning others' leaves, to see if thence would flow
Some fresh and fruitful showers upon my sun-burned brain.
But words came halting forth, wanting Invention's stay,
Invention, Nature's child, fled step-dame Study's blows,
And others' feet still seemed but strangers in my way.
Thus, great with child to speak, and helpless in my throes,
Biting my truant pen, beating myself for spite—
'Fool,' said my Muse to me, 'look in thy heart and write.'

Not at first sight, nor with a **dribbed** shot
Love gave the wound, which while I breathe will bleed;
But known worth did in mine of time proceed,
Till by degrees it had full conquest got:
I saw and liked, I liked but loved not;
I loved, but straight did not what Love decreed.
At length to love's decrees I, forced, agreed,
Yet with repining at so partial lot.
Now even that footstep of lost liberty
Is gone, and now like **slave-born Muscovite**
I call it praise to suffer tyranny;
And now employ the remnant of my wit
To make myself believe that all is well,
While with a feeling skill I paint my hell.

Let the dainty wits cry on the **Sisters nine**,
That bravely masked, their fancies may be told:

Or, **Pindar**'s apes, flaunt they in phrases fine,
Enam'ling with pied flowers their thoughts of gold.
Or else let them in statelier glory shine,
Ennobling new found tropes with problems old,
Or with strange similes enrich each line,
Of herbs or beasts with **Inde** or Afric' hold.
For me in sooth, no Muse but one I know:
Phrases and problems from my reach do grow,
And strange things cost too dear for my poor sprites.
How then? Even thus: in Stella's face I read
What love and beauty be, then all my deed
But copying is, what in her Nature writes.

Virtue, alas, now let me take some rest.
Thou set'st a bate between my soul and wit.
If vain love have my simple soul oppressed,
Leave what thou likest not, deal not thou with it.
The scepter use in some old **Cato's** breast;
Churches or schools are for thy seat more fit.
I do confess, pardon a fault confessed,
My mouth too tender is for thy hard bit.
But if that needs thou wilt usurping be,
The little reason that is left in me,
And still th'effect of thy persuasions prove:
I swear, my heart such one shall show to thee
That shrines in flesh so true a deity,
That Virtue, thou thyself shalt be in love.

It is most true, that eyes are formed to serve
The inward light; and that the heavenly part
Ought to be king, from whose rules who do swerve,
Rebels to Nature, strive for their own smart.
It is most true, what we call Cupid's dart,
An image is, which for ourselves we carve:
And, fools, adore in temple of our heart,
Till that good God make Church and churchman starve.
True, that true beauty virtue is indeed,
Whereof this beauty can be but a shade,
Which elements with mortal mixture breed:
True, that on earth we are but pilgrims made,
And should in soul up to our country move:
True, and yet true that I must Stella love.

Some lovers speak when they their Muses entertain,
Of hopes begot by fear, of wot not what desires:
Of force of heav'nly beams, infusing hellish pain:
Of living deaths, dear wounds, fair storms, and freezing fires.

Some one his song in **Jove**, and Jove's strange tales attires,
Broidered with bulls and swans, powdered with golden rain;
Another humbler wit to shepherd's pipe retires,
Yet hiding royal blood full oft in rural vein.
To some a sweetest plaint a sweetest style affords,
While tears pour out his ink, and sighs breathe out his words:
His paper pale despair, and pain his pen doth move.
I can speak what I feel, and feel as much as they,
But think that all the map of my state I display,
When trembling voice brings forth that I do Stella love.

When Nature made her chief work, Stella's eyes,
In colour black why wrapped she beams so bright?
Would she in beamy black, like painter wise,
Frame daintiest lustre, mixed of shades and light?
Or did she else that sober hue devise,
In object best to knit and strength our sight,
Lest if no veil those brave gleams did disguise,
They sun-like should more dazzle than delight?
Or would she her miraculous power show,
That whereas black seems Beauty's contrary,
She even if black doth make all beauties flow?
Both so and thus, she minding Love shoud be
Placed ever there, gave him this mourning weed,
To honour all their deaths, who for her bleed.

Queen Virtue's court, which some call Stella's face,
Prepared by Nature's choicest furniture,
Hath his front built of alabaster pure;
Gold in the covering of that stately place.
The door by which sometimes comes forth her Grace
Red **Porphir** is, which lock of pearl makes sure,
Whose porches rich (which name of cheeks endure)
Marble mixed red and white do interlace.
The windows now through which this heav'nly guest
Looks o'er the world, and can find nothing such,
Which dare claim from those lights the name of best,
Of touch they are that without touch doth touch,
Which Cupid's self from Beauty's mine did draw:
Of touch they are, and poor I am their straw.

Cupid, because thou shin'st in Stella's eyes,
That from her locks, thy day-nets, none scapes free,
That those lips swell, so full of thee they be,
That her sweet breath makes oft thy flames to rise,
That in her breast thy pap well sugared lies,
That her Grace gracious makes thy wrongs, that she

What words so ere she speak persuades for thee,
That her clear voice lifts thy fame to the skies:
Thou countest Stella thine, like those whose powers
Having got up a breach by fighting well,
Cry, 'Victory, this fair day all is ours.'
Oh no, her heart is such a citadel,
So fortified with wit, stored with disdain,
That to win it, is all the skill and pain.

The curious wits seeing dull pensiveness
Bewray itself in my long settled eyes,
Whence those same fumes of melancholy rise,
With idle pains, and missing aim, do guess.
Some that know how my spring I did address,
Deem that my Muse some fruit of knowledge plies:
Others, because the Prince my service tries,
Think that I think state errors to redress.
But harder judges judge ambition's rage,
Scourge of itself, still climbing slipp'ry place,
Holds my young brain catived in golden cage.
Oh Fools, or over-wise, alas the race
Of all my thoughts hath neither stop nor start,
But only Stella's eyes and Stella's heart.

Come, let me write. 'And to what end?' To ease
A burthened heart. 'How can words ease, which are
The glasses of thy daily vexing care?'
Oft cruel fights well pictured forth do please.
'Art not ashamed to publish thy disease?'
Nay, that may breed my fame, it is so rare.
'But will not wise men think thy words fond ware?'
Then be they close, and so none shall displease.
'What idler thing than speak and not be heard?'
What harder thing than smart, and not to speak?
Peace, foolish wit, with wit my wit is marred.
Thus write I while I doubt to write, and wreak
My harms on ink's poor loss; perhaps some find
Stella's great powers, that so confuse my mind.

What may words say, or what may words not say,
Where truth itself must speak like flattery?
Within what bounds can one his liking stay,
Where Nature doth with infinite agree?
What **Nestor's** counsel can my flames allay,
Since Reason's self doth blow the coal in me?
And ah what hope, that hope should once see day,
Where Cupid is sworn page to Chastity?

Honour is honoured, that thou dost possess
Him as thy slave, and now long needy Fame
Doth even grow rich, naming my Stella's name.
Wit learns in thee perfection to express,
Not thou by praise, but praise in thee is raised:
It is a praise to praise, when thou art praised.

Having this day my horse, my hand, my lance
Guided so well, that I obtained the prize,
Both by the judgment of the English eyes,
And of some sent from that sweet enemy France;
Horsemen my skill in horsemanship advance,
Town-folks my strength; a daintier judge applies
His praise to sleight, which from good use doth rise;
Some lucky wits impute it but to chance;
Others, because of both sides I do take
My blood from them who did escel in this,
Think Nature me a man of arms did make.
How far they shot awry! the true cause is,
Stella looked on, and from her heav'nly face
Sent forth the beams, which made so fair my race.

Oh eyes, which do the spheres of beauty move,
Whose beams be joys, whose joys all virtues be,
Who while they make Love conquer, conquer Love,
The schools where Venus hath learned chastity;
Oh eyes, whose humble looks most glorious prove,
Only loved tyrants, just in cruelty,
Do not, oh do not from poor me remove,
Keep still my zenith, ever shine on me.
For though I never see them, but straightways
My life forgets to nourish languished sprites;
Yet still on me, oh eyes, dart down your rays:
And if from majesty of sacred lights,
Oppressing mortal sense, my death proceed,
Wracks triumphs be, which Love (high set) doth breed.

Notes

Astrophel: from 'Aster' (star) and 'phil' (lover) **Stella:** Latin for 'star'; the 'Stella' of Sidney's sonnet sequence is possibly Penelope Rich **dribbed:** to crop, or cut a little **slave-born Muscovite:** This refers to Moscow which, during Sidney's time, was under the reign of the tyrannical Ivan the Terrible. **Sisters nine:** the Muses **Pindar:** ancient Greek poet, known mainly for his odes **Inde:** East Indies **Cato:** ancient Greek statesman, often referred to as Cato the Censorious for his frugal lifestyle and strong sense of discipline **Jove:** Jupiter **Porphir:** a kind of crystalline rock, used to make jewellery **Bewray:** betray **Nestor:** from Greek myth, an Argonaut who helped fight the Centaurs, later King of Pylos, known for his wisdom

Elizabeth I

Queen of England, Elizabeth was born in 1533 to Henry VIII and Anne Boleyn, who was executed. After several years of messy succession intrigues with Edward VI, and Mary I, Elizabeth came to the throne of England in 1558. She developed the Protestant faith into what would eventually become the Church of England. Refusing to marry, Elizabeth set about establishing her authority over the country, even as her iconic status as the Virgin Queen, 'married to her country', grew. She thwarted rebellions, most notably by Mary, Queen of Scots, and won major wars, like that against the Spanish Armada in 1588. Known for her dramatic speeches and careful rhetoric – in which she would present herself as having 'the body but of a weak and feeble woman, but … the heart and stomach of a king, and of a King of England', as she put it in her speech to the troops setting out to battle the Armada – Elizabeth won the hearts of her countrymen. She also established relations with Russian and Ottoman Empires. Elizabeth died in 1603.

On Monsieur's Departure

I grieve and dare not show my discontent;
I love, and yet am forced to seem to hate;
I do, yet dare not say I ever meant;
I seem stark mute, but inwardly do prate.
    I am, and not; I freeze and yet am burned,
    Since from myself another self I turned.

My care is like my shadow in the sun —
Follows me flying, flies when I pursue it,
Stands, and lies by me, doth what I have done;
His too familiar care doth make me rue it.
    No means I find to rid him from my breast,
    Till by the end of things it be supprest.

Some gentler passion slide into my mind,
For I am soft, and made of melting snow;
Or be more cruel, Love, and so be kind.
Let me or float or sink, be high or low;
    Or let me live with some more sweet content,
    Or die, and so forget what love e'er meant.

In Defiance of Fortune

Never think you Fortúne can bear the sway
Where virtue's force can cause her to obey.

The Doubt of Future Foes

The doubt of future foes exiles my present joy,
And wit me warns to shun such snares as threaten mine annoy;
For falsehood now doth flow, and subjects' faith doth ebb,
Which should not be if reason ruled or wisdom weaved the web.
But clouds of joys untried do cloak aspiring minds,
Which **turn to rain of late** repent by changèd course of winds.
The top of hope supposed, the root of rue shall be,
And fruitless all their grafted guile, as shortly ye shall see.
The dazzled eyes with pride, which great ambition blinds,
Shall be unsealed by worthy **wights** whose foresight falsehood finds.
The **daughter of debate** that discord **aye** doth sow
Shall reap no gain where former rule **still** peace hath taught to know.
No **foreign banished wight** shall anchor in this port;
Our realm brooks not seditious sects, let them elsewhere resort.
My rusty sword through rest shall first his edge employ
To **poll their tops** that seek such change or gape for future joy.

Notes:

turn to rain of late: tears of repentance **The top of hope supposed:** the full flowering of hope **wights:** fellows **daughter of debate:** possible reference to Mary, Queen of Scots **aye:** always **still:** always **foreign banished wight:** possible reference to Philip II of Spain **My rusty sword through rest:** 'my sword which is rusty through rest' **poll their tops:** cut off their heads

Michael Drayton

Born in Warwickshire in 1563, Drayton was a page with Sir Henry Goodeere of Polesworth with whose daughter, Anne, he fell in love. Not much is known of his early years but it is speculated that he served in the army. His first published book was *Harmonie of the Church* in 1591. He published *Endymion and Phoebe*, which would later offer Keats the source for his own *Endymion*. Drayton also wrote some plays of which only *The First Part of Sir John Oldcastle* (1600) survives. Drayton tried to get employed at the Court, but was rejected by James I. His literary circle included Ben Jonson, William Drummond and George Wither. It is also a matter of some speculation that he was a friend of Shakespeare's as well. In 1627, he published an epic poem, *The Battle of Agincourt*, although he is now known mostly for his *Poly-Olbion*, a poem that maps the history and geography of England. The first part of the poem appeared in 1613 and the full poem in 1622.

Poly-Olbion (extracts)

From: The First Song

Of Albion's glorious Isle the wonders whilst I write,
The sundry varying soils, the pleasures infinite,
(Where heat kills not the cold, nor cold expells
the heat,
The calms too mildly small, nor winds too roughly great.
Nor night doth hinder day, nor day the night doth wrong,
The summer not too short, the winter not too long)
What help shall I invoke to aid my Muse the while?
Thou Genius of the place (this most renowned Isle)
Which livedst long before the all-earth-drowning Flood,
Whilst yet the world did swarm with her Gigantic brood,
Go thou before me still thy circling shores about,
And in this wand'ring maze help to conduct me out:
Direct my course so right, as with thy hand to show
Which way thy Forests range, which way thy Rivers flow . . .

Upon the utmost end of Cornwalls furrowing beak,
Where **Bresnan** from the land the tilting waves doth break;
The shore let her transcend, the promont to descry,
And view about the Point th' unnumb'red fowl that fly.
Some, rising like a storm from off the troubled sand,
Seem in their hovering flight to shadow all the land ;
Some, sitting on the beach to prune their painted breasts,
As if both earth and air they only did possess.
Whence, climbing to the cleeves, herself she firmly sets
The Bourns, the Brooks, the Becks, the Rills, the Rivelets,
Exactly to derive; receiving in her way,

That straight'ned tongue of land, where, at **Mount-Michael's**
Rude Neptune, cutting in, a cantle forth doth take;

And, on the other side, **Hayles'** vaster mouth doth make
A **chersonese** thereof, the corner clipping in;
Where to the industrious Muse the Mount doth thus begin:
Before thou further pass, and leave this setting shore,
Whose towns unto the Saints that lived here of yore
(Their fasting, works, and pray'rs, remaining to our shames,)
Were rear'd, and justly call'd by their peculiar names,
The builders honour still; this due and let them have,
As deign to drop a tear upon each holy grave; so

Whose charity and zeal instead of knowledge stood:
For surely in themselves they were right simply good.
If credulous too much, thereby they offended heaven,
In their devout intents yet be their sins forgiven.
Then from his rugged top the tears down trickling fell;
And, in his passion stirr'd, again began to tell,

Strange things, that in his days Time's course had brought to
That forty miles now sea, sometimes firm fore-land was;
And that a forest then, which now with him is flood,
Whereof he first was call'd the **Hoar-Rock in the Wood,**

Let **Camell**, of her course, and curious windings boast,
In that her greatness reigns sole mistress of that coast
'Twixt **Tamer** and that Bay, where Hayle pours forth her pride:
And let us (nobler Nymphs) upon the mid-day side,
Be frolic with the best. Thou Foy, before us all,
By thine own named Town made famous in thy fall,

As Low, amongst us here; a most delicious brook,
With all our sister Nymphs, that to the noon-sted look.
Which gliding from the hills, upon the tinny ore,
Betwixt your high-rear'd banks, resort to this our shore:
Lov'd streams, let us exult, and think ourselves no less
Than those upon their side, the setting that possess.

Which Camell overheard: but what doth she respect
Their taunts, her proper course that loosely doth neglect
As frantic, ever since her British Arthur's blood
By **Mordreds** murtherous hand was mingled with her flood.
For, as that river best might boast that Conqueror's breath,
So sadly she bemoans his too untimely death;
Who, after twelve proud fields against the Saxon fought,
Yet back unto her banks by fate was lastly brought:
As though no other place, on Britain's spacious earth,
Were worthy of his end, but where he had his birth:
And careless ever since how she her course do steer,

This mutt'reth to herself, in wand'ring here and there:
Ev'n in the agedst face, where beauty once did dwell,
And nature (in the least) but seemed to excell,
Time cannot make such waste, but something will appear.
To show some little tract of delicacy there.

Or some religious work, in building many a day,
That this penurious age hath suffer'd to decay . . .

Upon the British coast, what ship yet ever came
That not of Plymouth hears,where those brave Navies lie,
From cannons' thund'ring throats that all the world defy
Which, to invasive spoil when th' English list to draw,
Have check'd Iberia's pride, and held her oft in awe:
Oft furnishing onr dames with India's rar'st devices,
And lent us gold, and pearl, rich silks, and dainty spices.
But Tamer takes the place, and all attend her here,

A faithful bound to both; and two that be so near
For likeliness of soil, and quantity they hold,
Before the Roman came; whose people were of old
Known by one general name, upon this point that dwell,
All other of this Isle in wrestling that excell

My Britain-founding **Brute**, when with his puissant fleet
At **Totnesse** first he touch'd: which shall renown my stream
(Which now the envious world doth slander for a dream.)
Whose fatal flight from Greece, his fortunate arrive
In happy Albion here whilst strongly I revive,
Dear **Harburne** at thy hands this credit let me win,
Quoth she, that as thou hast my faithful handmaid been
So now (my only brook) assist me with thy spring,
Whilst of the god-like Brute the story thus I sing:

Next **Silvius** him succeeds, begetting Brute again:
Who in his mother's womb whilst yet he did remain,
The Oracles gave out, that next-born **Brute** should be
His parents' only death: which soon they liv'd to see.
For, in his painful birth his mother did depart;
And ere his fifteenth year, in hunting of a hart,
He with a luckless shaft his hapless father slew:
For which, out of his throne, their king the Latins threw.

Notes

Bresnan: an island off the Cornish coast **Mount-Michael's:** St Michael's Mount, an island off Moutn's bay, Cornwall **Hayles:** a small town in western Cornwall **chersonese:** a Latin word, derived from the Greek name for 'peninsula' **Hoar-Rock in the**

Wood: from the Cornish name of St Michael's Mount, 'carrec loys en coys' **Camell:** a river in Cornwall **Tamer:** or Tamar, a river in Cornwall **Mordred:** a character in the Arthurian legends, a traitor who fought Arthur, and fatally injured him (Mordred was killed) and is believed to have been Arthur's illegitimate son **Brute:** Brutus of Troy, the supposed founder of Britain **Totnesse:** or Totnes, a town in Devon; it is supposed to be the place where Brutus of Troy first arrived. Its first castle dates back to 900 AD and it is mentioned in Geoffrey of Monmouth's chronicle of England. A stone, supposedly the one he stepped on when alighting from his ship, is a major tourist attraction still. **Harburne:** a place in Birmingham whose records go back to 1086, and where traces of a Roman city are found **Silvius:** according to some histories, the second son of Ascanius **Brute:** His mother died in childbirth, and he later accidentally killed his father with an arrow. After being exiled, and spending several years wandering, Brute came to Britain and settled it.

Thomas Campion

Born in 1567 in London, Campion went to Cambridge but left without a degree. He later studied for the law. Campion's reputation rests primarily on his poems for musical accompaniment, although his first works appeared in a pirated edition of Philip Sidney's *Astrophel and Stella* in 1591. In 1601 *A Booke of Ayres* was published, and many of the lyrics set to music, and performed at royal events. Campion also published a work of criticism, *Observations in the Art of English Poesie* (1602). In 1605 he received a medical degree from the University of Caen in France and practised as a physician in London. He may have died of plague in 1620. Campion also wrote masques that were performed for James I.

My Sweetest Lesbia

My sweetest Lesbia, let us live and love,
And though the sager sort our deeds reprove,
Let us not way them: heaven's great lamps do dive
Into their west, and straight again revive,
But soon as once set is our little light,
Then must we sleep one **ever-during** night.

If all would lead their lives in love like me,
Then bloody swords and armour should not be,

No drum nor trumpet peaceful sleeps should moue,
Unless alarm came from the camp of love:
But fools do live, and waste their little light,
And seek with pain their ever-during night.

When timely death my life and fortune ends,
Let not my hearse be vexed with mourning friends,
But let all lovers rich in triumph come,
And with sweet pastimes grace my happy tomb;
And Lesbia close up thou my little light,
And crown with love my ever-during night.

Notes

ever-during: everlasting

Now Winter Nights Enlarge

Now winter nights enlarge
    The number of their hours;
And clouds their storms discharge
    Upon the **airy** towers.
Let now the chimneys blaze
    And cups overflow with wine,
Let well-tuned words amaze
    With harmony divine.
Now yellow waxen lights
    Shall wait on honey Love
While youthful Revels, Masks, and Courtly sights,
    Sleeps leaden spells remove.

    This time **doth well dispense**
    With lovers long discourse;
Much speech hath some defence,
    Though beauty no remorse.
All doe not all things well;
    Some measures comely tread;
Some knotted Riddles tell;
    Some Poems smoothly read.
The Summer hath his joys,
    And Winter his delights;
Though Love and all his pleasures are but toys,
    They shorten tedious nights.

Notes

airy: lofty **doth well dispense:** allows for, enables

Aemilia Lanyer

Born in Bishopsgate, London, in 1569, Aemilia Lanyer may have grown up in the household of Susan Bertie Wingfield, the Countess Dowager of Kent. She was later attached to the household of Margaret, the Countess of Cumberland, and her daughter, Anne Clifford, whose house she described in 'The Description of Cooke-ham', the first country-house poem in English. She was also a visitor at the court of the Queen and was mistress to Henry Carey. She later married Alphonso Lanyer, a court musician. Lanyer published her first collection of poetry called *Salve Deus Rex Judaeorum* in 1611. In later life, as a widow, she ran a school. She died in 1645. The few biographical details about Lanyer are embedded in speculations – where she is sometimes Shakespeare's mistress and sometimes the dark-eyed lady of Milton's sonnets.

To the Queen's Most Excellent Majesty

Renowned Empress, and great Britain's Queen,

Most gracious Mother of succeeding Kings;
Vouchsafe to view that which is seldom seen,
A Womans writing of divinest things:
    Reade it faire Queen, though it defective be,
    Your Excellence can grace both It and Me.

For you have rifled Nature of her store,

And all the Goddesses have dispossessed
Of those rich gifts which they enjoyed before,
But now great Queen, in you they all doe rest.
    If now they strived for the golden Ball,
    Paris would give it you before them all.

From Juno you have State and Dignities,

From warlike Pallas, Wisdom, Fortitude;
And from faire Venus all her Excellencies,
With their best parts your Highness is endowed:
    How much are we to honour those that springs
    From such rare beauty, in the blood of Kings?

The Muses doe attend upon your Throne,

With all the Artists at your beck and call;

The Sylvan Gods, and Satyrs every one,
Before your faire triumphant Chariot fall:
    And shining Cynthia with her nymphs attend
    To honour you, whose Honour hath no end.

From your bright sphere of greatness where you sit,
Reflecting light to all those glorious stars
That wait upon your Throne; to virtue yet
Vouchsafe that splendor which my meanness bars:
    Be like faire Phoebe, who doth love to grace
    The darkest night with her most beauteous face.

Apollo's beams doe comfort every creature,
And shines upon the meanest things that be;
Since in Estate and Virtue none is greater,
I humbly wish that yours may light on me:
    That so these rude unpolished lines of mine,
    Graced by you may seem the more divine.

Look in this Mirror of a worthy Mind,
Where some of your fair Virtues will appear;
Though all it is impossible to find,
Unless my Glass were crystal, or more clear:
    Which is dim steel, yet full of spotless truth,
    And for one look from your faire eyes it su'th.

Here may your sacred Majesty behold
That mighty Monarch both of heaven and earth,
He that all Nations of the world controlled,
Yet took our flesh in base and meanest berth:
    Whose days were spent in poverty and sorrow,
    And yet all Kings their wealth of him do borrow.

For he is Crown and Crowner of all Kings,
The hopeful haven of the meaner sort,
Its he that all our joy full tidings brings
Of happy reign within his royal Court:
    Its he that in extremity can give
    Comfort to them that have no time to live.

And since my wealth within his Region stands,
And that his Crosse my chiefest comfort is,
Yea in his kingdom only rests my lands,

Of honour there I hope I shall not miss:
    Though I on earth doe live unfortunate,
    Yet there I may attain a better state.

In the mean time, accept most gracious Queen

This holy work, Virtue presents to you,
In poor apparel, shaming to be seen,
Or once to appear in your judicial view:
    But that faire Virtue, though in mean attire,
    All Princes of the world doe most desire.

And sit all royal virtues are in you,

The Natural, the Moral, and Divine,
I hope how plain soever, being true,
You will accept even of the meanest line
    Faire Virtue yields; by whose rare gifts you are
    So highly graced, to exceed the fairest faire.

Behold, great Queen, faire Eves Apology,

Which I have writ in honour of your sex,
And doe refer unto your Majesty,
To judge if it agree not with the Text:
    And if it do, why are poor Women blamed,
    Or by more faulty Men so much defamed?

And this great Lady I have here attired,

In all her richest ornaments of Honour,
That you faire Queen, of all the world admired,
May take the more delight to look upon her:
    For she must entertain you to this Feast,
    To which your Highness is the welcomest guest.

For here I have prepared my Paschal Lamb,

The figure of the living Sacrifice;
Who dying, all the Infernal powers overcame,
That we with him to Eternity might rise:
    This precious Passover feed upon, O Queen,
    Let your faire Virtues in my Glass be seen.

And she that is the pattern of all Beauty,

The very model of your Majesty,
Whose rarest parts enforces Love and Duty,
The perfect pattern of all Piety:

O let my Book by her faire eyes be blest,
In whose pure thoughts all Innocence rests.

Then shall I think my Glass a glorious Sky,

When two such glittering Suns at once appear;
The one replete with sovereign majesty,
Both shining brighter than the clearest clear:
And both reflecting comfort to my spirits,
To find their grace so much above my merit;

Whose untuned voice the doleful notes doth sing

Of sad Affliction in an humble strain;
Much like unto a Bird that wants a wing,
And cannot fly, but warbles forth her pain:
Or he that barred from the Suns bright light,
Wanting days comfort, doth commend the night.

So I that live closed up in Sorrows Cell,

Since great Eliza's favour blest my youth;
And in the confines of all cares doe dwell,
Whose grieved eyes no pleasure ever vieweth:
But in Christs sufferings, such sweet taste they have,
As makes me praise pale Sorrow and the Grave.

And this great Lady whom I love and honour,

And from my very tender years have known,
This holy habit still to take upon her,
Still to remain the same, and still her own:
And what our fortunes doe enforce us to,
She of Devotion and mere Zeal doth do.

Which makes me think our heavy burden light,

When such a one as she will help to bear it:
Treading the paths that make our way go right,
What garment is so faire but she may wear it;
Especially for her that entertains
A Glorious Queen, in whom all worth remains.

Whose power may raise my sad dejected Muse,

From this love Mansion of a troubled mind;
Whose princely favour may such grace infuse,
That I may spread Her Virtues in like kind:
But in this trial of my slender skill,
I wanted knowledge to perform my will.

For even as they that doe behold the Stars,

Not with the eye of Learning, but of Sight,
To find their motions, want of knowledge bars
Although they see them in their brightest light:
So, though I see the glory of her State,
It's she that must instruct and elevate.

My weak distempered brain and feeble spirits,

Which all unlearned have adventured, this
To writ of Christ, and of his sacred merits,
Desiring that this Book Her hands may kiss:
And though I be unworthy of that grace,
Yet let her blessed thoughts this book embrace.

And pardon me (faire Queen) though I presume,

To doe that which so many better can;
Not that I Learning to my self assume,
Or that I would compare with any man:
But as they are Scholars, and by Art do write,
So Nature yields my Soule a sad delight.
And since all Arts at first from Nature came,

That Goodly Creature, Mother of Perfection,

Whom loves almight hand at first did frame,
Taking both her and hers in his protection:
Why should not She now grace my barren Muse,
And in a Woman all defects excuse.
So peerless Princess humbly I desire,

That your great wisdom would vouchsafe to omit
All faults; and pardon if my spirits retire,
Leaving to aim at what they cannot hit:
To write your worth, which no pen can express,
Were but to eclipse your Fame, and make it less.

The Description of Cooke-ham

Farewell (sweet *Cooke-ham*) where I first obtained
Grace from that Grace where perfect Grace remained;
And where the Muses gave their full consent,
I should have power the virtuous to content:
Where **princely Palace** willed me to **indite**,

The sacred Story of the Souls delight,
Farewell (sweet Place) where Virtue then did rest,
And all delights did harbour in her breast:
Never shall my sad eyes again behold
Those pleasures which my thoughts did then unfold:
Yet you (great Lady) **Mistress of that Place**,
From whose desires did spring this work of Grace;
Vouchsafe to think upon those pleasures past
As fleeting worldly joys that could not last:
Or, as dim shadows of celestial pleasures,
Which are desired above all earthly treasures.
Oh how (me thought) against you thither came,
Each part did seem some new delight to frame!
The House received all ornaments to grace it,
And would endure no foulness to deface it.
The Walks put on their summer Liveries,
And all things else did hold like similies:
The Trees with leaves, with fruits, with flowers clad,
Embraced each other, seeming to be glad,
Turning themselves to beauteous Canopies,
To shade the bright Sun from your brighter eyes:
The crystal Streams with silver spangles graced,

While by the glorious Sun they were embraced:
The little Birds in chirping notes did sing,
To entertain both You and that sweet Spring.
And **Philomela** with her sundry lays,
Both You and that delightful Place did praise.
Oh how me thought each plant, each flour, each tree
Set forth their beauties then to welcome thee!
The very Hills right humbly did descend,
When you to tread upon them did intend,
And as you set your feet, they still did rise,
Glad that they could receive so rich a prize.
The gentle Winds did take delight to be
Among those woods that were so graced by thee.
And in sad murmur uttered pleasing sound,
That Pleasure in that place might more abound:
The swelling Banks delivered all their pride,
When such a *Phoenix* once they had espied.
Each Arbor, Bank, each Seat, each stately Tree,
Thought themselves honored in supporting thee.
The pretty Birds would oft come to attend thee,
Yet fly away for fear they should offend thee:
The little creatures in the Burrough by
Would come abroad to sport them in your eye;

Yet fearful of the Bowe in your faire Hand
Would run away when you did make a stand.
Now let me come unto that stately Tree,
Wherein such goodly Prospects you did see;
That Oak that did in height his fellows pass,
As much as lofty trees, low growing grass:
Much like a comely Cedar straight and tall,
Whose beauteous stature far exceeded all:
How often did you visit this fair tree,
Which seeming joyful in receiving thee,
Would like a Palme tree spread his arms abroad,

Desirous that you there should make abode:
Whose faire green leaves much like a comely veil,
Defended **Phoebus** when he would assail:
Whose pleasing boughs did yield a cool fresh air,
Joying his happiness when you were there.
Where being seated, you might plainly see,
Hills, vales, and woods, as if on bended knee
They had appeared, your honour to salute,
Or to prefer some strange unlooked for suit:
All interlaced with brooks and crystal springs,
A Prospect fit to please the eyes of Kings:
And thirteen shires appeared all in your sight,
Europe could not afford much more delight.
What was there then but gave you all content,
While you the time in meditation spent,
Of their Creators power, which there you saw,
In all his Creatures held a perfect Law;
And in their beauties did you plain descry,
His beauty, wisdom, grace, love, majesty.
In these sweet woods how often did you walke,
With Christ and his Apostles there to talk;
Placing his holy Writ in some faire tree,
To meditate what you therein did see:
With *Moses* you did mount his holy Hill,
To know his pleasure, and perform his Will.
With lovely *David* did you often sing,
His holy Hymns to Heavens Eternal King.
And in sweet music did your soul delight,
To sound his praises, morning, noon, and night.
With blessed *Joseph* you did often feed
Your pined brethren, when they stood in need.
And that sweet Lady sprung from **Cliffords race**,
Of noble *Bedfords* blood, faire steam [*sic*] of Grace;
To honourable *Dorset* now espoused,

In whose faire breast true virtue then was housed:
Oh what delight did my weak spirits find,
In those pure parts of her well framed mind:
And yet it grieves me that I cannot be
Near unto her, whose virtues did agree
With those faire ornaments of outward beauty,
Which did enforce from all both love and duty.
Unconstant Fortune, thou art most too blame,
Who casts us down into so low a frame:
Where our great friends we cannot daily see,

So great a difference is there in degree.
Many are placed in those Orbs of state,
Parters in honour, so ordained by Fate;
Nearer in show, yet farther off in love,
In which, the lowest always are above.
But whither am I carried in conceit?
My Wit too weak to **conster** of the great.
Why not? although we are but borne of earth,
We may behold the Heavens, despising death;
And loving heaven that is so far above,
May in the end vouchsafe us entire love.
Therefore sweet Memory doe thou retain
Those pleasures past, which will not turn again:
Remember beauteous *Dorsets* former sports,
So far from being touched by ill reports;
Wherein my self did always bear a part,
While reverend Love presented my true heart:
Those recreations let me bear in mind,
Which her sweet youth and noble thoughts did find:
Whereof deprived, I evermore must grieve,
Hating blind Fortune, careless to relieve.
And you sweet Cooke-ham, whom these Ladies leave,
I now must tell the grief you did conceive
At their departure; when they went away,

How every thing retained a sad dismay:
Nay long before, when once an **inkling** came,
Me thought each thing did unto sorrow frame:
The trees that were so glorious in our view,
Forsook both flowers and fruit, when once they knew,
Of your depart, their very leaves did wither,
Changing their colours as they grew together.
But when they saw this had no power to stay you,
They often wept, though speechless, could not pray you;
Letting their tears in your faire bosoms fall,

As if they said, Why will ye leave us all?
This being vain, they cast their leaves away,
Hoping that pity would have made you stay:
Their frozen tops, like Ages hoary hairs,
Shows their disaster, languishing in fears:
A swarthy **rivelled rine** all over spread,
Their dying bodies half alive, half dead.
But your occasions called you so away,
That nothing there had power to make you stay:
Yet did I see a noble grateful mind,
Requiting each according to their kind,
Forgetting not to turn and take your leave
Of these sad creatures, powerless to receive
Your favour, when with grief you did depart,
Placing their former pleasures in your heart;
Giving great charge to noble Memory,
There to preserve their love continually:
But specially the love of that faire tree,
That first and last you did vouchsafe to see:
In which it pleased you oft to take the air,
With noble *Dorset*, then a virgin faire:
Where many a learned Book was read and scanned
To this faire tree, taking me by the hand,
You did repeat the pleasures which had past,

Seeming to grieve they could no longer last.
And with a chaste, yet loving kiss took leave,
Of which sweet kiss I did it soon bereave:
Scorning a **senseless creature** should possess
So rare a favour, so great happiness.
No other kiss it could receive from me,
For fear to give back what it took of thee:
So I ungrateful Creature did deceive it,
Of that which you vouchsafed in love to leave it.
And though it oft had given me much content,
Yet this great wrong I never could repent:
But of the happiest made it most forlorn,
To show that nothing's free from Fortunes scorn,
While all the rest with this most beauteous tree,
Made their sad consort sorrows harmony.
The Flowers that on the banks and walks did grow,
Crept in the ground, the Grass did weep for woe.
The Winds and Waters seemed to chide together,
Because you went away they knew not whither:
And those sweet Brookes that ran so faire and clear,
With grief and trouble wrinkled did appear.

Those pretty Birds that wonted were to sing,
Now neither sing, nor chirp, nor use their wing;
But with their tender feet on some bare spray,
Warble forth sorrow, and their own dismay.
Faire *Philomela* leaves her mournful Ditty,
Drowned in dead sleep, yet can procure no pity:
Each arbor, bank, each seat, each stately tree,
Looks bare and desolate now for want of thee;
Turning green tresses into frosty gray,
While in cold grief they wither all away.
The Sun grew weak, his beams no comfort gave,
While all green things did make the earth their grave:
Each brier, each bramble, when you went away,

Caught fast your clothes, thinking to make you stay:
Delightful Echo wonted to reply
To our last words, did now for sorrow die:
The house cast off each garment that might grace it,
Putting on Dust and Cobwebs to deface it.
All desolation then there did appear,
When you were going whom they held so dear.
This last farewell to *Cooke-ham* here I give,
When I am dead thy name in this may live
Wherein I have performed her noble hest,
Whose virtues lodge in my unworthy breast,
And ever shall, so long as life remains,
Tying my heart to her by those rich chains.

Notes

Cooke-ham: Cookham was leased by the brother of Margaret, Countess of Cumberland and her daughter. Margaret would occasionally reside there. It was also the place where Anne, later the Countess of Dorset, grew up. **princely Palace:** archaism for princely palate **indite:** to compose **Mistress of that Place:** a reference to Lady Margaret **Philomela:** a reference from Ovid, the Athenian princess who was raped and had her tongue cut off, and was transformed into a nightingale **Phoebus:** another name for Apollo **Cliffords' race:** Lady Anne was related to the Cliffords on her father's side. **Many are placed . . . love:** individuals removed to centres of power, they pretend to be close but are not truly affectionate **conster:** construe **inkling:** rumour 10 **rivelled:** wrinkled **rine:** rind/bark **senseless creature:** here, refers to the trees, taken to be lacking in a soul

John Donne

John Donne (1572–1631) was born into a family of writers – his mother was the daughter of the playwright John Heywood, and descended from Thomas More. His mother married soon after the death of his father, when Donne was four years old. Donne went to Oxford and Cambridge, but did not get any degree because he was a Roman Catholic and refused to accept Protestantism.

After some years of travel in Europe, he joined service with the Earl of Essex and later travelled with Sir Walter Raleigh and Essex on their voyages hunting for treasure. On his return he secretly married Anne More, whose uncle George More, Chancellor of the Garter, had Donne imprisoned. Donne led an impoverished life with no useful employment and five children (they had twelve; five survived). After another spell of travel on the Continent, he returned to live with his family on Robert Drury's estate. His first theological tract, *Essays in Divinity*, appeared in 1611. Donne took the orders in 1615, possibly because James I made it clear that he would not grant him any other employment. Anne died in 1617. Donne turned more towards his religious duties, and he quickly acquired the reputation of being a formidable preacher, with royalty being among his admirers. Donne's health failed, from around 1623, and during the process of recovery he composed his *Devotions upon Emergent Occasions*. In 1631 he fell ill again, possibly from stomach cancer. One of his final sermons was 'Death's Duell', which many deem to be his epitaph. John Donne died in March of the same year. His famous sermons appeared in 1640, 1649 and 1661 – one hundred and fifty six in all – though his poems had appeared earlier in 1633 and 1635 after circulation for several years in manuscript form.

Sonnet X

Death, be not proud, though some have called thee
Mighty and dreadful, for thou art not so;
For those, whom thou thinkest thou dost overthrow,
Die not, poor Death, nor yet canst thou kill me.
From rest and sleep, which but **thy pictures be**,
Much pleasure, then from thee much more must flow,
And soonest **our best men with thee do go**,
Rest of their bones, and soul's delivery.
Thou art slave to Fate, chance, kings, and desperate men,

And dost with poison, war, and sickness dwell,
And poppy, or charms can make us sleep as well,
And better than thy stroke; why **swellest thou** then?
One short sleep past, we wake eternally,
And Death shall be no more; Death, thou shalt die.

Notes

thy pictures be: that death is another *image* for sleep

our best men with thee do go: a reference to the proverb that the good die young

swellest thou: a reference to the idiomatic expression, 'to swell with pride'

Sonnet XIX

Oh, to vex me, contraries meet in one:
Inconstancy unnaturally hath begot
A constant habit; that when I would not
I change in vows, and in devotion.
As **humorous** is my contrition
As my profane love, and as soon forgot:
As riddlingly **distempered**, cold and hot,
As praying, as mute; as infinite, as none.
I durst not view heaven yesterday; and today
In prayers and flattering speeches I court God:
Tomorrow I quake with true fear of his rod.
So my devout fits come and go away
Like a fantastic ague; save that here
Those are my best days, when I shake with feare.

Notes

humorous: here, frivolous, whimsical, but the suggestion is that we are at the mercy of our bodies

distempered: reference to the theory of humours, where a change in the balance results in 'distemper'

Sonnet XIV

Batter my heart, three-personed God; for you
As yet but knock; breathe, shine, and seek to mend;
That I may rise, and stand, overthrow me, and bend
Your force, to break, blow, burn, and make me new.
I, like an usurped town, **to another due**,
Labour to admit you, but O, to no end.
Reason, your viceroy in me, me should defend,
But is **captived**, and proves weak or untrue.
Yet dearly I love you, and would be loved fain,

But am betrothed unto **your enemy**;
Divorce me, untie, or break that **knot** again,
Take me to you, imprison me, for I,
Except you enthrall me, never shall be free,
Nor ever chaste, except you ravish me.

Notes

to another due: belonging to another **captived:** captured **your enemy:** here refers to the world, which is presented as the enemy to both God and the heavens **knot:** marriage

The Good-Morrow

I wonder by my troth, what thou and I
Did, till we loved? were we not weaned till then?
But sucked on **country pleasures**, childishly?
Or snorted we in the **Seven Sleepers'** den?
'Twas so; but this, all pleasures fancies be;
If ever any beauty I did see,
Which I desired, and got, 'twas but a dream of thee.

And now good-morrow to our waking souls,
Which watch not one another out of fear;
For love all love of other sights controls,
And makes one little room an everywhere.
Let sea-discoverers to new worlds have gone;
Let maps to other, worlds on worlds have shown;
Let us possess **one world**; each hath one, and is one.

My face in thine eye, thine in mine appears,
And true plain hearts do in the faces rest;
Where can we find two better hemispheres
Without sharp north, without declining west?
Whatever dies, was not mixed equally;
If our two loves be one, or thou and I
Love so alike that none can slacken, none can die.

Notes

country pleasures: rustic pleasures, but also suggestive of sexual pleasures **Seven Sleepers:** a reference to the seven young men of Ephesus who, to escape persecution, went into a cave and emerged two centuries later when the world had turned Christian **one world:** a possible reference to the plurality of worlds theory that was disturbing the intellectual climate of the time; here the one world of lovers, as opposed to all the other possible worlds

The Sun Rising

Busy old fool, unruly Sun,
    Why dost thou thus,
Through windows, and through curtains, call on us ?
Must to thy motions lovers' seasons run?
    Saucy pedantic wretch, go chide
    Late school-boys and sour prentices,
  Go tell court-huntsmen that the **King will ride**,
  Call country ants to harvest offices;
Love, all alike, no season knows nor clime,
Nor hours, days, months, which are the rags of time.

    Thy beams so reverend, and strong
    Why shouldst thou think?
I could eclipse and cloud them with a wink,
But that I would not lose her sight so long.
    If her eyes have not blinded thine,
    Look, and to-morrow late tell me,
  Whether both the **Indias of spice** and mine
  Be where thou left'st them, or lie here with me.
Ask for those kings whom thou sawest yesterday,
And thou shalt hear, 'All here in one bed lay.'

    She's all states, and all princes I;
    Nothing else is;
Princes do but play us; compared to this,
All honour's mimic, all wealth **alchemy**.
    Thou, Sun, art half as happy as we,
    In that the **world's contracted** thus;
  Thine age asks ease, and since thy duties be
  To warm the world, that's done in warming us.
Shine here to us, and thou art everywhere;
This bed thy center is, these walls thy sphere.

Notes

King will ride: a reference to James I's passion for hunting **Indias of spice:** a reference to spice in East Indies (India) and the gold of the West (the Americas) **alchemy:** here, suggests illusion **world's contracted:** the world becoming closer (a possible reference to the discoveries of new worlds, but also the private world of the lovers into which the outside world does not intrude

Air and Angels

Twice or thrice had I loved thee,
  Before I knew thy face or name;

So in a voice, so in a shapeless flame
Angels affect us oft, and worshipped be.
Still when, to where thou wert, I came,
Some lovely glorious nothing did I see.
But since my soul, whose child love is,
Takes limbs of flesh, and else could nothing do,
More subtle than the parent is
Love must not be, but take a body too;
And therefore what thou wert, and who,
I bid Love ask, and now
That it assume thy body, I allow,
And fix itself in thy lip, eye, and brow.

Whilst thus to ballast love I thought,
And so more steadily to have gone,
With **wares which would sink admiration**,
I saw I had love's **pinnace** overfraught;
Thy every hair for love to work upon
Is much too much ; some fitter must be sought;
For, nor in nothing, nor in things
Extreme, and scattering bright, can love inhere;
Then as an angel face and wings
Of air, not pure as it, yet pure doth wear,
So thy love may be my love's sphere;
Just such disparity
As is 'twixt air's and angels' purity,
'Twixt women's love, and men's, will ever be.

Notes

'Air and Angels': a reference to Thomas Aquinas' idea that angels assume bodies of air and converse with humans **pinnace:** small boat **wares which would sink admiration:** The boat is so overloaded with lovely cargo that the admirers would be mesmerised, confounded ('sink').

The Canonization

For God's sake hold your tongue, and let me love;
Or chide my palsy, or my gout;
My five gray hairs, or ruin'd fortune flout;
With wealth your state, your mind with arts improve;
Take you a course, get you a place,
Observe his Honour, or his Grace;
Or the king's real, or his stamp'd face
Contemplate; what you will, approve,
So you will let me love.

Alas ! alas ! who's injured by my love?
What merchant's ships have my sighs drown'd?
Who says my tears have overflow'd his ground?
When did my colds a forward spring remove?
When did the heats which my veins fill
Add one more to the plaguy bill?
Soldiers find wars, and lawyers find out still
Litigious men, which quarrels move,
Though she and I do love.

Call's what you will, we are made such by love;
Call her one, me another fly,
We're tapers too, and at our own cost die,
And we in us find th' eagle and the dove.
The phoenix riddle hath more wit
By us; we two being one, are it ;
So, to one neutral thing both sexes fit.
We die and rise the same, and prove
Mysterious by this love.

We can die by it, if not live by love,
And if unfit for tomb or hearse
Our legend be, it will be fit for verse;
And if no piece of chronicle we prove,
We'll build in sonnets pretty rooms;
As well a well-wrought urn becomes
The greatest ashes, as half-acre tombs,
And by these hymns, all shall approve
Us canonized for love;

And thus invoke us, 'You, whom reverend love
Made one another's hermitage;
You, to whom love was peace, that now is rage;
Who did the whole world's soul contract, and drove
Into the glasses of your eyes;
So made such mirrors, and such spies,
That they did all to you epitomize—
Countries, towns, courts beg from above
A pattern of your love.'

Notes

Take you a course, get you a place: flatter the rich and the powerful

A Valediction Forbidding Mourning

As virtuous men pass mildly away,
And whisper to their souls to go,

Whilst some of their sad friends do say,
　　'Now his breath goes,' and some say, 'No.'

So let us melt, and make no noise,
　　No tear-floods, nor sigh-tempests move;
'Twere profanation of our joys
　　To tell the laity our love.

Moving of th' earth brings harms and fears;
　　Men reckon what it did, and meant;
But trepidation of the spheres,
　　Though greater far, is innocent.

Dull sublunary lovers' love
　　—Whose soul is sense—cannot admit
Of absence, 'cause it doth remove
　　The thing which elemented it.

But we by a **love so much refined**,
　　That ourselves know not what it is,
Inter-assurèd of the mind,
　　Care less, eyes, lips and hands to miss.

Our two souls therefore, which are one,
　　Though I must go, endure not yet
A breach, but an expansion,
　　Like gold to **airy thinness** beat.

If they be two, they are two so
　　As stiff twin compasses are two;
Thy soul, **the fix'd foot**, makes no show
　　To move, but doth, if th' other do.

And though it in the centre sit,
　　Yet, when the other far doth roam,
It leans, and hearkens after it,
　　And grows erect, as that comes home.

Such wilt thou be to me, who must,
　　Like th' other foot, obliquely run;
Thy firmness makes my circle just,
　　And makes me end where I begun.

Notes

love so much refined: love described as refined, pure **airy thinness:** lightness, flexibility, but also perhaps suggests a purity that is not of the earth (where earth is regarded as a baser element) **the fix'd foot:** the fixed foot of the compass, here suggesting the constancy of the lover, but also the companionship where one foot moves when the other does

Hymn to God, in My Sickness

Since I am coming to that Holy room,
Where, with Thy choir of saints for evermore,
I shall be made Thy music; as I come
I tune the instrument here at the door,
And what I must do then, think here before;

Whilst my physicians by their love are grown
Cosmographers, and I their **map**, who lie
Flat on this bed, that by them may be shown
That this is my south-west discovery,
Per fretum febris, by these straits to die;

I joy, that in these straits I see my west ;
For, though those currents yield return to none,
What shall my west hurt me? As west and east
In all flat maps—and I am one—are one,
So death doth touch the resurrection.

Is the Pacific sea my home?Or are
The eastern riches? Is Jerusalem?
Anian, and Magellan, and Gibraltar?
All straits, and none but straits, are ways to them
Whether where **Japhet** dwelt, or **Cham**, or **Shem**.

We think that Paradise and Calvary,
Christ's cross and Adam's tree, stood in one place;
Look, Lord, and find both Adams met in me;
As the first Adam's sweat surrounds my face,
May the last Adam's blood my soul embrace.

So, in His purple wrapp'd, receive me, Lord;
By these His thorns, give me His other crown;
And as to others' souls I preach'd Thy word,
Be this my text, my sermon to mine own, 'rows down.'
'Therefore that He may raise, the Lord throws down.'

Notes

map: man as the map of the world *Per fretum febris*: 'fretum' is both 'fever' and 'channel'; here fever is the channel that leads to the final destination, and rest; 'febris' is also 'fever'. Here Donne refers to various 'straits' connecting lands. **Anian:** strait of the Northwest passage via the Arctic circle connecting the Atlantic and Pacific oceans **Japhet, Cham, Shem:** the sons of Noah who inherited various continents (Japheth got Europe, Ham, Africa and Seth, Asia)

To His Mistress, Going to Bed

Come, madam, come, all rest my powers defy;
Until I labour, I in labour lie.
The foe ofttimes, having the foe in sight,
Is tired with standing, though he never fight.
Off with that girdle, like heaven's zone glittering,
But a far fairer world encompassing.
Unpin that spangled breast-plate, which you wear,
That th' eyes of busy fools may be stopp'd there.
Unlace yourself, for that harmonious chime
Tells me from you that now it is bed-time.
Off with that happy busk, which I envy,
That still can be, and still can stand so nigh.
Your gown going off such beauteous state reveals,
As when from flowery meads th' hill's shadow steals.
Off with your wiry coronet, and show
The hairy diadems which on you do grow.
Off with your hose and shoes; then softly tread
In this love's hallow'd temple, this soft bed.
In such white robes heaven's angels used to be
Revealed to men; thou, angel, bring'st with thee
A heaven-like Mahomet's paradise; and though
Ill spirits walk in white, we easily know
By this these angels from an evil sprite;
Those set our hairs, but these our flesh upright.

Licence my roving hands, and let them go
Before, behind, between, above, below.
O, my America, my Newfoundland,
My kingdom, safest when with one man mann'd,
My mine of precious stones, my empery;
How am I blest in thus discovering thee!
To enter in these bonds, is to be free;
Then, where my hand is set, my soul shall be.

Full nakedness! All joys are due to thee;
As souls unbodied, bodies unclothed must be
To taste whole joys. Gems which you women use
Are like Atlanta's ball cast in men's views;
That, when a fool's eye lighteth on a gem,
His earthly soul might court that, not them.
Like pictures, or like books' gay coverings made
For laymen, are all women thus array'd.

•

Themselves are only mystic books, which we
—Whom their imputed grace will dignify—

Must see reveal'd. Then, since that I may know,
As liberally as to thy midwife show
Thyself; cast all, yea, this white linen hence;
There is no penance due to innocence:
To teach thee, I am naked first; why then,
What needst thou have more covering than a man

The Ecstasy

Where, like a pillow on a bed,
  A **pregnant** bank swell'd up, to rest
The violet's reclining head,
  Sat we two, one another's best.

Our hands were firmly cemented
  By a fast balm, which thence did spring;
Our eye-beams twisted, and did thread
  Our eyes upon one double string.

So to engraft our hands, as yet
  Was all the means to make us one;
And pictures in our eyes to get
  Was all our propagation.

As, 'twixt two equal armies, Fate
  Suspends uncertain victory,
Our souls—which to advance their state,
  Were gone out—hung 'twixt her and me.

And whilst our souls negotiate there,
  We like sepulchral statues lay;
All day, the same our postures were,
  And we said nothing, all the day.

If any, so by love refined,
  That he soul's language understood,
And by good love were grown all mind,
  Within convenient distance stood,

He—though he knew not which soul spake,
  Because both meant, both spake the same—
Might thence a new concoction take,
  And part far purer than he came.

This ecstasy doth unperplex
  (We said) and tell us what we love;

We see by this, it was not sex;
We see, we saw not, what did move:

But as all several souls contain
Mixture of things they know not what,
Love these mix'd souls doth mix again,
And makes both one, each this, and that.

A single **violet transplant,**
The strength, the colour, and the size—
All which before was poor and scant—
Redoubles still, and **multiplies**.

When love with one another so
Interanimates two souls,
That abler soul, which thence doth flow,
Defects of loneliness controls.

We then, who are this new soul, know,
Of what we are composed, and made,
For th' atomies of which we grow
Are souls, whom no change can invade.

But, O alas! so long, so far,
Our bodies why do we forbear?
They are ours, though not we; we are
Th' intelligences, they the spheres.

We owe them thanks, because they thus
Did us, to us, at first convey,
Yielded their senses' force to us,
Nor are dross to us, but allay.

On man heaven's influence works not so,
But that it first imprints the air;
For soul into the soul may flow,
Though it to body first repair.

As our blood labours to beget
Spirits, as like souls as it can;
Because such fingers need to knit
That subtle knot, which makes us man;

So must pure lovers' souls descend
To affections, and to faculties,
Which sense may reach and apprehend,
Else a great prince in prison lies.

To our bodies turn we then, that so
  Weak men on love reveal'd may look;
Love's mysteries in souls do grow,
  But yet the body is his book.

And if some lover, such as we,
  Have heard this dialogue of one,
  Let him still mark us, he shall see
Small change when we're to bodies gone.

Notes

pregnant: swelled **violet transplant . . . multiplies:** Violets are improved by transplantation. **interanimates:** to animate **Defects of loneliness:** the problems of being single **Spirits, as like souls as it can:** spirits as the instruments of the soul

Ben Jonson

Shakespeare's contemporary, and one whose reputation might have been truly formidable but for the presence of the former, Ben Jonson (1572–1637) went to Westminster school. Later he travelled on the continent as a soldier with the English army. On his return he took up acting and writing plays, and may have played a role in Kyd's *The Spanish Tragedy*. Many of his earlier plays are now lost, and only two tragedies from the period – *Sejanus* and *Catiline* – survive. He married in 1594, though his wife's identity has never been clear, but was possibly Ann Lewis. With the success of *Every Man in his Humour* (1598) Jonson's reputation as a playwright was established, which Jonson promptly ruined by killing a man in a pub fight. Jonson was branded though, by pleading 'benefit of the clergy' – the ability to read the Bible in Latin – he escaped execution. Jonson had three children, all of whom died early, with the second one dying of the plague. He began writing masques for the royal court, collaborating with designer Inigo Jones, eventually being appointed Poet Laureate. He was also patronised by royalty such as Elizabeth Sidney (Philip Sidney's daughter). Jonson had problems, however, due to his refusal to accept the Anglican faith. Some of his most successful plays came from this period, with *Volpone* (1606), *The Alchemist* (1610) and *Bartholomew Fair* (1614). His play on fellow poets and dramatists, notably Thomas Dekker and John Marston, *The Poetaster*, remains a popular literary satire to this day. Oxford bestowed him with an honorary Masters degree and his reputation grew, slowly causing an entire group of disciples – the 'sons of Ben' or the 'tribe of Ben' – to form around him. After a stroke in 1628 Jonson remained bedridden till his death in 1637. Shakespeare acted in many of Jonson's plays, and the two are believed to have had learned, witty debates. Later, Jonson would write a prefatory poem for Shakespeare's First Folio in which while he presented Shakespeare as a natural genius, he also claimed that the younger playwright has a great sense of craft:

> Yet must I not give Nature all: Thy Art,
> My gentle Shakespeare, must enjoy a part.

To Penshurst

Thou art not, PENSHURST, built to envious show
Of touch, or marble; nor canst boast a row
Of polish'd pillars, or a roof of gold:
Thou hast no lantern whereof tales are told;
Or stair, or courts; but stand'st an ancient pile,
And these grudg'd at, art reverenced the while.
Thou joy'st in **better marks**, of soil, of air,
Of wood, of water; therein thou art fair.
Thou hast thy walks for health, as well as sport:
Thy mount, to which thy **Dryads** do resort,
Where **Pan** and **Bacchus** their high feasts have made,
Beneath the broad beech, and the chestnut shade;
That taller tree, which of a nut was set,
At his great birth, where all the **Muses** met.
There, in the writhed bark, are cut the names
Of many a sylvan, taken with his flames;
And thence the ruddy satyrs oft provoke
The lighter fauns, to reach thy lady's oak.
Thy copse too, named of **Gamage**, thou hast there,
That never fails to serve thee season'd deer,
When thou wouldst feast or exercise thy friends.
The lower land, that to the river bends,
Thy sheep, thy bullocks, kine, and calves do feed;
The middle grounds thy mares and horses breed.
Each bank doth yield thee conies; and the tops
Fertile of wood, Ashore and Sydney's copse,
To crown thy open table, doth provide

The purpled pheasant, with the speckled side:
The painted partridge lies in ev'ry field,
And for thy mess is willing to be kill'd.
And if the high-swollen **Medway** fail thy dish,
Thou hast thy ponds, that pay thee tribute fish,
Fat aged carps that run into thy net,
And pikes, now weary their own kind to eat,
As loath the second draught or cast to stay,
Officiously at first themselves betray.
Bright eels that emulate them, and leap on land,
Before the fisher, or into his hand,
Then hath thy orchard fruit, thy garden flowers,
Fresh as the air, and new as are the hours.
The early cherry, with the later plum,
Fig, grape, and quince, each in his time doth come:
The blushing apricot, and woolly peach
Hang on thy walls, that every child may reach.
And though thy walls be of the country stone,
They're rear'd with no man's ruin, no man's groan;
There's none, that dwell about them, wish them down;
But all come in, the farmer and the clown;
And no one empty-handed, to salute
Thy lord and lady, though they have no suit.

Some bring a **capon**, some a rural cake,
Some nuts, some apples; some that think they make
The better cheeses, bring them; or else send
By their ripe daughters, whom they would commend
This way to husbands; and whose baskets bear
An emblem of themselves in plum, or pear.
But what can this (more than express their love)
Add to thy free provisions, far above
The need of such? whose liberal board doth flow
With all that hospitality doth know!

Where comes no guest, but is allow'd to eat,
Without his fear, and of thy lord's own meat:
Where the same beer and bread, and self-same wine,
That is his lordship's, shall be also mine.
And I not fain to sit (as some this day,
At great men's tables) and yet dine away.
Here no man tells my cups; nor standing by,
A waiter, doth my gluttony envy:
But gives me what I call, and lets me eat,
He knows, below, he shall find plenty of meat;
Thy tables hoard not up for the next day,

Nor, when I take my lodging, need I pray
For fire, or lights, or livery; all is there;
As if thou then wert mine, or I reign'd here:
There's nothing I can wish, for which I stay.
That found King JAMES, when hunting late, this way,
With his brave son, the prince; they saw thy fires
Shine bright on every hearth, as the desires
Of thy **Penates** had been set on flame,
To entertain them; or the country came,
With all their zeal, to warm their welcome here.
What (great, I will not say, but) sudden cheer
Didst thou then make 'em! and what praise was heap'd
On thy good lady, then! who therein reap'd
The just reward of her high housewifery;
To have her linen, plate, and all things nigh,
When she was far; and not a room, but drest,
As if it had expected such a guest!
These, Penshurst, are thy praise, and yet not all.
Thy lady's noble, fruitful, chaste withal.
His children thy great lord may call his own;
A fortune, in this age, but rarely known.
They are, and have been taught religion; thence
Their gentler spirits have suck'd innocence.
Each morn, and even, they are taught to pray,
With the whole household, and may, every day,
Read in their virtuous parents' noble parts,
The **mysteries** of manners, arms, and arts.
Now, Penshurst, they that will proportion thee
With other edifices, when they see
Those proud ambitious heaps, and nothing else,
May say, their lords have built, but thy lord dwells.

Notes

Penshurst: The country home of Robert Sidney and his wife, Barbara, was the centre of cultural activities and famous for its hospitality – this latter is of course the subject of the poem. **Of touch, or marble:** black and white marble **better marks:** indicating distinction, markers of prestige **Dryads:** In Greek mythology, these are tree nymphs. **Pan:** Greek god of the wilds, but also of shepherds and nature **Bacchus:** Roman God of wine **Muses:** the nine muses of poetry **Gamage:** Lady Barbara **Medway:** a river in Kent **capon:** a chicken castrated to improve the quality of its flesh (as food) **Without his fear:** without being afraid of the owner, but also to indicate that the house owner will not fear so many people partaking of his food **With his brave son, the prince:** Prince Henry died in 1612. **Penates:** the fires of the household; here, indicative of warmth **mysteries:** professions

William Shakespeare

The most translated and studied author in the history of world literature, Shakespeare's biography remains sketchy and speculative and mostly draws upon official documents. References to him in the writings of other authors and playwrights have been a key source as well. A record of his baptism in Stratford-upon-Avon survives from 1564, and his marriage to Anna Hathaway is recorded for 1582. He would have attended the local school, and acquired adequate learning in the classics and Latin. There is a missing period in his life and we then hear of him as part of the London theatre scene.

Shakespeare seems to have become successful fairly quickly, especially after he joined the Lord Chamberlain's Men (later called the King's Men), a theatre group. He was producing plays steadily during the London years, which at the time of his death came to 38 extant plays, and several whose authorship is uncertain and disputed. His son Hamnet died in 1596, aged eleven. Shakespeare spent most of his life away from his family, living mainly in London. After his career, however, Shakespeare retired to his Stratford-upon-Avon house having made secure his finances, his family well-settled (the mystery of his legacy of the 'second-best bed' to Anne Hathaway remains unresolved). He died in 1616. There is no name on his gravestone. Shakespeare also published two narrative poems, *Venus and Adonis* and *The Rape of Lucrece*, and a large number of sonnets, in addition to the poems in several of the plays.

Sonnet 1

From fairest creatures we desire **increase**,
That thereby beauty's rose might never die,
But as the riper should by time decease,
His tender heir might bear his memory:
But thou, **contracted** to thine own bright eyes,
Feed'st thy light's flame with self-substantial fuel,
Making a famine where abundance lies,
Thyself thy foe, to thy sweet self too cruel.
Thou that art now the world's fresh ornament
And **only** herald to the **gaudy** spring,
Within thine own bud buriest thy content
And, tender churl, makest waste in **niggarding**.

Pity the world, or else this glutton be,
To eat the world's due, by the grave and thee.

Notes

increase: here, offspring **contracted:** bound **Feed'st thy light's . . . fuel:** Let your eyes feast on yourself. **only:** chief **gaudy:** showy and decorative, but not in a negative sense **niggarding:** to hoard

Sonnet 18

Shall I compare thee to a summer's day?
Thou art more lovely and more **temperate**:
Rough winds do shake the darling buds of May,
And summer's lease hath all too short a date:
Sometime too hot the **eye of heaven** shines,
And often is his gold complexion dimm'd;
And **every fair from fair sometime declines**,
By chance or nature's changing course untrimm'd;
But thy eternal summer shall not fade
Nor lose possession of that fair thou owest;
Nor shall Death brag thou wander'st in his shade,
When **in eternal lines to time thou growest**:
So long as men can breathe or eyes can see,
So long lives this and this gives life to thee.

Notes

temperate: even-tempered **the eye of heaven:** the sun **every fair from fair sometime declines:** beauty fades **in eternal lines . . . growest:** a botanical image, referring to grafting where two plants are joined to grow as one. The idea is that in the poem the beloved is joined to time, and becomes immortal.

Sonnet 55

Not marble, nor the gilded monuments
Of princes, shall outlive this powerful rhyme;
But you shall shine more bright in these contents
Than unswept stone besmear'd with **sluttish** time.
When wasteful war shall statues overturn,
And **broils** root out the work of masonry,
Nor Mars his sword nor war's quick fire shall burn
The living record of your memory.
'Gainst death and **all-oblivious enmity**
Shall you pace forth; your praise shall still find room

Even in the eyes of all posterity
That wear this world out to the ending doom.
So, till the judgment that yourself arise,
You live in this, and dwell in lovers' eye.

Notes

sluttish: here, 'filthy' **broils:** quarrels or riots **all-oblivious enmity:** war or decay that cause the subject of the poem to be forgotten

Sonnet 97

How like a winter hath my absence been
From thee, the pleasure of the fleeting year!
What freezings have I felt, what dark days seen!
What old December's bareness every where!
And yet this time removed was summer's time,
The teeming autumn, big with rich increase,
Bearing the wanton burden of the prime,
Like widow'd wombs after their lords' decease:
Yet this abundant issue seem'd to me
But hope of orphans and unfather'd fruit;
For summer and his pleasures wait on thee,
And, thou away, the very birds are mute;
Or, if they sing, 'tis with so dull a cheer
That leaves look pale, dreading the winter's near.

Sonnet 116

Let me not to the marriage of true minds
Admit **impediments**. Love is not love
Which alters when it alteration finds,
Or **bends** with the remover to **remove**:
O no! it is an **ever-fixed mark**
That looks on tempests and is never shaken;
It is **the star** to every wandering bark,
Whose worth's unknown, although his height be taken.
Love's not Time's fool, though rosy lips and cheeks
Within **his bending sickle's** compass come:
Love alters not with his brief hours and weeks,
But bears it out even to the edge of doom.
If this be error and upon me proved,
I never writ, nor no man ever loved.

Notes

impediments: might refer to the banns which asks anybody who has an objection to the announced wedding to come and register their protest **bends:** deviates **remove:** here, to alter its course **ever-fixed mark:** a lighthouse **the star:** Polaris, the star that guides lost ships **Love's not Time's fool:** love is not at Time's mercy **his bending sickle:** refers to Death, the scythe wielding personification of death.

Sonnet 144

Two loves I have of comfort and despair,
Which like **two spirits** do suggest me still:
The better angel is a man right fair,
The worser spirit a woman colour'd ill.
To win me soon to hell, my female evil
Tempteth my better angel from my side,
And would corrupt my saint to be a devil,
Wooing his purity with her foul pride.
And whether that my angel be turn'd fiend
Suspect I may, but not directly tell;
But being both from me, both to each friend,
I guess one angel in another's hell:
Yet this shall I ne'er know, but live in doubt,
Till my bad angel fire my good one out.

Notes

two spirits: in traditional psychomachia where Virtue and Vice prompt and persuade the Man

Mary Wroth

A cousin of Walter Raleigh, and the niece of Philip Sidney, Lady Mary Wroth (1587?–1651) grew up on Montgomery estate. James I made her father, Robert, the Earl of Leicester. After her marriage to Robert Wroth she moved in court circles. Mary played a role – that of an Ethiopian woman – in Ben Jonson's *Masque of Blackness*. She was Jonson's patron, and *The Alchemist* is dedicated to her. Robert Wroth died in 1614 and left Mary in considerable debt. As the mistress of William Herbert, the Earl of Pembroke, she had two children. Using the scandals of the court as a basis, Mary Wroth published a romance, *The Countess of Montgomeries Urania*, in 1621. The consequences of this work – in which she portrayed a jealous and petty Queen Anne – were serious, and Mary Wroth, already criticised for her illegitimate children, had no more court patronage. Many royals accused her of slandering them, and the work was withdrawn from publication later in the same year. There is little information about her later life. Her *Pamphilia to Amphilanthus* is the first known sonnet sequence in English by a woman.

The Spring Now Come at Last

The Spring now come at last
    To Trees, Fields, to Flowers,
And Meadows makes to taste
    His pride, while sad showers
Which from mine eyes doe flow
    Makes known with cruel pains,
    Cold Winter yet remains,
No sign of Spring we know.

The Sun which to the Earth
    Gives heat, light, and pleasure,
Joys in Spring hates Dearth,
    Plenty makes his Treasure.
His heat to me is cold,
    His light all darkness is,
    Since I am barred of bliss,
I heat nor light behold.

A Shepherdess thus said,
    Who was with grief oppressed,
For truest Love betrayed,
    Barrd her from quiet rest:
And weeping thus, said she,
    My end approaches near,
    Now Willow must I wear,
My Fortune so will bee.

With Branches of this tree
    Ile dress my hapless head,
Which shall my witness bee,
    My hopes in Love are dead:
My clothes embroidered all,

Shall be with Garlands round,
Some scattered, others bound;
Some tide, some like to fall.

The Bark my Book shall bee,
Where daily I will write,
This tale of hapless me,
True slave to Fortunes spite.
The root shall be my bed,
Where nightly I will lye
Wailing inconstancy,
Since all true love is dead.

And these Lines I will leave,
If some such Lover come,
Who may them right conceive,
and place them on my Tomb:
She who still constant loved
Now dead with cruel care,
Killed with unkind Despair,
And change, her end hear proved.

Sweet Silvia in a Shady Wood

Sweet Silvia in a shady wood,
With her faire Nymphs laid down,
Saw not fare off where Cupid stood,
The Monarch of Loves Crown,
All naked, playing with his wings,
Within a Myrtle Tree,
Which sight a sudden laughter brings,
His Godhead so to see.

An fondly they began to jest,
With scoffing, and delight,
Not knowing he did breed unrest,
And that his will's his right:
When he perceiving of their scorn,
Grew in such desperate rage,
Who but for honour first was borne,
Could not his rage assuage.

Till shooting of his murdering dart,
Which not long lighting was,
Knowing the next way to the heart,

Did through a poor Nymph pass:
This shot the others made to bow,
Besides all those to blame,
Who scorners be, or not allow
Of powerful Cupid's name.

Take heed then nor doe idly smile,
Nor Loves commands despise,
For soon will be your strength beguile,
Although he want his eyes.

Fie Tedious Hope

Fie tedious Hope, why do you still rebel?
Is it not yet enough you flattered me,
But cunningly you seek to use a Spell
How to betray; must these your Trophies be?

I looked from you far sweeter fruit to see,
But blasted were your blossoms when they fell:
And those delights expected from hands free,
Withered and dead, and what seemed bliss proves hell.

No Towne was won by a more plotted slight,
Then I by you, who may my fortune write,
In embers of that fire which ruined me:
Thus Hope your falsehood calls you to be tried,
Your loth, I see, the trial to abide;
Prove true at last, and gain your liberty.

Like to the Indians Scorched with the Sun

Like to the Indians scorched with the Sun,
The Sun which they do as their God adore:
So am I used by Love, for evermore
I worship him, less favours have I won.

Better are they who thus to blackness run,
And so can only whiteness want deplore:
Then I who pale and white am with griefs store,
Nor can have hope, but to see hopes undone.

Besides their sacrifice received in sight,
Of their chose Saint, mine hid as worthless rite,
Grant me to see where I my offerings give.

Then let me wear the mark of *Cupids* might,
In heart, as they in skin of *Phoebus* light,
Not ceasing offerings to Love while I live.

Come, Darkest Night

Come darkest Night, becoming sorrow best,
Light leave thy light, fit for a lightsome soul:
Darkness doth truly suit with me oppressed,
Whom absence power doth from mirth control.

The very trees with hanging heads condole
Sweet Summers parting, and of leaves **distressed**,
In dying colours make a grief-full role;
So much (alas) to sorrow are they pressed.

Thus of dead leaves, her farewell carpets made,
Their fall, their branches, all their mournings prove,
With leaveless naked bodies, whose hues **vade**
From hopeful green to wither in their love.

If trees, and leaves for absence mourners be,
No marvel that I grieve, who **like want see**.

Notes

distressed: here, afflicted **vade:** fade **like want see:** to experience a similar absence

George Wither

Born in 1588 in Hampshire, Wither went to Magdalene College, Oxford, but left without a degree before turning to the law. During this period he produced satiric pieces which resulted in imprisonment. *The Shepherd's Hunting* (1615), a set of eclogues, was written in prison. *Wither's Motto*, another collection of satires appeared in 1621. Wither published *Britain's Remembrancer*, a poem that documented the London plague of 1625. He joined the forces of Charles I, but took the Parliament's side during the Civil War. After the Restoration Wither's poem satirising the House of Commons earned him another long spell in prison. Wither's position in literary history as a pamphleteer and poet is sometimes subsumed under his role in asserting intellectual property rights: his *Hymnes and Songs of the Church* was the first book in which an author successfully asserted his copyright to own work. He died in 1667.

A Widow's Hymn

How near me came the hand of Death,
When at my side he struck my dear,
And took away the precious breath
Which quicken'd my belovàd peer!
How helpless am I thereby made!
By day how grieved, by night how sad!
And now my life's delight is gone,
—Alas! how am I left alone!
The voice which I did more esteem
Than music in her sweetest key,
Those eyes which unto me did seem
More comfortable than the day;
Those now by me, as they have been,
Shall never more be heard or seen;
But what I once enjoy'd in them
Shall seem hereafter as a dream.
Lord! keep me faithful to the trust
Which my dear spouse reposed in me:
To him now dead preserve me just
In all that should performàd be!
For though our being man and wife
Extendeth only to this life,
Yet neither life nor death should end
The being of a faithful friend.

Her Beauty

Her true beauty leaves behind
Apprehensions in my mind
Of more sweetness than all art
Or inventions can impart;
Thoughts too deep to be expressed,
And too strong to be suppressed . . .
. . . What pearls, what rubies can

Seem so lovely fair to man,
As her lips whom he doth love
When in sweet discourse they move:
Or her lovelier teeth, the while
She doth bless him with a smile!
Stars indeed fair creatures be;
Yet amongst us where is he
Joys not more the whilst he lies
Sunning in his mistress' eyes.
Than in all the glimmering light
Of a starry winter's night?
Note the beauty of an eye,
And if aught you praise it by
Leave such passion in your mind,
Let my reason's eye be blind.
Mark if ever red or white
Anywhere gave such delight
As when they have taken place
In a worthy woman's face.

Lilies Without, Lilies Within

Can I think the Guide of Heaven
Hath so beautifully given
Outward features, 'cause He meant
To have made less excellent
Your divine part? Or suppose
Beauty, goodness doth oppose;
Like those fools, who do despair
To find any, good and fair?
Rather there I seek a mind
Most excelling, where I find
God hath to the body lent
Most-beseeming ornament,
And I do believe it true,
That, as we the body view
Nearer to perfection grow;
So, the soul herself doth show:
Other more and more excelling
In her powers; as in her dwelling.

Robert Herrick

Born in London in 1591 into a goldsmith's family, Robert Herrick lost his father the very next year – Nicholas Herrick committed suicide in 1592. Robert became an apprentice to his uncle, also a goldsmith, in 1607, but quit to join Cambridge in 1613. After his Masters in 1620 Herrick began moving in the London literary circles, and became part of the 'sons of Ben', the acolytes and admirers of Ben Jonson. Soon however, he took the orders and was appointed by Charles I to a priory in the diocese of Exeter. Herrick was not fond of country life and sought the pleasures of London. His refusal to accept the Solemn League and Covenant caused his expulsion from the priory, thus bringing him back to where he wanted to be – London. Soon after he published his mammoth *Hesperides*, consisting of 1200 poems, in 1648, though some of his poetry had appeared in collections published as early as the 1620s. After the Restoration, he returned to Devon where he died in 1674. 'Gather ye rosebuds while ye may' from his 'To the Virgins, to Make Much of Time' has remained one of the English language's most famous lines.

To the Virgins, to Make Much of Time

Gather ye rosebuds while ye may,
Old time is still a-flying:
And this same flower that smiles to-day
To-morrow will be dying.

The glorious lamp of heaven, the sun,
The higher he's a-getting,
The sooner will his race be run,
And nearer he's to setting.

That age is best which is the first,
When youth and blood are warmer;
But being spent, the worse, and worst
Times still succeed the former.

Then be not coy, but use your time,
And while ye may go marry:
For having lost but once your prime
You may for ever tarry.

Notes

Gather ye rosebuds while ye may: This is an echo of Spenser's 'gather therefore the rose, whilst yet is time.' (*Faerie Queene* 1.12.75)

Upon Julia's Clothes

Whenas in silks my Julia goes,
Then, then, methinks, how sweetly flows
That liquefaction of her clothes.

Next, when I **cast mine eyes** and see
That brave vibration each way free;
O how that glittering taketh me!

Notes

cast mine eyes: to glance with his eyes, but also as in 'casting' his net for fish

The Frozen Zone

Whither? Say, whither shall I fly,
To slack these flames wherein I fry?
To the treasures, shall I go,
Of the rain, frost, hail, and snow?
Shall I search the underground,
Where all damps and mists are found?
Shall I seek (for speedy ease)
All the floods and frozen seas?
Or descend into the deep,
Where eternal cold does keep?
These may cool; but there's a zone
Colder yet than anyone:
That's my Julia's breast, where dwells
Such destructive icicles,
As that the **congelation** will
Me sooner starve than those can kill.

Notes

congelation: to congeal, to thicken

To his Valentine on St Valentine's Day

Oft have I heard both youths and virgins say
Birds choose their mates, and couple too this day;

But by their flight I never can divine
When I shall couple with my valentine.

Francis Quarles

Quarles (1592–1644), was born into a highly connected family, educated at Cambridge and Lincoln's Inn, later worked as the secretary to Archbishop James Ussher in Ireland. Quarles' main claim to fame is as an emblematist. In 1613 he was appointed cupbearer to Queen Elizabeth. Quarles married Ursula Woodgate in 1618, and they had eighteen children. His *Emblemes* (1635) with its carvings and visuals accompanied by verse or prose commentaries proved hugely successful. Together with the later work, *Hieroglyphikes*, Quarles produced what might have been the most popular book of poetry of the age. His book of aphorisms, *Enchiridion* (1640) was also very successful. In 1640 Quarles became chronologer to London, virtually abandoning poetry to employ his pen more lucratively. He died in relative poverty.

On Time

Time's an hand's-breadth; 'tis a tale;
'Tis a vessel under sail;
'Tis an eagle in its way,
Darting down upon its prey;
'Tis an arrow in its flight,
Mocking the pursuing sight;
'Tis a short-lived fading flower;
'Tis a rainbow on a shower;
'Tis a momentary ray,
Smiling in a winter's day;
'Tis a torrent's rapid stream;
'Tis a shadow; 'tis a dream;
'Tis the closing watch of night,
Dying at the rising light;
'Tis a bubble; 'tis a sigh;
Be prepared, O! man, to die.

On the Life and Death of Man

The world's a theatre. The earth, a stage
Placed in the midst: where both prince and page,
Both rich and poor, fool, wise man, base and high,
All act their parts in life's short tragedy.
Our life's a tragedy. Those secret rooms,
Wherein we 'tire us, are our mothers' wombs.
The music ushering in the play is mirth
To see a man-child brought upon the earth.
That fainting gasp of breath which first we vent,
Is a dumb show; presents the argument.
Our new-born cries, that new-born griefs bewray,
Are the sad prologue of the ensuing play.
False hopes, true fears, vain joys, and fierce distracts,
Are like the music that divides the Acts.
Time holds the glass, and when the hour's outrun,
Death strikes the epilogue, and the play is done.

George Herbert

Born to Edward Herbert, first Baron Herbert of Cherbury, George Herbert (1593–1633) attended Westminster School and Trinity College, Cambridge, being elected orator to the University in 1620, with some influence in court circles. He resigned as orator in 1627 and in 1630 was ordained priest and became rector at Bemerton. Even though he wrote poetry throughout his life, his famous volume *The Temple* only appeared after his death. The volume went through eight editions by 1690, and established Herbert's reputation.

The Collar

I struck the **board**, and cried, 'No more;
        I will abroad!
What? shall I ever sigh and pine?
My **lines** and life are free, free as the road,

Loose as the wind, as large as **store**.
Shall I be still **in suit**?
Have I no harvest but **a thorn**
To let me blood, and not **restore**
What I have lost with cordial fruit?
Sure there was wine
Before my sighs did dry it; there was corn
Before my tears did drown it.
Is the year only lost to me?
Have I no **bays** to crown it,
No flowers, no garlands gay? All blasted?
All wasted?
Not so, my heart; but there is fruit,
And thou hast hands.
Recover all thy sigh-blown age
On **double** pleasures: leave thy cold dispute
Of what is fit and not. Forsake thy cage,
Thy rope of sands,
Which petty thoughts have made, and made to thee
Good cable, to enforce and draw,
And be thy law,
While thou didst wink and wouldst not see.
Away! take heed;
I will abroad.
Call in thy death's-head there; tie up thy fears;
He that forbears
To suit and serve his need
Deserves his load.'
But as I raved and grew more fierce and wild
At every word,
Methought I heard one calling, *Child!*
And I replied *My Lord*.

Notes

board: communion table **lines:** directions **store:** indicating plenty **in suit:** to be a complainant, petitioner or litigant **a thorn/To let me blood:** to have his blood drained by his guilt **restore/What I have lost with cordial fruit:** restore the blood lost with wine, cordial here is 'grape' **bays:** the evergreen bay as crown for poets **double:** Unused pleasures double due to increased interest, but they are also deceitful.

The Pulley

When God at first made man,
Having a glass of blessings standing by;
Let us (said he) pour on him all we can:

Let the worlds riches, which dispersed lie,
        Contract into a **span**.

        So strength first made a way;
Then beauty flowed, then wisdom, honour, pleasure:
When almost all was out, God made a stay,
Perceiving that alone, of all his treasure,
        Rest in the bottom lay.

        For if I should (said he)
Bestow this jewel also on my creature,
He would adore my gifts in stead of me,
And rest in Nature, not the God of Nature:
        So both should losers be.

        Yet let him keep the rest,
But keep them with repining restlessness:
Let him be rich and weary, that at least,
If goodness lead him not, yet weariness
        May toss him to my breast.

Notes

span: the length of a man's days, but might also be a reference to his size

Affliction I

When first Thou didst entice to Thee my heart,
        I thought the service brave:
So many joys I writ down for my part,
        Besides what I might have
Out of my stock of naturall delights,
Augmented with Thy gracious benefits.

I lookèd on Thy furniture so fine,
        And made it fine to me;
Thy glorious household stuff did me entwine,
        And 'tice me unto Thee.
Such stars I counted mine: both heaven and earth
Paid me my wages in a world of mirth.

What pleasures could I want, whose King I served,
        Where joys my fellows were?
Thus argued into hopes, my thoughts reserved
        No place for grief or fear;
Therefore my sudden soul caught at the place,
And made her youth and fierceness seek Thy face:

At first thou gavest me milk and sweetnesses;
I had my wish and way:
My days were strewed with flowers and happiness:
There was no month but May.
But with my years sorrow did twist and grow,
And made a party unawares for woe.

My flesh began unto my soul in pain,
Sicknesses clave my bones,
Consuming agues dwell in every vein,
And tune my breath to groans,
Sorrow was all my soul; I scarce believed,
Till grief did tell me roundly, that I lived.

When I got health, Thou took'st away my life—
And more; for my friends die:
My mirth and edge was lost: a blunted knife
Was of more use than I.
Thus, thin and lean, without a fence or friend,
I was blown through with every storm and wind.

Whereas my birth and spirit rather took
The way that takes the town,
Thou didst betray me to a lingering book,
And wrap me in a gown.
I was entangled in the world of strife,
Before I had the power to change my life.

Yet, for I threatened oft **the siege to raise**,
Not simpering all mine age,
Thou often didst **with academic praise**
Melt and dissolve my rage.
I took thy sweetened pill, till I came near;
I could nor go away, nor persevere.

Yet, lest perchance I should too happy be
In my unhappiness,
Turning my purge to food, Thou throwest me
Into more sicknesses.
Thus doth Thy power cross-bias me, not making
Thine own gift good, yet me from my ways taking.

Now I am here, what thou wilt do with me
None of my books will show:
I read, and sigh, and wish I were a tree—
For sure, then, I should grow
To fruit or shade; at least, some bird would trust
Her household to me, and I should be just.

Yet, though Thou troublest me, I must be meek;
In weakness must be stout:
Well, I will change the service, and go seek
Some other master out.
Ah, my dear God ! though I am clean forgot,
Let me not love Thee, if I love Thee not.

Notes

I thought the service: employment **the siege to raise:** to end the confinement **with academic praise/Melt and dissolve my rage:** Having taken to academics, I forgot my political aims. But then due to praise received I could not give up academics nor continue with it.

Thomas Carew

Born around 1594 in Kent to Sir Matthew Carew, the master in chancery, Carew went to Oxford and the Middle Temple, Oxford. He later was attached to the embassies in Venice, The Hague and Paris. Eventually he came back to England to become server at the King's table, and began to acquire a reputation as a wit with his love poetry circulated in manuscript form. He could count among his friends Ben Jonson and John Suckling. Carew translated a number of the psalms as well. Carew died in London around 1639.

To Saxham

Though frost and snow lock'd from mine eyes
That beauty which without door lies,
Thy gardens, orchards, walks, that so
I might not all thy pleasures know;
Yet, Saxham, thou within thy gate
Art of thyself so **delicate**,
So full of native sweets, that bless
Thy **roof** with inward happiness,
As neither from, nor to thy store

Winter takes aught, or spring adds more.
The cold and frozen air had **starved**
Much poor, if not by thee preserved,
Whose prayers have made thy table blest
With plenty, far above the rest.
The season hardly did afford
Coarse cates unto thy neighbours' board,
Yet thou hadst dainties, as the sky
Had only been thy **volary**;
Or else the birds, fearing the snow
Might to another deluge grow,
The pheasant, partridge, and the lark
Flew to thy house, as to the Ark.
The willing ox of himself came
Home to the slaughter with the lamb,
And every beast did thither bring
Himself, to be an offering.
The **scaly herd** more pleasure took,
Bathed in thy dish than in the brook;
Water, earth, air, did all conspire
To pay their tributes to thy **fire**,
Whose cherishing flames themselves divide
Through every room, where they deride
The night and cold abroad; whilst they,
Like suns within, keep endless day.
Those cheerful beams send forth their light
To all that wander in the night,
And seem to beckon from **aloof**
The weary pilgrim to thy roof,
Where if, refresh'd, he will away,
He's faily welcome; or, if stay,
Far more; which he shall hearty find
Both from the master and the hind:
The stranger's welcome each man there
Stamp'd on his cheerful brow doth wear,
Nor doth this welcome or his cheer
Grow less, 'cause he stays longer here:
There's none observes, much less repines,
How often this man sups or dines.
Thou hast no porter at thy door
T' examine or keep back the poor;
Nor locks nor bolts: thy gates have bin
Made only to let strangers in;
Untaught to shut, they do not fear
To stand wide open all the year,
Careless who enters, for they know

Thou never didst deserve a foe:
And as for thieves, thy bounty's such,
They cannot steal, thou giv'st so much.

Notes

Saxham: the house of John Crofts, Crew's friend, in Suffolk **delicate**: here, delightful **roof**: synecdoche for 'house' **starved**: killed **volary**: aviary **scaly herd**: fish **fire**: synecdoche for 'hearth' **aloof**: here, afar

Persuasions to Enjoy

If the quick spirits in your eye
  Now languish and anon must die;
If every sweet and every grace
Must fly from that forsaken face;
  Then, Celia, let us reap our joys
  Ere time such goodly fruit destroys.

Or, if that golden fleece must grow
  For ever free from aged snow;
If those bright suns must know no shade,
Nor your fresh beauties ever fade;
Then fear not, Celia, to bestow
What, still being gather'd, still must grow.
  Thus, either Time his sickle brings
  In vain, or else in vain his wings.

To My Mistress, I Burning in Love

I burn; and cruel you, in vain
Hope to quench me with disdain;
If from your eyes those sparkles came
That have kindled all this flame,
What boots it me, though now you shroud
Those fierce comets in a cloud?
Since all the flames that I have felt
Could your snow yet never melt;
Nor can your snow, though you should take
Alps into your bosom, slake
The heat of my enamoured heart.
But, with wonder, learn Love's art:
No seas of ice can cool desire,
Equal flames must quench Love's fire.
Then, think not that my heat can die,
Till you burn as well as I.

Edmund Waller

Born in 1606 in Hertfordshire, Waller, noted for his development of the heroic couplet as a form, attended King's College, Cambridge but left without a degree. He became a Member of Parliament in 1624 when he was barely in his late teens, and continued to be a Member through the 1630s and turbulent 1640s. He married Anne Banks in 1631 and, after her death in 1634 and an unsuccessful wooing of Lady Dorothy Sidney, he married Mary Bracey in 1644. During the Civil War Waller was involved in many intrigues and barely managed to escape execution for his activities in support of the King. He was fined and banished to the Continent in 1643 where he lived till 1651. His *Poems* were published in 1645. In 1661 he became Member of Parliament for Hastings and proved to be popular as a Parliamentarian. In 1677, after the death of his wife, Waller returned to his home in Beaconsfield. Waller died in 1687.

Go, Lovely Rose

Go, lovely Rose—
Tell her that wastes her time and me,
That now she knows,
When I resemble her to thee,
How sweet and fair she seems to be.

Tell her that's young,
And shuns to have her graces spied,
That hadst thou sprung
In deserts where no men abide,
Thou must have uncommended died.

Small is the worth
Of beauty from the light retired:
Bid her come forth,
Suffer herself to be desired,
And not blush so to be admired.

Then die—that she
The common fate of all things rare
May read in thee;
How small a part of time they share
That are so wondrous sweet and fair!

Notes

In deserts where no men abide: fertile places now laid waste

To a Very Young Lady

Why came I so untimely forth
Into a world, which wanting thee
Could entertain us with no worth
Or shadow of felicity?
  That time should me so far remove
  From that which I was born to love.

Yet fairest blossom do not slight
That age which you may know so soon;
That Rosy Morn resigns her light,
And milder Glory to the Noon:
  And then what wonders shall you do,
  whose dawning Beauty warms us so?

Hope waits upon the flowry prime,
And Summer though it be less gay,
Yet is not lookt on as a time
Of declination or decay.
  For with a full hand that does bring
  All that was promis'd by the Spring

William Davenant

William Davenant (1606–1668), born in Oxford, had as his godfather, William Shakespeare. He went to Oxford but left without a degree. In 1637 he succeeded Ben Jonson as the Poet Laureate of England. Tried for treason for support of King Charles I, Davenant exiled himself to Paris. He was later knighted for running supplies across the English Channel. Charles II appointed him Treasurer of Virginia, and later Lieutenant Governor of Maryland. He was later arrested and imprisoned in the Tower of London. Constantly under surveillance for his supposed seditious writings – he put up his plays in a converted auditorium in his house – Davenant later fled to France again, returning to London in 1660 and producing Shakespeare's plays for the stage there. Davenant introduced the opera to the English stage. He founded the new Duke of York's Playhouse in Lincoln's Inn Fields and co-authored an adaptation of *The Tempest* with John Dryden. Davenant's epic poem, *Gondibert*, was published in 1650.

Aubade

The lark now leaves his wat'ry nest,
  And climbing shakes his dewy wings.
He takes this window for the East,
  And to implore your light he sings—
Awake, awake! the morn will never rise
Till she can dress her beauty at your eyes.

The merchant bows unto the seaman's star,
  The ploughman from the sun his season takes,
But still the lover wonders what they are
  Who look for day before his mistress wakes.
Awake, awake! break thro' your veils of lawn!
Then draw your curtains, and begin the dawn!

Weep no more for what is past

Weep no more for what is past,
For time in motion makes such haste
He hath no leisure to descry
Those errors which he passeth by.
If we consider accident,
And how repugnant unto sense
It pays desert with bad event,
We shall disparage Providence.

John Milton

Often described as the greatest poet of the English language, John Milton was born in London in 1608. He was privately tutored and later went to St Paul's School and finally to Christ's College, Cambridge from where he was briefly suspended for arguing too much with his tutor. During his Cambridge years he composed his famous 'On the Morning of Christ's Nativity'. After acquiring an MA, Milton returned to his family home in Hammersmith to read and write. From this period during which Milton steeped himself in classical reading, wrote 'L'Allegro', 'Il Penseroso' and the masque *Comus*, which was performed at Ludlow Castle in 1634. Milton also acquired a command over Latin, Greek, Hebrew, French, Spanish, Old English and Dutch (he already knew Italian). The death of his close friend Edward King in 1637 produced his great elegy *Lycidas*.

After a tour of Europe, Milton returned to England on the cusp of civil war. He began publishing radical pamphlets. There was a short-lived marriage to Mary Powell in 1642, which caused Milton to write his famous divorce tracts. Mary Powell returned and the two lived together for a while. He was appointed Secretary for Foreign Tongues by the Council of State in 1649, the year in which he published his defence of the regicide, *Eikonoklastes*. In 1652, the year he published his *Defence of the English People*, in Latin, Milton became blind, and lost his wife, his newborn daughter and his son, John, all in the same year. Milton continued writing his tracts, and when *A Treatise of Civil Power* was published in 1659 he was forced into hiding and eventually arrested to be released later by the Parliament. In 1653 Milton married Elizabeth Minshull.

Meanwhile Milton was working on *Paradise Lost*, composing the work in his head at night and dictating the lines to his aides the next morning. It appeared finally in 1667, and was instantly recognised as a masterpiece. *Paradise Regain'd* and *Samson Agonistes* were published together in 1671. In 1674, the second edition of *Paradise Lost* was published, in twelve books. Milton died in November of the same year.

On His Blindness

When I consider how my light is spent
Ere half my days in this dark world and wide,
And that one talent which is death to hide

Lodg'd with me useless, though my soul more bent
To serve therewith my Maker, and present
My true account, lest he returning chide,
'Doth God exact day-labour, light denied?'
I fondly ask. But Patience, to prevent
That murmur, soon replies: 'God doth not need
Either man's work or his own gifts: who best
Bear his mild yoke, they serve him best. His state
Is kingly; thousands at his bidding speed
And post o'er land and ocean without rest:
They also serve who only stand and wait.'

L'Allegro

Hence loathed Melancholy
Of **Cerberus**, and blackest midnight born,
In **Stygian** Cave forlorn
'Mongst horrid shapes, and shrieks, and sights unholy,
Find out some uncouth cell,
Wher brooding darknes spreads his jealous wings,
And the night-Raven sings;
There under **Ebon** shades, and low-brow'd Rocks,
As ragged as thy Locks,
In dark **Cimmerian** desert ever dwell.

But come thou Goddes fair and free,
In Heav'n **ycleap'd Euphrosyne**,
And by men, heart-easing Mirth,
Whom lovely **Venus** at a birth
With two sister **Graces** more
To **Ivy-crowned Bacchus** bore;
Or whether (as som **Sager** sing)
The frolick Wind that breathes the Spring,
Zephir with **Aurora** playing,
As he met her once **a-Maying**,
There on Beds of Violets blew,
And fresh-blown Roses washt in dew,
Fill'd her with thee a daughter fair,
So bucksom, blith, and debonair.
Haste thee nymph, and bring with thee
Jest and youthful Jollity,
Quips and **Cranks**, and wanton Wiles,
Nods, and Becks, and Wreathed Smiles,
Such as hang on **Hebe's** cheek,
And love to live in dimple sleek;

Sport that wrincled Care derides,
And Laughter holding both his sides.
Com, and **trip** it as ye go
On the light fantastick toe,
And in thy right hand lead with thee,
The Mountain Nymph, sweet Liberty;
And if I give thee honour due,
Mirth, admit me of thy crue
To live with her, and live with thee,
In unreproved pleasures free;
To hear the Lark begin his flight,
And singing startle the dull night,
From his watch-towre in the skies,
Till the dappled dawn doth rise;
Then to com in spight of sorrow,
And at my window bid good morrow,
Through the Sweet-Briar, or the Vine,
Or the twisted **Eglantine**.
While the Cock with lively din,
Scatters the rear of darknes thin,
And to the stack, or the Barn dore,
Stoutly struts his **Dames** before,
Oft list'ning how the **Hounds and horn**,
Chearly rouse the slumbring morn,
From the side of som Hoar Hill,
Through the high wood echoing shrill.
Som time walking not unseen
By Hedge-row Elms, on Hillocks green,
Right against the Eastern gate,
Wher the great Sun begins his **state**,
Rob'd in flames, and Amber light,
The clouds in thousand Liveries **dight**.
While the Plowman neer at hand,
Whistles ore the Furrow'd Land,
And the Milkmaid singeth blithe,
And the Mower whets his sithe,
And every Shepherd **tells his tale**
Under the Hawthorn in the dale.
Streit mine eye hath caught new pleasures
Whilst the **Lantskip** round it measures,
Russet Lawns, and Fallows Gray,
Where the nibling flocks do stray,
Mountains on whose barren brest
The labouring clouds do often rest:
Meadows trim with Daisies pide,
Shallow Brooks, and Rivers wide.

Towers, and Battlements it sees
Boosom'd high in tufted Trees,
Wher perhaps som beauty lies,
The Cynosure of neighbouring eyes.
Hard by, a Cottage chimney smokes,
From **betwixt** two aged Okes,
Where **Corydon and Thyrsis** met,
Are at their savory dinner set
Of Hearbs, and other Country Messes,
Which the neat-handed Phillis dresses;
And then in haste her Bowre she leaves,
With **Thestylis** to bind the Sheaves;
Or if the earlier season lead
To the tann'd **Haycock** in the Mead,
Som times with secure delight
The up-land Hamlets will invite,
When the merry Bells ring round,
And the jocond **rebecks** sound
To many a youth, and many a maid,
Dancing in the Chequer'd shade;
And young and old com forth to play
On a Sunshine Holyday,
Till the live-long day-light fail,
Then to the Spicy Nut-brown Ale,
With stories told of many a feat,
How **Faery Mab** the **junkets** eat,
She was pincht, and pull'd she sed,
And he by Friars **Lanthorn** led
Tells how the drudging Goblin swet
To ern his Cream-bowle duly set,
When in one night, ere glimps of morn,
His shadowy Flale hath thresh'd the Corn
That ten day-labourers could not end,
Then lies him down the **Lubbar Fiend.**
And stretch'd out all the Chimney's length,
Basks at the fire his hairy strength;
And Crop-full out of dores he flings,
Ere the first Cock his **Matin** rings.
Thus don the Tales, to bed they creep,
By whispering Windes soon lull'd asleep.
Towred Cities please us then,
And the busie humm of men,
Where throngs of Knights and Barons bold,
In **weeds** of Peace high triumphs hold,
With store of Ladies, whose bright eies
Rain influence, and judge the prise

Of Wit, or Arms, while both contend
To win her Grace, whom all commend.
There let **Hymen** oft appear
In Saffron robe, with Taper clear,
And pomp, and feast, and revelry,
With mask, and antique Pageantry,
Such sights as youthfull Poets dream
On Summer eeves by haunted stream.
Then to the well-trod stage anon,
If **Jonson's** learned **Sock** be on,
Or sweetest Shakespear fancies childe,
Warble his native Wood-notes wilde,
And ever against eating Cares,
Lap me in soft **Lydian Aires**,
Married to immortal verse,
Such as the meeting soul may pierce
In notes, with many a winding bout
Of lincked sweetnes long drawn out,
With wanton heed, and giddy cunning,
The melting voice through mazes running;
Untwisting all the chains that ty
The hidden soul of harmony.
That **Orpheus** self may heave his head
From golden slumber on a bed
Of heapt **Elysian** flowres, and hear
Such streins as would have won the ear
Of **Pluto**, to have quite set free
His half regain'd Eurydice.
These delights, if thou canst give,
Mirth with thee, I mean to live.

Notes

Cerberus: the three-headed dog which guards the gates of Hades **Stygian:** refers to the river Styx, the river of Hades **Ebon:** ebony **Cimmerian:** gloomy **ycleap'd:** named **Euphrosyne:** one of the three Graces, the goddess of joy **Venus:** Roman name for Aphrodite, the goddess of love in Greek mythology **Graces:** the three sisters: Aglaia the goddess of brightness; Euphrosyne, the goddess of joy and Thalia, the goddess of festivity **Ivy-crownèd:** wearing an ivy wreath as a crown **Bacchus:** another name for Dionysus, the god of wine and revelry **Sager:** a wise person **Zephir:** god of the west wind **Aurora:** the goddess of dawn **a-Maying:** celebrating the month of May **Cranks:** here, fanciful speech, but also caprice **Hebe:** the goddess of youth **trip:** here, dance **Eglantine:** wild rose **Dames:** hens **Hounds and horn:** refers to the hunt with hounds and horns **state:** reign **dight:** dressed **tells his tale:** counts his sheep **Lantskip:** old form of 'landscape' **pide:** colourful **betwixt:** between **Corydon and Thyrsis:** Corydon, the goatherd in Theocritus the Greek pastoral poet. Thyrsis is a shepherd in Theocritus. Corydon and

Thyrsis appear together in Eclogue VII of the Roman poet Virgil (70–19 BC), who used the works of Theocritus as a source. **Thestylis:** a servant girl in Theocritus **Haycock:** pile of hay **rebecks:** stringed musical instrument **Faery Mab:** in English folklore, a fairy queen **junkets:** sweetened milk curds **Lanthorn:** lantern **Lubbar Fiend:** originating from English folklore, a huge manlike figure with a tail who does household/farm chores at night in exchange for a bowl of cream **Matin:** morning song **weeds:** here, attire, clothing **Hymen:** the god of marriage **Jonson's:** Ben Jonson (1572–1637) **Sock:** footwear of comic actors in ancient Greek and Roman drama; here, uses it for drollery. **Lydian Aires:** soothing Lydian music; Lydia was an ancient kingdom in what is now Turkey. **Orpheus:** a musician from Greek mythology. Pluto, the god of the underworld, allowed Orpheus to attempt to lead his wife, Eurydice, out of the underworld. Orpheus failed because he disobeyed Pluto's order to not look back at her until they reached the upper world. **Elysian:** heavenly **Pluto:** Roman name for Hades, the Greek god of the underworld. **Mirth:** addressing Euphrosyne, the goddess of joy

Il Penseroso

Hence vain deluding joyes,
The brood of folly without father bred,
How little you **bested**,
Or fill the fixed mind with all your toyes;
Dwell in som idle brain,
And fancies fond with gaudy shapes possess,
As thick and numberless
As the gay motes that people the Sun Beams,
Or likest hovering dreams
The fickle **Pensioners** of **Morpheus** train.

But hail thou Goddes, sage and holy,
Hail divinest Melancholy,
Whose Saintly visage is too bright
To hit the Sense of human sight;
And therfore to our weaker view,
Ore laid with black staid Wisdoms hue.
Black, but such as in esteem,
Prince **Memnons sister** might beseem,
Or that **Starr'd Ethiope Queen** that strove
To set her beauties praise above
The Sea Nymphs, and their powers offended.
Yet thou art higher far descended,
Thee bright- hair'd **Vesta** long of yore,
To solitary Saturn bore;
His daughter she (in **Saturns** raign,
Such mixture was not held a stain).
Oft in glimmering Bowres, and glades

He met her, and in secret shades
Of woody **Ida's** inmost grove,
While yet there was no fear of Jove.
Com pensive **Nun**, devout and pure,
Sober, stedfast, and demure,
All in a robe of darkest grain,
Flowing with majestick train,
And sable stole of **Cipres Lawn**,
Over thy **decent** shoulders drawn.
Com, but keep thy wonted state,
With eev'n step, and musing gate,
And looks **commercing** with the skies,
Thy rapt soul sitting in thine eyes:
There held in holy passion still,
Forget thy self to Marble, till
With a sad Leaden downward cast,
Thou fix them on the earth as fast.
And joyn with thee calm Peace, and Quiet,
Spare Fast, that oft with gods doth diet,
And hears the **Muses** in a ring,
Ay round about Joves Altar sing.
And adde to these retired leasure,
That in trim Gardens takes his pleasure;
But first, and chiefest, with thee bring,
Him that yon soars on golden wing,
Guiding the fiery-wheeled throne,
The Cherub Contemplation,
And the mute Silence **hist along**,
'Less Philomel will daign a Song,
In her sweetest, saddest plight,
Smoothing the rugged brow of night,
While **Cynthia** checks her Dragon yoke,
Gently o're th' accustom'd Oke;
Sweet Bird that shunn'st the noise of folly,
Most musicall, most melancholy!
Thee **Chauntress** oft the Woods among,
I woo to hear thy eeven-Song;
And missing thee, I walk unseen
On the dry smooth-shaven Green,
To behold the wandring Moon,
Riding neer her highest noon,
Like one that had bin led astray
Through the Heav'ns wide pathles way;
And oft, as if her head she bow'd,
Stooping through a fleecy cloud.
Oft on a **Plat** of rising ground,

I hear the far-off Curfeu sound,
Over som wide-water'd shoar,
Swinging slow with sullen roar;
Or if the Ayr will not permit,
Som still removed place will fit,
Where glowing Embers through the room
Teach light to counterfeit a gloom,
Far from all resort of mirth,
Save the Cricket on the hearth,
Or the **Belmans** drousie charm,
To bless the dores from nightly harm:
Or let my Lamp at midnight hour,
Be seen in som high lonely Towr,
Where I may oft out-watch the **Bear**,
With thrice great **Hermes**, or unsphear
The spirit of Plato to unfold
What Worlds, or what vast Regions hold
The **immortal mind** that hath forsook
Her mansion in this fleshly nook:
And of those Dæmons that are found
In fire, air, flood, or under ground,
Whose power hath a true **consent**
With Planet, or with Element.
Som time let Gorgeous **Tragedy**
In **Scepter'd Pall** com sweeping by,
Presenting **Thebs, or Pelops line,**
Or the tale of Troy divine.
Or what (though rare) of later age,
Ennobled hath the **Buskin'd** stage.
But, O **sad Virgin**, that thy power
Might raise **Musæus** from his bower,
Or bid the soul of **Orpheus** sing
Such notes as warbled to the string,
Drew Iron tears down **Pluto's** cheek,
And made Hell grant what Love did seek.
Or call up him that left half told
The story of Cambuscan bold,
Of Camball, and of Algarsife,
And who had Canace to wife,
That own'd the vertuous Ring and Glass,
And of the wondrous Hors of Brass,
On which the Tartar King did ride;
And if ought els, great Bards beside,
In sage and solemn tunes have sung,
Of Turneys and of Trophies hung;
Of Forests, and inchantments drear,

Where more is meant then meets the ear.
Thus night oft see me in thy pale career,
Till civil-suited **Morn** appeer,
Not trickt and **frounc't** as she was wont,
With the **Attick Boy** to hunt,
But Cherchef't in a comly Cloud,
While rocking Winds are Piping loud,
Or usher'd with a shower still,
When the gust hath blown his fill,
Ending on the russling Leaves,
With minute drops from off the **Eaves**.
And when the Sun begins to fling
His flaring beams, me Goddess bring
To arched walks of twilight groves,
And shadows brown that **Sylvan** loves
Of Pine, or monumental Oake,
Where the rude Ax with heaved stroke,
Was never heard the Nymphs to daunt,
Or fright them from their hallow'd haunt.
There in close **covert** by som Brook,
Where no profaner eye may look,
Hide me from Day's **garish eye**,
While the Bee with Honied thie,
That at her flowry work doth sing,
And the Waters murmuring
With such consort as they keep,
Entice the dewy-feather'd Sleep;
And let som strange mysterious dream,
Wave at his Wings in Airy stream,
Of lively portrature display'd,
Softly on my eye-lids laid.
And as I wake, sweet musick breath
Above, about, or underneath,
Sent by som spirit to **mortals good**,
Or th' unseen **Genius** of the Wood.
But let my due feet never fail,
To walk the studious Cloysters pale,
And love the high embowed Roof,
With antick Pillars massy proof,
And storied Windows richly dight,
Casting a dimm religious light.
There let the pealing Organ blow,
To the full voic'd Quire below,
In Service high, and Anthems cleer,
As may with sweetnes, through mine ear,
Dissolve me into extasies,

And bring all Heav'n before mine eyes.
And may at last my weary age
Find out the peacefull hermitage,
The **Hairy Gown** and Mossy Cell,
Where I may sit and rightly spell,
Of every Star that Heav'n doth shew,
And every Herb that sips the dew;
Till old experience do attain
To somthing like Prophetic strain.
These pleasures Melancholy give,
And I with thee will choose to live.

Notes

bested: to satisfy **Pensioners:** here, attendants. **Morpheus:** the god of dreams **Memnon's sister:** the king of Ethiopia. Because he was very handsome, Milton assumes that his sister was also extremely attractive. Thus, the comparison of Melancholy to Memnon's sister is a high compliment to the former. **Starr'd Ethiop queen:** Cassiopeia, the wife of Cepheus, a king of Ethiopia. Cassiopeia boasted that she was more attractive than the Nereids, the sea nymphs. Angered, Poseidon, the god of the sea, had her country destroyed by a sea monster. After her death, she was changed into a constellation. **Vesta:** Hestia, the goddess of the hearth **Saturn:** alternatively, Cronus, the first king of the gods in Greek myth, later overthrown by his son Zeus (or Jove) **Ida:** the highest mountain in Crete **While . . . Jove:** the overthrow of Saturn by his son Jove **Nun:** refers here to Melancholy **cipres lawn:** black silk or cotton fabric used to make mourning clothes **decent:** here, attractive **commércing:** communicating **Forget . . . marble:** still as a marble statue **Muses:** the daughters of Zeus and Mnemosyne. There were nine of them, and together, they were considered sources of inspiration for writers, musicians, dancers, and artists: Calliope (epic poetry), Euterpe (lyric poetry), Clio (history), Terpsichore (choral singing and dance), Melpomene (tragic plays), Thalia (tragic comedies), Polyhymnia (sacred poetry) and Urania (astronomy). **hist along:** came along quietly **'Less:** unless **Philomel:** Philomela, the princess of Athens. Her brother-in-law, Tereus of Thrace, raped her. To prevent her from revealing his crime, he cut out her tongue. However, Philomel embroidered a tapestry depicting his brutality and showed it to her sister. The two women took revenge by serving Tereus his own son, Utys, cooked in a stew. Tereus hunted out the women, but the gods turned Philomela into a nightingale and Procne into a swallow. **Cynthia:** Artemis, the goddess of the moon and hunting, also known as Diana **Chauntress:** singer **Plat:** a plot of ground **Belman:** the town crier **Bear:** the constellation Ursa Major **Hermes:** Hermes Trismegistus, Egyptian alchemist and author of works on magic, the soul, and philosophy **immortal mind:** This refers to Plato's soul or mind. **And . . . demons:** and unsphere the spirits of those demons **consent:** here, connection **Tragedy:** tragic play **Sceptr'd Pall:** black robe **Thebs . . . divine:** subjects of Greek tragedies **buskin'd:** derived from buskin, the boot worn by actors in ancient Greek and Roman tragedies **sad virgin:** refers to Melancholy **Musæus:** poet and singer **Orpheus:** a musician, whom the god of the underworld, Pluto, allowed to lead his wife, Eurydice, out of the underworld. But Orpheus disobeyed Pluto's order not to look back at her until they reached the upper world. **Pluto:** the god of the underworld **Or**

call . . . wife: refers to 'The Squire's Tale' in *The Canterbury Tales* of Geoffrey Chaucer. 'Call up him' refers to Chaucer. 'Half-told story': Chaucer did not complete this tale. **Morn:** Aurora, the Roman name for Eos, the goddess of dawn **frounc't:** wrinkled **Attick Boy:** Cephalus, a great hunter in Greek mythology **Eaves:** edge of the leaves **Sylvan:** could refer to a person who lives in a forest or Sylvanus, the Roman god of the forest **covert:** sheltered place **garish eye:** the sun **Entice . . . Sleep:** the murmuring waters that lull the listener to sleep **mortals good:** here, good mortals **Genius:** guardian spirit **Hairy Gown:** a hair shirt, which monks and other religious persons wore to cause themselves discomfort as a form of repentance

On the Morning of Christ's Nativity

His is the Month, and this the happy morn
Wherein the Son of Heav'ns eternal King,
Of wedded Maid, and Virgin Mother born,
Our great redemption from above did bring;
For so the **holy sages** once did sing,
That he our deadly forfeit should release,
And with his Father work us a perpetual peace.

II
That glorious Form, that Light unsufferable,
And that far-beaming blaze of Majesty,
Wherwith he wont at Heav'ns high Councel-Table,
To sit the midst of **Trinal Unity**,
He laid aside; and here with us to be,
Forsook the Courts of everlasting Day,
And chose with us a darksom House of mortal Clay.

III
Say Heav'nly Muse, shall not thy sacred vein
Afford a present to the Infant God?
Hast thou no vers, no hymn, or solemn strein,
To welcom him to this his new abode,
Now while the Heav'n by the Suns team untrod,
Hath took no print of the approching light,
And all the **spangled host** keep watch in squadrons bright?

IV
See how from far upon the Eastern rode
The Star-led **Wisards** haste with odours sweet:
O run, **prevent** them with thy humble ode,

And lay it lowly at his blessed feet;
Have thou the honour first, thy Lord to greet,
And joyn thy voice unto the Angel Quire,
From out his secret Altar toucht with hallow'd fire.

The Hymn

I

It was the Winter wilde,
While the Heav'n-born-childe,
All meanly wrapt in the rude manger lies;
Nature in aw to him
Had doff't her gawdy trim,
With her great Master so to sympathize:
It was no season then for her
To wanton with the Sun her lusty Paramour.

II

Onely with speeches fair
She woo's the gentle Air
To hide her guilty front with innocent Snow,
And on her naked shame,
Pollute with sinfull blame,
The Saintly Vail of Maiden white to throw,
Confounded, that her Makers eyes
Should look so neer upon her foul deformities.

III

But he her fears to cease,
Sent down the meek-eyd Peace,
She crown'd with Olive green, came softly sliding
Down through the turning **sphear**,
His ready Harbinger,
With Turtle wing the **amorous clouds** dividing,
And waving wide her **mirtle** wand,
She strikes a universall Peace through Sea and Land.

IV

No War, or Battails sound
Was heard the World around:
The idle spear and shield were high up hung;
The hooked Chariot stood

Unstain'd with hostile blood,
The Trumpet spake not to the armed throng,
And Kings sate still with awfull eye,
As if they surely knew their sovran Lord was by.

V

But peacefull was the night
Wherein the Prince of light
His raign of peace upon the earth began:
The Windes, with wonder **whist**,
Smoothly the waters kist,
Whispering new joyes to the milde Ocean,
Who now hath quite forgot to rave,
While **Birds of Calm** sit brooding on the charmed wave.

VI

The Stars with deep amaze
Stand fixt in stedfast gaze,
Bending one way their pretious influence,
And will not take their flight,
For all the morning light,
Or **Lucifer** that often warn'd them thence;
But in their glimmering Orbs did glow,
Untill their Lord himself bespake, and bid them go.

VII

And though the shady gloom
Had given day her room,
The Sun himself with-held his wonted speed,
And hid his head for shame,
As his inferiour flame,
The new-enlightn'd world no more should need;
He saw a greater Sun appear
Then his bright Throne, or burning **Axletree** could bear.

VIII

The Shepherds on the Lawn,
Or ere the point of dawn,
Sate simply chatting in a rustick row;
Full little thought they than,
That the mighty **Pan**
Was kindly com to live with them below;
Perhaps their loves, or els their sheep,
Was all that did their silly thoughts so busie keep.

IX
When such musick sweet
Their hearts and ears did greet,
As never was by mortall finger strook,
Divinely-warbled voice
Answering the stringed noise,
As all their souls in blisfull rapture took:
The Air such pleasure loth to lose,
With thousand echo's still prolongs each heav'nly close.

X
Nature that heard such sound
Beneath the **hollow round**
Of Cynthia's seat, the Airy region thrilling,
Now was almost won
To think her part was don,
And that her raign had here its last fulfilling;
She knew such harmony alone
Could hold all Heav'n and Earth in happier union.

XI
At last surrounds their sight
A Globe of circular light,
That with long beams the shame-fac't night array'd,
The helmed Cherubim
And sworded Seraphim
Are seen in glittering ranks with wings displaid,
Harping in loud and solemn quire,
With unexpressive notes to Heav'ns new-born Heir.

XII
Such Musick (as 'tis said)
Before was never made,
But when of old the sons of morning sung,
While the Creator Great
His constellations set,
And the well-balanc't world on hinges hung,
And cast the dark foundations deep,
And bid the weltring waves their oozy channel keep.

XIII
Ring out ye Crystall sphears,
Once bless our human ears,

(If ye have **power to touch our senses** so)
And let your silver chime
Move in melodious time;
And let the Base of Heav'ns deep Organ blow,
And with your ninefold harmony
Make up full consort to th' Angelike symphony.

XIV
For if such holy Song
Enwrap our fancy long,
Time will run back, and fetch the **age of gold**,
And speckl'd vanity
Will sicken soon and die,
And leprous sin will melt from earthly mould,
And Hell itself will pass away,
And leave her dolorous mansions to the peering day.

XV
Yea Truth, and Justice then
Will down return to men,
Th' enameld Arras of the Rainbow wearing,
And Mercy set between,
Thron'd in Celestiall sheen,
With radiant feet the tissued clouds down stearing,
And Heav'n as at som festivall,
Will open wide the Gates of her high Palace Hall.

XVI
But wisest Fate sayes no,
This must not yet be so,
The Babe lies yet in smiling Infancy,
That on the bitter cross
Must redeem our loss;
So both himself and us to glorifie:
Yet first to those ychain'd in sleep,
The wakefull trump of doom must thunder through the deep,

XVII
With such a horrid clang
As on mount **Sinai** rang
While the red fire, and smouldring clouds out brake:
The aged Earth agast

With terrour of that blast,
Shall from the surface to the center shake,
When at the worlds last session,
The dreadfull Judge in middle Air shall spread his throne.

XVIII
And then at last our bliss
Full and perfect is,
But now begins; for from this happy day
Th' old **Dragon** under ground,
In straiter limits bound,
Not half so far casts his usurped sway,
And wrath to see his Kingdom fail,
Swindges the scaly Horrour of his foulded tail.

XIX
The Oracles are dumm,
No voice or hideous humm
Runs through the arched roof in words deceiving.
Apollo from his shrine
Can no more divine,
With hollow shreik the steep of Delphos leaving.
No nightly trance, or breathed spell,
Inspire's the pale-ey'd Priest from the prophetic cell.

XX
The lonely mountains o're,
And the resounding shore,
A voice of weeping heard, and loud lament;
From haunted spring and dale
Edg'd with poplar pale,
The parting **Genius** is with sighing sent,
With flowre-inwov'n tresses torn
The Nimphs in twilight shade of tangled thickets mourn.

XXI
In consecrated Earth,
And on the holy Hearth,
The **Lars, and Lemures** moan with midnight plaint,
In Urns, and Altars round,
A drear, and dying sound
Affrights the **Flamins** at their service quaint;
And the chill Marble seems to sweat,
While each peculiar power forgoes his wonted seat.

XXII
Peor, and Baalim,
Forsake their Temples dim,
With that twise-batter'd god of Palestine,
And mooned **Ashtaroth**,
Heav'ns Queen and Mother both,
Now sits not girt with Tapers holy shine,
The Libyc **Hammon** shrinks his horn,
In vain the Tyrian Maids their wounded **Thamuz** mourn.

XXIII
And sullen **Moloch** fled,
Hath left in shadows dred.
His burning Idol all of blackest hue,
In vain with Cymbals ring,
They call the grisly king,
In dismall dance about the furnace blue;
The brutish **gods of Nile** as fast,
Isis and Orus, and the Dog Anubis hast.

XXIV
Nor is **Osiris** seen
In Memphian Grove, or Green,
Trampling the unshowr'd Grasse with lowings loud:
Nor can he be at rest
Within his sacred chest,
Naught but profoundest Hell can be his shroud:
In vain with Timbrel'd Anthems dark
The sable-stoled Sorcerers bear **his worshipt Ark.**

XXV
He feels from Juda's land
The dredded Infants hand,
The rayes of Bethlehem blind his dusky eyn;
Nor all the gods beside,
Longer dare abide,
Nor **Typhon** huge ending in snaky twine:
Our Babe, to shew **his Godhead true,**
Can in his swadling bands controul the damned crew.

XXVI
So when the Sun in bed,
Curtain'd with cloudy red,

Pillows his chin upon an Orient wave.
The flocking shadows pale
Troop to th' infernall jail,
Each fetter'd Ghost slips to his severall grave,
And the yellow-skirted Fayes
Fly after the Night-steeds, leaving their Moon-lov'd maze.

XXVII
But see the Virgin blest,
Hath laid her Babe to rest.
Time is our tedious Song should here have ending,
Heav'ns youngest-teemed Star
Hath fixt her polisht Car,
Her sleeping Lord with Handmaid Lamp attending.
And all about the Courtly Stable,
Bright-harnest Angels sit in order serviceable.

Notes

holy sages: the ancient prophets **Trinal Unity:** the doctrine of the Holy Trinity **spangled host:** stars, which are believed to be angels **Wisards:** the three wise men from Matthew 2('Now when Jesus was born in Bethlehem of Judaea in the days of Herod the king, behold, there came wise men from the east to Jerusalem') **prevent:** here, come before **sphear:** the Ptolemaic model of the universe with the earth at the centre and the stars revolving around it **amorous clouds:** a reference to Jupiter's seduction of Io by appearing as a cloud (Ovid's *Metamorphoses)* **mirtle:** traditionally associated with Venus (also from Ovid) **whist:** hushed **Birds of Calm:** the halcyons or kingfishers nesting on seas that have been calmed for their sake (Ovid) **Lucifer:** Venus, the morning star **Axletree:** the sun's chariot **Pan:** Pan here is an image of Christ as Edmund Spenser depicts it in his *Shepheardes' Calendar.* **hollow round/ Of Cynthia's seat:** the moon; Cynthia is the moon. **power to touch our senses:** the Pythagorean theory that heavenly spheres make music as they turn. Humans cannot hear this music. **age of gold:** from Virgil's *Eclogues* **Sinai:** where Moses received the Law **Dragon:** here, the devil **Genius:** the guardian spirit of a place **Lars and Lemures:** Roman gods of home, and spirits of the dead **Flamins:** priests **Peor and Baalim:** Mount Peor housed the Phoenician deity Baal-peor. Baalim in general are Phoenician deities. **Ashtaroth:** or Astarte, goddess of the moon and fertility **Hammon:** the Lybian god Jupiter-Ammon **Thamuz:** alternatively, Dammuzi, the Phoenician god whose death was celebrated annually because the cycle of his death and re-birth symbolised the seasons **Moloch:** The name is Ammonite for 'king'. **gods of Nile:** Isis, the Egyptian moon goddess; Horus, the sun god, and Anubis, his son **Osiris:** The principal Egyptian ('Memphian') god also known as Apis, usually figured as a black bull with a white triangle on its forehead **his worshipt Ark:** According to Herodotus, the Egyptian festival of Ares in Pampremis included carrying an image of Apis or Osirus in a gilt wooden shrine or ark. **Typhon:** a fire-breathing giant with hundred heads and a serpentine body **his Godhead true:** Christ is compared to Hercules, who strangled two serpents when he was a baby. **teemed:** here, born

Paradise Lost

Book 1

THE ARGUMENT

This first Book proposes, first in brief, the whole Subject, Mans disobedience, and the loss thereupon of Paradise wherein he was plac't: Then touches the prime cause of his fall, the Serpent, or rather Satan in the Serpent; who revolting from God, and drawing to his side many Legions of Angels, was by the command of God driven out of Heaven with all his Crew into the great Deep. Which action past over, the Poem hasts into the midst of things, presenting Satan with his Angels now fallen into Hell, describ'd here, not in the Center (for Heaven and Earth may be suppos'd as yet not made, certainly not yet accurst) but in a place of utter darkness, fitliest call'd Chaos: Here Satan with his Angels lying on the burning Lake, thunder-struck and astonisht, after a certain space recovers, as from confusion, calls up him who next in Order and Dignity lay by him; they confer of thir miserable fall. Satan awakens all his Legions, who lay till then in the same manner confounded; They rise, thir Numbers, array of Battel, thir chief Leaders nam'd, according to the Idols known afterwards in Canaan and the Countries adjoyning. To these Satan directs his Speech, comforts them with hope yet of regaining Heaven, but tells them lastly of a new World and new kind of Creature to be created, according to an ancient Prophesie or report in Heaven; for that Angels were long before this visible Creation, was the opinion of many ancient Fathers. To find out the truth of this Prophesie, and what to determin thereon he refers to a full Councel. What his Associates thence attempt. Pandemonium the Palace of Satan rises, suddenly built out of the Deep: The infernal Peers there sit in Councel.

Of Mans First Disobedience, and the Fruit
Of that Forbidden Tree, whose mortal tast
Brought **Death into the World, and all our woe,**
With loss of Eden, till **one greater Man**
Restore us, and regain the blissful Seat,
Sing **Heav'nly Muse**, that on the secret top
Of **Oreb**, or of Sinai, didst inspire
That Shepherd, who first taught the **chosen Seed,**
In the Beginning how the Heav'ns and Earth
Rose **out of Chaos**: Or if **Sion** Hill
Delight thee more, and Siloa's Brook that flow'd
Fast by the Oracle of God; I thence

Invoke thy aid to my adventrous Song,
That with no middle flight intends to soar
Above th' **Aonian Mount**, while it pursues
Things unattempted yet in Prose or Rhime.
And chiefly Thou O Spirit, that dost prefer
Before all Temples th' upright heart and pure,
Instruct me, for Thou know'st; Thou from the first
Wast present, and with mighty wings outspread
Dove-like satst brooding on the vast Abyss
And mad'st it pregnant: What in me is dark
Illumin, what is low raise and support;
That to the highth of this great Argument
I may assert Eternal Providence,
And justifie the wayes of God to men.

Say first, for Heav'n hides nothing from thy view
Nor the deep Tract of Hell, say first what cause
Mov'd our Grand Parents in that happy State,
Favour'd of Heav'n so highly, to fall off
From thir Creator, and transgress his Will
For **one restraint,** Lords of the World besides?
Who first seduc'd them to that foul revolt?
Th' infernal Serpent; he it was, whose guile
Stird up with Envy and Revenge, deceiv'd
The Mother of Mankind, what time his Pride
Had cast him out from Heav'n, with all his Host
Of Rebel Angels, by whose aid aspiring
To set himself in Glory above his Peers,
He trusted to have equal'd the most High,
If he oppos'd; and with ambitious aim
Against the Throne and Monarchy of God
Rais'd impious War in Heav'n and Battel proud
With vain attempt. Him the Almighty Power
Hurld headlong flaming from th' Ethereal Skie
With hideous ruine and combustion down
To bottomless perdition, there to dwell
In **Adamantine** Chains and penal Fire,
Who durst defie th' Omnipotent to Arms.
Nine times the Space that measures Day and Night
To mortal men, he with his horrid crew
Lay vanquisht, rowling in the fiery Gulfe
Confounded though immortal: But his doom
Reserv'd him to more wrath; for now the thought
Both of lost happiness and lasting pain
Torments him; round he throws his baleful eyes
That witness'd huge affliction and dismay

Mixt with obdurate pride and stedfast hate:
At once as far as Angels kenn he views
The dismal Situation waste and wilde,
A Dungeon horrible, on all sides round
As one great Furnace flam'd, yet from those flames
No light, but rather darkness visible
Serv'd onely to discover sights of woe,
Regions of sorrow, doleful shades, where peace
And rest can never dwell, hope never comes
That comes to all; but torture without end
Still urges, and a fiery Deluge, fed
With ever-burning Sulphur unconsum'd:
Such place Eternal Justice had prepar'd
For those rebellious, here thir Prison ordain'd
In utter darkness, and thir portion set
As far remov'd from God and light of Heav'n
As **from the Center thrice to th' utmost Pole.**
O how unlike the place from whence they fell!
There the companions of his fall, o'rewhelm'd
With Floods and Whirlwinds of tempestuous fire,
He soon discerns, and weltring by his side
One next himself in power, and next in crime,
Long after known in Palestine, and nam'd
Beelzebub. To whom th' Arch-Enemy,
And thence in Heav'n **call'd Satan,** with bold words
Breaking the horrid silence thus began.

If thou beest he; But O how fall'n! how chang'd
From him, who in the happy Realms of Light
Cloth'd with transcendent brightness didst out-shine
Myriads though bright: If he Whom mutual league,
United thoughts and counsels, equal hope
And hazard in the Glorious Enterprize,
Joynd with me once, now misery hath joynd
In equal ruin: into what Pit thou seest
From what highth fall'n, so much the stronger prov'd
He with his Thunder: and till then who knew
The force of those dire Arms? yet not for those,
Nor what the Potent Victor in his rage
Can else inflict, do I repent or change,
Though chang'd in outward lustre; that fixt mind
And high disdain, from sence of injur'd merit,
That with the mightiest rais'd me to contend,
And to the fierce contention brought along
Innumerable force of Spirits arm'd
That durst dislike his reign, and me preferring,

His utmost power with adverse power oppos'd
In dubious Battel on the Plains of Heav'n,
And shook his throne. What though the field be lost?
All is not lost; the unconquerable Will,
And study of revenge, immortal hate,
And courage never to submit or yield:
And what is else not to be overcome?
That Glory never shall his wrath or might
Extort from me. To bow and sue for grace
With suppliant knee, and deifie his power,
Who from the terrour of this Arm so late
Doubted his Empire, that were low indeed,
That were an ignominy and shame beneath
This downfall; since by Fate the strength of Gods
And this Empyreal substance cannot fail,
Since through experience of this great event
In Arms not worse, in foresight much advanc't,
We may with more successful hope resolve
To wage by force or guile eternal Warr
Irreconcileable, to our grand Foe,
Who now triumphs, and in th' excess of joy
Sole reigning holds the Tyranny of Heav'n.

So spake th' Apostate Angel, though in pain,
Vaunting aloud, but rackt with deep despare:
And him thus answer'd soon his bold Compeer.

O Prince, O Chief of many Throned Powers,
That led th' imbattelld Seraphim to Warr
Under thy conduct, and in dreadful deeds
Fearless, endanger'd Heav'ns perpetual King;
And put to proof his high Supremacy,
Whether upheld by strength, or Chance, or Fate,
Too well I see and rue the dire event,
That with sad overthrow and foul defeat

Hath lost us Heav'n, and all this mighty Host
In horrible destruction laid thus low,
As far as Gods and Heav'nly Essences
Can perish: for the mind and spirit remains
Invincible, and vigour soon returns,
Though all our Glory extinct, and happy state
Here swallow'd up in endless misery.
But what if he our Conquerour, (whom I now
Of force believe Almighty, since no less
Then such could hav orepow'rd such force as ours)

Have left us this our spirit and strength intire
Strongly to suffer and support our pains,
That we may so suffice his vengeful ire,
Or do him mightier service as his **thralls**
By right of Warr, what e're his business be
Here in the heart of Hell to work in Fire,
Or do his Errands in the gloomy Deep;
What can it then avail though yet we feel
Strength undiminisht, or eternal being
To undergo eternal punishment?
Whereto with speedy words th' Arch-fiend reply'd.

Fall'n Cherube, to be weak is miserable
Doing or Suffering: but of this be sure,
To do ought good never will be our task,
But ever to do ill our sole delight,
As being the contrary to his high will
Whom we resist. If then his Providence
Out of our evil seek to bring forth good,
Our labour must be to pervert that end,
And out of good still to find means of evil;
Which oft times may succeed, so as perhaps
Shall grieve him, if I fail not, and disturb
His inmost counsels from thir destind aim.
But see the angry Victor hath recall'd
His Ministers of vengeance and pursuit
Back to the Gates of Heav'n: The Sulphurous Hail
Shot after us in storm, oreblown hath laid
The fiery Surge, that from the Precipice
Of Heav'n receiv'd us falling, and the Thunder,
Wing'd with red Lightning and impetuous rage,
Perhaps hath spent his shafts, and ceases now
To bellow through the vast and boundless Deep.
Let us not slip th' occasion, whether scorn,
Or satiate fury yield it from our Foe.
Seest thou yon dreary Plain, forlorn and wilde,
The seat of desolation, voyd of light,
Save what the glimmering of these livid flames
Casts pale and dreadful? Thither let us tend
From off the tossing of these fiery waves,
There rest, if any rest can harbour there,
And reassembling our afflicted Powers,
Consult how we may henceforth most offend
Our Enemy, our own loss how repair,
How overcome this dire Calamity,
What reinforcement we may gain from Hope,

If not what resolution from despare.

Thus Satan talking to his neerest Mate
With Head up-lift above the wave, and Eyes
That sparkling blaz'd, his other Parts besides
Prone on the Flood, extended long and large
Lay floating many a **rood**, in bulk as huge
As whom the Fables name of monstrous size,
Titanian, or Earth-born, that warr'd on Jove,
Briareos or **Typhon**, whom the Den
By ancient Tarsus held, or that Sea-beast
Leviathan, which God of all his works
Created hugest that swim th' Ocean stream:
Him haply slumbring on the Norway foam
The Pilot of some small night-founder'd Skiff,
Deeming some Island, oft, as Sea-men tell,
With fixed Anchor in his skaly rind
Moors by his side under the Lee, while Night
Invests the Sea, and wished Morn delayes:
So stretcht out huge in length the Arch-fiend lay
Chain'd on the burning Lake, nor ever thence
Had ris'n or heav'd his head, but that the will
And high permission of all-ruling Heaven
Left him at large to his own dark designs,
That with reiterated crimes he might
Heap on himself damnation, while he sought
Evil to others, and enrag'd might see
How all his malice serv'd but to bring forth
Infinite goodness, grace and mercy shewn
On Man by him seduc't, but on himself
Treble confusion, wrath and vengeance pour'd.
Forthwith upright he rears from off the Pool
His mighty Stature; on each hand the flames
Drivn backward slope thir pointing spires, and rowld
In billows, leave i'th' midst a horrid Vale.
Then with expanded wings he stears his flight
Aloft, **incumbent** on the dusky Air
That felt unusual weight, till on dry Land
He lights, if it were Land that ever burn'd
With solid, as the Lake with liquid fire;
And such appear'd in hue, as when the force
Of subterranean wind transports a Hill
Torn from **Pelorus**, or the shatter'd side
Of thundring Ætna, whose combustible
And fewel'd entrals thence conceiving Fire,
Sublim'd with Mineral fury, aid the Winds,

And leave a singed bottom all involv'd
With stench and smoak: Such resting found the sole
Of unblest feet. Him followed his next Mate,
Both glorying to have scap't the **Stygian** flood
As Gods, and by thir own recover'd strength,
Not by the sufferance of supernal Power.

Is this the Region, this the Soil, the Clime,
Said then the lost Arch-Angel, this the seat
That we must change for Heav'n, this mournful gloom
For that celestial light? Be it so, since he
Who now is Sovran can dispose and bid
What shall be right: fardest from him is best
Whom reason hath equald, force hath made supream
Above his equals. Farewel happy Fields
Where Joy for ever dwells: Hail horrours, hail
Infernal world, and thou profoundest Hell
Receive thy new Possessor: One who brings
A mind not to be chang'd by Place or Time.
The mind is its own place, and in it self
Can make a Heav'n of Hell, a Hell of Heav'n.
What matter where, if I be still the same,
And what I should be, all but less then he
Whom Thunder hath made greater? Here at least
We shall be free; th' Almighty hath not built
Here for his envy, will not drive us hence:
Here we may reign secure, and in my choyce
To reign is worth ambition though in Hell:
Better to reign in Hell, then serve in Heav'n.
But wherefore let we then our faithful friends,
Th' associates and copartners of our loss
Lye thus astonisht on th' oblivious Pool,
And call them not to share with us their part
In this unhappy Mansion, or once more
With rallied Arms to try what may be yet
Regaind in Heav'n, or what more lost in Hell?

So Satan spake, and him Beelzebub
Thus answer'd. Leader of those Armies bright,
Which but th' Onmipotent none could have foyld,
If once they hear that voyce, thir liveliest pledge
Of hope in fears and dangers, heard so oft

In worst extreams, and on the perilous edge
Of battel when it rag'd, in all assaults
Thir surest signal, they will soon resume

New courage and revive, though now they lye
Groveling and prostrate on yon Lake of Fire,
As we erewhile, astounded and amaz'd,
No wonder, fall'n such a pernicious highth.

He scarce had ceas't when the superiour Fiend
Was moving toward the shoar; his ponderous shield
Ethereal temper, massy, large and round,
Behind him cast; the broad circumference
Hung on his shoulders like the Moon, whose Orb
Through **Optic Glass** the **Tuscan Artist** views
At Ev'ning from the top of **Fesole**,
Or in **Valdarno**, to descry new Lands,
Rivers or Mountains in her spotty Globe.
His Spear, to equal which the tallest Pine
Hewn on Norwegian hills, to be the Mast
Of some great **Ammiral**, were but a wand,
He walkt with to support uneasie steps
Over the burning **Marle**, not like those steps
On Heavens Azure, and the torrid Clime
Smote on him sore besides, vaulted with Fire;
Nathless he so endur'd, till on the Beach
Of that inflamed Sea, he stood and call'd
His Legions, Angel Forms, who lay intrans't
Thick as Autumnal Leaves that strow the Brooks
In **Vallombrosa**, where th' **Etrurian shades**
High overarch't imbowr; or scatterd **sedge**
Afloat, when with fierce Winds **Orion** arm'd
Hath vext the Red-Sea Coast, whose waves orethrew
Busiris and his Memphian Chivalry,
While with perfidious hatred they pursu'd
The **Sojourners of Goshen**, who beheld
From the safe shore thir floating Carkases
And broken Chariot Wheels, so thick bestrown
Abject and lost lay these, covering the Flood,
Under amazement of thir hideous change.
He call'd so loud, that all the hollow Deep
Of Hell resounded. Princes, Potentates,
Warriers, the Flowr of Heav'n, once yours, now lost,
If such astonishment as this can sieze
Eternal spirits; or have ye chos'n this place
After the toyl of Battel to repose
Your wearied vertue, for the ease you find
To slumber here, as in the Vales of Heav'n?
Or in this abject posture have ye sworn
To adore the Conquerour? who now beholds

Cherube and Seraph rowling in the Flood
With scatter'd Arms and Ensigns, till anon
His swift pursuers from Heav'n Gates discern
Th' advantage, and descending tread us down
Thus drooping, or with linked Thunderbolts
Transfix us to the bottom of this Gulfe.
Awake, arise, or be for ever fall'n.

They heard, and were abasht, and up they sprung
Upon the wing, as when men wont to watch
On duty, sleeping found by whom they dread,
Rouse and bestir themselves ere well awake.
Nor did they not perceave the evil plight
In which they were, or the fierce pains not feel;
Yet to thir Generals Voyce they soon obeyd
Innumerable. As when the potent Rod
Of **Amrams Son** in Egypts evill day
Wav'd round the Coast, up call'd a pitchy cloud
Of Locusts, warping on the Eastern Wind,
That ore the Realm of impious Pharaoh hung
Like Night, and darken'd all the Land of Nile:
So numberless were those bad Angels seen
Hovering on wing under the **Cope** of Hell
'Twixt upper, nether, and surrounding Fires;
Till, as a signal giv'n, th' uplifted Spear
Of thir **great Sultan** waving to direct
Thir course, in even ballance down they light
On the firm brimstone, and fill all the Plain;
A multitude, like which the **populous North**
Pour'd never from her frozen loyns, to pass
Rhene or the Danaw, when her barbarous Sons
Came like a Deluge on the South, and spread
Beneath Gibralter to the Lybian sands.
Forthwith from every Squadron and each Band
The Heads and Leaders thither hast where stood
Thir great Commander; Godlike shapes and forms
Excelling human, Princely Dignities,
And Powers that earst in Heaven sat on Thrones;
Though of thir Names in heav'nly Records now
Be no memorial blotted out and ras'd
By thir Rebellion, from the Books of Life.
Nor had they yet among the Sons of Eve
Got them new Names, till wandring ore the Earth,
Through Gods high sufferance for the tryal of man,
By falsities and lyes the greatest part
Of Mankind they corrupted to forsake

God thir Creator, and th' invisible
Glory of him that made them, to transform
Oft to the Image of a Brute, adorn'd
With gay Religions full of Pomp and Gold,
And **Devils to adore for Deities:**
Then were they known to men by various Names,
And various Idols through the Heathen World.
Say, Muse, thir Names then known, who first, who last,
Rous'd from the slumber,on that fiery Couch,
At thir great Emperors call, as next in worth
Came singly where he stood on the bare strand,
While the promiscuous croud stood yet aloof?
The chief were those who from the Pit of Hell
Roaming to seek thir prey on earth, durst fix
Thir Seats long after next the Seat of God,
Thir Altars by his Altar, Gods ador'd
Among the Nations round, and durst abide
Jehovah thundring out of Sion, thron'd
Between the Cherubim; yea, often plac'd
Within his Sanctuary it self thir Shrines,
Abominations; and with cursed things
His holy Rites, and solemn Feasts profan'd,
And with thir darkness durst affront his light.
First **Moloch**, horrid King besmear'd with blood
Of human sacrifice, and parents tears,
Though for the noyse of Drums and Timbrels loud
Thir **childrens cries unheard**, that past through fire
To his grim Idol. Him the **Ammonite**
Worshipt in **Rabba** and her watry Plain,
In **Argob** and in **Basan**, to the stream
Of utmost **Arnon**. Nor content with such
Audacious neighbourhood, the wisest heart
Of Solomon he led by fraud to build
His Temple right against the Temple of God
On that opprobrious Hill, and made his Grove
The pleasant Vally of **Hinnom**, Tophet thence
And black Gehenna call'd, the Type of Hell.
Next **Chemos**, th' obscene dread of Moabs Sons,
From **Aroar** to **Nebo**, and the wild
Of Southmost **Abarim**; in **Hesebon**
And Horonaim, Seons Realm, beyond
The flowry Dale of **Sibma** clad with Vines,
And **Eleale** to th' **Asphaltick Pool**.
Peor his other Name, when he entic'd
Israel in Sittim on thir march from Nile
To do him wanton rites, which cost them woe.

Yet thence his lustful Orgies he enlarg'd
Even to that **Hill of Scandal**, by the Grove
Of Moloch homicide, lust hard by hate;
Till good Josiah drove them thence to Hell.
With these came they, who from the bordring flood
Of old Euphrates to the Brook that parts
Egypt from Syrian ground, had general Names
Of **Baalim and Ashtaroth**, those male,
These Feminine. For Spirits when they please
Can either Sex assume, or both; so soft
And uncompounded is thir **Essence pure,**
Not ti'd or manacl'd with joynt or limb,
Nor founded on the brittle strength of bones,
Like cumbrous flesh; but in what shape they choose
Dilated or condens't, bright or obscure,
Can execute thir aerie purposes,
And works of love or enmity fulfill.
For those the Race of Israel oft forsook
Thir living strength, and unfrequented left
His righteous Altar, bowing lowly down
To bestial Gods; for which thir heads as low
Bow'd down in Battel, sunk before the Spear
Of despicable foes. With these in troop
Came Astoreth, whom the Phoenicians call'd
Astarte, Queen of Heav'n, with crescent Horns;
To whose bright Image nightly by the Moon
Sidonian Virgins paid thir Vows and Songs,
In **Sion** also not unsung, where stood
Her Temple on **th' offensive Mountain**, built
By that **uxorious King**, whose heart though large,
Beguil'd by fair Idolatresses, fell
To Idols foul. **Thammuz** came next behind,
Whose annual wound in Lebanon allur'd
The Syrian Damsels to lament his fate
In amorous dittyes all a Summers day,
While smooth **Adonis** from his native Rock
Ran purple to the Sea, suppos'd with blood
Of Thammuz yearly wounded: the Love-tale
Infected **Sions daughters** with like heat,
Whose wanton passions in the sacred Porch
Ezekiel saw, when by the Vision led
His eye survay'd the dark Idolatries
Of **alienated** Judah. Next came one
Who mourn'd in earnest, when the Captive Ark
Maim'd his brute Image, head and hands lopt off
In his own Temple, on the **grunsel** edge,

Where he fell flat, and sham'd his Worshipers:
Dagon his Name, Sea Monster, upward Man
And downward Fish: yet had his Temple high
Rear'd in **Azotus**, dreaded through the Coast
Of Palestine, in Gath and Ascalon
And Accaron and Gaza's frontier bounds.
Him follow'd **Rimmon**, whose delightful Seat
Was fair Damascus, on the fertil Banks
Of Abbana and Pharphar, lucid streams.
He also against the house of God was bold:
A Leper once he lost and gain'd a King,
Ahaz his sottish Conquerour, whom he drew
Gods Altar to disparage and displace
For one of Syrian mode, whereon to burn
His odious off'rings, and adore the Gods
Whom he had vanquisht. After these appear'd
A crew who under Names of old Renown,
Osiris, Isis, Orus and their Train
With monstrous shapes and sorceries abus'd
Fanatic Egypt and her Priests, to seek
Thir wandring Gods disguis'd in brutish forms
Rather then human. Nor did Israel scape
Th' infection when thir borrow'd Gold compos'd
The Calf in Oreb: and the **Rebel King**
Doubl'd that sin in Bethel and in Dan,
Lik'ning his Maker to the Grazed Ox,
Jehovah, who in one Night when he pass'd
From Egypt marching, equal'd with one stroke
Both her first born and all her bleating Gods.
Belial came last, then whom a Spirit more lewd
Fell not from Heaven, or more gross to love
Vice for it self: To him no Temple stood
Or Altar smoak'd; yet who more oft then hee
In Temples and at Altars, when the Priest
Turns Atheist, as did **Ely's Sons**, who fill'd
With lust and violence the house of God.
In Courts and Palaces he also Reigns
And in luxurious Cities, where the noyse
Of riot ascends above thir loftiest Towrs,
And injury and outrage: And when Night
Darkens the Streets, then wander forth the Sons
Of Belial, **flown** with insolence and wine.
Witness the Streets of Sodom, and that night
In Gibeah, when the hospitable door
Expos'd a Matron to avoid **worse rape**.
These were the prime in order and in might;

The rest were long to tell, though far renown'd,
Th' Ionian Gods, of **Javans** Issue held
Gods, yet confest later then Heav'n and Earth
Thir **boasted Parents**; Titan Heav'ns first born
With his enormous brood, and birthright seis'd
By younger Saturn, he from mightier Jove
His own and Rhea's Son like measure found;
So Jove usurping reign'd: these first in **Creet**
And Ida known, thence on the Snowy top
Of cold **Olympus** rul'd the middle Air
Thir highest Heav'n; or on the **Delphian** Cliff,
Or in Dodona, and through all the bounds
Of **Doric Land**; or who with Saturn old
Fled over **Adria** to th' **Hesperian Fields,**
And ore the Celtic roam'd the **utmost Isles.**
All these and more came flocking; but with looks
Down cast and damp, yet such wherein appear'd
Obscure some glimps of joy, to have found thir chief
Not in despair, to have found themselves not lost
In loss it self; which on his count'nance cast
Like doubtful hue: but he his wonted pride
Soon recollecting, with high words, that bore
Semblance of worth, not substance, gently rais'd
Thir fainting courage, and dispel'd thir fears.
Then strait commands that at the warlike sound
Of Trumpets loud and Clarions bc upreard
His mighty Standard; that proud honour claim'd
Azazel as his right, a Cherube tall:
Who forthwith from the glittering Staff unfurld
Th' Imperial Ensign, which full high advanc't
Shon like a Meteor streaming to the Wind
With Gemms and Golden lustre rich imblaz'd,
Seraphic arms and Trophies: all the while
Sonorous mettal blowing Martial sounds:
At which the universal Host upsent
A shout that tore Hells Concave, and beyond
Frighted the Reign of **Chaos** and old Night.
All in a moment through the gloom were seen
Ten thousand Banners rise into the Air
With Orient Colours waving: with them rose
A Forest huge of Spears: and thronging Helms
Appear'd, and serried shields in thick array
Of depth immeasurable: Anon they move
In perfect **Phalanx** to the Dorian mood
Of Flutes and soft Recorders; such as rais'd
To hight of noblest temper Hero's old

Arming to Battel, and in stead of rage
Deliberate valour breath'd, firm and unmov'd
With dread of death to flight or foul retreat,
Nor wanting power to mitigate and **swage**
With solemn touches, troubl'd thoughts, and chase
Anguish and doubt and fear and sorrow and pain
From mortal or immortal minds. Thus they
Breathing united force with fixed thought
Mov'd on in silence to soft Pipes that charm'd
Thir painful steps o're the burnt soyle; and now
Advanc't in view, they stand, a horrid Front
Of dreadful length and dazling Arms, in guise
Of Warriers old with order'd Spear and Shield,
Awaiting what command thir mighty Chief
Had to impose: He through the armed Files
Darts his experienc't eye, and soon traverse
The whole Battalion views, thir order due,
Thir visages and stature as of Gods,
Thir number last he summs. And now his heart
Distends with pride, and hardning in his strength
Glories: For never since created man,
Met such imbodied force, as nam'd with these
Could merit more then that small infantry
Warr'd on by Cranes: though all the Giant brood
Of **Phlegra** with th' Heroic Race were joyn'd
That fought at **Theb's** and Ilium, on each side
Mixt with auxiliar Gods; and what resounds
In Fable or Romance of **Uthers** Son
Begirt with British and **Armoric** Knights;
And all who since, Baptiz'd or Infidel
Jousted in **Aspramont** or **Montalban**,
Damasco, or **Morocco, or Trebisond**,
Or whom **Biserta** sent from Afric shore
When Charlemain with all his Peerage fell
By Fontarabbia. Thus far these beyond
Compare of mortal prowess, yet observ'd
Thir dread commander: he above the rest
In shape and gesture proudly eminent
Stood like a Towr; his form had yet not lost
All her Original brightness, nor appear'd
Less then Arch Angel ruind, and th' excess
Of Glory obscur'd: As when the Sun new ris'n
Looks through the Horizontal misty Air
Shorn of his Beams, or from behind the Moon
In dim Eclips disastrous twilight sheds
On half the Nations, and with fear of change

Perplexes Monarchs. Dark'n'd so, yet shon
Above them all th' Arch Angel: but his face
Deep scars of Thunder had intrencht, and care
Sat on his faded cheek, but under Browes
Of dauntless courage, and considerate Pride
Waiting revenge: cruel his eye, but cast
Signs of remorse and passion to behold
The fellows of his crime, the followers rather
(Far other once beheld in bliss) condemn'd
For ever now to have thir lot in pain,
Millions of Spirits for his fault **amerc't**
Of Heav'n, and from Eternal Splendors flung
For his revolt, yet faithfull how they stood,
Thir Glory witherd. As when Heavens Fire
Hath scath'd the Forrest Oaks, or Mountain Pines,
With singed top thir stately growth though bare
Stands on the blasted Heath. He now prepar'd
To speak; whereat thir doubl'd Ranks they bend
From wing to wing, and half enclose him round
With all his Peers: attention held them mute.
Thrice he assayd, and thrice in spight of scorn,
Tears such as Angels weep, burst forth: at last
Words interwove with sighs found out thir way.
O Myriads of immortal Spirits, O Powers
Matchless, but with th' Almighty, and that strife
Was not inglorious, though **th' event** was dire,
As this place testifies, and this dire change
Hateful to utter: but what power of mind
Foreseeing or presaging, from the Depth
Of knowledge past or present, could have fear'd,
How such united force of Gods, how such
As stood like these, could ever know repulse?
For who can yet beleeve, though after loss,
That all these **puissant** Legions, whose exile
Hath emptied Heav'n, shall fail to re-ascend
Self-rais'd, and repossess thir native seat?
For mee be witness all the Host of Heav'n,
If counsels different, or danger shun'd
By me, have lost our hopes. But he who reigns
Monarch in Heav'n, till then as one secure
Sat on his Throne, upheld by old repute,
Consent or custome, and his Regal State
Put forth at full, but still his strength conceal'd,
Which tempted our attempt, and wrought our fall.
Henceforth his might we know, and know our own
So as not either to provoke, or dread

New warr, provok't; our better part remains
To work in close design, by fraud or guile
What force effected not: that he no less
At length from us may find, who overcomes
By force, hath overcome but half his foe.
Space may produce new Worlds; whereof so rife
There went a **fame** in Heav'n that he ere long
Intended to create, and therein plant
A generation, whom his choice regard
Should favour equal to the Sons of Heaven:
Thither, if but to pry, shall be perhaps
Our first eruption, thither or elsewhere:
For this Infernal Pit shall never hold
Cælestial Spirits in Bondage, nor th' Abyss
Long under darkness cover. But these thoughts
Full Counsel must mature: Peace is despaird,
For who can think Submission? Warr then, Warr
Open or understood must be resolv'd.

He spake: and to confirm his words, out-flew
Millions of flaming swords, drawn from the thighs
Of mighty **Cherubim**; the sudden blaze
Far round illumin'd hell: highly they rag'd
Against the Highest, and fierce with grasped arms
Clash'd on thir sounding Shields the din of war,
Hurling defiance toward the vault of Heav'n.

There stood a Hill not far whose griesly top
Belch'd fire and rowling smoak; the rest entire
Shon with a glossie scurff, undoubted sign
That in his womb was hid metallic Ore,
The work of Sulphur. Thither wing'd with speed
A numerous Brigad hasten'd. As when Bands
Of **Pioners** with Spade and Pickax arm'd
Forerun the Royal Camp, to trench a Field,
Or cast a Rampart. **Mammon** led them on,
Mammon, the least erected Spirit that fell
From heav'n, for ev'n in heav'n his looks and thoughts
Were always downward bent, admiring more
The riches of Heav'ns pavement, trod'n Gold,
Then aught divine or holy else enjoy'd
In vision beatific: by him first
Men also, and by his suggestion taught,
Ransack'd the Center, and with impious hands
Rifl'd the bowels of thir mother Earth
For Treasures better hid. Soon had his crew

Op'nd into the Hill a spacious wound
And dig'd out ribs of Gold. Let none admire
That riches grow in Hell; that soyle may best
Deserve the precious bane. And here let those
Who boast in mortal things, and wond'ring tell
Of Babel, and the works of **Memphian** Kings
Learn how thir greatest Monuments of Fame,
And Strength and Art are easily out-done
By Spirits reprobate, and in an hour
What in an age they with incessant toyle
And hands innumerable scarce perform.
Nigh on the Plain in many cells prepar'd,
That underneath had veins of liquid fire
Sluc'd from the Lake, a second multitude
With wondrous Art found out the massie Ore,
Severing each kind, and scum'd the Bullion dross:
A third as soon had form'd within the ground
A various mould, and from the boyling cells
By strange conveyance fill'd each hollow nook,
As in an Organ from one blast of wind
To many a row of Pipes the sound-board breaths.
Anon out of the earth a Fabrick huge
Rose like an Exhalation, with the sound
Of Dulcet Symphonies and voices sweet,
Built like a Temple, where Pilasters round
Were set, and Doric pillars overlaid
With Golden Architrave; nor did there want
Cornice or Freeze, with **bossy** Sculptures grav'n,
The Roof was **fretted Gold**. Not Babilon,
Nor great **Alcairo** such magnificence
Equal'd in all thir glories, to inshrine
Belus or Serapis thir Gods, or seat
Thir Kings, when Ægypt with Assyria strove
In wealth and luxurie. Th' ascending pile
Stood fixt her stately highth, and strait the dores
Op'ning thir brazen foulds discover wide
Within, her ample spaces, o're the smooth
And level pavement: from the arched roof
Pendant by suttle Magic many a row
Of Starry Lamps and blazing **Cressets** fed
With Naphtha and Asphaltus yeilded light
As from a sky. The hasty multitude
Admiring enter'd, and the work some praise
And some the Architect: his hand was known
In Heav'n by many a Towred structure high,
Where Scepter'd Angels held thir residence,

And sat as Princes, whom the supreme King
Exalted to such power, and gave to rule,
Each in his Hierarchie, the Orders bright.
Nor was his name unheard or unador'd
In ancient Greece; and in **Ausonian land**
Men call'd him **Mulciber**; and how he fell
From Heav'n, they fabl'd, thrown by angry Jove
Sheer o're the Chrystal Battlements: from Morn
To Noon he fell, from Noon to dewy Eve,
A Summers day; and with the setting Sun
Dropt from the Zenith like a falling Star,
On Lemnos th' Ægean Ile: thus **they relate,**
Erring; for he with this rebellious rout
Fell long before; nor aught avail'd him now
To have built in Heav'n high Towrs; nor did he scape
By all his Engins, but was headlong sent
With his industrious crew to build in hell.
Meanwhile the winged Haralds by command
Of Sovran power, with **awful** Ceremony
And Trumpets sound throughout the Host proclaim
A solemn Councel forthwith to be held
At **Pandæmonium**, the high Capital
Of Satan and his Peers: thir summons call'd
From every Band and squared Regiment
By place or choice the worthiest; they anon
With hunderds and with thousands trooping came
Attended: all access was throng'd, the Gates
And Porches wide, but chief the spacious Hall
(Though like a cover'd field, where Champions bold
Wont ride in arm'd, and at the Soldans chair
Defi'd the best of **Paynim** chivalry
To mortal combat or carreer with Lance)
Thick swarm'd, both on the ground and in the air,
Brusht with the hiss of russling wings. As **Bees**
In spring time, when the Sun with Taurus rides,
Pour forth thir populous youth about the Hive
In clusters; they among fresh dews and flowers
Flie to and fro, or on the smoothed Plank,
The suburb of thir Straw-built Cittadel,
New rub'd with Baum, expatiate and confer
Thir State affairs. So thick the aerie crowd
Swarm'd and were straitn'd; till the Signal giv'n.
Behold a wonder! they but now who seemd
In bigness to surpass Earths Giant Sons
Now less then smallest Dwarfs, in narrow room
Throng numberless, like that **Pigmean Race**

Beyond the Indian Mount, or Faerie Elves,
Whose midnight Revels, by a Forrest side
Or Fountain **some belated Peasant** sees,
Or dreams he sees, while over-head the Moon
Sits Arbitress, and neerer to the Earth
Wheels her pale course, they on thir mirth and dance
Intent, with jocond Music charm his ear;
At once with joy and fear his heart rebounds.
Thus incorporeal Spirits to smallest forms
Reduc'd thir shapes immense, and were at large,
Though without number still amidst the Hall
Of that infernal Court. But far within
And in thir own dimensions like themselves
The great Seraphic Lords and Cherubim
In close recess and secret **conclave** sat
A thousand Demi-Gods on golden seats,
Frequent and full. After short silence then
And summons read, the great consult began.

Notes

Death into the World, and all our woe: Death follows nuptials in classical myth; this is a reference to the wedding of Aeneas and Dido in the *Aeneid*. **one greater Man:** the Messiah **Heav'nly Muse:** possibly the Holy Spirit, or even Urania **Oreb:** Moses **chosen Seed:** the Israelites **In the beginning:** the opening lines of *Genesis*: 'In the Beginning was the Word' **Sion:** Mt Sion, here represented as Parnassus or its equivalent **Out of chaos:** unformed matter **Aonian Mount:** Mt Helicon, Aonia, sacred to the classical muses **Dove-like:** the Holy Spirit which appeared as a dove according to the Bible **one restraint:** the prohibition against eating from the tree of knowledge **Adamantine:** unbreakable **Nine times the Space:** The Titans in classical mythology had fallen likewise. **from the Center thrice to the utmost Pole:** Milton asks us to refer to the Ptolemaic model of the universe with the earth at the centre of nine concentric spheres. **Beelzebub:** 'Chief of the devils' **call'd Satan:** Milton is referring to the renaming of Lucifer ('bringer of light') as Satan ('enemy'). **thralls:** slaves **rood:** a rod of about six inches **Titanian:** the Titans who warred with Jove and the gods **Briareos:** who sided with the Titans **Typhon:** Typhon is the offspring of Gaia and Tartarus. His mate is Echidna and both were so fearful that when the gods saw them they changed into animals and fled in terror. **Leviathan:** a sea monster referred to in the Bible. He is one of the seven princes of Hell and its gatekeeper. The word has become synonymous with any large sea monster or creature. **incumbent:** pressing upon **Pelorus:** peninsula in Sicily; Mount Aetna is located here. **Stygian:** refers to Styx, one of the rivers of hell **Ethereal temper:** tempered in heavenly fire, like Aeneas' shield **Optic glass:** the telescope **Tuscan artist:** Galileo (Milton is known to have visited him) **Fesole:** Fiesole, a town near Florence **Valdarno:** the Arno valley, where Florence is located **Ammiral:** flagship **Marle:** a kind of clay **Vallombrosa:** a shady valley near Florence **Etrurian shades:** Etrurian is 'Etruscan', from the Tuscany region of Italy **sedge:** seaweed **Orion:** constellation **Busirus:** Greek name for Pharaoh **Sojourners of Goshen:** the Israelites **Cherube and Seraph:** the two orders of angels **Amrams son**: Moses **Cope:** canopy of heaven **great Sultan:** Satan as Sultan (Here Milton equates Islam with demonism.) **populous North:** refers to the northern parts of Europe from where the barbarian supposedly came to plunder Rome **Rhene or the Danaw:** Rhine and Danube **Devils…for Deities:** Traditionally, fallen angels became pagan deities. **Moloch:** king **children's cries unheard:** The cries of children being sacrificed to Moloch were drowned out by drums. **Ammonite:** Israelites destroyed the Ammonite tribes. **Rabba:** the capital of the Ammonites, now Amman **Argob, Basan, Arnon**: lands east of the Dead Sea, where Moloch was worshipped, known today as Jordan **Hinnom:** also known as Gehinnom, the valley where human sacrifices were made to Moloch **Chemos:** a deity to whom Solomon built a shrine **Aroar:** Aroer, now Arair in modern Jordan **Nebo:** southern Moabite town; also, the name of the mountain from which Moses first glimpsed the promised land of Canaan **Abarim:** hill of western Moab, overlooking the Jordan and the Dead Sea **Hesebon:** Heshbon and Horonaim were Amorite cities. Sihon (Milton's Seon) was king of the Amorites. **Sibma:** region east of the Jordan famous for its wine **Eleale:** a city in Jordan **Asphaltick Pool:** the Dead Sea **Israel in Sittim:** Israelites who slept with the daughters of Moab at Shittim **Hill of Scandal:** the Mount of Olives, east of the Jerusalem temple, where Solomon erected temples to deities like Moloch, Baal, Chemosh, and Ashtoreth. Later these were destroyed by King Josiah. **Baalim and Ashtaroth:** Baal and Astarte. Baal-Peor was a place of worship of Baal, Astarte was the goddess of fertility and war. **Essence pure:** Angels are non-corporeal, being pure spirit. **Sidonian:** Phoenician **Sion:** Israel's promised land **th' offensive Mountain:** the 'Hill of Scandal', the Mount of Olives, east of the Jerusalem temple, where Solomon erected temples to deities such as Moloch, Baal, Chemosh, and Ashtoreth. Later these were destroyed by King Josiah. **uxorious King:** Solomon, who had several hundred wives **Thammuz:** lover and spouse of Sumerian Inanna; identified with Adonis **Adonis:** Lebanese river **Sions daughters:** Israelite women **alienated:** alienated from God; apostate **grunsel:** threshold **Dagon:** a Philistine sea-God **Azotus:** or Ashdod, one of the five cities of Philistia (the others are Askelon, Ekron, Gath and Gaza) **Rimmon:** Hadad, the west Semitic god of weather **A Leper once he lost:** When the prophet Elisha told the Syrian Naaman that bathing in the Jordan would cure his leprosy, Naaman scoffed. Later he bathed in the Jordan and was cured and then he began to worship the God of Israel. **Osiris, Orus, Isis:** Osiris was the Egyptian god; Isis was his consort and mother of Horus. **Rebel King:** Jereboam **Belial:** usually a synonym for Satan **Ely's sons:** Hophni and Phinehas, notorious for their wild revelries **flown:** a sheet or sail that flies in the wind **worse rape:** Milton suggests that rape of men is 'worse' than the rape of women. **Javan:** Japhet's son and therefore Noah's grandson **boasted Parents:** here Heaven and Earth, believed to be the parents of the Titans **Creet:** Crete Rhea, pregnant with Zeus, feared that Chronus would try to destroy the child prophesied to supplant him; so she hid in Crete and bore Zeus in a cave there. **Olympus:** the home of the gods **Delphian:** the oracle of Delphi **Doric Land:** Greece **Adria:** Adriatic Sea **Hesperian Fields:** Italy **utmost Isles:** British isles **Azazel:** Hebrew for 'scapegoat' **Chaos:** In Miltonian cosmology, Chaos and Night reigned over the 'eternal anarchy', the void between hell and heaven. **Phalanx:** a body of infantry **swage:** assuage **Warr'd on by Cranes:** Homer compares the cries of the Trojans to the sound made by cranes in their annual rush to the sea. **Phlegra:** place in Macedonia where the giants battle with the gods (from Ovid) **Theb's:** the

'Heroic Race', the seven heroes of the Trojan war **Uthers Son:** King Arthur, son of Uther Pendragon **Armoric:** Brittany, north France **Aspramont or Montalban:** castles in romances; these were the sites of tournaments. **Damasco, Morocco, Trebisond:** sites from romances where tournaments between Christian and pagans were held **Biserta:** The Muslims supposedly set out from Bizerte in Tunisia to conquer Carolingian Spain. **Perplexes monarchs:** Eclipses were traditionally believed to portend the fall of monarchs. **amerc't:** deprived **th' event:** the result **puissant:** powerful **fame:** here, rumour **Pioners:** trench-diggers **Mammon:** Aramaic term for 'wealth' **Memphian:** Egyptian **bossy:** embossed or engraved **fretted Gold:** adorned with carving **Alcairo:** Cairo **Belus or Serapis:** Belus, Latin form of Bel, Mesopotamian god of the air, also known as Baal; Sarapis is the Greco-Egyptian god of the sun. **Cressets:** iron basket lamps **Ausonian land:** Italy **Mulciber:** Vulcan, the gods' smith **they relate:** This refers to Homer's and Lucretius' accounts of Hephaistos's fall. **awful:** here, awe-inspiring **Pandæmonium:** Milton's coinage from the Greek 'pan' ('all'), daimon ('demon' or 'mortal-to-god go-between') and ion ('assembly'). **Paynim:** another name for 'pagan' **Bees:** Homeric description of the Achaean assembly as 'busy bees' in the *Iliad.* Virgil does this for the Carthaginians in *Aeneid.* **Pigmean Race:** In ancient geography pygmies came from lands beyond the Ganges. **some belated Peasant:** Milton echoes the episode of Bottom's dream in Shakespeare's *A Midsummer Night's Dream.* **conclave:** the conclave of cardinals who elect the pope. Milton suggests a demonic character to such conclaves.

Book 9

THE ARGUMENT

Satan having compast the Earth, returns as a mist by Night into Paradise, enters into the Serpent sleeping. Adam and Eve in the Morning go forth to thir labours, which Eve proposes to divide in several places, each labouring apart: Adam consents not, alledging the danger, lest that Enemy, of whom they were forewarn'd, should attempt her found alone: Eve loath to be thought not circumspect or firm enough, urges her going apart, the rather desirous to make tryal of her strength; Adam at last yields: The Serpent finds her alone; his subtle approach, first gazing, then speaking, with much flattery extolling Eve above all other Creatures. Eve wondring to hear the Serpent speak, asks how he attain'd to human speech and such understanding not till now; the Serpent answers, that by tasting of a certain Tree in the Garden he attain'd both to Speech and Reason, till then void of both: Eve requires him to bring her to that Tree, and finds it to be the Tree of Knowledge forbidden: The Serpent now grown bolder, with many wiles and arguments induces her at length to eat; she pleas'd with the taste deliberates a while whether to impart thereof to Adam or not, at last brings him of the Fruit, relates what perswaded her to eat thereof: Adam at first amaz'd, but perceiving her lost, resolves through vehemence of love to perish with her; and extenuating the trespass, eats also of the Fruit: The Effects thereof in them both; they seek to cover thir nakedness; then fall to variance and accusation of one another.

No more of talk where God or Angel Guest
With Man, as with his Friend, familiar us'd
To sit indulgent, and with him partake
Rural repast, permitting him the while
Venial discourse unblam'd: I now must change
Those Notes to Tragic; foul distrust, and breach
Disloyal on the part of Man, revolt,
And disobedience: On the part of Heav'n
Now alienated, distance and distaste,
Anger and just rebuke, and judgement giv'n,
That brought **into this World a world of woe**,
Sinne and her shadow Death, and Miserie
Deaths Harbinger: Sad task, yet **argument**
Not less but more Heroic then **the wrauth**
Of stern Achilles on **his Foe** pursu'd
Thrice Fugitive about Troy Wall; or rage
Of **Turnus for Lavinia** disespous'd,
Or Neptun's ire or Juno's, that so long
Perplex'd **the Greek** and **Cytherea's Son**;
If **answerable** style I can obtaine
Of my **Celestial Patroness**, who deignes
Her nightly visitation unimplor'd,
And dictates to me slumb'ring, or inspires
Easie my unpremeditated Verse:
Since first this Subject for Heroic Song
Pleas'd me long choosing, and **beginning late**;
Not sedulous by Nature to indite
Warrs, hitherto the onely Argument
Heroic deem'd, chief maistrie to dissect
With long and tedious havoc fabl'd Knights
In Battels feign'd; the better fortitude
Of Patience and Heroic Martyrdom
Unsung; or to describe Races and Games,
Or **tilting Furniture**, emblazon'd Shields,
Impreses quaint, Caparisons and Steeds;
Bases and tinsel Trappings, gorgious Knights
At Joust and Torneament; then marshal'd Feast
Serv'd up in Hall with **Sewers, and Seneschals**;
The **skill of Artifice** or Office mean,
Not that which justly gives Heroic name
To Person or to Poem. Mee of these

Nor skilld nor studious, higher Argument
Remaines, sufficient of it self to raise
That name, unless an age too late, or **cold**
Climat, or Years damp my intended wing
Deprest, and much they may, if all be mine,
Not Hers who brings it nightly to my Ear.

The Sun was sunk, and after him the Starr
Of **Hesperus**, whose Office is to bring
Twilight upon the Earth, short Arbiter
Twixt Day and Night, and now from end to end
Nights Hemisphere had veild the Horizon round:
When Satan who late fled before the threats
Of Gabriel out of Eden, now improv'd
In meditated fraud and malice, bent
On mans destruction, maugre what might hap
Of heavier on himself, fearless return'd.
By Night he fled, and at Midnight return'd.
From compassing the Earth, cautious of day,
Since **Uriel** Regent of the Sun descri'd
His entrance, and forewarnd the **Cherubim**
That kept thir watch; thence full of anguish driv'n,
The space of seven continu'd Nights he rode
With darkness, thrice the Equinoctial Line
He circl'd, four times cross'd the **Carr of Night**
From Pole to Pole, traversing each **Colure**;
On the eighth return'd, and on the Coast averse
From entrance or Cherubic Watch, by stealth
Found unsuspected way. There was a place,
Now not, though Sin, not Time, first wraught the change,
Where **Tigris** at the foot of Paradise
Into a Gulf shot under ground, till part
Rose up a Fountain by the Tree of Life;
In with the River sunk, and with it rose
Satan involv'd in rising Mist, then sought
Where to lie hid; Sea he had searcht and Land
From Eden over **Pontus**, and the **Poole**
Mæotis, up beyond the **River Ob**;
Downward as farr Antartic; and in length
West from **Orontes** to the Ocean **barr'd**
At **Darien**, thence to the Land where flowes
Ganges and Indus: thus the **Orb** he roam'd
With narrow search; and with inspection deep
Consider'd every Creature, which of all
Most opportune might serve his Wiles, and found

The Serpent suttlest Beast of all the Field.
Him after long debate, irresolute
Of thoughts revolv'd, his final sentence chose
Fit Vessel, fittest Imp of fraud, in whom
To enter, and his dark suggestions hide
From sharpest sight: for in the wilie Snake,
Whatever sleights none would suspicious mark,
As from his wit and native suttletie
Proceeding, which in other Beasts observ'd
Doubt might beget of Diabolic pow'r
Active within beyond the sense of brute.
Thus he resolv'd, but first from inward griefe
His bursting passion into plaints thus pour'd:

O Earth, how like to Heav'n, if not preferr'd
More justly, Seat worthier of Gods, as built
With **second thoughts**, reforming what was old!
For what God after better worse would build?
Terrestrial Heav'n, danc't round by other Heav'ns
That shine, yet bear thir bright **officious** Lamps,
Light above Light, for thee alone, as seems,
In thee concentring all thir precious beams
Of sacred influence: As God in Heav'n
Is Center, yet extends to all, so thou
Centring receav'st from all those Orbs; in thee,
Not in themselves, all thir known vertue appeers
Productive in Herb, Plant, and nobler birth
Of Creatures animate with gradual life
Of Growth, Sense, Reason, all summ'd up in Man.
With what delight could I have walkt thee round,
If I could joy in aught, sweet interchange
Of Hill, and Vallie, Rivers, Woods and Plaines,
Now Land, now Sea, and Shores with Forrest crownd,
Rocks, Dens, and Caves; but I in none of these
Find place or refuge; and the more I see
Pleasures about me, so much more I feel
Torment within me, as from the hateful siege
Of contraries; all good to me becomes
Bane, and in Heav'n much worse would be my state.
But neither here seek I, no nor in Heav'n
To dwell, unless by maistring Heav'ns Supreame;
Nor hope to be my self less miserable
By what I seek, but others to make such
As I, though thereby worse to me redound:
For onely in destroying I find ease
To my relentless thoughts; and him destroyd,

Or won to what may work his utter loss,
For whom all this was made, all this will soon
Follow, as to him linkt in weal or woe,
In wo then: that destruction wide may range:
To mee shall be the glorie sole among
The infernal Powers, in one day to have marr'd
What he Almightie styl'd, six Nights and Days
Continu'd making, and who knows how long
Before had bin contriving, though perhaps
Not longer then since I in one Night freed
From servitude inglorious welnigh half
Th' Angelic Name, and thinner left the throng
Of his adorers: hee to be aveng'd,
And to repaire his numbers thus impair'd,
Whether such **vertue** spent of old now faild
More Angels to Create, **if they at least**
Are his Created, or to spite us more,
Determin'd to advance **into our room**
A Creature form'd of Earth, and him endow,
Exalted from so base original,
With Heav'nly spoils, **our spoils**: What he decreed
He effected; Man he made, and for him built
Magnificent this World, and Earth his seat,
Him Lord pronounc'd, and, O indignitie!
Subjected to his service Angel wings,
And flaming Ministers to watch and tend
Thir earthy Charge: Of these the vigilance
I dread, and to elude, thus wrapt in mist
Of midnight vapor glide obscure, and prie
In every Bush and Brake, where hap may finde
The Serpent sleeping, in whose mazie foulds
To hide me, and the dark intent I bring.
O foul descent! that I who erst contended
With Gods to sit the highest, am now constraind
Into a Beast, and mixt with bestial slime,
This essence to **incarnate and imbrute**,
That to the hight of Deitie aspir'd;
But what will not Ambition and Revenge
Descend to? who aspires must down as low
As high he soard, **obnoxious** first or last
To basest things. Revenge, at first though sweet,
Bitter ere long back on it self recoiles;
Let it; I reck not, so it light well aim'd,
Since higher I fall short, on him who next
Provokes my envie, this new Favorite
Of Heav'n, this Man of Clay, Son of despite,

Whom us the more to **spite** his Maker rais'd
From dust: spite then with spite is best repaid.

So saying, through each Thicket Danck or Drie,
Like a black mist low creeping, he held on
His midnight search, where soonest he might finde
The Serpent: him fast sleeping soon he found
In Labyrinth of many a round self-rowld,
His head the midst, well stor'd with suttle wiles:
Not yet in horrid Shade or dismal Den,
Nor nocent yet, but on the grassie Herbe
Fearless unfeard he slept: in at his Mouth
The Devil enterd, and his brutal sense,
In heart or head, possessing soon inspir'd
With act intelligential; but his sleep
Disturbd not, waiting **close** th' approach of Morn.
Now **when as** sacred Light began to dawne
In Eden on the humid Flours, that breathd
Thir morning incense, when all things that breath,
From th' Earths great Altar send up silent praise
To the Creator, and his Nostrils fill
With grateful Smell, forth came the human pair
And joind thir vocal Worship to the Quire
Of Creatures **wanting** voice, that done, partake
The season, prime for sweetest Sents and Aires:
Then commune how that day they best may ply
Thir growing work: for much thir work outgrew
The hands dispatch of two Gardning so wide.
And Eve first to her Husband thus began.

Adam, well may we labour still to dress
This Garden, still to tend Plant, Herb and Flour,
Our pleasant task enjoyn'd, but till more hands
Aid us, the work under our labour grows,
Luxurious by restraint; what we by day
Lop overgrown, or prune, or prop, or bind,
One night or two with wanton growth derides
Tending to wilde. Thou therefore now advise
Or hear what to my minde first thoughts present,
Let us divide our labours, thou where choice
Leads thee, or where most needs, whether to wind
The Woodbine round this Arbour, or direct
The clasping Ivie where to climb, while I
In yonder **Spring** of Roses intermixt
With Myrtle, find what to redress till Noon:
For while so near each other thus all day

Our taske we choose, what wonder if so near
Looks intervene and smiles, or object new
Casual discourse draw on, which intermits
Our dayes work brought to little, though begun
Early, and th' hour of Supper comes unearn'd.

To whom mild answer Adam thus return'd.
Sole Eve, Associate sole, to me beyond
Compare above all living Creatures deare,
Well hast thou **motion'd**, well thy thoughts imployd
How we might best fulfill the work which here
God hath assign'd us, nor of me shalt pass
Unprais'd: for nothing lovelier can be found
In Woman, then to studie houshold good,
And good workes in her Husband to promote.
Yet not so strictly hath our Lord impos'd
Labour, as to debarr us when we need
Refreshment, whether food, or talk between,
Food of the mind, or this sweet intercourse
Of looks and smiles, for smiles from Reason flow,
To brute deni'd, and are of Love the food,
Love not the lowest end of human life.
For not to irksom toile, but to delight
He made us, and delight to Reason joyn'd.
These paths and Bowers doubt not but our joynt hands
Will keep from Wilderness with ease, as wide
As we need walk, till younger hands ere long
Assist us: But if much converse perhaps
Thee satiate, to short absence I could yield.
For solitude somtimes is best societie,
And short retirement urges sweet returne.
But other doubt possesses me, least harm
Befall thee sever'd from me; for thou knowst
What hath bin warn'd us, what malicious Foe
Envying our happiness, and of his own
Despairing, seeks to work us woe and shame
By sly assault; and somwhere nigh at hand
Watches, no doubt, with greedy hope to find
His wish and best advantage, us asunder,
Hopeless to circumvent us joynd, where each
To other speedie aide might lend at need;
Whether his first design be to withdraw
Our fealtie from God, or to disturb
Conjugal Love, then which perhaps no bliss
Enjoy'd by us excites his envie more;
Or this, or worse, leave not the faithful side

That gave thee being, still shades thee and protects.
The Wife, where danger or dishonour lurks,
Safest and seemliest by her Husband staies,
Who guards her, or with her the worst endures.

To whom the **Virgin** Majestie of Eve,
As one who loves, and some unkindness meets,
With sweet austeer composure thus reply'd,

Ofspring of Heav'n and Earth, and all Earths Lord,
That such an Enemie we have, who seeks
Our ruin, both by thee informd I learne,
And from the parting Angel over-heard
As in a shadie nook I stood behind,
Just then returnd at shut of Evening Flours.
But that thou shouldst my firmness therfore doubt
To God or thee, because we have a foe
May tempt it, I expected not to hear.
His violence thou fear'st not, being such,
As wee, not capable of death or paine,
Can either not receave, or can repell.
His fraud is then thy fear, which plain inferrs
Thy equal fear that my firm Faith and Love
Can by his fraud be shak'n or seduc't;
Thoughts, which how found they harbour in thy brest
Adam, **misthought** of her to thee so dear?

To whom with healing words Adam replyd.
Daughter of God and Man, immortal Eve,
For such thou art, from sin and blame **entire**:
Not diffident of thee do I dissuade
Thy absence from my sight, but to avoid
Th' attempt itself, intended by our Foe.
For hee who tempts, though in vain, at least asperses
The tempted with dishonour foul, suppos'd
Not incorruptible of Faith, not prooff
Against temptation: thou thy self with scorne
And anger wouldst resent the offer'd wrong,
Though ineffectual found: misdeem not then,
If such affront I labour to avert
From thee alone, which on us both at once
The Enemie, though bold, will hardly dare,
Or daring, first on mee th' assault shall light.
Nor thou his malice and false guile contemn;
Suttle he needs must be, who could seduce
Angels nor think superfluous others aid.

I from the influence of thy looks receave
Access in every Vertue, in thy sight
More wise, more watchful, stronger, if need were
Of outward strength; while shame, thou looking on,
Shame to be overcome or over-reacht
Would utmost vigor raise, and rais'd unite.
Why shouldst not thou like sense within thee feel
When I am present, and thy trial choose
With me, best witness of thy Vertue tri'd.

So spake domestick Adam in his care
And Matrimonial Love; but Eve, who thought
Less attributed to her Faith sincere,
Thus her reply with accent sweet renewd.

If this be our condition, thus to dwell
In narrow circuit **strait'nd** by a Foe,
Suttle or violent, we not endu'd
Single with like defence, wherever met,
How are we happie, still in fear of harm?
But harm precedes not sin: onely our Foe
Tempting affronts us with his foul esteem
Of our integritie: his foul esteeme
Sticks no dishonor on our **Front**, but turns
Foul on himself; then wherefore shund or feard
By us? who rather double honour gaine
From his surmise prov'd false, find peace within,
Favour from Heav'n, our witness from th' event.
And what is Faith, Love, Vertue unassaild
Alone, without exterior help sustaind?
Let us not then suspect our happie State
Left so imperfet by the Maker wise,
As not secure to single or combin'd.
Fraile is our happiness, if this be so,
And Eden were no Eden thus expos'd.

To whom thus Adam fervently repli'd.
O Woman, best are all things as the will
Of God ordain'd them, his creating hand
Nothing imperfet or deficient left
Of all that he Created, much less Man,
Or aught that might his happie State secure,
Secure from outward force; within himself
The danger lies, yet lies within his power:
Against his will he can receave no harme.
But God left free the Will, for what obeyes
Reason, is free, and Reason he made right

But bid her well beware, and still **erect**,
Least by some faire appeering good surpris'd
She dictate false, and misinforme the Will
To do what God expresly hath forbid,
Not then mistrust, but tender love enjoynes,
That I should mind thee oft, and mind thou me.
Firm we subsist, yet possible to swerve,
Since Reason not impossibly may meet
Some specious object by the Foe subornd,
And fall into deception unaware,
Not keeping strictest watch, as she was warnd.
Seek not temptation then, which to avoide
Were better, and most likelie if from mee
Thou sever not: Trial will come unsought.
Wouldst thou **approve** thy constancie, approve
First thy obedience; th' other who can know,
Not seeing thee attempted, who attest?
But if thou think, trial unsought may finde
Us both securer then thus warnd thou seemst,
Go; for thy stay, not free, absents thee more;
Go in thy native innocence, relie
On what thou hast of vertue, summon all,
For God towards thee hath done his part, do thine.

So spake the Patriarch of Mankinde, but Eve
Persisted, yet **submiss**, though last, repli'd.

With thy permission then, and thus forewarnd
Chiefly by what thy own last reasoning words
Touchd onely, that our trial, when least sought,
May finde us both perhaps farr less prepar'd,
The willinger I goe, nor much expect
A Foe so proud will first the weaker seek,
So bent, the more shall shame him his repulse.
Thus saying, from her Husbands hand her hand
Soft she withdrew, and like a Wood-Nymph light
Oread or Dryad, or of **Delia's** Traine,
Betook her to the Groves, but Delia's self
In gate surpass'd and Goddess-like **deport**,
Though not as shee with Bow and Quiver armd,

But with such Gardning Tools as Art yet rude,
Guiltless of fire had formd, or Angels brought.
To **Pales**, or **Pomona**, thus adornd,
Likeliest she seemd, Pomona when she fled
Vertumnus, or to **Ceres** in her Prime,

Yet Virgin of Proserpina from Jove.
Her long with ardent look his Eye pursu'd
Delighted, but desiring more her stay.
Oft he to her his charge of quick returne
Repeated, shee to him as oft engag'd
To be returnd by Noon amid the Bowre,
And all things in best order to invite
Noontide repast, or Afternoons repose.
O much deceav'd, much failing, hapless Eve,
Of thy presum'd return! event perverse!
Thou never from that houre in Paradise
Foundst either sweet repast, or sound repose;
Such ambush hid among sweet Flours and Shades
Waited with hellish rancour imminent
To intercept thy way, or send thee back
Despoild of Innocence, of Faith, of Bliss.
For now, and since first break of dawne the Fiend,
Meer Serpent in appearance, forth was come,
And on his Quest, where likeliest he might finde
The onely two of Mankinde, but in them
The whole included Race, his purposd prey.
In Bowre and Field he sought, where any tuft
Of Grove or Garden-Plot more pleasant lay,
Thir **tendance** or Plantation for delight,
By Fountain or by shadie Rivulet

He sought them both, but wish'd his hap might find
Eve separate, he wish'd, but not with hope
Of what so seldom chanc'd, when to his wish,
Beyond his hope, Eve separate he spies,
Veild in a Cloud of Fragrance, where she stood,
Half spi'd, so thick the Roses bushing round
About her glowd, oft stooping to support
Each Flour of slender stalk, whose head though gay
Carnation, Purple, Azure, or spect with Gold,
Hung drooping unsustaind, them she upstaies
Gently with Mirtle band, mindless the while,
Her self, though fairest unsupported Flour,
From her best prop so farr, and storm so nigh.
Neerer he drew, and many a walk travers'd
Of stateliest Covert, Cedar, Pine, or Palme,
Then **voluble** and bold, now hid, now seen
Among thick-wov'n Arborets and Flours
Imborderd on each Bank, the hand of Eve:
Spot more delicious then those Gardens feign'd
Or of reviv'd Adonis, or renownd

Alcinous, host of old **Laertes Son**,
Or that, **not Mystic**, where the **Sapient King**
Held dalliance with his fair Egyptian Spouse.
Much hee the Place admir'd, the Person more.
As one who long in populous City pent,
Where Houses thick and Sewers annoy the Aire,
Forth issuing on a Summers Morn to breathe
Among the pleasant Villages and Farmes
Adjoynd, from each thing met conceaves delight,
The smell of Grain, or **tedded** Grass, or Kine,
Or Dairie, each rural sight, each rural sound;
If chance with Nymphlike step fair Virgin pass,
What pleasing seemd, for her now pleases more,
She most, and in her look summs all Delight.
Such Pleasure took the Serpent to behold
This Flourie **Plat**, the sweet recess of Eve
Thus earlie, thus alone; her Heav'nly forme
Angelic, but more soft, and Feminine,
Her graceful Innocence, her every Aire
Of gesture or lest action overawd
His Malice, and with rapine sweet bereav'd
His fierceness of the fierce intent it brought:
That space the Evil one abstracted stood
From his own evil, and for the time remaind
Stupidly good, of enmitie disarm'd,

Of guile, of hate, of envie, of revenge;
But the hot Hell that alwayes in him burnes,
Though in mid Heav'n, soon ended his delight,
And tortures him now more, the more he sees
Of pleasure not for him ordain'd: then soon

Fierce hate he recollects, and all his thoughts
Of mischief, gratulating, thus excites.

Thoughts, whither have ye led me, with what sweet
Compulsion thus transported to forget
What hither brought us, hate, not love, nor hope

Of Paradise for Hell, hope here to taste
Of pleasure, but all pleasure to destroy,
Save what is in destroying, other joy
To me is lost. Then let me not let pass
Occasion which now smiles, behold alone
The Woman, opportune to all attempts,
Her Husband, for I view far round, not nigh,
Whose **higher intellectual** more I shun,

And strength, of courage hautie, and of limb
Heroic built, though of terrestrial mould,
Foe not informidable, exempt from wound,
I not; so much hath Hell debas'd, and paine
Infeebl'd me, to what I was in Heav'n.
Shee fair, divinely fair, fit Love for Gods,
Not terrible, though terrour be in Love
And beautie, not approacht by stronger hate,
Hate stronger, under shew of Love well feign'd,
The way which to her ruin now I tend.

So spake the Enemie of Mankind, enclos'd
In Serpent, Inmate bad, and toward Eve
Address'd his way, not with indented wave,
Prone on the ground, as since, but on his reare,
Circular base of rising foulds, that **tour'd**
Fould above fould a surging Maze, his Head
Crested aloft, and Carbuncle his Eyes;
With burnisht Neck of verdant Gold, erect
Amidst his circling **Spires**, that on the grass
Floted redundant: pleasing was his shape,
And lovely, never since of Serpent kind
Lovelier, not those that in Illyria **chang'd**
Hermione and Cadmus, or **the God**
In Epidaurus; nor to which transformd
Ammonian Jove, or Capitoline was seen,
Hee with Olympias, this with her who bore
Scipio the highth of Rome. With tract oblique
At first, as one who sought access, but feard
To interrupt, side-long he works his way.
As when a Ship by skilful Stearsman wrought
Nigh Rivers mouth or Foreland, where the Wind
Veres oft, as oft so steers, and shifts her Saile;
So varied hee, and of his tortuous Traine
Curld many a wanton wreath in sight of Eve,
To lure her Eye; shee busied heard the sound
Of rusling Leaves, but minded not, as us'd
To such disport before her through the Field,
From every Beast, more duteous at her call,
Then at Circean call the **Herd disguis'd**.
Hee boulder now, uncall'd before her stood;
But as in gaze admiring: Oft he bowd
His turret Crest, and sleek enamel'd Neck,
Fawning, and lick'd the ground whereon she trod.
His gentle dumb expression turnd at length
The Eye of Eve to mark his play; he glad

Of her attention gaind, with Serpent Tongue
Organic, or impulse of vocal Air,
His fraudulent temptation thus began.
Wonder not, sovran Mistress, if perhaps
Thou canst, who art sole Wonder, much less arm
Thy looks, the Heav'n of mildness, with disdain,
Displeas'd that I approach thee thus, and gaze
Insatiate, I thus single, nor have feard
Thy awful brow, more awful thus retir'd.
Fairest resemblance of thy Maker faire,
Thee all things living gaze on, all things thine
By gift, and thy Celestial Beautie adore
With ravishment beheld, there best beheld
Where universally admir'd; but here
In this enclosure wild, these Beasts among,
Beholders rude, and shallow to discerne
Half what in thee is fair, one man except,
Who sees thee? (and what is one?) who shouldst be seen
A Goddess among Gods, ador'd and serv'd
By Angels numberless, thy daily Train.

So gloz'd the Tempter, and his **Proem** tun'd;
Into the Heart of Eve his words made way,
Though at the voice much marveling; at length
Not unamaz'd she thus in answer spake.
What may this mean? Language of Man pronounc't
By Tongue of Brute, and human sense exprest?
The first at lest of these I thought deni'd
To Beasts, whom God on thir Creation-Day
Created mute to all articulat sound;
The latter I demurre, for in thir looks
Much reason, and in thir actions oft appeers.
Thee, Serpent, suttlest beast of all the field
I knew, but not with human voice endu'd;
Redouble then this miracle, and say,
How cam'st thou speakable of mute, and how
To me so friendly grown above the rest
Of brutal kind, that daily are in sight?
Say, for such wonder claims attention due.

To whom the guileful Tempter thus reply'd.
Empress of this fair World, resplendent Eve,
Easie to mee it is to tell thee all
What thou commandst and right thou shouldst be obeyd:
I was at first as other Beasts that graze
The trodden Herb, of abject thoughts and low,

As was my food, nor aught but food discern'd
Or Sex, and **apprehended nothing high**:
Till on a day roaving the field, I chanc'd
A goodly Tree farr distant to behold
Loaden with fruit of fairest colours mixt,
Ruddie and Gold: I nearer drew to gaze;
When from the boughes a savorie odour blow'n,
Grateful to appetite, more pleas'd my sense,
Then smell of sweetest **Fenel or the Teats**
Of Ewe or Goat dropping with Milk at Eevn,
Unsuckt of Lamb or Kid, that tend thir play.
To satisfie the sharp desire I had
Of tasting those fair Apples, I resolv'd
Not to deferr; hunger and thirst at once,
Powerful perswaders, quick'nd at the scent
Of that alluring fruit, urg'd me so keene.
About the mossie Trunk I wound me soon,
For high from ground the branches would require
Thy utmost reach or Adams: Round the Tree
All other Beasts that saw, with like desire
Longing and envying stood, but could not reach.
Amid the Tree now got, where plenty hung
Tempting so nigh, to pluck and eat my fill
I spar'd not, for such pleasure till that hour
At Feed or Fountain never had I found.
Sated at length, ere long I might perceave
Strange alteration in me, to degree
Of Reason in my inward Powers, and Speech
Wanted not long, though to this shape retain'd.
Thenceforth to Speculations high or deep
I turnd my thoughts, and with capacious mind
Considerd all things visible in Heav'n,
Or Earth, or **Middle**, all things fair and good;
But all that fair and good in thy Divine
Semblance, and in thy Beauties heav'nly Ray
United I beheld; no Fair to thine
Equivalent or second, which compel'd
Mee thus, though importune perhaps, to come
And gaze, and worship thee of right declar'd
Sovran of Creatures, universal Dame.

So talk'd the **spirited** sly Snake; and Eve
Yet more amaz'd unwarie thus reply'd.
Serpent, thy overpraising leaves in doubt
The vertue of that Fruit, in thee first prov'd:
But say, where grows the Tree, from hence how far?

For many are the Trees of God that grow
In Paradise, and various, yet unknown
To us, in such abundance lies our choice,
As leaves a greater store of Fruit untoucht,
Still hanging incorruptible, till men
Grow up to **thir provision**, and more hands
Help to disburden Nature of her **Bearth**.

To whom the wilie Adder, blithe and glad.
Empress, the way is readie, and not long,
Beyond a row of Myrtles, on a Flat,
Fast by a Fountain, one small Thicket past
Of **blowing** Myrrh and Balme; if thou accept
My conduct, I can bring thee thither soon.

Lead then, said Eve. Hee leading swiftly rowld
In tangles, and made intricate seem strait,
To mischief swift. Hope elevates, and joy
Bright'ns his Crest, as when a **wandring Fire**
Compact of unctuous vapor, which the Night
Condenses, and the cold invirons round,
Kindl'd through agitation to a Flame,
Which oft, they say, some evil Spirit attends
Hovering and blazing with delusive Light,
Misleads th' amaz'd Night-wanderer from his way
To Boggs and Mires, and oft through Pond or Poole,
There swallow'd up and lost, from succour farr.
So glister'd the dire Snake, and into fraud
Led Eve our credulous Mother, to the Tree
Of prohibition, root of all our woe;
Which when she saw, thus to her guide she spake.

Serpent, we might have spar'd our coming hither,
Fruitless to mee, though Fruit be here to excess,
The credit of whose vertue rest with thee,
Wondrous indeed, if cause of such effects.
But of this Tree we may not taste nor touch;
God so commanded, and left that Command
Sole Daughter of his voice; the rest, we live
Law to our selves, our Reason is our Law.

To whom the Tempter guilefully repli'd.
Indeed? hath God then said that of the Fruit
Of all these Garden Trees ye shall not eate,
Yet Lords declar'd of all in Earth or Aire?

To whom thus Eve yet sinless. Of the Fruit
Of each Tree in the Garden we may eate,

But of the Fruit of this fair Tree amidst
The Garden, God hath said, Ye shall not eate
Thereof, nor shall ye touch it, least ye die.

She scarse had said, though brief, when now more bold
The Tempter, but with shew of Zeale and Love
To Man, and indignation at his wrong,
New part puts on, and as to passion mov'd,
Fluctuats disturbd, yet comely and in act
Rais'd, as of som great matter to begin.
As when of old som Orator renound
In Athens or free Rome, where Eloquence
Flourishd, since mute, to som great cause addrest,
Stood in himself collected, while each part,
Motion, each act won audience ere the tongue,
Somtimes in highth began, as no delay
Of Preface **brooking** through his Zeal of Right.
So standing, moving, or to highth upgrown
The Tempter all impassiond thus began.

O Sacred, Wise, and Wisdom-giving Plant,
Mother of **Science**, Now I feel thy Power
Within me cleere, not onely to discerne
Things in thir Causes, but to trace the wayes
Of **highest Agents**, deemd however wise.
Queen of this Universe, doe not believe
Those rigid threats of Death; ye shall not Die:
How should ye? by the Fruit? it gives you Life
To Knowledge, By the Threatner, look on mee,
Mee who have touch'd and tasted, yet both live,
And life more perfet have attaind then Fate
Meant mee, by ventring higher then my Lot.
Shall that be shut to Man, which to the Beast
Is open? or will God incense his ire
For such a petty Trespass, and not praise
Rather your dauntless vertue, whom the pain
Of Death denounc't, whatever thing Death be,
Deterrd not from atchieving what might leade
To happier life, knowledge of Good and Evil;
Of good, how just? of evil, if what is evil
Be real, why not known, since easier shunnd?
God therefore cannot hurt ye, and be just;
Not just, not God; not feard then, nor obeyd:
Your feare it self of Death removes the feare.
Why then was this forbid? Why but to awe,
Why but to keep ye low and ignorant,

His worshippers; he knows that in the day
Ye Eate thereof, your Eyes that seem so cleere,
Yet are but dim, shall perfetly be then
Op'nd and cleerd, and ye shall be as Gods,
Knowing both Good and Evil as they know.
That ye should be as Gods, since I as Man,
Internal Man, is but proportion meet,
I of brute human, yee of human Gods.
So ye shall die perhaps, by putting off
Human, to put on Gods, death to be wisht,
Though threat'nd, which no worse then this can bring.
And what are Gods that Man may not become
As they, participating God-like food?
The Gods are first, and that advantage use
On our belief, that all from them proceeds;
I question it, for this fair Earth I see,
Warm'd by the Sun, producing every kind,
Them nothing: If they all things, who enclos'd
Knowledge of Good and Evil in this Tree,
That whoso eats thereof, forthwith attains
Wisdom without their leave? and wherein lies
Th' offence, that Man should thus attain to know?
What can your knowledge hurt him, or this Tree
Impart against his will if all be his?
Or is it envie, and can envie dwell
In Heav'nly brests? these, these and many more
Causes import your need of this fair Fruit.
Goddess humane, reach then, and freely taste.

He ended, and his words replete with guile
Into her heart too easie entrance won:
Fixt on the Fruit she gaz'd, which to behold
Might tempt alone, and in her ears the sound
Yet rung of his perswasive words, **impregn'd**
With Reason, to her seeming, and with Truth;
Mean while the hour of Noon drew on, and wak'd
An eager appetite, rais'd by the smell
So savorie of that Fruit, which with desire,
Inclinable now grown to touch or taste,
Sollicited her longing eye; yet first
Pausing a while, thus to her self she mus'd.
Great are thy Vertues, doubtless, best of Fruits,
Though kept from Man, and worthy to be admir'd,
Whose taste, too long forborn, at first assay
Gave elocution to the mute, and taught
The Tongue not made for Speech to speak thy praise:

Thy praise hee also who forbids thy use,
Conceales not from us, naming thee the Tree
Of Knowledge, knowledge both of good and evil;
Forbids us then to taste, but his forbidding
Commends thee more, while it inferrs the good
By thee communicated, and our want:
For good unknown, sure is not had, or had
And yet unknown, is as not had at all.
In plain then, what forbids he but to know,
Forbids us good, forbids us to be wise?
Such prohibitions binde not. But if Death
Bind us with after-bands, what profits then
Our inward freedom? In the day we eate
Of this fair Fruit, our doom is, we shall die.
How dies the Serpent? hee hath eat'n and lives,
And knows, and speaks, and reasons, and discerns,
Irrational till then. For us alone
Was death invented? or to us deni'd
This intellectual food, for beasts reserv'd?
For Beasts it seems: yet that one Beast which first
Hath tasted, envies not, but brings with joy
The good befall'n him, Author unsuspect,
Friendly to man, farr from deceit or guile.
What fear I then, rather what know to feare
Under this ignorance of good and Evil,
Of God or Death, of Law or Penaltie?
Here grows the Cure of all, this Fruit Divine,
Fair to the Eye, inviting to the Taste,
Of vertue to make wise: what hinders then
To reach, and feed at once both Bodie and Mind?

So saying, her rash hand in evil hour
Forth reaching to the Fruit, she pluck'd, she eat:
Earth felt the wound, and Nature from her seat
Sighing through all her Works gave signs of woe,
That all was lost. Back to the Thicket slunk
The guiltie Serpent, and well might, for Eve
Intent now wholly on her taste, naught else
Regarded, such delight till then, as seemd,
In Fruit she never tasted, whether true
Or fansied so, through expectation high
Of knowledg, nor was God-head from her thought.
Greedily she ingorg'd without restraint,
And knew not eating Death: Satiate at length,
And hight'nd as with Wine, jocond and **boon**,
Thus to her self she pleasingly began.

O Sovran, vertuous, precious of all Trees
In Paradise, of operation blest
To Sapience, hitherto obscur'd, infam'd,
And thy fair Fruit let hang, as to no end
Created; but henceforth my early care,
Not without Song, each Morning, and due praise
Shall tend thee, and the fertil burden ease
Of thy full branches offer'd free to all;
Till dieted by thee I grow mature
In knowledge, as the Gods who all things know;
Though others envie what they cannot give;
For had the gift bin theirs, it had not here
Thus grown. Experience, next to thee I owe,
Best guide; not following thee, I had remaind
In ignorance, thou op'nst Wisdoms way,
And giv'st access, though secret she retire.
And I perhaps am secret; Heav'n is high,
High and remote to see from thence distinct
Each thing on Earth; and other care perhaps
May have diverted from continual watch
Our great Forbidder, safe with all his Spies
About him. But to Adam in what sort
Shall I appeer? shall I to him make known
As yet my change, and give him to partake
Full happiness with mee, or rather not,
But keep the odds of Knowledge in my power
Without Copartner? so to add what wants
In Femal Sex, the more to draw his Love,
And render me more equal, and perhaps,
A thing not undesireable, somtime
Superior: for inferior who is free?
This may be well: but what if God have seen
And Death ensue? then I shall be no more,
And Adam wedded to another Eve,
Shall live with her enjoying, I extinct;
A death to think. Confirm'd then I resolve,
Adam shall share with me in bliss or woe:
So dear I love him, that with him all deaths
I could endure, without him live no life.

So saying, from the Tree her step she turnd,
But first low Reverence don, as to the power
That dwelt within, whose presence had infus'd
Into the plant **sciential** sap, deriv'd
From Nectar, drink of Gods. Adam the while
Waiting desirous her return, had wove

Of choicest Flours a Garland to adorne
Her Tresses, and her rural labours crown,
As Reapers oft are wont thir Harvest Queen.
Great joy he promis'd to his thoughts, and new
Solace in her return, so long delay'd;
Yet oft his heart, **divine** of somthing ill,
Misgave him; hee the faultring measure felt;
And forth to meet her went, the way she took
That Morn when first they parted; by the Tree
Of Knowledge he must pass, there he her met,
Scarse from the Tree returning; in her hand
A bough of fairest fruit that downie smil'd,
New gatherd, and ambrosial smell diffus'd.
To him she hasted, in her face excuse
Came Prologue, and Apologie to prompt,
Which with bland words at will she thus addrest.

Hast thou not wonderd, Adam, at my stay?
Thee I have misst, and thought it long, depriv'd
Thy presence, **agonie of love** till now
Not felt, nor shall be twice, for never more
Mean I to trie, what rash untri'd I sought,
The pain of absence from thy sight. But strange
Hath bin the cause, and wonderful to heare:
This Tree is not as we are told, a Tree
Of danger tasted, nor to evil unknown
Op'ning the way, but of Divine effect
To open Eyes, and make them Gods who taste;
And hath bin **tasted** such: the Serpent wise,
Or not restraind as wee, or not obeying,
Hath eat'n of the fruit, and is become,
Not dead, as we are threatn'd, but thenceforth
Endu'd with human voice and human sense,
Reasoning to admiration, and with mee
Perswasively hath so prevaild, that I
Have also tasted, and have also found
Th' effects to correspond, opener mine Eyes
Dimm erst, dilated Spirits, ampler Heart,
And growing up to Godhead; which for thee
Chiefly I sought, without thee can despise.
For bliss, as thou hast part, to me is bliss,
Tedious, unshar'd with thee, and odious soon.
Thou therefore also taste, that equal Lot
May joyne us, equal Joy, as equal Love;
Least thou not tasting, different degree
Disjoyne us, and I then too late renounce

Deitie for thee, when Fate will not permit.

Thus Eve with Countnance blithe her storie told;
But in her Cheek distemper flushing glowd.
On th' other side, Adam, soon as he heard
The fatal Trespass don by Eve, amaz'd,
Astonied stood and Blank, while horror chill
Ran through his veins, and all his joynts relax'd;
From his slack hand the Garland wreath'd for Eve
Down drop'd, and all the faded Roses shed:
Speechless he stood and pale, till thus at length
First to himself he inward silence broke.

O fairest of Creation, **last and best**
Of all Gods works, Creature in whom excell'd
Whatever can to sight or thought be formd,
Holy, divine, good, amiable, or sweet!
How art thou lost, how on a sudden lost,
Defac't, deflourd, and now to Death **devote**?
Rather how hast thou yeelded to transgress
The strict forbiddance, how to violate
The sacred Fruit forbidd'n! som cursed fraud
Of Enemie hath beguil'd thee, yet unknown,
And mee with thee hath ruind, for with thee
Certain my resolution is to Die;
How can I live without thee, how forgoe
Thy sweet Converse and Love so dearly joyn'd,
To live again in these wilde Woods forlorn?
Should God create another Eve, and I
Another Rib afford, yet loss of thee
Would never from my heart; no no, I feel
The Link of Nature draw me: Flesh of Flesh,
Bone of my Bone thou art, and from thy State
Mine never shall be parted, **bliss or woe**.

So having said, as one from sad dismay
Recomforted, and after thoughts disturbd
Submitting to what seemd remediless,
Thus in calm mood his Words to Eve he turnd.

Bold deed thou hast presum'd, adventrous Eve
And peril great provok't, who thus hath dar'd
Had it been onely coveting to Eye
That sacred Fruit, sacred to abstinence,
Much more to taste it under banne to touch
But past who can recall, or don undoe?
Not God Omnipotent, nor Fate, yet so

Perhaps thou shalt not Die, perhaps the Fact
Is not so hainous now, foretasted Fruit,
Profan'd first by the Serpent, by him first
Made common and unhallowd ere our taste;
Nor yet on him found deadly, he yet lives,
Lives, as thou saidst, and gaines to live as Man
Higher degree of Life, inducement strong
To us, as likely tasting to attaine
Proportional ascent, which cannot be
But to be Gods, or Angels Demi-gods.
Nor can I think that God, Creator wise,
Though threatning, will in earnest so destroy
Us his prime Creatures, dignifi'd so high,
Set over all his Works, which in our Fall,
For us created, needs with us must faile,
Dependent made; so God shall uncreate,
Be frustrate, do, undo, and labour loose,
Not well conceav'd of God, who though his Power
Creation could repeate, yet would be loath
Us to abolish, least the **Adversary**
Triumph and say; Fickle their State whom God
Most Favors, who can please him long; Mee first
He ruind, now Mankind; whom will he next?
Matter of scorne, not to be given the Foe,
However I with thee have fixt my Lot,
Certain to undergoe like doom, if Death
Consort with thee, Death is to mee as Life;
So forcible within my heart I feel
The Bond of Nature draw me to my owne,
My own in thee, for what thou art is mine;
Our State cannot be severd, we are one,
One Flesh; to loose thee were to loose my self.

So Adam, and thus Eve to him repli'd.
O glorious trial of exceeding Love,
Illustrious evidence, example high!
Ingaging me to emulate, but short
Of thy perfection, how shall I attaine,
Adam, from whose deare side I boast me sprung,
And gladly of our Union heare thee speak,
One Heart, one Soul in both; whereof good prooff
This day affords, declaring thee resolvd,
Rather then Death or aught then Death more dread
Shall separate us, linkt in Love so deare,
To undergoe with mee one Guilt, one Crime,
If any be, of tasting this fair Fruit,

Whose vertue, for of good still good proceeds,
Direct, or by occasion hath presented
This happie trial of thy Love, which else
So eminently never had bin known.
Were it I thought Death menac't would ensue
This my attempt, I would sustain alone
The worst, and not perswade thee, rather die
Deserted, then **oblige** thee with a **fact**
Pernicious to thy Peace, chiefly assur'd
Remarkably so late of thy so true,
So faithful Love unequald; but I feel
Farr otherwise th' event, not Death, but Life
Augmented, op'nd Eyes, new Hopes, new Joyes,
Taste so Divine, that what of sweet before
Hath toucht my sense, flat seems to this, and harsh.
On my experience, Adam, freely taste,
And fear of Death deliver to the Windes.

So saying, she embrac'd him, and for joy
Tenderly wept, much won that he his Love
Had so enobl'd, as of choice to incurr
Divine displeasure for her sake, or Death.
In recompence (for such compliance bad
Such recompence best merits) from the bough
She gave him of that fair enticing Fruit
With liberal hand: he scrupl'd not to eat
Against his better knowledge, not deceav'd,
But fondly overcome with Femal charm.
Earth trembl'd from her entrails, as again
In pangs, and Nature gave a second groan,
Skie lowr'd, and muttering Thunder, som sad drops
Wept at compleating of the mortal Sin
Original; while Adam took no thought,
Eating his fill, nor Eve to iterate
Her former trespass fear'd, the more to soothe
Him with her lov'd societie, that now
As with new Wine intoxicated both
They swim in mirth, and fansie that they feel
Divinitie within them breeding wings
Wherewith to scorne the Earth: but that false Fruit
Farr other operation first displaid,
Carnal desire enflaming, hee on Eve
Began to cast lascivious Eyes, she him
As wantonly repaid; **in Lust they burne:**
Till Adam thus 'gan Eve to dalliance move,

Eve, now I see thou art exact of taste,
And elegant, of Sapience no small part,
Since to each meaning savour we apply,
And Palate call judicious; I the praise
Yeild thee, so well this day thou hast purvey'd.
Much pleasure we have lost, while we abstain'd
From this delightful Fruit, nor known till now
True relish, tasting; if such pleasure be
In things to us forbidden, it might be wish'd,
For this one Tree had bin forbidden ten.
But come, so well refresh't, now let us play,
As meet is, after such delicious Fare;
For never did thy Beautie since the day
I saw thee first and wedded thee, adorn'd
With all perfections, so enflame my sense
With ardor to enjoy thee, fairer now
Then ever, bountie of this vertuous Tree.

So said he, and forbore not glance or toy
Of amorous intent, well understood
Of Eve, whose Eye darted contagious Fire.
Her hand he seis'd, and to a shadie bank,
Thick overhead with verdant roof imbowr'd
He led her nothing loath; Flours were the Couch,
Pansies, and Violets, and Asphodel,
And Hyacinth, Earths freshest softest lap.
There they thir fill of Love and Loves disport
Took largely, of thir mutual guilt the Seale,
The solace of thir sin, till dewie sleep
Oppress'd them, wearied with thir amorous play.
Soon as the force of that fallacious Fruit,
That with exhilerating vapour **bland**
About thir spirits had plaid, and inmost powers
Made erre, was now exhal'd, and grosser sleep
Bred of **unkindly** fumes, with **conscious** dreams
Encumberd, now had left them, up they rose
As from unrest, and each the other viewing,
Soon found thir Eyes how op'nd, and thir minds
How dark'nd; innocence, that as a veile
Had shadow'd them from knowing ill, was gon,
Just confidence, and native righteousness
And honour from about them, naked left
To guiltie shame **hee cover'd**, but his Robe
Uncover'd more, so rose the **Danite** strong
Herculean Samson from the Harlot-lap

Of Philistean Dalilah, and wak'd
Shorn of his strength, They destitute and bare
Of all thir vertue: silent, and in face
Confounded long they sate, as struck'n mute,
Till Adam, though not less then Eve abasht,
At length gave utterance to these words constraind.

O Eve, in evil hour thou didst give eare
To that false Worm, of whomsoever taught
To counterfet Mans voice, true in our Fall,
False in our promis'd Rising; since our Eyes
Op'nd we find indeed, and find we know
Both Good and Evil, Good lost, and Evil got,
Bad Fruit of Knowledge, if this be to know,
Which leaves us naked thus, of Honour void,
Of Innocence, of Faith, of Puritie,
Our wonted Ornaments now soild and staind,
And in our Faces evident the signes
Of foul concupiscence; whence evil store;
Even shame, the last of evils; of the first
Be sure then. How shall I behold the face
Henceforth of God or Angel, earst with joy
And rapture so oft beheld? those heav'nly shapes
Will dazle now this earthly, with thir blaze
Insufferably bright. O might I here
In solitude live savage, in some glade
Obscur'd, where highest Woods impenetrable
To Starr or Sun-light, spread thir umbrage broad,
And brown as Evening: Cover me ye Pines,
Ye Cedars, with innumerable boughs
Hide me, where I may never see them more.
But let us now, as in bad plight, devise
What best may for the present serve to hide
The Parts of each from other, that seem most
To shame obnoxious, and unseemliest seen,
Some Tree whose broad smooth Leaves together sowd,
And girded on our loyns, may cover round
Those middle parts, that this new commer, Shame,
There sit not, and reproach us as unclean.

So counsel'd hee, and both together went
Into the thickest Wood, there soon they chose
The Figtree, not that kind for Fruit renown'd,
But such as at this day to Indians known
In Malabar or Decan spreds her Armes

Braunching so broad and long, that in the ground
The bended Twigs take root, and Daughters grow
About the Mother Tree, a Pillard shade
High overarch't, and echoing Walks between;
There oft the Indian Herdsman shunning heate
Shelters in coole, and tends his pasturing Herds
At Loopholes cut through thickest shade: Those Leaves
They gatherd, broad as **Amazonian Targe**,
And with what skill they had, together sowd,
To gird thir waste, vain Covering if to hide
Thir guilt and dreaded shame; O how unlike
To that first naked Glorie. Such of late
Columbus found **th' American so girt**
With featherd Cincture, naked else and wilde
Among the Trees on Iles and woodie Shores.
Thus fenc't, and as they thought, thir shame in part
Coverd, but not at rest or ease of Mind,
They sate them down to weep, nor onely Teares
Raind at thir Eyes, but high Winds worse within
Began to rise, high Passions, Anger, Hate,
Mistrust, Suspicion, Discord, and shook sore
Thir inward State of Mind, calm Region once
And full of Peace, now tost and turbulent:
For Understanding rul'd not, and the Will
Heard not her lore, both in subjection now
To sensual Appetite, who from beneathe
Usurping over sovran Reason claimd
Superior sway: From thus distemperd brest,
Adam, estrang'd in look and alterd stile,
Speech intermitted thus to Eve renewd.

Would thou hadst heark'nd to my words, and stai'd
With me, as I besought thee, when that strange
Desire of wandring this unhappie Morn,
I know not whence possessd thee; we had then
Remaind still happie, not as now, despoild
Of all our good, sham'd, naked, miserable.
Let none henceforth seek needless cause to approve
The Faith they owe; when earnestly they seek
Such proof, conclude, they then begin to faile.

To whom soon mov'd with touch of blame thus Eve.
What words have past thy Lips, Adam severe,
Imput'st thou that to my default, or will
Of wandring, as thou call'st it, which who knows

But might as ill have happ'nd thou being by,
Or to thy self perhaps: hadst thou been there,
Or here th' attempt, thou couldst not have discernd
Fraud in the Serpent, speaking as he spake;
No ground of enmitie between us known,
Why hee should mean me ill, or seek to harme.
Was I to have never parted from thy side?
As good have grown there still a liveless Rib.
Being as I am, why didst not thou the **Head**
Command me absolutely not to go,
Going into such danger as thou saidst?
Too facil then thou didst not much gainsay,
Nay, didst permit, approve, and fair dismiss.
Hadst thou bin firm and fixt in thy dissent,
Neither had I transgress'd, nor thou with mee.

To whom then first incenst Adam repli'd,
Is this the Love, is this the recompence
Of mine to thee, ingrateful Eve, exprest
Immutable when thou wert lost, not I,
Who might have liv'd and joyd immortal bliss,
Yet willingly chose rather Death with thee:
And am I now upbraided, as the cause
Of thy transgressing? not enough severe,
It seems, in thy restraint: what could I more?
I warn'd thee, I admonish'd thee, foretold
The danger, and the lurking Enemie
That lay in wait; beyond this had bin force,
And force upon free Will hath here no place.
But confidence then bore thee on, secure
Either to meet no danger, or to finde
Matter of glorious trial; and perhaps
I also err'd in overmuch admiring
What seemd in thee so perfet, that I thought
No evil durst attempt thee, but I rue
That errour now, which is become my crime,
And thou th' accuser. Thus it shall befall
Him who to worth in Women overtrusting
Lets her Will rule; restraint she will not brook,
And left to her self, if evil thence ensue,
Shee first his weak indulgence will accuse.

Thus they in mutual accusation spent
The fruitless hours, but neither self-condemning,
And of thir vain contest appeer'd no end.

Notes

Venial: erroneous, but not sinful. One commits error in ignorance but sin, as Milton proposes it, is here disobedience because it is committed with prior knowledge. **into this World a world of woe:** refers to death that followed the wedding celebrations of Aeneas and Dido **argument:** here, subject **the wrauth:** Achilles' wrath **his Foe:** Hector, whom Achilles pursued and finally killed **Turnus for Lavinia:** In Virgil's *Aeneid* Turnus loses Lavinia to Aeneas. **the Greek:** refers to Odysseus, harassed by Neptune **Cytherea's son:** Aeneas, harassed by Juno **answerable:** adequate **Celestial Patroness:** Urania, the muse of astronomy, but here, also the Holy Spirit **beginning late:** Milton wrote *Paradise Lost* nearly seventeen years after he first made the notes for it, but also refers to his own age: he was fifty-nine when he wrote it. **sedulous:** eager **tilting:** jousting **furniture:** here, instruments **Impreses:** or Imprezas, the symbols on the shields of knights **Bases:** cloth coverings of horses **Sewers and Seneschals:** 'seater', but also waiter-like servants; 'seneschal' was the chief steward of a medieval household. **skill of Artifice:** implies that the poem is not chiefly a matter of art, but divinely inspired **cold Climat or Years:** the traditional belief that cold climate reduced human intelligence **Hesperus:** Venus **Uriel:** Uriel spotted Satan in Eden. **Cherubim:** one of the ranks of angels **Carr of Night:** Night moving around the earth, Satan circling the earth, stayed ahead of the sun and therefore moved around in the night **Colure:** an imaginary circle in space; two circles are believed to intersect at the celestial poles **Tigris:** The Tigris is believed to be a part of the river that emerged from Eden **Pontus:** Latin name for the Black Sea **Poole Mæotis:** the Sea of Azov, north of the Black Sea **River Ob:** a river in Siberia **Orontes** ; a river in Lebanon, Syria, and Turkey **barr'd:** bounded **Darien:** a narrow strip of land linking Central and South America **Orb:** globe, here, earth **second thoughts:** the early modern belief that things created second or last must be better or more perfect, an idea used by women **officious:** here, dutiful **vertue:** power **if they at least:** Satan admits that he was created by God. **into our room:** on the indignity of earthly creatures taking his place **our spoils:** the Israelites' spoliation of Egypt as they fled Pharaoh **incarnate and imbrute:** Satan's incarnation as a beast, where the Son of God incarnates as a man **obnoxious:** exposed **spite:** Satan and Beelzebub pledged to spite the Creator **Nor nocent:** innocent **close:** secretly **when as:** when **wanting:** lacking **Spring:** Grove **motion'd:** suggested **Virgin:** perhaps taken to mean innocent of sin **misthought:** misjudged **entire:** entirely free **Access:** increase **strait'nd:** limited **Front:** brow **erect:** here, alert **approve:** prove **submiss:** submissively **Oread or Dryad:** wood nymph **Delia:** Diana **deport:** bearing **Pales:** goddess of pasture **Pomona:** goddess of orchards or fruit **Ceres:** According to myth, Ceres taught men to use the plow. **tendance:** care **voluble:** undulating **Laertes' son:** Odysseus **not Mystic:** Solomon's garden, which was real and not mythological **Sapient King:** Solomon **tedded:** scattered prior to hay-making **Plat:** plot **higher intellectual:** might refer to either Satan or Adam, touted as possessing a higher intellect **tour'd:** towered **Spires:** (serpentine) loops **chang'd:** Ovid's account of the metamorphosis of Cadmus and Harmonia into serpents **the God:** Æsculapius, the god of healing **Lines 510–14:** The first letters of these lines, read vertically from top to bottom (beginning with the *S* of 'Scipio'), spell S A T A N. **Herd disguis'd:** Circe turned her victims into swine. **Organic:** being used as an organ or instrument **Proem:**

preamble **apprehended nothing high:** where they cannot have pleasures greater than those of the body **Fenel . . . teats . . . Milt at Eevn:** the myth that snakes sucked milk directly from the teats of goats and sheep, but couldnot really reach them **Middle:** air between Earth and Heav'n **spirited:** possessed **thir provision:** Men grow up in numbers proportional to the available resources. **Bearth:** birth **blowing:** blooming **wandring Fire:** swamp gas which spontaneously combusts **brooking:** not waiting **Science:** here, simply 'knowledge' **highest Agents:** angels **Internal Man:** Satan implies that the serpent has become a man internally. **impregn'd:** impregnated **boon:** jovial **To Sapience:** to produce knowledge, but also 'taste' **sciential:** knowledge **divine:** foreseeing **agonie of love:** Eve's punishment is pain in childbirth and a simultaneous desire for her husband. **tasted:** proven by tasting **Not dead:** Satan is devoted to death but never dies. **last and best:** Human beings are the 'last and best' creation. **devote:** here, doomed **bliss or woe:** refers to the marriage vows, 'for better or for worse' **Adversary:** literal meaning of 'Satan' **Certain:** resolved **oblige:** Milton is using it in the Latin sense of 'to be involved in guilt' **fact:** deed **in Lust they burne:** Milton described another kind of burning, a rational burning, in his divorce tract (*Doctrine and Discipline of Divorce*); here Milton is suggesting a lustful burning, in contrast. **bland:** pleasing to the senses **unkindly:** unnatural **conscious:** here, conscious of sin **hee cover'd:** covered, or clothed in shame **Danite:** Samson **Amazonian Targe:** Amazons' shields **th' American so girt:** Milton compares the New World to the newly-fallen Adam. **Head:** Eve refers to Adam as her Head.

John Suckling

Born in 1609 in Middlesex to a wealthy family, John Suckling studied at Cambridge and joined Gray's Inn in 1627. He travelled briefly on the Continent. Suckling was knighted in 1630 and became a popular figure at the Court. He was close to Charles I and was part of the literary circle with Carew, Lovelace and Davenant. His play *Aglaura*, was staged, and printed at his own expense in 1637. He fought with Charles I against the Scots in 1639–40, often supplying horses and men at his own cost to the army. In 1641 Suckling was implicated in an attempt to rescue Thomas Wentworth, the first Earl of Strafford, from the Tower of London. He may have fled to Europe and later eloped with a lady to Spain. It is believed he committed suicide around 1642. His poetry, embodying the Cavalier tone, was made famous with lines such as, 'Why so pale and wan, fond lover?'

Why so pale and wan, fond lover?

Why so pale and wan fond lover?
Prithee why so pale?
Will, when looking well can't move her,
Looking ill prevail?
Prithee why so pale?

Why so dull and mute young **sinner**?
Prithee why so mute?
Will, when speaking well can't win her,
Saying nothing do't?
Prithee why so mute?

Quit, quit for shame, this will not move,
This cannot take her;
If of herself she will not love,
Nothing can make her;
The devil take her.

Notes

sinner: perhaps meant to be 'signor'

There never yet was woman made

There never yet was woman made,
Nor shall, but to be curst;
And O, that I, fond I, should first,
Of any lover,
This truth at my own charge to other fools discover!

You, that have promis'd to yourselves
Propriety in love,
Know women's hearts like straw do move,
And what we call
Their sympathy, is but love to jet in general.

All mankind are alike to them;
And, though we iron find
That never with a loadstone join'd,
'Tis not the iron's fault,
It is because near the loadstone it was never brought.

If where a gentle bee hath fall'n,
And laboured to his power,
A new succeeds not to that flower,

But passes by,
'Tis to be thought, the gallant elsewhere loads his thigh.

For still the flowers ready stand:
One buzzes round about,
One lights, one tastes, gets in, gets out;
All all ways use them,
Till all their sweets are gone, and all again refuse them.

Out upon it, I have loved

Out upon it, I have loved
Three whole days together;
And am like to love three more,
If it prove fair weather.

Time shall moult away his wings,
Ere he shall discover
In the whole wide world again
Such a constant lover.

But the spite on't is, no praise
Is due at all to me;
Love with me had **made no stay**,
Had it any been but she.

Had it any been but she,
And that very face,
There had been at least ere this
A dozen dozen in her place.

Notes

made no stay: has not stayed with me

Richard Crashaw

Born into the family of a Puritan minister in London, in 1613, Crashaw studied at Pembroke, Cambridge, eventually leaving with an MA in 1638. He was ordained and became the minister for the Church of St Mary the Less, Cambridge, in 1638. He fled to France during the period of the Civil War and turned Catholic there. His first work, *Steps to the Temple* and *The Delights of the Muses*, in one volume, appeared anonymously in 1646. With Abraham Cowley's support, he got a job, serving a Cardinal in Rome, a post he held till 1649. In 1649, he was made a sub-canon of the Cathedral of Santa Casa in Loretto, but died soon after taking up the post.

Saint Mary Magdalene, or the Weeper

Lo where a wounded heart with bleeding hearts conspire.
Is she a flaming fountain or a weeping fire!

Hail sister springs,
Parents of silver-footed rills!
Ever bubbling things!
Thawing crystal! Snowy hills!
Still spending, never spent; I mean
Thy fair eyes, sweet Magdalene.

Heavens thy fair eyes be;
Heavens of ever-falling stars;
'Tis seed-time still with thee,
And stars thou sow'st, whose harvest dares
Promise the earth to countershine
Whatever makes Heaven's forehead fine.

But we're deceived all:
Stars indeed they are too true,
For they but seem to fall
As Heaven's other spangles do:
It is not for our earth and us,
To shine in things so precious.

Upwards thou dost weep;
Heaven's bosom drinks the gentle stream.
Where the milky rivers creep,
Thine floats above and is the cream.

Waters above the heavens, what they be,
We are taught best by thy tears and thee.

Every morn from hence,
A **brisk** cherub something sips,
Whose soft influence
Adds sweetness to his sweetest lips;
Then to his music: and his song
Tastes of this breakfast all day long.

Not in the evening's eyes,
When they read with weeping are
For the Sun that dies,
Sits Sorrow with a face so fair.
Nowhere but here did ever meet
Sweetness so sad, sadness so sweet.

When Sorrow would be seen
In her brightest majesty,
For she is a Queen,
Then is she drest by none but thee.
Then, and only then, she wears
Her **proudest** pearls, I mean thy tears.

The dew no more will weep,
The primrose's pale cheek to deck;
The dew no more will sleep,
Nuzzled in the lily's neck.
Much rather would it tremble here,
And leave them both to be thy tear.

There is no need at all,
That the balsam-sweating bough
So coyly should let fall
His med'cinable tears; for now
Nature hath learnt t'extract a dew
More sovereign and sweet from you.

Yet let the poor drops weep,
Weeping is the case of woe;
Softly let them creep,
Sad that they are vanquish'd so;
They, though to others no relief,
May balsam be for their own grief.

Such the maiden gem
By the wanton spring put on,
Peeps from her parent stem,

And blushes on the watery sun:
This watery blossom of thy **eyen**
Ripe, will make the richer wine.

When some new bright guest
Takes up among the stars a room,
And Heaven will make a feast,
Angels with crystal vials come;
And draw from these full eyes of thine
Their Master's water, their own wine.

Golden though he be,
Golden **Tagus** murmurs though;
Were his way by thee,
Content and quiet he would go;
So much more rich would he esteem
Thy silver, than his golden stream.

Well does the May that lies
Smiling in thy cheeks, confess
The April in thine eyes;
Mutual sweetness they express.
No April ever lent kinder showers,
Nor May returned more faithful flowers.

O cheeks! Beds of chaste loves,
By your own showers seasonably dash'd.
Eyes! nests of milky doves,
In your own wells decently wash'd.
O wit of love! that thus could place
Fountain and garden in one face.

O sweet contest; of woes
With loves, of tears with smiles disporting!
O fair and friendly foes,
Each other kissing and comforting!
While rain and sunshine, cheeks and eyes,
Close in kind contrarieties.

But can these fair floods be
Friends with the bosom fires that fill ye!
Can so great flames agree
Eternal tears should thus distil thee!
O floods, O fires, O suns, O showers!
Mix'd and made friends by love's sweet pow'rs.

'Twas his well-pointed dart
That digged these wells, and dressed this vine;

And taught that wounded heart
The way into these weeping eyen.
Vain loves **avaunt**! bold hands forbear!
The lamb hath dipped his white foot here.

And now wherever he strays
Among the Galilean mountains,
Or more unwelcome ways,
He's follow'd by two faithful fountains;
Two walking baths, two weeping motions,
Portable and compendious oceans.

O thou, thy Lord's fair store,
In thy so rich and large expenses,
Even when he showed most poor,
He might provoke the wealth of princes.
What prince's wanton'st pride ever could
Wash with silver, wipe with gold?

Who is that King, but he
Who call'st his crown to be called thine,
Thus can boast to be
Waited on by a wandering mine,—
A voluntary mint, that strews
Warm silver showers wherever he goes?

O precious prodigal!
Fair spendthrift of thyself! thy measure,
Merciless love! is all
Even to the last pearl in thy treasure.
All places, times, and objects be
Thy tear's sweet opportunity.

Does the day-star rise?
Still thy stars do fal, and fall;
Does day close his eyes?
Still the fountain weeps for all.
Let night or day do what they will,
Thou hast thy task, thou weepest still.

Does thy song lull the air?
Thy falling tears keep faithful time.
Does thy sweet-breath'd prayer
Up in clouds of incense climb?
Still at each sigh, that is, each stop,
A bead, that is, a tear, does drop.

At these thy weeping gates,

Watching their wat'ry motion,
Each winged moment waits,
Takes his tear, and gets him gone.
By thine eye's tinct ennobled thus,
Time lay's him up: he's precious.

Not, *so long she lived*,
Shall thy tomb report of thee;
But, *so long she breathed*,
Thus must we date thy memory.
Others by moments, months, and years,
Measure their ages; thou, by tears.

So do perfumes expire;
So sigh tormented sweets, oppress'd
With proud unpitying fires;
Such tears the suff'ring rose that's vex'd
With ungentle flames does shed,
Sweating in a too warm bed.

Say, ye bright brothers,
The fugitive sons of those fair eyes
Your fruitful mothers,
What make you here? What hopes can 'tice
You to be born? What cause can borrow
You from those nests of noble sorrow?

Whither away so fast?
For sure the sordid earth
Your sweetness cannot taste,
Nor does the dust deserve their birth.
Sweet, whither haste you then? O, say
Why you trip so fast away?

We go not to seek
The darlings of Aurora's bed,
The rose's modest cheek,
Nor the violet's humble head.
Though the field's eyes, too, weepers be,
Because they want such tears as we.

Much less mean we to trace
The fortune of inferior gems,
Preferred to some proud face,
Or perch'd upon fear'd diadems.
Crowned heads are toys. We go to meet
A worthy object, our Lord's feet.

Notes

brisk: a swallow **proudest:** here, richest **eyen:** here, eyes **Tagus:** a Spanish river famous for its golden sands **avaunt:** forward **The lamb hath dipped his white foot here:** the fountain Hippocrene on Mt Helicon, created when the white, winged horse, Pegasus, struck the mountain with his foot. Here, the apocalyptic lamb of God is merged with Pegasus. **Preferred:** here, elevated

A Hymn to the Honour and Name of the Admirable Saint Theresa

Love, thou are absolute, sole Lord
Of life and death. To prove the word,
We'll now appeal to none of all
Those thy old soldiers, great and tall,
Ripe men of martyrdom, that could reach down
With strong arms their triumphant crown:
Such as could with lusty breath
Speak loud, unto the face of death,
Their great Lord's glorious name; to none
Of those whose spacious bosoms spread a throne
For love at large to fill. Spare blood and sweat:
We'll see Him take a private seat,
And make His mansion in the mild
And milky soul of a soft child.
Scarce has she learnt to lisp a name
Of martyr, yet she thinks it shame
Life should so long play with that breath
Which spent can buy so brave a death.
She never undertook to know
What death with love should have to do.
Nor has she e'er yet understood
Why, to show love, she should shed blood;
Yet, though she cannot tell you why,
She can love, and she can die.
Scarce has she blood enough to make
A guilty sword blush for her sake;
Yet has a heart dares hope to prove
How much less strong is death than love.
Be love but there; let poor six years
Be posed with the matures fears
Man trembles at, you straight shall find
Love knows no nonage, nor the mind.
'Tis Love, not years or limbs that can
Make the martyr, or the man.

Love touched her heart, and lo it beats.
High, and burns with such brave heats;
Such thirsts to die, as dares drink up.
a thousand cold deaths **in one cup**.
Good reason. For she breathes all fire.
Her weak breast heaves with strong desire
Of what she may with fruitless wishes
Seek for amongst her mother's kisses.
Since 'tis not to be had at home,
She'll travel for a martyrdom.
No home for her, confesses she,
But where she may a martyr be.
She'll to the Moors, and trade with them
For this **unvalued diadem**;
She offers them her dearest breath,
With Christ's name in't, in charge for death:
She'll bargain with them, and will give
Them God, and teach them how to live
In Him; or, if they this deny,
For Him she'll teach them how to die.
So shall she leave amongst them sown
Her Lord's blood, or at least her own.
Farewell then, all the world, adieu!
Teresa is no more for you.
Farewell all pleasures, sports, and joys,
Never till now esteemed toys!
Farewell whatever dear may be–
Mother's arms, or father's knee!
Farewell house, and farewell home!
She's for the Moors and Martyrdom.
Sweet, not so fast; lo! thy fair spouse,
Whom thou seek'st with so swift vows,
Calls thee back, and bids thee come
T' embrace a milder martyrdom . . .
Blest powers forbid thy tender life
Should bleed upon a barbarous knife;
Or some base hand have power to rase
Thy breast's chaste cabinet, and uncase
A soul kept there so sweet; oh no,
Wise Heav'n will never have it so;
Thou art Love's victim, and must die
A death more mystical and high;
Into Love's arms thou shalt let fall
A still-surviving funeral.
He is the dart must make the death
Whose stroke shall taste thy hallow'd breath;

A dart thrice dipp'd in that rich flame
Which writes thy spouse's radiant name
Upon the roof of heav'n, where aye
It shines, and with a sovereign ray
Beats bright upon the burning faces
Of souls, which in that name's sweet graces
Find everlasting smiles. So rare,
So spiritual, pure, and fair
Must be th' immortal instrument
Upon whose choice point shall be sent
A life so lov'd; and that there be
Fit executioners for thee,
The fair'st and first-born sons of fire,
Blest Seraphim, shall leave their quire
And turn Love's soldiers, upon thee
To exercise their archery.
O how oft shalt thou complain
Of a sweet and subtle pain!
Of intolerable joys!
Of a death, in which who dies
Loves his death, and dies again,
And would for ever so be slain;
And lives and dies, and knows not why
To live, but that he still may die!
How kindly will thy gentle heart
Kiss the sweetly-killing dart!
And close in his embraces keep
Those delicious wounds, that weep
Balsam, to heal themselves with thus,
When these thy deaths, so numerous,
Shall all at once die into one,
And melt thy soul's sweet mansion;
Like a soft lump of incense, hasted
By too hot a fire, and wasted
Into perfuming clouds, so fast
Shalt thou exhale to heaven at last
In a resolving sigh, and then,—
O what? Ask not the tongues of men.
Angels cannot tell; suffice,
Thyself shalt feel thine own full joys,
And hold them fast for ever there.
So soon as thou shalt first appear,
The moon of maiden stars, thy white
Mistress, attended by such bright
Souls as thy shining self, shall come,
And in her first ranks make thee room;

Where, 'mongst her snowy family,
Immortal welcomes wait for thee.
 O what delight, when she shall stand
And teach thy lips heaven, with her hand,
On which thou now may'st to thy wishes
Heap up thy consecrated kisses!
What joy shall seize thy soul, when she,
Bending her blessed eyes on thee,
Those second smiles of heaven, shall dart
Her mild rays through thy melting heart!
 Angels, thy old friends, there shall greet thee,
Glad at their own home now to meet thee.
 All thy good works which went before,
And waited for thee at the door,
Shall own thee there; and all in one
Weave a constellation
Of crowns, with which the King, thy spouse,
Shall build up thy triumphant brows.
 All thy old woes shall now smile on thee,
And thy pains sit bright upon thee:
All thy sorrows here shall shine,
And thy sufferings be divine.
Tears shall take comfort, and turn gems,
And wrongs repent to diadems.
Even thy deaths shall live, and new
Dress the soul which late they slew.
Thy wounds shall blush to such bright scars
As keep account of the Lamb's wars.
 Those rare works, where thou shalt leave writ
Love's noble history, with wit
Taught thee by none but Him, while here
They feed our souls, shall clothe thine there.
Each heavenly word by whose hid flame
Our hard hearts shall strike fire, the same
Shall flourish on thy brows, and be
Both fire to us and flame to thee;
Whose light shall live bright in thy face
By glory, in our hearts by grace.
 Thou shalt look round about, and see
Thousands of crown'd souls throng to be
Themselves thy crown, sons of thy vows,
The virgin-births with which thy spouse
Made fruitful thy fair soul; go now,
And with them all about thee bow
To Him; put on, He'll say, put on,
My rosy Love, that thy rich zone,

Sparkling with the sacred flames
Of thousand souls, whose happy names
Heaven keeps upon thy score: thy bright
Life brought them first to kiss the light
That kindled them to stars; and so
Thou with the Lamb, thy Lord, shalt go.
And, wheresoe'er He sets His white
Steps, walk with Him those ways of light,
Which who in death would live to see,
Must learn in life to die like thee.

Notes

Love . . . prove the word: The poem seeks to examine the words, or proposition, that life and death are determined by love. **in one cup:** a reference to John the Evangelist whose faith was tested by drinking from a poisoned cup **unvalued diadem:** crown of martyrdom

Samuel Butler

Famous mainly for his satiric poem, *Hudibras* (1662–1678), Samuel Butler was born in 1612 in Worcestershire, educated at King's school, Worcester. When employed in the household of the Countess of Kent, Butler was given access to the libraries and made the most of it, reading voraciously. Later he joined the service of Sir Samuel Luke, a colonel in the Parliamentary army. The puritan fanatics who formed Luke's army would offer Butler the subject matter of his most famous poem. Later Butler became secretary to Richard Vaughan, the Earl of Carbery, who, pleased with his services, made him steward of Ludlow castle. Butler possibly married during this period, but may have squandered his wife's fortunes. The second part of *Hudibras* appeared in 1663. The two parts, plus 'The Heroical Epistle of Hudibras to Sidrophel' were printed together in 1674. Butler found a patron in Charles II who, thrilled with the poem, issued an order that anybody copying or publishing the poem without license would be penalised. Charles II also bestowed upon Butler an annual pension. The final part of the poem appeared in 1678. Later Butler joined the service of George Villiers, the second Duke of Buckingham. Despite the annual pension, Butler died in poverty in 1680.

An Heroic Epistle of Hudibras to His Lady

I who was once as great as Caesar,
Am now reduced to Nebuchadnezzar;
And from as famed a conqueror
As ever took degree in war,
Or did his exercise in battle,
By you turned out to grass with cattle:
For since I am denied access
To all my earthly happiness
Am fallen from the paradise
Of your good graces, and fair eyes;
Lost to the world, and you, I'm sent
To everlasting banishment;
Where all the hopes I had t' have won
Your heart, being dashed, will break my own.

Yet if you were not so severe
To pass your doom before you hear,
You'd find, upon my just defence,
How much y' have wronged my innocence.
That once I made a vow to you,
Which yet is unperformed, 'tis true:
But not because it is unpaid,
'Tis violated, though delayed;
Or, if it were, it is no fau't,
So heinous as you'd have it thought;
To undergo the loss of ears,
Like vulgar hackney perjurers
For there's a difference in the case,
Between the noble and the base,
Who always are observed t' have done it
Upon as different an account:
The one for great and weighty cause,
To salve in honour ugly flaws;
For none are like to do it sooner
Than those who are nicest of their honour:
The other, for base gain and pay,
Forswear, and perjure by the day;
And make the exposing and retailing
Their souls and consciences a calling.

It is no scandal, nor aspersion,
Upon a great and noble person,
To say he naturally abhorred
Th' old-fashioned trick, To keep his word;
Though 'tis perfidiousness and shame
In meaner men to do the same:
For to be able to forget,
Is found more useful to the great,
Than gout, or deafness, or bad eyes,
To make 'em pass for wondrous wise.
But though the law on perjurers
Inflicts the forfeiture of ears,
It is not just that does exempt
The guilty, and punish th' innocent;
To make the ears repair the wrong
Committed by th' ungoverned tongue;
And when one member is forsworn,
Another to be cropped or torn.
And if you should, as you design,
By course of law, recover mine,
You're like, if you consider right,
To gain but little honour by it.
For he that for his lady's sake
Lays down his life or limbs at stake,
Does not so much deserve her favour,
As he that pawns his soul to have her,
This y' have acknowledged I have done,
Although you now disdain to own;
But sentence what you rather ought
T' esteem good service than a fau't.
Besides, oaths are not bound to bear
That literal sense the words infer,
But, by the practice of the age,
Are to be judged how far the engage;
And, where the sense by custom's checkt,
Are found void, and of none effect.
For no man takes or keeps a vow
But just as he sees others do;
Nor are the obliged to be so brittle,
As not to yield and bow a little:
For as best-tempered blades are found,
Before they break, to bend quite round,
So truest oaths are still most tough,
And though they bow, are breaking proof.
Then wherefore should they not b' allowed
In love a greater latitude?

For as the law of arms approves
All ways to conquest, so should love's;
And not be tied to true or false,
But make that justest that prevails
For how can that which is above
All empire, high and mighty love,
Submit its great prerogative
To any other power alive?
Shall love, that to no crown gives place,
Become the subject of a case?
The fundamental law of nature,
Be over-ruled by those made after?
Commit the censure of its cause
To any but its own great laws?
Love, that's the world's preservative,
That keeps all souls of things alive;
Controls the mighty power of fate,
And gives mankind a longer date;
The life of nature, that restores
As fast as time and death devours;
To whose free-gift the world does owe,
Not only earth, but heaven too;
For love's the only trade that's driven,
The interest of state in heaven,
Which nothing but the soul of man
Is capable to entertain.
For what can earth produce, but love
To represent the joys above?
Or who but lovers can converse,
Like angels, by the eye-discourse?
Address and compliment by vision;
Make love and court by intuition?
And burn in amorous flames as fierce
As those celestial ministers?
Then how can any thing offend,
In order to so great an end?
Or heaven itself a sin resent,
That for its own supply was meant?
That merits, in a kind mistake,
A pardon for the offence's sake.
Or if it did not, but the cause
Were left to the injury at laws,
What tyranny can disapprove
There should be equity in love;
For laws that are inanimate,
And feel no sense of love or hate,

That have no passion of their own,
Nor pity to be wrought upon,
Are only proper to inflict
Revenge on criminals as strict
But to have power to forgive,
Is empire and prerogative;
And 'tis in crowns a nobler gem
To grant a pardon than condemn.
Then since so few do what they ought,
'Tis great t' indulge a well-meant fau't.
For why should he who made address,
All humble ways, without success,
And met with nothing, in return,
But insolence, affronts, and scorn,
Not strive by wit to countermine,
And bravely carry his design?
He who was used so unlike a soldier,
Blown up with philters of love-powder?
And after letting blood, and purging,
Condemned to voluntary scourging;
Alarmed with many a horrid fright,
And clawed by goblins in the night;
Insulted on, reviled, and jeered,
With rude invasion of his beard;
And when your sex was foully scandaled,
As foully by the rabble handled;
Attacked by despicable foes,
And drubbed with mean and vulgar blows;
And, after all, to be debarred
So much as standing on his guard;
When horses, being spurred and pricked,
Have leave to kick for being kicked?

Or why should you, whose mother-wits
Are furnished with all perquisites,
That with your breeding-teeth begin,
And nursing babies, that lie in,
B' allowed to put all tricks upon
Our cully sex, and we use none?
We, who have nothing but frail vows
Against your stratagems t' oppose;
Or oaths more feeble than your own,
By which we are no less put down?
You wound, like **Parthians**, while you fly,
And kill with a retreating eye:
Retire the more, the more we press

To draw us into ambushes.
As pirates all false colours wear
T' entrap the unwary mariner,
So women, to surprise us, spread
The borrowed flags of white and red;
Display 'em thicker on their cheeks
Than their old grandmothers, the **Picts**;
And raise more devils with their looks,
Than conjurer's less subtle books;
Lay trains of amorous intrigues,
In towers, and curls, and perriwigs,
With greater art and cunning rear'd,
Than **PHILIP NYE's** thanksgiving beard,
Preposterously to entice, and gain
Those to adore 'em they disdain;
And only draw 'em in, to clog
With idle names a catalogue.

A lover is, the more he's brave,
T' his mistress but the more a slave;
And whatsoever she commands,
Becomes a favour from her hands;
Which he's obliged t' obey, and must,
Whether it be unjust or just.
Then when he is compelled by her
T' adventures he would else forbear,
Who with his honour can withstand,
Since force is greater than command?
And when necessity's obeyed,
Nothing can be unjust or bad
And therefore when the mighty powers
Of love, our great ally and yours,
Joined forces not to be withstood
By frail enamoured flesh and blood,
All I have done, unjust or ill,
Was in obedience to your will;
And all the blame that can be due,
Falls to your cruelty and you.
Nor are those scandals I confest,
Against my will and interest,
More than is daily done of course
By all men, when they're under force;
When some upon the rack confess
What th' hangman and their prompters please;
But are no sooner out of pain,
Than they deny it all again.

But when the Devil turns confessor,
Truth is a crime he takes no pleasure
To hear, or pardon, like the founder
Of liars, whom they all claim under
And therefore, when I told him none,
I think it was the wiser done.
Nor am I without precedent,
The first that on the adventure went
All mankind ever did of course,
And daily dues the same, or worse.
For what romance can show a lover,
That had a lady to recover,
And did not steer a nearer course,
To fall a-board on his amours?
And what at first was held a crime,
Has turned to honourable in time.

To what a height did I infant ROME,
By ravishing of women, come
When men upon their spouses seized,
And freely married where they pleased,
They ne'er forswore themselves, nor lied.
Nor, in the mind they were in, died;
Nor took the pains t' address and sue,
Nor played the masquerade to woo;
Disdained to stay for friends' consents;
Nor juggled about settlements:
Did need no license, nor no priest,
Nor friends, nor kindred, to assist;
Nor lawyers, to join land and money
In the holy state of matrimony,
Before they settled hands and hearts,
Till alimony or death them parts:
Nor would endure to stay until
The' had got the very bride's good will;
But took a wise and shorter course
To win the ladies, downright force.
And justly made 'em prisoners then,
As they have often since, us men,
With acting plays, and dancing jigs,
The luckiest of all love's intrigues;
And when they had them at their pleasure,
Then talked of love and flames at leisure;
For after matrimony's over,
He that holds out but half a lover,
Deserves for every minute more

Than half a year of love before;
For which the dames in contemplation
Of that best way of application,
Proved nobler wives than ever was known,
By suit or treaty to be won;
And such as all posterity
Could never equal nor come nigh.

For women first were made for men,
Not men for them. — It follows, then,
That men have right to every one,
And they no freedom of their own
And therefore men have power to choose,
But they no charter to refuse.
Hence 'tis apparent, that what course
Soever we take to your amours,
Though by the indirectest way,
'Tis no injustice, nor foul play;
And that you ought to take that course,
As we take you, for better or worse;
And gratefully submit to those
Who you, before another, chose.
For why should every savage beast
Exceed his great lord's interest?
Have freer power than he in grace,
And nature, o'er the creature has?
Because the laws he since has made
Have cut off all the power he had;
Retrenched the absolute dominion
That nature gave him over women;
When all his power will not extend
One law of nature to suspend;
And but to offer to repeal
The smallest clause, is to rebel.
This, if men rightly understood
Their privilege, they would make good;
And not, like sots, permit their wives
T' encroach on their prerogatives;
For which sin they deserve to be
Kept, as they are, in slavery:
And this some precious Gifted Teachers,
Unreverently reputed leachers,
And disobeyed in making love,
Have vowed to all the world to prove,
And make ye suffer, as you ought,
For that uncharitable fau't.

But I forget myself, and rove
Beyond th' instructions of my love.

Forgive me (Fair) and only blame
Th' extravagancy of my flame,
Since 'tis too much at once to show
Excess of love and temper too.
All I have said that's bad and true,
Was never meant to aim at you,
Who have so sovereign a control
O'er that poor slave of yours, my soul,
That, rather than to forfeit you,
Has ventured loss of heaven too:
Both with an equal power possessed,
To render all that serve you blest:
But none like him, who's destined either
To have, or lose you, both together.
And if you'll but this fault release
(For so it must be, since you please)
I'll pay down all that vow, and more,
Which you commanded, and I swore,
And expiate upon my skin
Th' arrears in full of all my sin.
For 'tis but just that I should pay
Th' accruing penance for delay,
Which shall be done, until it move
Your equal pity and your love.

The Knight, perusing this Epistle,
Believed h' had brought her to his whistle;
And read it like a jocund lover,
With great applause t' himself, twice over;
Subscribed his name, but at a fit
And humble distance to his wit;
And dated it with wondrous art,
Given from the bottom of his heart;
Then sealed it with his Coat of Love,
A smoking faggot — and above,
Upon a scroll — I burn, and weep;
And near it — For her Ladyship;
Of all her sex most excellent,
These to her gentle hands present.
Then gave it to his faithful Squire,
With lessons how t' observe and eye her.

She first considered which was better,

To send it back, or burn the letter.
But guessing that it might import,
Though nothing else, at least her sport,
She opened it, and read it out,
With many a smile and leering flout:
Resolved to answer it in kind,
And thus performed what she designed.

Notes

Parthians: the Parthian Empire, in the north of Iran, from 250 BC to about 250 AD **Picts:** people of the medieval age in Scotland **Philip Nye:** a Cromwell adviseor who pleaded for toleration

John Denham

Born in Dublin in 1615, educated at Oxford, Denham was called to the Bar, but never practised law. His early work consisted of translations of Greek epics such as the *Aeneid*. In 1642 he published *Cooper's Hill*, a topographical poem that inaugurated a genre in English, to be imitated later by major writers like Alexander Pope. During the war he was the Sheriff of Surrey. He supported the cause of Charles II and was made first a Surveyor of the King's works (he succeeded Inigo Jones in the position), a knight of the Bath and later elected to the Royal Society after the Restoration. He was made a member of Parliament in 1661. He may have suffered from dementia in the last years. John Denham died in 1669. Almost his entire reputation today rests on *Cooper's Hill.*

Cooper's Hill (extracts)

Sure we have poets that did never dream
Upon **Parnassus**, nor did taste the stream
Of **Helicon**, and therefore I suppose
Those made not poets, but the poets those.
And as Courts make not Kings, but Kings the Court,

So where the Muses and their troops resort,
Parnassus stands, if I can be to thee
A poet, thou Parnassus art to me.
Nor wonder, if (**advantaged in my flight**,
By taking wing from thy auspicious height)
Through untraced ways and airy paths I fly,
More boundless in my fancy than my eye.
Exalted to this height, I first look down
On Paul's, as men from thence upon the town.
Paul's, the late theme of such a muse whose flight
Has bravely reached and soared above thy height:
Now shalt thou stand, though time, or sword, or fire,
Or zeal (more fierce than they) thy fall conspire,
Secure, whilst thee the best of poets sings,
Preserved from ruin by the best of kings.
As those who raised in body, or in thought
Above the earth, or the air's middle vault,
Behold how winds, and storms and meteors grow,
How clouds condense to rain, congeal to snow,
And see the thunder formed, before it tear
The air, secure from danger and from fear,
So raised above the tumult and the crowd
I see the city, in a thicker cloud
Of business, than of smoke, where men like ants
Toil to prevent imaginary wants;
Yet all in vain, increasing with their store,
Their vast desires, but make their wants the more.
As food to unsound bodies, though it please
The appetite, feeds only the disease.
Where, with like haste, though several ways they run,
Some to undo, and some to be undone;
While luxury, and wealth, like war and peace,
Are each the other's ruin, and increase;
As rivers lost in seas, some secret vein
Thence reconveys, there to be lost again.
Some study plots, and some those plots t' undo,
Others to make 'em, and undo 'em too,
False to their hopes, afraid to be secure,
Those mischiefs only which they make, endure,
Blinded with light, and sick of being well,
In tumults seek their peace, their Heaven in Hell.
Oh happiness of sweet retired content!
To be at once secure, and innocent.
Windsor the next (where Mars with Venus dwells,
Beauty with strength) above the valley swells
Into my eye, as the late married dame

(Who proud, yet seems to make that pride her shame)
When nature quickens in her pregnant womb
Her wishes past, and now her hopes to come:
With such an easy, and unforced ascent,
Windsor her gentle bosom doth present;
Where no stupendous cliff, no threatening heights
Access deny, no horrid steep affrights,
But such a rise, as doth at once invite
A pleasure, and a reverence from the sight.
   Thy master's emblem, in whose face I saw
A friend-like sweetness, and a king-like awe,
Where majesty, and love so mixed appear,
Both gently kind, both royally severe.
So Windsor, humble in itself, seems proud,
To be the base of that majestic load,
   Than which no hill a nobler burden bears,
But Atlas only, that supports the spheres.
Nature this mount so fitly did advance,
We might conclude, that nothing is by chance
So placed, as if she did on purpose raise
The hill, to rob the builder of his praise.
For none commends his judgment, that doth choose
That which a blind man only could refuse;
Such are the towers which th' hoary temples graced
   Of Cybele, when all her heavenly race
Do homage to her, yet she cannot boast
Amongst that numerous, and celestial host
More heroes than can Windsor, nor doth fame's
Immortal book record more noble names.
Nor to look back so far, to whom this isle
Must owe the glory of so brave a pile,
Whether to Caesar, **Albanact**, or Brute,
The British Arthur, or the Danish Knute,
(Though this of old no less contest did move,
Than when for Homer's birth seven cities strove)
(Like him in birth, thou should'st be like in fame,
As thine his fate, if mine had been his flame)
But whosoever it was, nature designed
First a brave place, and then as brave a mind.
No to recount those several kings, to whom
It gave a cradle, or to whom a tomb,
   But thee (great Edward) and thy greater son,
   He that the lilies wore, and he that won,
   And thy **Bellona** who deserves her share
In all thy glories, of that royal pair
Which waited on thy triumph, she brought one.

Thy son the other brought, and she that son
Nor of less hopes could her great off-spring prove;
A royal eagle cannot breed a dove.

Then didst thou found that order, whether love
Or victory thy royal thoughts did move,
Each was a noble cause, nor was it less
I' th' institution, than the great success
Whilst every part conspires to give it grace,
The King, the cause, the patron, and the place,
Which foreign kings, and emperors esteem
The second honour to their diadem.

So having tasted Windsor, casting round
My wandering eye, an emulous hill doth bound
My more contracted sight, whose top of late
A chapel crowned, till in the common fate,
The adjoining abbey fell: (may no such storm
Fall on our times, where ruin must reform)
Tell me, (my muse) what monstrous dire offence,
What crime could any Christian king incense
To such a rage? Was't luxury, or lust?
Was he so temperate, so chaste, so just?
Were these their crimes? they were his own, much more;
But they (alas) were rich, and he was poor;
And having spent the treasures of his crown,
Condemns their luxury to feed his own;
And yet this act, to varnish o'er the shame
Of sacrilege, must bear devotion's name.
And he might think it just, the cause and time
Considered well, for none commits a crime
Appearing such, but as 'tis understood,
A real, or at least a seeming good.
While for the Church his learned pen disputes
His much more learned sword his pen confutes,
Thus to the ages past he makes amends,
Their charity destroys, their faith defends.
Then did religion in a lazy cell,
In empty, airy contemplation dwell;
And like the block unmoved lay: but ours,
As much too active like the stork devours.
Is there no temperate region can be known.
Betwixt their frigid, and our torrid zone?
Could we not wake from that lethargic dream,
But to be restless in a worse extreme?

And for that lethargy was there no cure,
  But to be cast into a calenture?
Can knowledge have no bound, but must advance
So far, to make us wish for ignorance?
And rather in the dark to grope our way,
Than led by a false guide to err by day?

Parting from thence 'twixt anger, shame and fear,
Those for what's past, and this for what's too near:
My eye descending from the hill, surveys
Where Thames among the wanton valleys strays.
Thames, the most loved of all the ocean's sons,
By his old sire to his embraces runs,
Hasting to pay his tribute to the sea,
  Like mortal life to meet eternity.
And though his clearer sand, no golden veins,
  Like Tagus and **Pactolus** streams, contains
His genuine, and less guilty wealth t' explore,
Search not his bottom, but survey his shore;
O'er which he kindly spreads his spacious wing
And hatches plenty for the ensuing spring.
Nor with a furious, and unruly wave,
Like profuse kings, resumes the wealth he gave,
No unexpected inundations spoil
  The mower's hopes, nor mock the ploughman's toil;
Then like a lover he forsakes his shores,
Whose stay with jealous eyes his spouse implores;
Till with a parting kiss he saves her tears,
And promising return, secures her fears;
As a wise king first settles fruitful peace
In his own realms, and with their rich increase,
Seeks wars abroad, and in triumph brings
The spoils of kingdoms, and the crowns of kings.
So Thames to London doth at first present
Those tributes, which neighbouring counties sent,
But as his second visit from the east,
  Spices he brings, and treasures from the west.
Finds wealth where 'tis, bestows it where it wants,
Cities in deserts, woods in cities plants.
Rounds the whole globe, and with his flying towers
Brings home to us, and makes both Indies ours;
So that to us no thing, no place is strange
While thy fair bosom is the world's exchange:
O could my verse freely and smoothly flow,
As thy pure flood, Heaven should no longer know

Her old **Eridanus**; thy purer stream
Should bathe the gods and be the poets' theme.

Here nature, whether more intent to please
Us or herself, with strange varieties,
(For things of wonder more, no less delight
To the wise maker's, than beholders' sight.
Though these delights from several causes move;
For so our children, thus our friends we love)
Wisely she knew the harmony of things,
As well as that of sounds, from discords springs.
Such was the discord, which did first disperse
Form, order, beauty through the universe;
While dryness moisture, coldness heat resists,
All that we have, and that we are, subsists.
While the steep horrid roughness of the wood
Strives with the gentle calmness of the flood.
Such huge extremes, when Nature doth unite,
Wonder from thence results, from thence delight.
The stream is so transparent, pure, and clear,
That had the self-enamoured youth gazed here,
So fatally deceived he had not been,
While he the bottom, not his face had seen.
And such the roughness of the hill, on which
Diana her toils, and Mars his tents might pitch
And as our surly supercilious lords,
Big in their frowns, and haughty in their words,
Look down on those, whose humble fruitful pain
Their proud, and barren greatness must sustain:
So looks the hill upon the stream; between
There lies a spacious, and a fertile green,
Where from the woods, the Dryads oft meet
Thy Nyads, and with their nimble feet,
Soft dances lead, although their airy shape
All but a quick poetic sight escape.
There **Faunus and Silvanus** keep their courts;
And thither all the horrid host resorts
(When like the elixir, with his evening beams,
The sun has turned to gold the silver streams)
To graze the ranker mead, that noble herd,
On whose sublime and shady fronts is reared
Nature's great master-piece; to show how soon
Great things are made, but sooner much undone.
Here have I seen our Charles, when great affairs
Give leave to slacken, and unbend his cares,

Chasing the royal stag, the gallant beast,
Roused with the noise, 'twist hope and fear distressed,
Resolves 'tis better to avoid, than meet
His danger, trusting to his winged feet:
But when he sees the dogs, now by the view,
Now by the scent, his speed with speed pursue,
He tries his friends, amongst the lesser herd,
Where he but lately was obeyed, and feared,
Safety he seeks: the herd, unkindly wise,
Or chases him from thence, or from him flies.
Like a declining statesman, left forlorn
To his friends' pity, and pursuers' scorn.
Wearied, forsaken, and pursued, at last
All safety in despair of safety placed,
Courage he thence assumes, resolved to bear
All their assaults, since 'tis in vain to fear.
But when he sees the eager chase renewed,
Himself by dogs, the dogs by men pursued.
When neither speed, nor art, nor friends, nor force
Could help him towards the stream he bends his course
Hoping those lesser beasts would not assay
An element more merciless than they.
But fearless they pursue, nor can the flood
Quench their dire thirst (alas) they thirst for blood.
As some brave hero, whom his baser foes
In troops surround, now these assail, now those,
Though prodigal of life, disdains to die
By vulgar hands; but if he can descry
Some nobler foes approach, to him he calls
And begs his fate, and then contented falls:
So the tall stag amidst the lesser hounds,
Repels their force, and wounds returns for wounds.
Till Charles from his unerring hand lets fly
A mortal shaft, then glad, and proud to die
By such a wound he falls, the crystal flood
Dying he dies, and purples with his blood.

This a more innocent, and happy chase,
Than when of old, but in the selfsame place,
Fair liberty pursued, and meant a prey
To tyranny, here turned, and stood at bay.
When in that remedy all hope was placed
Which was, or should have been at least the last;
For armed subjects can have no pretence
Against their princes, but their just defence,

And whether then, or no, I leave to them
To justify, who else themselves condemn:
Yet might the fact be just, if we may guess
The justness of an action from success.

Here was that charter sealed, wherein the Crown
All marks of arbitrary power lays down:
Tyrant and slave, those names of hate and fear,
The happier style of king and subject bear:
Happy, when both to the same centre move,
When kings give liberty, and subjects love.
Therefore not long in force this charter stood;
Wanting that seal, it must be sealed in blood.
The subjects armed, the more their princes gave,
But this advantage took, the more to crave:
Till kings by giving, give themselves away.
And even that power, that should deny, betray.
'Who gives constrained, but his own fear reviles
Nor thanked, but scorned; nor are they gifts, but spoils.
And they, whom no denial can withstand,
Seem but to ask, while thy indeed command.
Thus all to limit royalty conspire,
While each forgets to limit his desire
Till kings like old **Antaeus** by their fall,
Being forced, their courage from despair recall.

When a calm river raised with sudden rains,
Or snows dissolved o'erflows the' adjoining plains,
The husbandmen with high-raised banks secure
Their greedy hopes, and this he can endure.
But if with bays and dams they strive to force
His channel to a new, or narrow course
No longer then within his banks he dwells,
First to a torrent, then a deluge swells:
Stronger and fiercer by restraint he roars,
And knows no bound, but makes his power his shores.
Thus kings by grasping more than they can hold,
First made their subjects by oppressions bold,
And popular sway by forcing kings to give
More, than was fit for subjects to receive,
Ran to the same extreme, and one excess
Made both by striving to be greater, less.
Nor any way, but seeking to have more
Makes either lose what each possessed before.
Therefore their boundless power till princes draw
Within the channel, and the shores of law,

And may the law, which teaches kings to sway
Their sceptres, teach their subjects to obey.

Notes

Parnassus: a mountain in Greece, supposedly home to the Muses **Helicon:** a river in Greece **advantaged in my flight:** a reference to Daedalus **Albanact:** Trojan prince who committed suicide **Bellona:** ancient Roman goddess of war **Pactolus:** a river near the Aegean coast of Turkey; it once contained electrum and according to myth King Midas ended his curse by washing himself in the river **Eridanus:** a constellation, represented as a river, named after the Greek river Po **Faunus and Silvanus:** the Roman gods of the woods and countryside **Antaeus:** a giant, the son of Poseidon and Gaia

Richard Lovelace

Richard Lovelace (1618–1657), born to a wealthy family that owned estates in Kent and shares in the Virginia Company, was educated at Oxford. He published a play at the age of sixteen, which was staged at Blackfriars. Due to the family's Royalist sympathies – he had fought in the King's wars against Scotland during 1639–40, Lovelace was imprisoned in 1642 after he gave a petition on their behalf to the Parliament. During this imprisonment, he wrote perhaps one of the most popular descriptions of incarceration in 'To Althea, from Prison': 'Stone walls do not a prison make/Nor iron bars a cage.' After leaving prison he joined the French army and fought in Europe. He returned to England in 1647 and was imprisoned in 1648. During his second term in prison he wrote the poems that collectively turned into the volume *Lucasta* (1649, the 'Lucasta' of the poems is Lucy Sacherevell). Lovelace sold most of his lands and may even have died in poverty.

To Althea, from Prison

When Love with unconfined wings
   Hovers within my Gates;
And my divine *Althea* brings
   To whisper at the Grates;

When I lye tangled in her hair
And fettered to her eye;
The *Gods* that wanton in the Air,
Know no such Liberty.

When flowing Cups run swiftly round
With no allaying *Thames*,
Our careless heads with Roses bound,
Our hearts with Loyal Flames;
When thirsty grief in Wine we steep,
When Healths and draughts go free,
Fishes that tipple in the Deep,
Know no such Liberty.

When (like committed linnets) I
With shriller throat shall sing
The sweetness, Mercy, Majesty,
And glories of my KING;
When I shall voice aloud, how Good
He is, how Great should be;
Enlarged Winds that curl the Flood,
Know no such Liberty.

Stone Walls do not a Prison make,
Nor Iron bars a Cage;
Minds innocent and quiet take
That for an Hermitage;
If I have freedom in my Love,
And in my soul am free;
Angels alone that sore above,
Enjoy such Liberty.

To Lucasta, Going to the Wars

Tell me not (Sweet) I am unkind,
That from the nunnery
Of thy chaste breast and quiet mind
To war and arms I fly.

True, a new mistress now I chase,
The first foe in the field;
And with a stronger faith embrace
A sword, a horse, a shield.

Yet this inconstancy is such
As you too shall adore;

I could not love thee (Dear) so much,
  Loved I not **Honour** more.

Notes

Loved I not Honour more: Lovelace casts 'honour' as the new mistress.

To Lucasta, Taking the Waters at Tunbridge

Ye happy floods! that now must pass
The sacred conducts of her womb,
Smooth and transparent as your face,
When you are deaf, and winds are dumb.

Be proud! and if your waters be
Fouled with a counterfeited tear,
Or some false sigh hath stained ye,
Haste, and be purified there.

And when her rosy gates y'have traced,
Continue yet some Orient wet,
'Till, turned into a gemme, y'are placed
Like diamonds with rubies set.

Yee drops, that dew th' Arabian bowers,
Tell me, did you e're smell or view
On any leaf of all your flowers
So sweet a scent, so rich a hiew?

But as through th' Organs of her breath
You trickle wantonly, beware:
Ambitious Seas in their just death
As well as Lovers, must have share

And see! you boil as well as I;
You, that to cool her did aspire,
Now troubled and neglected lye,
Nor can your selves quench your own fire.

Yet still be happy in the thought,
That in so small a time as this,
Through all the Heavens you were brought
Of Virtue, Honour, Love and Bliss.

Abraham Cowley

Abraham Cowley (1618–1667) is believed to have read *The Faerie Queene* in his parents' house before he started school. At the age of ten he wrote the *Tragicall History of Piramus and Thisbe*, an epic romance. A precocious student, Cowley continued to produce poetry through his school years. At King's College, Cambridge, he distinguished himself as an extraordinary pupil, and continued with his writing, producing epic texts and poetry in English and Latin. During the Civil War, Cowley stayed in Paris in exile, and often made journeys to other parts of Europe on missions for the royal family. In 1647 a collection of his love poetry, *The Mistress*, was published. After the Restoration he retired to the country but was active in promoting the Royal Society's efforts, publishing pamphlets such as *The Advancement of Experimental Philosophy.*

To The Royal Society (Extracts)

Philosophy the great and only heir
Of all that human knowledge which has bin
Unforfeited by man's rebellious sin,
Though full of years he do appear,
(Philosophy, I say, and call it, he,
For whatso'ere the painter's fancy be,
It a male-virtue seems to me)
Has still been kept in nonage till of late,
Nor managed or enjoyed his vast estate:
Three or four thousand years one would have thought,
To ripeness and perfection might have brought
A science so well bred and nursed,
And of such hopeful parts too at the first.
But, oh, the guardians and the tutors then,
(Some negligent, and some ambitious men)
Would ne'er consent to set him free,
Or his own natural powers to let him see,
Lest that should put an end to their authority.

That his own business he might quite forget,
They amused him with the sports of wanton wit,
With the desserts of poetry they fed him,
Instead of solid meats t' increase his force;
Instead of vigorous exercise they led him

Into the pleasant labyrinths of ever-fresh discourse:
Instead of carrying him to see
The riches which do hoarded for him lie
In Nature's endless treasury,
They chose his eye to entertain
(His curious but not covetous eye)
With painted scenes, and pageants of the brain.
Some few exalted spirits this latter age has shown,
That laboured to assert the liberty
(From guardians, who were now usurpers grown)
Of this old minor still, captived Philosophy;
But 'twas rebellion called to fight
For such a long oppressed right.
Bacon at last, a mighty man, arose
Whom a wise King and Nature chose
Lord Chancellor of both their laws,
And boldly undertook the injured pupil's cause.

Authority, which did a body boast,
Though 'twas but air condensed, and stalked about,
Like some old giant's more gigantic ghost,
To terrify the learned rout
With the plain magic of true reason's light,
He chased out of our sight,
Nor suffered living men to be misled
By the vain shadows of the dead:
To graves, from whence it rose, the conquered phantom fled;
He broke that monstrous god which stood
In midst of th' orchard, and the whole did claim,
Which with a useless scythe of wood,
And something else not worth a name,
(Both vast for show, yet neither fit
Or to defend, or to beget;
Ridiculous and senseless terrors!) made
Children and superstitious men afraid.
The orchard's open now, and free;
Bacon has broke that scarecrow deity;
Come, enter, all that will,
Behold the ripened fruit, come gather now your fill.
Yet still, methinks, we fain would be
Catching at the forbidden tree,
We would be like the Deity,
When truth and falsehood, good and evil, we
Without the senses aid within our selves would see;
For 'tis God only who can find
All Nature in his mind.

From words, which are but pictures of the thought,
Though we our thoughts from them perversely drew
To things, the mind's right object, he it brought,
Like foolish birds to painted grapes we flew;
He sought and gathered for our use the true;
And when on heaps the chosen bunches lay,
He pressed them wisely the mechanic way,
Till all their juice did in one vessel join,
Ferment into a nourishment divine,
The thirsty soul's refreshing wine.
Who to the life an exact piece would make,
Must not from other's work a copy take;
No, not from Rubens or Vandyke;
Much less content himself to make it like
Th' ideas and the images which lie
In his own fancy, or his memory.
No, he before his sight must place
The natural and living face;
The real object must command
Each judgment of his eye, and motion of his hand.
From these and all long errors of the way,
In which our wandering predecessors went,
And like th' old Hebrews many years did stray
In deserts but of small extent;
Bacon, like Moses, led us forth at last,
The barren wilderness he past,
Did on the very border stand
Of the blest promised land,
And from the mountain's top of his exalted wit,
Saw it himself, and showed us it.
But life did never to one man allow
Time to discover worlds, and conquer too;
Nor can so short a line sufficient be
To fathom the vast depths of Nature's sea:
The work he did we ought t' admire,
And were unjust if we should more require
From his few years, divided 'twixt th' excess
Of low affliction, and high happiness.
For who on things remote can fix his sight,
That's always in a triumph, or a fight?

From you, great champions, we expect to get
These spacious countries but discovered yet;
Countries where yet in stead of Nature, we
Her images and idols worshipped see:
These large and wealthy regions to subdue,

Though learning has whole armies at command,
Quartered about in every land,
A better troop she never together drew.
Methinks, like Gideon's little band,
God with design has picked out you,
To do these noble wonders by a few:
When the whole host he saw, they are (said he)
Too many to overcome for me;
And now he chooses out his men,
Much in the way that he did then:
Not those many whom he found
Idly extended on the ground,
To drink with their dejected head
The stream just so as by their mouths it fled:
No, but those few who took the waters up,
And made of their laborious hands the cup.

With courage and success you the bold work begin;
Your cradle has not idle bin:
None e're but Hercules and you could be
At five years age worthy a history.
And never did fortune better yet
Th' historian to the story fit:
As you from all old errors free
And purge the body of philosophy;
So from all modern follies he
Has vindicated eloquence and wit.
His candid style like a clean stream does slide,
And his bright fancy all the way
Does like the sun-shine in it play;
It does like Thames, the best of rivers, glide,
Where the god does not rudely overturn,
But gently pour the crystal urn,
And with judicious hand does the whole current guide.
'T has all the beauties Nature can impart,
And all the comely dress without the paint of art.

On the Death of William Hervey

It was a dismal and a fearful night:
Scarce could the Morn drive on th' unwilling Light,
When Sleep, Death's image, left my troubled breast
By something liker Death possest.
My eyes with tears did uncommanded flow,
And on my soul hung the dull weight

Of some intolerable fate.
What bell was that? Ah me! too much I know!

My sweet companion and my gentle peer,
Why hast thou left me thus unkindly here,
Thy end for ever and my life to moan?
O, thou hast left me all alone!
Thy soul and body, when death's agony
Besieged around thy noble heart,
Did not with more reluctance part
Than I, my dearest Friend, do part from thee.

My dearest Friend, would I had died for thee!
Life and this world henceforth will tedious be:
Nor shall I know hereafter what to do
If once my griefs prove tedious too.
Silent and sad I walk about all day,
As sullen ghosts stalk speechless by
Where their hid treasures lie;
Alas! my treasure's gone; why do I stay?

Say, for you saw us, ye immortal lights,
How oft unwearied have we spent the nights,
Till the Ledaean stars, so famed for love,
Wonder'd at us from above!
We spent them not in toys, in lusts, or wine;
But search of deep Philosophy,
Wit, Eloquence, and Poetry—
Arts which I loved, for they, my Friend, were thine.

Ye fields of Cambridge, our dear Cambridge, say
Have ye not seen us walking every day?
Was there a tree about which did not know
The love betwixt us two?
Henceforth, ye gentle trees, for ever fade;
Or your sad branches thicker join
And into darksome shades combine,
Dark as the grave wherein my Friend is laid!

Large was his soul: as large a soul as e'er
Submitted to inform a body here;
High as the place 'twas shortly in Heaven to have,
But low and humble as his grave.
So high that all the virtues there did come,
As to their chiefest seat
Conspicuous and great;
So low, that for me too it made a room.

Knowledge he only sought, and so soon caught
As if for him Knowledge had rather sought;
Nor did more learning ever crowded lie
   In such a short mortality.
Whenever the skilful youth discoursed or writ,
   Still did the notions throng
   About his eloquent tongue;
Nor could his ink flow faster than his wit.

His mirth was the pure spirits of various wit,
Yet never did his God or friends forget;
And when deep talk and wisdom came in view,
   Retired, and gave to them their due.
For the rich help of books he always took,
   Though his own searching mind before
   Was so with notions written o'er,
As if wise Nature had made that her book.

With as much zeal, devotion, piety,
He always lived, as other saints do die.
Still with his soul severe account he kept,
   Weeping all debts out ere he slept.
Then down in peace and innocence he lay,
   Like the Sun's laborious light,
   Which still in water sets at night,
Unsullied with his journey of the day.

But happy Thou, taken from this frantic age,
Where ignorance and hypocrisy does rage!
A fitter time for Heaven no soul ever chose—
   The place now only free from those.
There among the blest thou dost for ever shine;
   And wheresoe'er thou casts thy view
   Upon that white and radiant crew,
See'st not a soul clothed with more light than thine.

Notes

What bell was that: the ringing of a bell to indicate a death

Andrew Marvell

Born in 1621 in Yorkshire, Andrew Marvell studied at Hull grammar school and later, at Trinity College, Cambridge.He spent some time travelling in Europe and on his return became a tutor to Mary, the daughter of Lord Fairfax, at Nun Appleton in Yorkshire. He later became tutor to Oliver Cromwell's ward, William Dutton. After a period of service as Latin secretary to John Milton in the foreign office, he was made the Member of Parliament for Hull, a post he held until his death. After the restoration of monarchy in 1660 Marvell wrote satires targeting members of the court, which were not published until his death (the most famous of these was *Last Instructions to a Painter*). Marvell died in 1678 in London.

Upon Appleton House (extracts)

Within this sober Frame expect
Work of no foreign *Architect*;
That unto Caves the Quarries drew,
And Forests did to Pastures hew;
Who of his great Design in pain
Did for a Model vault his Brain,
Whose Columns should so high be raised
To arch the Brows that on them gazed.

Why should of all things Man unruled
Such unproportioned dwellings build?
The Beasts are by their Dens expressed:
And Birds contrive an equal Nest;
The low roofed Tortoises do dwell
In cases fit of Tortoise-shell:
No Creature loves an empty space;
Their Bodies measure out their Place.

But He, superfluously spread,
Demands more room alive then dead.
And in his hollow Palace goes
Where Winds as he themselves may lose.
What need of all this Marble Crust
T'impark the wanton Mose of Dust,
That thinks by Breadth the World t'unite
Though the **first Builders fail'd in Height**?

But all things are composed here
Like Nature, orderly and near:
In which we the Dimensions find
Of that more sober Age and Mind,
When larger sized Men did stoop
To enter at a narrow loop;
As practising, in doors so strait,
To strain themselves through *Heavens Gate*.

Humility alone designs
Those short but admirable Lines,
By which, ungirt and unconstrain'd,
Things greater are in less contain'd.
Let others vainly strive t'immure
The *Circle* in the *Quadrature!*
These *holy Mathematicks* can
In ev'ry Figure equal Man.

Yet thus the laden House does sweat,
And scarce endures the *Master* great:
But where he comes the swelling Hall
Stirs, and the *Square* grows *Spherical;*
More by his *Magnitude* distrest,
Than he is by its straitness prest:
And too officiously it slights
That in it self which him delights.

So Honour better Lowness bears,
Then That unwonted Greatness wears
Height with a certain *Grace* does bend,
But low Things clownishly ascend.
And yet what needs there here Excuse,
Where ev'ry Thing does answer Use?
Where neatness nothing can condemn,
Nor Pride invent what to contemn?

A Stately *Frontispice Of Poor*
Adorns without the open Door:
Nor less the Rooms within commends
Daily new *Furniture Of Friends.*
The House was built upon the Place
Only as for **a Mark Of Grace**;
And for an *Inn* to entertain
Its *Lord* a while, but not remain.

While with slow Eyes we these survey,
And on each pleasant footstep stay,

We opportunly may relate
The progress of this Houses Fate.
A *Nunnery* first gave it birth.
For *Virgin Buildings* oft brought forth.
And all that Neighbour-Ruine shows
The Quarries whence this dwelling rose.

Near to this gloomy Cloysters Gates
There dwelt the blooming Virgin *Thwates,*
Fair beyond Measure, and an Heir
Which might Deformity make fair.
And oft She spent the Summer Suns
Discoursing with the *Suttle Nunns.*
Whence in these Words one to her weav'd,
(As 'twere by Chance) Thoughts long conceiv'd

'Within this holy leisure we
Live innocently as you see.
these Walls restrain the World without,
But hedge our Liberty about.
These Bars inclose the wider Den
Of those wild Creatures, called Men.
The Cloyster outward shuts its Gates,
And, from us, locks on them the Grates.

'But much it to our work would add
If here your hand, your Face we had:
By it we would our Lady touch;
Yet thus She you resembles much.
Some of your Features, as we sow'd,
Through ev'ry Shrine should be bestow'd.
And in one Beauty we would take
Enough a thousand Saints to make.

'Nor is our *Order* yet so nice,
Delight to banish as a Vice.
Here Pleasure Piety doth meet;
One perfecting the other Sweet.
So through the mortal fruit we boyl
The Sugars uncorrupting Oyl:
And that which perish while we pull,
Is thus preserved clear and full.

'For such indeed are all our Arts;
Still handling Natures finest Parts.
Flow'rs dress the Altars; for the Clothes,
The Sea-born Amber we compose;

Balms for the griv'd we draw; and pasts
We mold, as Baits for curious tasts.
What need is here of Man? unless
These as sweet Sins we should confess.

'Each Night among us to your side
Appoint a fresh and Virgin Bride;
Whom if *Our Lord* at midnight find,
Yet Neither should be left behind.
Where you may lye as chast in Bed,
As Pearls together billeted.
All Night embracing Arm in Arm,
Like Chrystal pure with Cotton warm.

'But what is this to all the store
Of Joys you see, and may make more!
Try but a while, if you be wise:
The Tryal neither Costs, nor Tyes.'
Now *Fairfax* seek her promis'd faith:
Religion that dispensed hath;
Which She hence forward does begin;
The *Nuns* smooth Tongue has suckt her in.

Oft, though he knew it was in vain,
Yet would he valiantly complain.
'Is this that *Sanctity* so great,
An Art by which you finly'r cheat
Hypocrite Witches, hence *avant*,
Who though in prison yet inchant!
Death only can such Theeves make fast,
As rob though in the Dungeon cast.

'Were there but, when this House was made,
One Stone that a just Hand had laid,
It must have fall'n upon her Head
Who first Thee from thy Faith misled.
And yet, how well soever ment,
With them 'twould soon grow fraudulent
For like themselves they alter all,
And vice infects the very Wall.

'But sure those Buildings last not long,
Founded by Folly, kept by Wrong.
I know what Fruit their Gardens yield,
When they it think by Night conceal'd.
Fly from their Vices. 'Tis thy 'state,
Not Thee, that they would consecrate.

Fly from their Ruine. How I fear
Though guiltless lest thou perish there.'

What should he do? He would respect
Religion, but not Right neglect:
For first Religion taught him Right,
And dazled not but clear'd his sight.
Sometimes resolv'd his Sword he draws,
But reverenceth then the Laws:
For **Justice still** that Courage led;
First from a Judge, then Souldier bred.

Small Honour would be in the Storm.
The *Court* him grants the lawful Form;
Which licens'd either Peace or Force,
To hinder the unjust Divorce.
Yet still the *Nuns* his Right debar'd,
Standing upon their holy Guard.
Ill-counsell'd Women, do you know
Whom you resist, or what you do?

Is not this he whose Offspring fierce
Shall fight through all the *Universe*;
And with successive Valour try
France, Poland, either *Germany;*
Till one, as long since prophecy'd,
His Horse through conquer'd *Britain* ride?
Yet, against Fate, his Spouse they kept;
And the great Race would intercept.

Some to the Breach against their Foes
Their *Wooden Saints* in vain oppose
Another bolder stands at push
With their old *Holy-Water Brush.*
While the disjointed *Abbess* threads
The gingling Chain-shot of her *Beads.*
But their lowd'st Cannon were their Lungs;
And sharpest Weapons were their Tongues.

But, waving these aside like Flyes,
Young *Fairfax* through the Wall does rise.
Then the unfrequented Vault appeared,
And superstitions vainly feared.
The *Relics false* were set to view;
Only the Jewels there were true.
But truly bright and holy **Thwaites**
That weeping at the *Altar* waites.

But the glad Youth away her bears,
And to the *Nuns* bequeaths her Tears:
Who guiltily their Prize bemoan,
Like Gipsies that a Child hath stoln.
Thenceforth (as when th' Inchantment ends
The Castle vanishes or rends)
The wasting Cloister with the rest
Was in one instant dispossest.

At the demolishing, this Seat
To *Fairfax* fell as by Escheat.
And what both *Nuns* and *Founders* will'd
'Tis likely better thus fulfill'd,
For if the *Virgin* prov'd not theirs,
The *Cloyster* yet remained hers.
Though many a *Nun* there made her vow,
'Twas no *Religious-House* till now.

From that blest Bed the *Heroe* came,
Whom *France* and *Poland* yet does fame:
Who, when retired here to Peace,
His warlike Studies could not cease;
But laid these Gardens out in sport
In the just Figure of a Fort;
And with five Bastions it did fence,
As aiming one for ev'ry Sense.

When in the *East* the Morning Ray
Hangs out the Colours of the Day,
The Bee through these known Allies hums,
Beating the *Dian* with its *Drums*.
Then Flowers their drowsy Eyelids raise,
Their Silken Ensigns each displays,
And dries its Pan yet dank with Dew,
And fills its Flask with Odours new.

These, as their *Governor* goes by,
In fragrant Volleys they let fly;
And to salute their *Governess*
Again as great a charge they press:
None for the *Virgin Nymph*; for She
Seems with the Flowers a Flower to be.
And think so still! though not compare
With Breath so sweet, or Cheek so faire.

Well shot ye Firemen! Oh how sweet,
And round your equal Fires do meet;

Whose shrill report no Ear can tell,
But Ecchoes to the Eye and smell.
See how the Flow'rs, as at *Parade*,
Under their *Colours* stand displaid:
Each *Regiment* in order grows,
That of the Tulip, Pinke, and Rose.

But when the vigilant *Patroul*
Of Stars walks round about the *Pole*,
Their Leaves, that to the stalks are curl'd,
Seem to their Staves the *Ensigns* furl'd.
Then in some Flow'rs beloved Hut
Each Bee as Sentinel is shut;
And sleeps so too: but, if once stir'd,
She runs you through, nor askes *the Word*.

Oh Thou, that dear and happy Isle
The Garden of the World ere while,
Thou *Paradise* of four Seas,
Which *Heaven* planted us to please,
But, to exclude the World, did guard
With watry if not flaming Sword;
What luckless Apple did we tast,
To make us Mortal, and Thee Waste.

Unhappy! shall we never more
That sweet *Militia* restore,
When Gardens only had their Towers,
And all the Garrisons were Flowers,
When Roses only Arms might bear,
And Men did rosy Garlands wear?
Tulips, in several Colours barred,
Were then the *Switzers* of our *Guard*.

The *Gardiner* had the *Souldiers* place,
And his more gentle Forts did trace.
The Nursery of all things green
Was then the only *Magazeen*.
The *Winter Quarters* were the Stoves,
Where he the tender Plants removes.
But War all this doth overgrow:
We Ord'nance Plant and Powder sow.

To see Men through this Meadow Dive,
We wonder how they rise alive.
As, under Water, none does know
Whether he fall through it or go.

But, as the Mariners that sound,
And show upon their Lead the Ground,
They bring up Flowers so to be seen,
And prove they've at the Bottom been.

No **Scene that turns with Engines strange**
Does oftener then these Meadows change,
For when the Sun the Grass hath vext,
The tawny Mowers enter next;
Who seem like *Israelites* to be,
Walking on foot through a green Sea.
To them the Grassy Deeps divide,
And crowd a Lane to either Side.

With whistling Sithe, and Elbow strong,
These Massacre the Grass along:
While one, unknowing, carves the *Rail*,
Whose yet unfeather'd Quils her fail.
The Edge all bloody from its Breast
He draws, and does his stroke detest;
Fearing the Flesh untimely mow'd
To him a Fate as black forebode.

But bloody **Thestylis**, that waites
To bring the mowing Camp their Cates,
Greedy as Kites has trust it up,
And forthwith means on it to sup:
When on another quick She lights,
And cryes, he call'd us *Israelites*;
But now, to make his saying true,
Rails rain for Quails, for Manna Dew.

Unhappy Birds! what does it boot
To build below the Grasses Root;
When Lowness is unsafe as Hight,
And Chance o'retakes what scapeth spight?
And now your Orphan Parents Call
Sounds your untimely Funeral.
Death-Trumpets creak in such a Note,
And 'tis the *Sourdine* in their Throat.

Or sooner hatch or higher build:
The Mower now commands the Field;
In whose new Traverse seemeth wrought
A Camp of Battail newly fought:
Where, as the Meads with Hay, the Plain
Lyes quilted ore with Bodies slain:

The Women that with forks it filing,
Do represent the Pillaging.

And now the careless Victors play,
Dancing the Triumphs of the Hay;
Where every Mowers wholesome Heat
Smells like an *Alexanders Sweat.*
Their Females fragrant as the Mead
Which they in *Fairy Circles* tread:
When at their Dances End they kiss,
Their new-made Hay not sweeter is.

When after this 'tis pil'd in Cocks,
Like a calm Sea it shews the Rocks:
We wondring in the River near
How Boats among them safely steer.
Or, like the *Desert Memphis Sand,*
Short *Pyramids* of Hay do stand.
And such the *Roman Camps* do rise
In Hills for Soldiers Obsequies.

This *Scene* again withdrawing brings
A new and empty Face of things;
A levell'd space, as smooth and plain,
As Clothes for *Lilly* strecht to stain.
The World when first created sure
Was such a Table rase and pure.
Or rather such is the *Toril*
Ere the Bulls enter at Madril.

For to this naked equal Flat,
Which *Levellers* take Pattern at,
The Villagers in common chase
Their Cattle, which it closer rase;
And what below the Sith increast
Is pincht yet nearer by the Breast.
Such, in the painted World, appear'd
Davenant with th'Universal Heard.

They seem within the polisht Grass
A landskip drawen in Looking-Glass.
And shrunk in the huge Pasture show
As spots, so shap'd, on Faces do.
Such Fleas, ere they approach the Eye,
In Multiplyiug Glasses lye.
They feed so wide, so slowly move,
As *Constellations* do above.

Then, to conclude these pleasant Acts,
Denton sets open its *Cataracts*;
And makes the Meadow truly be
(What it but seem'd before) a Sea.
For, jealous of its *Lords* long stay,
It tries to invite him thus away.
The River in it self is drowned,
And Isl's the astonish Cattle round.

Let others tell the *Paradox*,
How Eels now bellow in the Ox;
How Horses at their Tails do kick,
Turned as they hang to Leeches quick;
How Boats can over Bridges sail;
And Fishes do the Stables scale.
How *Salmons* trespassing are found;
And Pikes are taken in the Pound.

But I, retiring from the Flood,
Take Sanctuary in the Wood;
And, while it lasts, my self imbark
In this yet green, yet growing Ark;
Where the first Carpenter might best
Fit Timber for his Keel have Prest.
And where all Creatures might have shares,
Although in Armies, not in Paires.

The double Wood of ancient Stocks
Link'd in so thick, an Union locks,
It like two *Pedigrees* appears,
On one hand *Fairfax*, th' other *Veres*:
Of whom though many fell in War,
Yet more to Heaven shooting are:
And, as they Natures Cradle deckt,
Will in green Age her Hearse expect.

When first the Eye this Forrest sees
It seems indeed as *Wood* not *Trees*:
As if their **Neighbourhood** so old
To one great Trunk them all did mold.
There the huge Bulk takes place, as ment
To thrust up a **Fifth Element**;
And stretches still so closely wedg'd
As if the Night within were hedg'd.

Dark all without it knits; within
It opens passable and thin;

And in as loose an order grows,
As the *Corinthean Porticoes.*
The Arching Boughs unite between
The Columnes of the Temple green;
And underneath the winged Quires
Echo about their tuned Fires.

The *Nightingale* does here make choice
To sing the Tryals of her Voice.
Low Shrubs she sits in, and adorns
With Musick high the squatted Thorns.
But highest Oakes stoop down to hear,
And listning Elders prick the Ear.
The Thorn, lest it should hurt her, draws
Within the Skin its shrunken claws.

But I have for my Musick found
A Sadder, yet more pleasing Sound:
The *Stock-doves* whose fair necks are grac'd
With Nuptial Rings their Ensigns chast;
Yet always, for some Cause unknown,
Sad pair unto the Elms they moan.
O why should such a Couple mourn,
That in so equal Flames do burn!

Then as I carless on the Bed
Of gelid *Straw-berryes* do tread,
And through the Hazles thick espy
The hatching *Thrastle's* shining Eye,
The *Heron* from the Ashes top,
The eldest of its young lets drop,
As if it **Stork-like did pretend**
That *Tribute* to *its Lord* to send.

But most the *Hewel's* wonders are,
Who here has the *Holt-felsters* care.
He walks still upright from the Root,
Meas'ring the Timber with his Foot;
And all the way, to keep it clean,
Doth from the Bark the Wood-moths glean.
He, with his Beak, examines well
Which fit to stand and which to fell.

The good he numbers up, and hacks;
As if he mark'd them with the Ax.
But where he, tinkling with his Beak,
Does find the hollow Oak to speak,

That for his building he designs,
And through the tainted Side he mines.
Who could have thought the *tallest Oak*
Should fall by such a *feeble Stroke!*

Nor would it, had the Tree not fed
A *Traitor-worm*, within it bred.
(As first our *Flesh* corrupt within
Tempts impotent and bashful *Sin.*)
And yet that *Worm* triumphs not long,
But serves to feed the *Hewels young*.
While the Oake seems to fall content,
Viewing the Treason's Punishment.

Thus I, *easie Philosopher*,
Among the *Birds* and *Trees* confer:
And little now to make me, wants
Or of the *Fowles*, or of the *Plants*.
Give me but Wings as they, and I
Streight floting on the Air shall fly:
Or turn me but, and you shall see
I was but an inverted Tree.

See how loose Nature, in respect
To her, it self doth recollect;
And every thing so whisht and fine,
Starts forth with to its *Bonne Mine*.
The *Sun* himself, of *Her* aware,
Seems to descend with greater Care,
And lest *She* see him go to Bed,
In blushing Clouds conceales his Head.

So when the Shadows laid asleep
From underneath these Banks do creep,
And on the River as it flows
With *Eben Shuts* begin to close;
The modest *Halcyon* comes in sight,
Flying betwixt the Day and Night;
And such an horror calm and dumb,
Admiring Nature does benum.

The viscous Air, wheres'ere She fly,
Follows and sucks her Azure dy;
The gellying Stream compacts below,
If it might fix her shadow so;
The Stupid Fishes hang, as plain
As *Flies* in *Chrystal* overt'ane,

And Men the silent Scene assist,
Charm'd with the *saphir-winged Mist*.

Maria such, and so doth hush
The *World*, and through the *Ev'ning* rush.
No new-born *Comet* such a Train
Draws through the Skie, nor Star new-slain.
For straight those giddy Rockets fail,
Which from the putrid Earth exhale,
But by her *Flames*, in *Heaven* try'd,
Nature is wholly *vitrifi'd*.

'Tis *She* that to these Gardens gave
That wondrous Beauty which they have;
She streightness on the Woods bestows;
To *Her* the Meadow sweetness owes;
Nothing could make the River be
So Chrystal-pure but only *She*;
She yet more Pure, Sweet, Straight, and Fair,
Then Gardens, Woods, Meads, Rivers are.

Therefore what first *She* on them spent,
They gratefully again present.
The Meadow Carpets where to tread;
The Garden Flowers to Crown *Her* Head;
And for a Glass the limpid Brook,
Where *She* may all *her* Beauties look;
But, since *She* would not have them seen,
The Wood about *her* draws a Screen.

For *She*, to higher Beauties raised,
Disdains to be for lesser praised.
She counts her Beauty to converse
In all the Languages as hers;
Not yet in those her self imployes
But for the *Wisdome*, not the *Noyse*;
Nor yet that *Wisdome* would affect,
But as 'tis *Heavens Dialect*.

Blest Nymph! that couldst so soon prevent
Those *Trains* by Youth against thee meant;
Tears (watry Shot that pierce the Mind;)
And *Sighs* (Loves Cannon charg'd with Wind;)
True Praise (That breaks through all defence;)
And *feign'd complying Innocence*;
But knowing where this *Ambush* lay,
She scap'd the safe, but roughest Way.

This 'tis to have been from the first
In a *Domestick Heaven* nurst,
Under the *Discipline* severe
Of *Fairfax*, and the starry *Vere*;
Where not one object can come nigh
But pure, and spotless as the Eye;
And *Goodness* doth it self intail
On *Females*, if there want a *Male*.

Go now fond Sex that on your Face
Do all your useless Study place,
Nor once at Vice your Brows dare knit
Lest the smooth Forehead wrinkled sit
Yet your own Face shall at you grin,
Thorough the Black-bag of your Skin;
When *knowledge* only could have fill'd
And *Virtue* all those *Furows till'd*.

Hence *She* with Graces more divine
Supplies beyond her *Sex* the *Line*;
And, like a *sprig of Misleto*,
On the *Fairfacian Oak* does grow;
Whence, for some universal good,
The *Priest* shall cut the sacred Bud;
While her *glad Parents* most rejoice,
And make their *Destiny* their *Choice*.

Mean time ye Fields, Springs, Bushes, Flow'rs,
Where yet She leads her studious Hours,
(Till Fate her worthily translates,
And find a *Fairfax* for our *Thwaites*)
Employ the means you have by Her,
And in your kind your selves preferr;
That, as all *Virgins* She preceds,
So you all *Woods, Streams, Gardens, Meads*.

'Tis not, what once it was, the *World*;
But a rude heap together hurl'd;
All negligently overthrown,
Gulfes, Deserts, Precipices, Stone.
Your lesser World contains the same.
But in more decent Order tame;
You Heaven's Center, Nature's Lap.
And Paradice's only Map.

But now the *Salmon-Fishers* moist
Their *Leathern Boats* begin to hoist;

And, like *Antipodes* in Shoes,
Have shod their *Heads* in their *Canoos*.
How Tortoise like, but not so slow,
These rational *Amphibii* go?
Let's in: for the dark *Hemisphere*
Does now like one of them appear.

Notes

Appleton House: Marvell was tutor to Mary Fairfax, daughter of Thomas Fairfax, at Appleton House around 1630. **first Builders fail'd in Height:** a reference to Babel **a mark of Grace:** merely to favour the neighbourhood **Justice still:** William Fairfax's father was a judge. **Thwaites:** Isabella Thwaites, Thomas Fairfax's ancestor who was kidnapped by William Fairfax from the nunnery **Scene that turns with Engines strange:** stage settings that were moved through mechanical devices **Thestylis:** a female slave, but also a rustic woman **Neighbourhood:** here, nearness **Fifth Element:** The four elements in the forest come together to create a fifth. **Stork-like did pretend:** In mythology, the stork gifts its first-born to the place it made its nest in.

The Garden

How vainly men themselves amaze
To win the **palm, the oak, or bays;**
And their uncessant labors see
Crowned from some single herb or tree,
Whose short and narrow-vergèd shade
Does prudently their toils upbraid;
While all the flowers and trees do close
To weave the garlands of repose.

Fair Quiet, have I found thee here,
And Innocence, thy sister dear!
Mistaken long, I sought you then
In busy companies of men:
Your sacred plants, if here below,
Only among the plants will grow;
Society is all but rude,
To this delicious solitude.

No **white nor red** was ever seen
So amorous as this lovely green;
Fond lovers, cruel as their flame,
Cut in these trees their mistress' name.
Little, alas, they know or heed,
How far these beauties hers exceed!
Fair trees! wheresoe'er your barks I wound
No name shall but your own be found.

When we have run our passion's heat,
Love hither makes his best retreat:
The gods who mortal beauty chase,
Still in a tree did end their race.
Apollo hunted Daphne so,
Only that she might laurel grow,
And Pan did after Syrinx speed,
Not as a nymph, but for a reed.

What wondrous life is this I lead!
Ripe apples drop about my head;
The luscious clusters of the vine
Upon my mouth do crush their wine;
The nectarine and curious peach
Into my hands themselves do reach;
Stumbling on melons as I pass,
Insnared with flowers, I fall on grass.

Meanwhile the mind, from pleasure less,
Withdraws into its happiness:
The mind, that ocean where each kind
Does straight its own resemblance find;
Yet it creates, transcending these,
Far other worlds, and other seas;
Annihilating all that's made
To a green thought in a green shade.

Here at the fountain's sliding foot,
Or at some fruit-tree's mossy root,
Casting the body's vest aside,
My soul into the boughs does glide:
There like a bird it sits and sings,
Then whets and combs its silver wings;
And, till prepared for longer flight,
Waves in its plumes the various light.

Such was that happy garden-state,
While man there walked without a mate:
After a place so pure and sweet,
What other help could yet be meet!
But 'twas beyond a mortal's share
To wander solitary there:
Two paradises 'twere in one
To live in Paradise alone.

How well the **skilful gardener** drew
Of flowers and herbs this dial new;

Where from above the milder sun
Does through a fragrant zodiac run;
And, as it works, the industrious bee
Computes its time as well as we.
How could such sweet and wholesome hours
Be reckoned but with herbs and flowers!

Notes

palm, the oak, or bays: symbols of honour **white nor red:** symbols of sexuality **skilful gardener:** a reference to God

To His Coy Mistress

Had we but world enough, and time,
This coyness, lady, were no crime.
We would sit down and think which way
To walk, and pass our long love's day;
Thou by the Indian Ganges' side
Shouldst rubies find; I by the tide
Of **Humber** would complain. I would
Love you **ten years before the Flood;**
And you should, if you please, refuse
Till the conversion of the Jews.
My **vegetable love should grow**
Vaster than empires, and more slow.
An hundred years should go to praise
Thine eyes, and on thy forehead gaze;
Two hundred to adore each breast,
But thirty thousand to the rest;
An age at least to every part,
And the last age should show your heart.
For, lady, you deserve this state,
Nor would I love at lower rate.

But at my back I always hear
Time's **winged** chariot hurrying near;
And yonder all before us lie
Deserts of vast eternity.
Thy beauty shall no more be found,
Nor, in thy marble vault, shall sound
My echoing song; then worms shall try
That long preserved virginity,
And your **quaint honour** turn to dust,
And into ashes all my lust.

The grave's a fine and private place,
But none I think do there embrace.

Now therefore, while the youthful hue
Sits on thy skin like morning dew,
And while thy willing soul transpires
At every pore with instant fires,
Now let us sport us while we may;
And now, like amorous birds of prey,
Rather at once our time devour,
Than languish in his slow-chapped power.
Let us roll all our strength, and all
Our sweetness, up into one ball;
And tear our pleasures with rough strife
Thorough the iron gates of life.
Thus, though we **cannot make our sun**
Stand still, yet we will make him run.

Notes

Humber: an estuary in the north of England; Marvell's father had drowned in it and hence the use of 'complain' **ten years before the Flood . . .Till the conversion of the Jews:** 1656 anno mundi (Noah) and 1656 anno domini (for the Conversion of the Jews, seen as a preliminary to the Second Coming of Christ) **vegetable love should grow:** taken from Virgil's eclogues where lovers inscribe their beloved's names on the barks of trees, and the name 'grows' with the tree **winged:** actually, the wings belong to Time and not to the chariot **quaint honour:** here, quaint implies both pleasingly unusual or anachronistic as well as skilful **cannot make our sun . . .Stand still:** In the Bible Joshua had stopped the sun.

Henry Vaughan

Born in 1622 in Wales, Vaughan studied at Oxford and trained for the law in London. Once the Civil War broke out, Vaughan returned home to the village of Llansantffraed where he lived the remainder of his life. He served as a secretary to Sir Marmaduke Lloyd during this period. Around 1646 he married Catherine Wise and had four children. After the death of Catherine he married her sister Elizabeth. As a result of the oppression visited upon the royalists, Vaughan lost his home briefly. He published his first volume, *Poems, with the Tenth Satyre of Juvenal Englished* in 1646, following it up quickly with a second volume in 1647. Vaughan also acknowledged his debt to George Herbert and the resultant conversion produced *Silex Scintillans* (1650), the volume that gave him serious attention as a religious poet. Vaughan later became a practitioner of medicine. He died in 1695.

The Retreat

Happy those early days, when I
Shined in my angel-infancy!
Before I understood this **place**
Appointed for my second **race**,
Or taught my soul to fancy ought
But a white, celestial thought;
When yet I had not walked above
A mile or two from my first love,
And looking back—at that short space—
Could see a glimpse of His bright face;
When on some gilded cloud, or flower,
My gazing soul would dwell an hour,
And in those weaker glories spy
Some shadows of eternity;
Before I taught my tongue to wound
My conscience with a sinful sound,
Or had the black art to dispense
A several sin to every sense,
But felt through all this fleshly dress
Bright shoots of everlastingness.
  O how I long to travel back,
And tread again that ancient track!
That I might once more reach that plain,
Where first I left my glorious train;

From whence th' enlightened spirit sees
That shady City of palm-trees.
But ah! my soul with too much stay
Is **drunk, and staggers in the way**!
Some men a forward motion love,
But I by backward steps would move;
And when this dust falls to the urn,
In that state I came, return.

Notes

place: earth **race:** the extent of one's life **drunk, and staggers in the way:** The image is from Plato's *Phaedrus* where he describes the soul as wandering around like a drunkard.

Regeneration

A **ward**, and still in bonds, one day
I stole abroad;
It was high-Spring, and all the way
Primrosed, and hung with shade:
Yet was it frost within,
And surly winds
Blasted my infant buds, and sin
Like clouds eclipsed my mind.

Stormed thus, I straight perceived my Spring
Mere stage and show;
My walk a monstrous, mountained thing,
Rough-cast with rocks, and snow;
And as a pilgrim's eye,
Far from relief,
Measures the melancholy sky,
Then drops, and rains for grief:

So sighed I upwards still; at last
'Twixt steps and falls,
I reached the pinnacle, where placed
I found a pair of scales;
I took them up, and laid
In th' one late pains;
The other smoke and pleasures weighed,
But proved the heavier grains.

With that, some cried, 'Away;' straight I
Obeyed, and led

Full East, a fair, fresh field could spy;
  Some called it, Jacob's Bed;
  A virgin soil, which no
    Rude feet ever trod;
Where – since He stept there – only go
  Prophets, and friends of God.

Here I reposed; but scarce well set,
    A grove descried
Of stately height, whose branches met
  And mixed, on every side;
  I entered, and once in,
    Amazed to see it,
Found all was changed, and a **new Spring**
  Did all my senses greet.

The unthrift sun shot vital gold,
    A thousand pieces;
And heaven its azure did unfold
  Chequered with snowy fleeces;
  The air was all in spice,
    And every bush
A garland wore: thus fed my eyes,
  But all the ear[th] lay hush.

Only a little Fountain lent
    Some use for ears,
And on the dumb shades language spent
  The music of her tears;
  I drew her near, and found
    The cistern full
Of divers stones, some bright and round,
  Others ill-shaped and dull.

The first, pray mark, as quick as light
    Danced through the flood;
But th' last, more heavy than the night,
  Nailed to the centre stood;
  I wondered much, but tired
    At last with thought,
My restless eye, that still desired,
  As strange an object brought.

It was a bank of flowers, where I descried,
    Though 'twas mid-day,
Some fast asleep, others broad-eyed,
  And taking in the ray;

Here musing long, I heard
A rushing wind,
Which still increased, but whence it stirred
Nowhere I could not find.

I turned me round, and to each shade
Dispatched an eye,
To see if any leaf had made
Least motion or reply;
But while I listening sought
My mind to ease
By knowing, where 'twas, or where not,
It whispered 'Where I please.'
'Lord,' then said I, 'on me one breath,
And let me die before my death!'

Notes

ward: a child, and therefore still under the control of parents or teachers **new Spring . . . greet:** the Church as ushering in new life (Spring)

Childhood

I cannot reach it; and my striving eye
Dazzles at it, as at eternity.

Were now that chronicle alive,
Those white designs which children drive,
And the thoughts of each harmless hour,
With their content too in my power,
Quickly would I make my path even,
And by mere playing go to heaven.

Why should men love
A wolf, more than a lamb or dove?
Or choose hell-fire and brimstone streams
Before bright stars and God's own beams?
Who kisseth thorns will hurt his face,
But flowers do both refresh and grace;
And sweetly living—fie on men !—
Are, when dead, medicinal then;
If seeing much should make staid eyes,
And long experience should make wise;
Since all that age doth teach is ill,
Why should I not love childhood still?
Why, if I see a rock or shelf,

Shall I from thence cast down myself?
Or by complying with the world,
From the same precipice be hurled?
Those observations are but foul,
Which make me wise to lose my soul.

And yet the practice worldlings call
Business, and weighty action all,
Checking the poor child for his play,
But gravely cast themselves away.

Dear, harmless age! the short, swift span
Where weeping Virtue parts with man;
Where love without lust dwells, and bends
What way we please without self-ends.

An age of mysteries! which he
Must live that would God's face see;
Which angels guard, and with it play,
Angels!which foul men drive away.

How do I study now, and scan
Thee more than ever I studied man,
And only see through a long night
Thy edges and thy bordering light!
O for thy centre and midday!
For sure that is the narrow way!

Margaret Cavendish

Born in 1623 into a royalist family, Margaret Lucas served as attendant of Queen Henrietta Maria. After the royalists were defeated in 1644 they were exiled to France, with Margaret continuing to be a part of the retinue. Later she became the second wife of William Cavendish, who would later become the first Duke of Newcastle-upon-Tyne. They lived in impoverished conditions in Paris and Antwerp. She is known to have started writing from a very early age. Margaret Cavendish wrote and published under her own name, an unusual feature for the age. She published *Poems and Fancies* and later *Philosophical Fancies* in the same year (1653). She also developed and maintained a strong interest in the sciences and natural philosophy, embodied in her work, *Observations upon Experimental Philosophy* (1666). She was one of the first women writers to try her hand at science fiction with her *The Description of a New World, Called the Blazing World* (1666). She died in 1673. In the twentieth century Margaret Cavendish has received considerable attention from feminist literary historians, starting with Virginia Woolf's mention of her in *The Common Reader*, while the *Stanford Encyclopedia of Philosophy* now carries an entry on her. In terms of philosophical thinking, she embodies the naturalists of her age.

A World Made By Atoms

Small Atoms of themselves a World may make,
As being subtle, and of every shape:
And as they dance about, fit places find,
Such Forms as best agree, make every kind.
For when we build a house of Brick, and Stone,
We lay them even, every one by one:
And when we find a gap that's big, or small,
We seek out Stones, to fit that place withal.
For when not fit, too big, or little be,
They fall away, and cannot stay we see.
So Atoms, as they dance, find places fit,
They there remain, lye close, and fast will stick.
Those that unfit, the rest that rove about,
Do never leave, until they thrust them out.
Thus by their several Motions, and their Forms,
As several work-men serve each others turns.
And thus, by chance, **may a New World create:**
Or else predestined to work by Fate.

Notes

may a New World . . . by Fate: may make the world by chance/accident, or are programmed by fate to do this

The Weight of Atoms

If atoms are as small, as small can bee,
They must in quantity of Matter all agree:
And if consisting Matter of the same (be right,)
Then every Atom must weigh just alike.
Thus Quantity, Quality and Weight, all

Together meets in every Atom small.

A World in an Ear-Ring

An Ear-ring round may well a Zodiac bee,
Where in a Sun goes round, and we not see.
And Planets seven about that Sun may move,
And He stand still, as some wise men would prove.
And fixed Stars, like twinkling Diamonds, placed
About this Ear-ring, which a World is vast.
That same which doth the Ear-ring hold, the hole,
Is that, which we do call the Pole.
There nipping Frosts may be, and Winter cold,
Yet never on the Ladies Ear take hold.
And Lightnings, Thunder, and great Winds may blow
Within this Ear-ring, yet the Ear not know.
There Seas may ebb, and flow, where Fishes swim,
And Islands be, where Spices grow therein.
There Crystal Rocks hang dangling at each Ear,
And Golden Mines as Jewels may they wear.
There Earth-quakes be, which Mountains vast down fling,
And yet never stir the Ladies Ear, nor Ring.
There Meadows bee, and Pastures fresh, and green,
And Cattle feed, and yet be never seen:
And Gardens fresh, and Birds which sweetly sing,
Although we hear them not in an Ear-ring.
There Night, and Day, and Heat, and Cold, and so
May Life, and Death, and Young, and Old, still grow.
Thus Youth may spring, and several Ages dye,
Great Plagues may be, and no Infections nigh,
There Cities be, and stately Houses built,
Their inside gay, and finely may be gilt.
There Churches bee, and Priests to teach therein,
And Steeple too, yet hear the Bells not ring.
From thence may pious Tears to Heaven run,
And yet the Ear not know which way they're gone.
There Markets bee, and things both bought, and sold,
Know not the price, nor how the Markets hold.
There Governors do rule, and Kings do Reign,
And Battles fought, where many may be slain.
And all within the Compass of this Ring,
And yet not tidings to the Wearer bring.
Within the Ring wise Counsellors may sit,
And yet the Ear not one wise word may get.
There may be dancing all Night at a Ball,

And yet the Ear be not disturbed at all.
There Rivals Duels fight, where some are slain;
There Lovers mourn, yet hear them not complain.
And Death may dig a Lovers Grave, thus were
A Lover Dead, in a Faire Ladies Ear.
But when the Ring is broke, the World is done,
Then Lovers they into Elysium run.

Of the Attraction of the Sun

When all those Atoms which in Rays do spread,
Are ranged long like to a slender thread,
They do not scattered fly but join in length,
And being joined, though small, add to their strength;
The further forth they stream, the more they waste
Their strength, though to the Sun they're tied fast:
For all those Rays, which Motion down doth send,
Sharp Atoms are, which from the Sun descend;
And as they flow in several Streams and Rays,
They stick their Points in all that stop their ways:
Like Needle points, whereon doth something Stick,
No way they make, having no force to prick,
And being stoppedt, they straight ways back do run,
Drawing those Bodies with them to the Sun.

Of the Sunne and the Earth

Through Earth's porous holes her sweat doth pass,
Which is the Dew that lies upon the Grasse:
Where (like a Lover kind) the Sun wipes clean,
That her faire face may to the Light be seen;
And for her sake that water he esteems,
Threading those drops upon his silver beams,
Like ropes of Pearle; he draws them to his sphere,
Turning those drops to Crystal when they're there.
Yet, what he gathers, cannot he keep all,
But down again some of those drops doe fall:
When turning back upon her head they run,
He clouds his brows, as if he had ill done.
But Lovers think they always do amiss,
Although those showers her refreshment is.
When she by sweat exhausted grows, and dry,
The Sun the moistest Clouds doth squeeze in sky;
Or else he takes some of his sharpest beams,

To break the Clouds, from whence pour Crystal streams.
Then Earth doth drink too much, yet doth not reel;
She cannot dizzy be, though sickness feel.

The Arithmetic of Passions

With Numeration Moralists begin
Upon the Passions, putting Quotients in;
Numbers divide with Figures, and Subtract,
And in their Definitions are exact;
As for Subtracting, take but one from three,
Add it to four, and it makes five to be:
Thus the odd Numbers to the even joined,
Will make the Passions rise within the mind.

Thomas Traherne

Thomas Traherne was born in Hereford in 1637, educated at Oxford. In 1657 he was appointed Rector of St Mary's Church at Credenhill and was ordained in 1660. Later he moved to Teddington, serving as chaplain to Sir Orlando Bridgeman. In 1672 Traherne was made minister of Teddington Church, but died soon after, in 1674. Traherne published only one work in his lifetime, the polemic *Roman Forgeries* (1673). His *Christian Ethicks* was published a few months after his death.The manuscripts of his poems were found in a London bookstore in 1896 and published to critical acclaim for the first time in 1903. Subsequent manuscripts were found through the twentieth century, one as recently as 1997.

The Vision

Flight is but preparative. The sight
    Is deep and infinite,
Ah me! 'tis all the glory, love, light, space,
    Joy, beauty and variety

That doth adorn the Godhead's dwelling-place;
'Tis all that eye can see.
Even trades themselves seen in celestial light,
And cares and sins and woes are bright.

Order the beauty even of beauty is,
It is the rule of bliss,
The very life and form and cause of pleasure;
Which if we do not understand,
Ten thousand heaps of vain confused treasure
Will but oppress the land.
In blessedness itself we that shall miss,
Being blind, which is the cause of bliss.

First then behold the world as thine, and well
Note that where thou dost dwell.
See all the beauty of the spacious case,
Lift up thy pleas'd and ravisht eyes,
Admire the glory of the Heavenly place
And all its blessings prize.
That sight well seen thy spirit shall prepare,
The first makes all the other rare.

Men's woes shall be but foils unto thy bliss,
Thou once enjoying this:
Trades shall adorn and beautify the earth,
Their ignorance shall make thee bright;
Were not their griefs **Democritus** his mirth?
Their faults shall keep thee right:
All shall be thine, because they all conspire
To feed and make thy glory higher.

To see a glorious fountain and an end,
To see all creatures tend
To thy advancement, and so sweetly close
In thy repose: to see them shine
In use, in worth, in service, and even foes
Among the rest made thine:
To see all these unite at once in thee
Is to behold felicity.

To see the fountain is a blessed thing,
It is to see the King
Of Glory face to face: but yet the end,
The glorious, wondrous end is more;
And yet the fountain there we comprehend,
The spring we there adore:

For in the end the fountain best is shown,
As by effects the cause is known.

From one, to one, in one to see all things,
To see the King of Kings
But once in two; to see His endless treasures
Made all mine own, myself the end
Of all his labours! 'Tis the life of pleasures!
To see myself His friend!
Who all things finds conjoined in Him alone,
Sees and enjoys the Holy One.

Notes

Democritus: ancient Greek philosopher who propounded that all matter consists of atoms

The Rapture

Sweet Infancy!
O Fire of heaven! O sacred Light
How fair and bright,
How great am I,
Whom all the world doth magnify!

O Heavenly Joy!
O great and sacred blessedness
Which I possess!
So great a joy
Who did into my arms convey?

From God above
Being sent, the Heavens me enflame:
To praise his Name
The stars to move!
The burning sun doth show His love.

O how divine
Am I! To all this sacred wealth,
This life and health,
Who raised? Who mine
Did make the same? What hand divine?

The Bible

That! That! There I was told
That I the son of God was made,

His image. O divine! And that fine gold,
With all the joys that here do fade,
Are but a toy, compared to the bliss
Which heavenly, God-like, and eternal is.

That we on earth are kings;
And, tho we're cloth'd with mortal skin,
Are inward cherubims, have angels' wings;
Affections, thoughts, and minds within,
Can soar through all the coasts of Heaven and earth;
And shall be sated with celestial mirth.

John Wilmot, Earl of Rochester

Born in 1647 in Oxford, John Wilmot succeeded his father's Earldom. He went to Oxford and graduated with an MA. Later he undertook the mandatory gentleman's 'grand tour' of Europe. He returned and joined the court, quickly becoming one of the most bohemian of its members, with a series of love affairs. He also distinguished himself as a soldier during the Dutch wars. In 1667 he married Elizabeth Malet and helped Dryden write his *Marriage a-la-Mode*. He was later appointed ranger of Woodstock Forest. Soon after his most famous volume, *A Satyr Against Mankind* (1675), Wilmot's health seriously declined and just before his death in 1680 he ranted and asked for his 'lewd' writings to be destroyed. Wilmot's reputation rests primarily on his satiric vision and his irony in works like 'Maim'd Debauchee'.

A Woman's Honour

Love bade me hope, and I obeyed;
Phyllis continued still unkind:
Then you may even despair, he said,
In vain I strive to change her mind.

Honour's got in, and keeps her heart,

Durst he but venture once abroad,
In my own right I'd take your part,
And show myself the mightier God.

This huffing Honour domineers
In breasts alone where he has place:
But if true generous Love appears,
The hector dares not show his face.

Let me still languish and complain,
Be most unhumanly denied:
I have some pleasure in my pain,
She can have none with all her pride.

I fall a sacrifice to Love,
She lives a wretch for Honour's sake;
Whose tyrant does most cruel prove,
The difference is not hard to make.

Consider real Honour then,
You'll find hers cannot be the same;
'Tis noble confidence in men,
In women, mean, mistrustful shame.

Satyr

Were I (who to my cost already am
One of those strange prodigious Creatures Man)
A Spirit free, to choose for my own share,
What Case of Flesh, and Blood, I pleased to wear,
I'd be a Dog, a Monkey, or a Bear,
Or any thing but that vain Animal,
Who is so proud of being rational.
The senses are too gross, and he'll contrive
A Sixth, to contradict the other Five;
And before certain instinct, will prefer
Reason, which Fifty times for one does err.
Reason, an **Ignis fatuus**, in the Mind,
Which leaving light of Nature, sense behind;
Pathless and dangerous wandering ways it takes,
Through errors Fenny – Boggs, and Thorny Brakes;
Whilst the misguided follower, climbs with pain,
Mountains of Whimseys, heaped in his own Brain:
Stumbling from thought to thought, falls headlong down,
Into doubts boundless Sea, where like to drown,
Books bear him up awhile, and make him try,
To swim with **Bladders of Philosophy**;

In hopes still t'oretake th'escaping light,
The Vapour dances in his dazzling sight,
Till spent, it leaves him to eternal Night.
Then Old Age, and experience, hand in hand,
Lead him to death, and make him understand,
After a search so painful, and so long,
That all his Life he has been in the wrong;
Huddled in dirt, the reasoning Engine lies,
Who was so proud, so witty, and so wise.
Pride drew him in, as Cheats, their **Bubbles** catch,
And makes him venture, to be made a Wretch.
His wisdom did his happiness destroy,
Aiming to know that World he should enjoy;
And Wit, was his vain frivolous pretence,
Of pleasing others, at his own expense.
For Wits are treated just like common Whores,
First they're enjoyed, and then kicked out of Doors:
The pleasure past, a threatening doubt remains,
That frights th'enjoyer, with succeeding pains:
Women and Men of Wit, are dangerous Tools,
And ever fatal to admiring Fools.
Pleasure allures, and when the Fops escape,
'Tis not that they're beloved, but fortunate,
And therefore what they fear, at heart they hate.
But now methinks some formal Band, and Beard,
Takes me to task, come on Sir I'm prepared.
Then by your favour, any thing that's writ
Against this gibing jingling knack called Wit,
Likes me abundantly, but you take care,
Upon this point, not to be too severe.
Perhaps my Muse, were fitter for this part,
For I profess, I can be very smart
On Wit, which I abhor with all my heart:
I long to lash it in some sharp Essay,
But your grand indiscretion bids me stay,
And turns my Tide of Ink another way.
What rage ferments in your degenerate mind,
To make you rail at Reason, and Mankind?
Blest glorious Man! to whom alone kind Heav'n,
An everlasting Soul has freely given;
Whom his great Maker took such care to make,
That from himself he did the Image take;
And this fair frame, in shining Reason drest,
To dignify his Nature, above Beast.
Reason, by whose aspiring influence,
We take a flight beyond material sense,

Dive into Mysteries, then soaring pierce,
The flaming limits of the Universe,
Search Heav'n and Hell, find out what's acted there,
And give the World true grounds of hope and fear.
Hold mighty Man, I cry, all this we know,
From the Pathetic Pen of **Ingello**;
From **Patricks** Pilgrim, **Stillingfleets** replies,
And 'tis this very reason I despise.
This supernatural gift, that makes a Mite —,
Think he's the Image of the Infinite:
Comparing his short life, void of all rest,
To the Eternal, and the ever blest.
This busy, puzzling, stirrer up of doubt,
That frames deep Mysteries, then finds 'em out;
Filling with Frantick Crowds of thinking Fools,
Those Reverend Bedlams, Colleges, and Schools;
Borne on whose Wings, each heavy Sot can pierce,
The limits of the boundless Universe.
So charming Ointments, make an Old Witch fly,
And bear a Crippled Carcass through the Sky.
'Tis this exalted Power, whose business lies,
In Nonsense, and impossibilities.
This made a Whimsical Philosopher,
Before the spacious World, his Tub prefer,
And we have modern Cloistered Coxcombs, who
Retire to think, cause they have naught to do.
But thoughts, are given, for Actions government,
Where Action ceases, thoughts impertinent:
Our Sphere of Action, is life's happiness,
And he who thinks Beyond, thinks like an Ass.
Thus, whilst against false reasoning I inveigh,
I own right Reason, which I would obey:
That Reason that distinguishes by sense,
And gives us Rules, of good, and ill from thence:
That bounds desires, with a reforming Will,
To keep 'em more in vigour, not to kill.
Your Reason hinders, mine helps t'enjoy,
Renewing Appetites, yours would destroy.
My Reason is my Friend, yours is a Cheat,
Hunger call's out, my Reason bids me eat;
Perversely yours, your Appetite does mock,
This asks for Food, that answers what's a Clock?
This plain distinction Sir your doubt secures,
'Tis not true Reason I despise but yours.
Thus I think Reason righted, but for Man,
I'le never recant defend him if you can.

For all his Pride, and his Philosophy,
'Tis evident, Beasts are in their degree,
As wise at least, and better far than he.
Those Creatures, are the wisest who attain,
By surest means, the ends at which they aim.
If therefore **Jowler**, finds, and Kills his Hares,
Better than **Meres**, supplies Committee Chairs;
Though one's a States-man, th'other but a Hound,
Jowler, in Justice, would be wiser found.
You see how far Mans wisdom here extends,
Look next, if humane Nature makes amends;
Whose Principles, most generous are, and just,
And to whose Morals, you would sooner trust.
Be judge your self, I'll bring it to the test,
Which is the basest Creature Man, or Beast?
Birds, feed on Birds, Beasts, on each other prey,
But Savage Man alone, does Man, betray:
Pressed by necessity, they Kill for Food,
Man, undoes Man, to do himself no good.
With Teeth, and Claws, by Nature armed they hunt,
Natures allowance, to supply their want.
But Man, with smiles, embraces, Friendships, praise,
Unhumanely his Fellows life betrays;
With voluntary pains, works his distress,
Not through necessity, but wantonness.
For hunger, or for Love, they fight, or tear,
Whilst wretched Man, is still in Arms for fear;
For fear he arms, and is of Armes afraid,
By fear, to fear, successively betrayed.
Base fear, the source whence his best passion came,
His boasted Honor, and his dear bought Fame.
That lust of Power, to which he's such a Slave,
And for the which alone he dares be brave:
To which his various Projects are designed,
Which makes him generous, affable, and kind.
For which he takes such pains to be thought wise,
And screws his actions, in a forced disguise:
Leading a tedious life in Misery,
Under laborious, mean Hypocrisy.
Look to the bottom, of his vast design,
Wherein Mans Wisdom, Power, and Glory join;
The good he acts, the ill he does endure,
'Tis all for fear, to make himself secure.
Merely for safety, after Fame we thirst,
For all Men, would be Cowards if they durst.
And honesty's against all common sense,

Men must be Knaves, 'tis in their own defence.
Mankind's dishonest, if you think it fair,
Amongst known Cheats, to play upon the square,
You'll be undone —
Nor can weak truth, your reputation save,
The Knaves, will all agree to call you Knave.
Wronged shall he live, insulted o're, oppressed,
Who dares be less a Villain, than the rest.
Thus Sir you see what humane Nature craves,
Most Men are Cowards, all Men should be Knaves:
The difference lies (as far as I can see)
Not in the thing it self, but the degree;
And all the subject matter of debate,
Is only who's a Knave, of the first Rate?
All this with indignation have I hurled,
At the pretending part of the proud World,
Who swollen with selfish vanity, devise,
False freedoms, holy Cheats, and formal Lies
Over their fellow Slaves to tyrannize.
But if in Court, so just a Man there be,
(In Court, a just Man, yet unknown to me)
Who does his needful flattery direct,
Not to oppress, and ruin, but protect;
Since flattery, which way so ever laid,
Is still a Tax on that unhappy Trade.
If so upright a States-Man, you can find,
Whose passions bend to his unbiased Mind;
Who does his Arts, and Policies apply,
To raise his Country, not his Family;
Nor while his Pride owned Avarice withstands,
Receives close Bribes, from Friends corrupted hands.
Is there a **Church-Man** who on God relies?
Whose Life, his Faith, and Doctrine Justifies?
Not one blown up, with vain Prelatic Pride,
Who for reproof of Sins, does Man deride:
Whose envious heart makes preaching a pretence
With his obstreperous saucy Eloquence,
To chide at Kings, and rail at Men of sense.
Who from his Pulpit, vents more peevish Lies,
More bitter railings, scandals, Calumnies,
Than at a Gossiping, are thrown about,
When the good Wives, get drunk, and then fall out.
None of that sensual Tribe, whose Talents lye,
In Avarice, Pride, Sloth, and Gluttony.
Who hunt good Livings, but abhor good Lives,
Whose Lust exalted, to that height arrives,

They act Adultery with their own Wives.
And e're a score of Years completed be,
Can from the lofty Pulpit proudly see,
Half a large Parish, their own Progeny.
Nor doting Bishop who would be adored,
For domineering at the Council Board;
A greater Fop, in business at Fourscore,
Fonder of serious Toys, affected more,
Than the gay glittering Fool, at Twenty proves,
With all his noise, his tawdry Cloths, and Loves.
But a meek humble Man, of honest sense,
Who Preaching peace, does practice continence;
Whose pious life's a proof he does believe,
Mysterious truths, which no Man can conceive.
If upon Earth there dwell such God-like Men,
I'll here recant my Paradox to them,
Adore those Shrines of Virtue, Homage pay,
And with the Rabble World, their Laws obey.
If such there are, yet grant me this at least,
Man differs more from Man, than Man from Beast.

Notes

Ignis fatuus: Thomas Hobbes' term for philosophy; it means 'vapour'; technically the exhalation of gas that is phosphorescent **Bladders of Philosophy:** Bladders are used to increase buoyancy but Rochester here gestures at the easy collapse of bladders as well. **Bubbles:** dupes **Ingello:** Nathaniel Ingello, author of moralistic prose romances **Patricks:** Simon Patrick, author of *Parable of the Pilgrim* (1665) **Stillingfleet:** Edward Stillingfleet, Anglican theologian and scholar, who participated in several polemical debates **Hunger . . . Reason bids me eat:** refers to the adage, 'hunger is a clock' **Jowler:** a hunting dog **Meres:** Thomas Meres, a distinguished parliamentarian of the time **Church-Man:** possible reference to Gilbert Sheldon, Archbishop of Canterbury, known to have been a philanderer but moralizer

Further Reading

Beal, Peter and Grace Ioppolo. Ed. *Elizabeth I and the Culture of Writing.* London: British Library, 2007.

Burke, Peter. *Popular Culture in Early Modern Europe.* Aldershot: Ashgate, 2009.

Chambers, E.K. *The Elizabethan Stage.* Oxford: Clarendon Press, 2009.

Cohen, Jeffrey Jerome. Ed. *The Postcolonial Middle Ages.* London: Palgrave Macmillan, 2000.

Cummings, Robert. Ed. *Seventeenth-Century Poetry: An Annotated Anthology.* Oxford: Blackwell, 2000.

Daybell, James and Peter Hinds. Ed. *Material Readings of Early Modern Culture: Texts and Social Practices, 1580–1730.* Basingstoke: Palgrave Macmillan, 2010.

De Grazia, Margaret, Margaret Quilligan and Peter Stallybrass. Eds. *Subject and Object in Renaissance Culture.* Cambridge: Cambridge Univ. Press, 1996.

Elsner, Jon and Cardinal, R. Eds. *The Cultures of Collecting.* London: Reaktion, 1994.

Evans, Robert C. and Eric J. Sterling. Eds. *The Seventeenth-century Literature Handbook.* London: Continuum, 2009.

Gillies, John. *Shakespeare and the Geography of Difference.* Cambridge: Cambridge Univ. Press, 1994.

Jardine, N. Secord, J.A. and Spary, E.C. Eds. *Cultures of Natural History.* Cambridge: Cambridge Univ. Press, 1996.

Kinney, Arthur F. Ed. *Elizabethan and Jacobean England: Sources and Documents of the English Renaissance.* Oxford: Wiley-Blackwell, 2011.

Loewenstein, David and Paul Stevens. Ed. *Early Modern Nationalism and Milton's England.* Toronto and London: Univ. of Toronto Press, 2008.

Robinson, Benedict. *Islam and Early Modern English Literature: The Politics of Romance from Spenser to Milton.* New York and Basingstoke: Palgrave–Macmillan, 2007.

Rowse, A.L. *The Elizabethan Renaissance: The Life of the Society.* London: Penguin, 2000.

Schultz, James. A. *Courtly Love, the Love of Courtliness, and the History of Sexuality.* Chicago, Ill. and London: Univ. of Chicago Press, 2006.

Singh, Jyotsna. Ed. *A Companion to the Global Renaissance: English Literature and Culture in the Era of Expansion.* Malden: Wiley-Blackwell, 2009.

Wheale, Nigel. *Writing and Society: Literacy, Print and Politics in Britain 1590–1660.* London and NY: Routledge, 1999.